PEACE
On That

The Peacemaker II

T.L. CRISWELL

outskirtspress
DENVER, COLORADO

This is a work of fiction. The events and characters described herein are imaginary and are not intended to refer to specific places or living persons. The opinions expressed in this manuscript are solely the opinions of the author and do not represent the opinions or thoughts of the publisher. The author has represented and warranted full ownership and/or legal right to publish all the materials in this book.

Peace On That
The Peacemaker II
All Rights Reserved.
Copyright © 2015 T.L. Criswell
v2.0

Cover Photo © 2015 thinkstockphotos.com. All rights reserved - used with permission.

This book may not be reproduced, transmitted, or stored in whole or in part by any means, including graphic, electronic, or mechanical without the express written consent of the publisher except in the case of brief quotations embodied in critical articles and reviews.

Outskirts Press, Inc.
http://www.outskirtspress.com

ISBN: 978-1-4787-6551-6

Library of Congress Control Number: 2015914496

Outskirts Press and the "OP" logo are trademarks belonging to Outskirts Press, Inc.

PRINTED IN THE UNITED STATES OF AMERICA

Acknowledgments

First I would like to thank my Creator for giving me the gift of writing and being able to share my voice with the world.

To my wonderful husband James Criswell; thank you for your patience, understanding, and dedication and commitment to our family. I love you more than words can express. To our boys, Mehki, Damon, and Keion, I love you all to pieces.

To my wonderful mother and stepfather, Jeanette and Samuel Kirkland. Thanks for being a great big part of our village. We love you very much.

Rest in peace to my daddy, Everett Gaines Parker Jr. I miss your face. I miss your smile. I miss your laughter. Your fun spirit will live on for eternity. ~Peace on That~

Thanking my siblings Terrance Parker, Yvette "Tresa" Brown, Shawntel Parker, and my sister–in-law Annette Rainer for always being supportive.

I want to thank my awesome mentor; advisor, teacher, and great friend Ben Smith for helping me find my creative voice and maximizing my potential. You're simply the greatest.

Sending a special thanks to Mr. John Moore (NY), a man who is a word master and a great teacher. I've learned so much from you.

Sending a special thank you to my creative aunt, Brenda Franklin, and Patricia Williams for their love and support. Rest in Peace to my beautiful aunt Selma Bell.

Thanks to my sister-friend Glenda Boyd, a woman who is as passionate about my writing as I am. I appreciate you.

Sending a special thanks to my soul sistah Valerie Bostic. Your wisdom and knowledge are so greatly appreciated.

I would also like to say thank you to my extended Tennessee and Georgia family for the outpouring of love and support and for helping to spread the word about my debut novel, *The Peacemaker*. Felicia Wilson, Orline Smith, Kasha Smith, Gwendolyn Brown and Algernetta Edwards, you guys rock!

I want to send a big thank you to The New Missionary Baptist Church (TN) book club and LeMoyne Gardens (MI) Book Club for embracing *The Peacemaker* and welcoming me to your meeting. It was truly heartwarming and a moment that I will cherish for a lifetime.

I want to send a special thank you to my test readers, Vincent Bennett and Teresa Furgerson Horn and my longtime friends Cheryl Burks-Jones and Chelita Robinson. I really appreciate you taking out the time to read my work. Thanks for a job well done.

I want to say thank you to all of my readers. I am deeply humbled and honored by your out pouring of love and support. I can't thank you enough for all the letters, texts, e-mails, phone calls, and reviews. You inspired me to complete this novel.

Much Love,

T. L. Criswell

Foreword by Ben Smith

My name is Benjamin C. Smith. Most people just call me "Ben." So who am I, and why should you care?

First of all, the author of this book T.L. Criswell, is one of my closest and dearest friends. We have known each other many years. Our friendship began in earnest when she sought my advice on her first book, *The Peacemaker*. At that time my life was full of turmoil and personal difficulties; being involved in something as complex as formulating a book was dubious at best. Both her faith and her confidence in my abilities along with her persistence convinced me to participate. (Besides, she would not take "No" for an answer.) Though she came to me for help, the relationship was mutually beneficial. I benefited greatly from her energetic and positive persona. Her enthusiasm rekindled a flame of mentoring and teaching that I thought was long dead.

Ms. Criswell knew of my background as a teacher and mentor. Some of my protégés are successful in the fields of politics, law, and the arts. But none of them equal her in humility, optimism, charm, and purity of character. She trusted my judgment and advice, and believed rightly that I had her best interests at heart.

Wherever she has gone, she has never failed to mention my involvement in her projects. I have made a point to stay out of sight whenever she has spoken publicly. I believe she should be the focal point. I view my role as that of a coach of a talented athlete or performer. She, however, is the star who puts in many long hours of work. One of my tasks is to help extract as much talent and potential from her as I can. From this she can find her true literary voice; she has not disappointed me yet.

Many of the main characters in her works are men. Yet as a woman she is able to articulate these characters as a man would. I often joke with her that she was probably a man in a previous life.

In my personal conversations with Ms. Criswell, I always come away impressed by her love for her husband and her children. They are a central part of who she is and how her moral compass is navigated and how she governs her life.

She has many passions; one is public awareness of Attention Deficit Disorder (ADD) and Attention Deficit Hyperactive Disorder (ADHD). These are afflictions that she struggles with as well as some family members. I think, however, it has aided in her creative writing abilities and a better understanding of others who struggle with it. She has a unique way of turning crisis into opportunity like few that I know.

Ms. Criswell had concerns about such a close friend as myself writing this foreword. She felt that it might be construed as self-serving propaganda. I insisted these words were not mere compliments, but facts. As facts they are valid and should be communicated as facts. Her modesty and humility are often excessive but most certainly refreshing.

I hope this book will inspire, entertain, and educate and leave you satisfied but also wanting more. As you read you will know that Ms. Criswell put her heart and soul into each and every word. Enjoy!

Peace on that, my friends:

Ben

In loving memory of my daddy
Everett Gaines Parker Jr.
~Peace on That~

Table of Contents

Big Man • 1
Courtroom Drama • 11
Fishing and Failure • 23
Pops and Uncle Buddy • 27
The Wedding • 37
The Motor City • 53
Lost Soul • 76
Same Buddy, Different City • 90
Detroit Riots • 104
Superstar • 114
Carla • 132
Jackie • 175
Moving Up • 185
Precious Gift • 192
The Boss • 195
Marriage and the Baby • 202
Apex • 209
Solitude • 239
Games • 254

Roller Coaster • 259
Fallacies • 275
The Devil's **Due** • **283**
Picking Up the Pieces • 305

Big Man

"Shorty, I'm so sorry. Please forgive me. I totally screwed up. I wasn't ready... I mean...I didn't know how to be a real father."

My lips tremble and the words come out broken. I take a deep breath and try to relax as I stare into the small bathroom mirror and continue to rehearse my apology.

"These last two years have been extremely painful. I've lost everyone and everything and you're all that I have left."

I pause and immediately retract those words after I say them. *That isn't going to work*. It sounded disingenuous coming from a man who once sat as a conqueror on top of the world, looking down on others as if they were prey. *Who am trying to fool? Actions speak louder than words*, and when it came to being a father, my past actions never made any real noise.

I turn around and catch a glimpse of my entire profile in the full-length mirror, behind the door. I look only like a fraction of the man I once was. My eyes have heavy bags, my skin is dry, my dreads are unkempt, and being down seventy-five pounds from two hundred and fifty pounds cause me to look emaciated. The image on the outside matches what is on the inside, *a man with a lost and broken soul.*

I eye the glass bottle of mouthwash sitting on top of the sink. I snatch it up and savagely throw it at the small mirror. It shatters. I stand entranced at the tiny pieces of glass. *It's just like my life.*

Minutes later, it sounds as if a Mack truck has rolled through the old two-family duplex house when Sharon, weighing over two hundred pounds and standing at about 5 foot 5 quickly stomps down the stairs. *I had forgotten that she'd spent the night.*

She rushes into the bathroom wearing nothing but her undergarments. Last night for the first time, we were intimate. I hadn't touched a woman in over two years. Although I really enjoyed her warm, soft, large frame, I could tell that for her it was awkward. She was uncomfortable with her size because she never fully exposed her body to me. When we were done, she immediately covered up and looked away. I thought that she was a beautiful full- figured woman. *Too bad I would never tell her that, though.* I was no longer in the business of making women feel good about themselves. They would somehow find a way to let their beauty and charm manipulate you.

She stands frozen as she observes me sitting in the middle of the bathroom floor, an absolute mess. I can tell by her expression that she doesn't know if she should cover up her body or wrap her arms around me.

The moment our eyes meet, she hurriedly snatches down the cheap shower curtain and covers up her partial nakedness. My voice sounds cold as I ask, "Please see yourself out."

She doesn't utter a word. She slowly steps back and turns around with the makeshift dress wrapped securely around her body, being sure to cover up every inch of her nice big butt.

***

Sharon Baker had shown up on my doorstep six months ago looking very professional, carrying a black leather briefcase and wearing black and gray business attire.

"Are you Mr. Jayson Jackson?" she asked.

I was reluctant to answer her question. Past experience had taught me that women who looked and dressed like her didn't come knocking on your door to sell Girl Scout cookies.

Once she noticed my hesitancy she quickly put my mind at ease. She extended her hand and said, "I'm Doctor Sharon Baker, but please call me Sharon." Her smile was warm and friendly causing me to return the gesture with a half smile.

Sharon was the therapist that Pops had been seeing before his untimely demise. He'd paid her in advance for family counseling and she was there to complete the job that she'd started. Our family had faced a tremendous amount of pain, devastation, and hardships over the past two years and he blamed himself. He wanted to mend the pieces to what was left of his broken family, so he sought out help. His plan was for him, his brother (Uncle Buddy) and me to seek family counseling. Pops was killed while on vacation in Africa before that could happen. His passing, along with the death of my ex-wife Jackie, had caused me to become despondent and depressed. I just couldn't move on. Uncle Buddy told Sharon where to find me.

In the beginning I was unwilling, but once I'd noticed the change in Uncle Buddy I became optimistic. She'd helped to functionalize a man that Pops deemed permanently dysfunctional. Before the devastation happened, Pops had pretty much given up on Uncle Buddy. He had a change of heart a few months before his death. Therapy would be his last resort.

I wished that Pops could have lived to see the change in his brother. I believe that he'd be proud. Uncle Buddy is sixty-two and for the first time ever, his life seems stable. He has a job working as a security guard for a local office building, he manages to keep up the duplex that Pops left to him, and he has a steady gig playing in a band on the weekends at various jazz bars.

I don't know if it was Pops' death that caused the change, or the fact that there was no one left to hold his hand. *It really didn't matter.* I was proud of the fact that someone in our family had found some sort of peace.

Since I wasn't comfortable with going to her office, Sharon agreed to come to me on a friendly and informal basis. She was a careful and compassionate listener and she didn't pass judgment. Six months later, I have no regrets. *She gives me hope.*

Our first visit was a microcosm of my life. I told her everything and I didn't hold anything back. I'd confessed all of my addictions, and the toxic relationships that I had had with my ex-wife Jackie, and Carla. She knew about my children and the status of my son Shorty, and the circumstances that led him to being in juvenile detention. I even confessed to her about the son James that I had with Carla. It's been over eight years and I still haven't had any written or verbal communication with the boy.

The next visit she asked me questions. "Jayson, what are you expecting to take away from our sessions? What are you hoping to gain? What are your goals? How far are you willing to go to achieve those goals? Are you prepared for rejection? Are you prepared to accept the things that you may not like?"

Her questions were tough. I had no idea if there were any right or wrong answers, so the only thing that I could do was to be honest and sincere.

"I really just want to mend the broken relationships with my sons. I want a second shot at life, *a normal life*. I no longer want the hustle and bustle of the fast life."

Sharon appeared empathetic and her soft smile let me know that she was pleased with my response.

"Jayson, I'm going to be straightforward with you. Getting over an addiction is never easy. It can take months, years--and most people will say it's a lifetime struggle. Although you may not indulge, you will still think about those addictions, crave those addictions, and you might even find yourself teetering with them. They are still a part of who you are. You must remain in control at all times. It really is one day at a time."

I listened very attentively because I'd heard this from every person who has ever suffered with any type of addiction.

Sharon did not stop there. She and I had become friends and we'd developed a bond and nothing was off limits. She warned me when we first started this journey that in order for her to help me, I was going to be administered a hard dose of reality. She was going to give it to me straight. No more telling me the things that I wanted to hear.

"Jayson, have you ever heard of the term making a deal with the devil?"

I didn't answer. Instead I somberly nodded my head yes and let out a nervous laugh. I loved and respected her honesty.

"Jayson, the main goal of making a deal with the devil is to obtain a favor or gift that a mere mortal could not possibly attain by himself. You give up part of your soul in exchange for diabolical favors like wealth, youth, knowledge, or power."

I closed my eyes when she said that because the lifestyle that I'd lived, I obtained all of those things.

I let her continue...

"Once you obtain all of those things, the deal is done. The devil will then make sure that you hold up your end of the bargain." My eyes were still closed as she said this.

She then whispered...

"Jayson, my friend... I believe that the devil has come to collect on that debt."

I bowed my head as the room fell silent.

I didn't take offense at her remark. I sat there trying to process everything that she'd said to me. With a remorseful and contrite heart, I asked the question, "How do I cash him out and settle that debt?"

She gave a soft smile.

"That's what I'm here for. I'm going to help you make peace with yourself before we move on to the other issues. As far as those young men, you will know when the time is right to reach out. We will then wrap up our final sessions talking about your relationship with your father and your Uncle Buddy."

I agreed because I was eager to talk about my Pops since I knew that he placed most of the blame on himself.

***

Last night was our sixth month since my healing journey had begun and we never got the chance to discuss Pops. Sharon also felt that I needed a little more time before I reached out to Shorty, but unfortunately the clock had run out. *His court hearing was the next morning.*

Sharon made an impromptu visit last night because she had some important information that she needed to disclose and it couldn't wait. When I opened the door and saw her standing there with a folder in her hand, I couldn't help but stare. I had never looked at her in a sexual way before, but last night I couldn't help myself. She looked so dynamic. Although her long wool coat was covered in snowflakes, it still couldn't hide her voluptuous figure. Her brown hair had tiny braids pinned up on top of her head, she was of light brown complexion with light brown eyes, and very large dimples, perfect white teeth, and she smelled so good. She gave full-figured a whole new meaning.

She then cleared her throat. "Are you going to let me in or leave me standing here in this cold?" I felt somewhat foolish. I was so overwhelmed by her beauty, that I completely lost sight of my manners. I apologized and invited her inside.

Once we sat down on the sofa, the mood quickly changed. She wore a look of sadness as she spoke in a low and somber tone.

"Jayson, after months and months of research, I ran across this today." She then handed me the folder. I reached out to grab it, but my hands started shaking. She placed her hands over my own and opened up the folder. She held up a photo of a big, tall, dark boy who looked to be well into his teens. I stared at the photo and I immediately recognized who it was. It was my son James. I smiled and became a bit emotional as I stared at his picture.

"I can't believe that you've found him!"

Sharon pressed her lips together and I sensed that she was holding back her own tears before she went on to explain.

***

His name was no longer James Jackson. It was Calvin Roberts and he's been housed in the juvenile detention facility for the past two years. When I left the little boy, Carla's uncle Carl adopted him. Calvin was a smart and gifted kid who suffered from a mental disorder and he never got over losing his mother. Carl and his wife provided a good life for him, and although they did seek medical treatment, he sometimes purposely failed to take his medicine. When this happened, his behavior would become unpredictable. He would often go days and even weeks without speaking and he didn't make friends very easily. Reading and drawing was what he enjoyed most.

When it came to academics, Calvin soared well beyond his peers. His uncle and aunt were extremely proud when he was accepted into a college preparatory high school. They felt he needed that challenge and maybe he would open up more and socialize with children who were more like him.

His teacher and counselor recognized his gifts right away. They took a special liking to him and did everything that they could to look out for him. They were on his side and rooted for his success. No one could prepare for what would happen at the end of his sophomore year.

Calvin was a big kid for his age and he was being bullied because of it. He told no one about it and kept it all bottled up inside. The last day of school, a student in the cafeteria made fun of his size and lack of communication skills. Calvin had finally had enough. He picked up a chair and smashed the boy over the head with it. Everyone in the lunchroom stepped away in shock. His teacher ran down the hall trying to stop Calvin, but it was too late. He pummeled the boy several times across the face before anyone could pull him off the student. Calvin was enraged and the only thing that could calm him down was the police.

He left school that day in handcuffs. The student was rushed to the ER and Calvin was taken down to a juvenile detention facility. His uncle Carl hired a lawyer, but it didn't seem to do any good because the minute Calvin was locked up, he continued to fight. He was ruining his own life and he didn't seem to care.

The boy's parents sued Carl for medical expenses and pain and suffering. This caused a strain on his marriage. He and his wife filed for an immediate separation in order to stop the boy's parents from taking all of their money. His wife had finally had enough and they later divorced. All of the stress caused Carl to have a stroke. He's seventy-five years old and is unable to care for himself so he now resides in a nursing home.

***

When Sharon told me all of this I had a meltdown. The pain on the inside was perdition and I couldn't speak. I was completely immobilized and I wished that I were dead. The devil was a cruel man.

As Sharon reached out to hug me, my head landed softly between her bosoms. She then said, "Jayson, I really hate to tell you this, but...." She hesitated and closed her eyes.

I pulled myself away and let out a heavy sigh. "Please say it. I don't believe that I can hurt much more than I'm hurting now. She steadied my face with her hands. "I'm so sorry, but he's due in court tomorrow." I instantly dropped my head and she held me once more, but this time even tighter.

That's how we ended up sleeping together last night. I don't remember much about the evening other than the fact that she was soft and warm and gave me the comfort I needed.

After our encounter, I never slept. My mind was heavily consumed with thoughts of my boys. I slipped out of bed early. I came to the bathroom in search of peace. I try and collect my thoughts. It's no use. There are no words. I realize; *there is no dress rehearsal for real life.*

As Sharon stomps up the stairs, I know that I can't afford to shut her out, but I have nothing to offer her. She is thirty years old, exactly ten years my junior. She comes from a wealthy family. Her grandfather is a doctor and so is her father. She has no children, a master's degree in psychology, and plans to open her own practice one day.

She returns several minutes later with her few belongings and heads toward the door. Before she exits, she turns around with a hurt look in her eyes. She hands me her business card. "I'll be in my office all day so please call me when it's over. It's imperative that we have our last few sessions. I owe that to your father."

I grab the card, but I won't make any promises. I'm not sure if I am going to go down to the courthouse. I am afraid of not being able to handle the outcome.

Sharon doesn't wait around. She offers one last meek smile and softly closes the door.

I stand, being careful not to cut myself on the glass. I make my way to the kitchen and put on a pot of coffee. I light a cigarette and turn the television on. That's when I see that Shorty's case is all over the news.

My decision is made at that time.

Courtroom Drama

"Adult crime. Adult time. Adult crime. Adult time." A group of raging protestors chant all in one accord. They march up and down the block in front of the juvenile courthouse. They carry large signs with the slogan " P.A.V.E" written across the top and the words "People Against Violence Everyday" was highlighted underneath. A few more protestors hold today's newspaper high above their heads with images of Michael and Shorty surrounded by other teenagers who were victims of juvenile gun violence. "Has Justice Been Served?" reads the top of the headlines.

I stop and stare in awe across the street.

Several police officers direct traffic and set up roadblocks as a means of trying to keep the agitated crowd in order. As the many news reporters and other media outlets descend upon the building, the scene starts to look and feel more like a circus. The sight alone makes my heart beat at a pace that is faster than normal.

It just doesn't seem fair. My Shorty is still a young kid who deserves a second chance. Michael was his friend, and I know and I believe that everyone knows that the shooting was unintentional. But this angry group doesn't seem to care. They are understandably tired of all the violence that's going on in this city and they just want it to end.

A female protestor, wearing African garb and matching head wrap, is the leader of this organization. I watched her do a live interview this morning as I contemplated whether I should show up. I couldn't help but notice how bold and strong she stood. She was a very dark woman of African descent and although she had a heavy accent, she still managed to articulate her words carefully. She held a photo of her deceased teenaged son up to the camera.

"This was my son Malik. Five years ago he lost his life because of teenage gun violence. The case went unsolved and got little media coverage. When I reached out to the many different groups and organizations for help, the only response that I received was 'I'm sorry, ma'am, but we'll see what we can do.' I felt that since this happens so often, I had to take a number and go to the back of the line. That's why I coalesced the P.A.V.E. organization, to make the courts and the politicians listen and hopefully bring about change. Since Jayson Jackson's case is high profile, our organization couldn't afford to pass on the opportunity to have our voices finally heard. It angers me to see a young teenage boy walking around carrying a gun instead of a textbook."

She paused and was very stern.

"We're not only seeking justice for Michael, but for my son and every other kid who has been a victim of violence as well." She then pumped her fist in the air and the protestors in the background became fired up. They waved their signs higher and applauded as she continued, "He altered the life of a young man who was a leader." The protestors all shouted "Yeah," sounding like modern-day Black Panthers. I even heard one say "Preach!!!"

This got her adrenaline going even more. "Not only was Michael Stephens academically inclined, but physically also. He had a promising basketball career ahead of him and by no fault of his own, that has all been taken away. We also want to send the strong message to any teenager out there who decides to carry a gun that there will be tough penalties and dire consequences to pay. The P.A.V.E. organization will continue to march until there is something done." The crowd roared once more before the reporter went to commercial break.

I sadly shook my head just thinking about the message this woman was conveying. I felt terrible that she'd lost a son and the perpetrator had never been captured, but did she know that throwing an innocent young man under the bus would not solve this problem? She was speaking solely from raw emotion and not a rational point of view. *What about rehabilitation?* She never even mentioned that word. What this lady really wanted was for every teenager probably in America to pay for what had happened to her son.

That speech is what brought me here. It made me realize that this really wasn't about me. My current struggles and insolvency seem of little importance compared to what my son is up against. There wasn't any room for foolish pride. I had to push forward. *"Although I don't like the beat of the music, I have no choice but to get out here and dance; to a song that doesn't have soul."*

My mind is flooded with thoughts of Shorty. It's been that way for quite some time, but today has to be the worst. I haven't reached out to him in almost two years. I didn't know what to say. I'd written him so many letters over the last year, but I never mailed them. I'd once read that "talk is cheap and anyone could afford it." It seemed as though those words were tailor-made for me. I knew that I had let him down, and a few words on a piece of paper wouldn't easily fix the damage that I'd caused.

My body rocks back and forth as I stand at the crosswalk impatiently waiting for the light to turn green. Once it does, I exit the curb out into the busy street. A distracted driver, gawking in the direction of all the pandemonium, nearly mows me down with his vehicle. I slip and fall, and land flat on my back. The careless driver leans on the horn and slams on his brakes when I faintly hear the words "Watch where you're going, asshole." I am in no condition to respond. The snow is thick and heavy, and I am tired and weak.

As I lie buried in the fresh few inches of snow, it suddenly feels as if the walls of my silhouette are going to cave in and suffocate me.

I slowly lift my head. My eyes manage to focus in on a black limo that pulls up to the curb. A tall muscular man wearing a black and grey fedora hat, and black overcoat, carrying a large briefcase, jumps out of the car. He helps an older, smaller-framed woman wearing a long black coat with a rain cap over her head out of the car. He tells the driver, "Don't worry about finding parking in this mess, we will call you when it's over." The driver pulls off.

The big, burly gentleman barely misses me. He suddenly looks down and sees me struggling with the snow. He hardly uses any energy as he quickly snatches my flimsy body up with one hand. "Are you all right?" He only asks out of courtesy because he never looked me in the face. "You could have gotten squashed out here." he says.

I mumble in a low voice, "I'm all right," being sure that my long dreadlocks mask the front of my face. He doesn't say anything else. He looks straight ahead, wearing a grave expression across his face as he awaits the light to change. When it does, he firmly holds onto the woman and his briefcase and they both cross the street in silence.

Anxiety suddenly kicks in and I pinch myself to make sure that I'm not hallucinating. Emphatically I'm not. Those were my ex-in laws Jeffery Scott and his mother Mrs. Scott. They hadn't recognized me. I look down at my hobo-like attire, and understand why.

I stand not knowing what to do next. For a split second, I contemplate turning around and running away forever. I immediately erase the thought from my mind. *Running is what actually caused all of this mess.* I then pick up the pace and hurry across the busy street.

I make sure that I stay about ten steps behind Jeff and his mother as I follow their lead. Suddenly, they walk in the opposite direction of the crowd. I move in closer.

We end up in the back of the building. "Attorney's entrance" read the sign on the door. Jeff holds the door for his mother and proceeds to walk through himself. He turns around to make sure that the private entrance door is closing when he notices me trying to enter. I bow my head so that he cannot see my face. He politely says, "I'm sorry sir, this is a private entrance." I remain silent and I can feel him stare me up and down. His heavy breathing indicates that he's irritated. "Damn drifter," he murmurs under his breath. He then reaches inside his pocket and pulls out a few bills and tries to hand them to me. "Go and grab something to eat." he says.

I don't accept the money. Instead, I slowly lift my head and remove my dreads from my face. We make eye contact. A look of bewilderment covers his face. He drops his heavy briefcase and the loud bang it makes hitting the floor echoes throughout the deserted hallway. His eyes grow extra wide and before I can duck, his hands are wrapped tightly around my throat. He looks deranged as he tries to choke all the air out my lungs. I am defenseless and almost certain that I will take my last breath right here in this hallway. He despises me. I understand. I abandoned my responsibilities as a father and he and Mrs. Scott were left holding the bag.

Mrs. Scott finally turns around and notices what is happening. "Jeffery Scott?" she whispers through clenched teeth. "What has gotten into you? Put that man down!" she demands.

He releases, but not before thrusting me backward a few feet. I bend over and start gasping for breath. He then storms off towards the elevator. Mrs. Scott stands over me and pats my back. After what just happened, I'm too ashamed to face her. Since I'd married her daughter, I had never been one of her favorite persons, and I am afraid that she just might finish the job herself.

Jeff calls out to his mother in vexation, "Let's go, Mother!" She's hesitant. I pull myself together and muster up the strength and courage to straighten my body and look her square in the eyes.

Stunned, she jerks backward and on instinct she places one hand over her heart and takes a quick deep breath. I close my eyes in anticipation for the slap. After seconds pass and I feel no sting, I realize that she's doing just the opposite. She makes a long sigh before she gently grabs my hand and we move toward the elevator that just closed shut with Jeffery Scott inside.

* * *

The floor of the courtroom mimics the outside of the building. It takes us several minutes to duck through the crowds and all the news reporters before we finally make it inside the courtroom. Once inside, the harassment from the media intensifies.

They whisper into their small tape recorders and report our every move…

"Jayson Jackson's grandmother just entered into the courtroom and she is being escorted by an unknown person. They will be sitting right behind from where the defendant will be standing."

Mrs. Scott doesn't pay them any mind. Anyone could clearly see the pain in her eyes and the nervousness in her walk, but she refuses to hang her head. She has always been a dignified woman and today will prove to be no different. She holds her head up high and tightly grips my hand and leads the way to our seats.

The bailiff enters from behind the judge's chambers and everyone in the courtroom begins to settle down. He says, "All rise" and introduces the judge.

I feel nauseous and my body feels warm. Mrs. Scott squeezes my hand before we take our seats.

A tall, young, lanky white man wearing wire-framed glasses and with messy brown hair takes the podium. He looks like he is fresh out of law school because he appears to be nervous. He knocks over his briefcase and papers go flying everywhere. The judge looks in his direction and grins. She then busies herself by looking over some papers.

The bailiff opens the door and my heart feels heavy. Shorty enters the room and looks in our direction. Shame and disgrace fill my insides because I cannot reach out and protect him. He's no longer my little Shorty. That kid is now a grown young man. He's so handsome. He has thick hair like I have, but it's cut low and it's very wavy. His face is clean-shaven and he has the build of an athlete. Other than my big brown eyes, he looks so much like Jackie. It scares me.

He smiles at Mrs. Scott and wears a puzzled look when he sees me. I feel ill at ease. The discomfort causes me to suspend all eye contact. I drop my head--burying myself deeper into the shadows of my guilt.

The judge calls the first name on her docket. "The State of Michigan versus Calvin Lee Roberts." All the blood seems to rush out of my body when I hear that name. I look around the room, hoping that an unrecognizable face answers. A few seconds go by and it doesn't happen. *There is no way that's him. That can't be him.* I try and psych myself out.

The tall, lanky white dude stands up and has a lost look on his face. The bailiff suddenly waves him over as he whispers something to the judge. Her facial expression turns sour and I could see her whisper the word "*Suicide.*" She bows her head and makes a cross sign over her forehead and her heart. Shorty drops his head while Mrs. Scott whispers the Lord's Prayer. I close my eyes and clasp my hands together and curse the devil. *Please leave me alone. I can't take any more pain.*

"Could the family of Calvin Lee Roberts, along with his counsel, step into my chambers?" the judge instructs in a grief-stricken voice.

I briefly stand up, but I quickly sit back down. *I have no rights. I gave them up years ago.* The judge repeats herself. "Could the family of Calvin Lee...." The lanky white dude cuts her off mid-sentence and replies, "Your honor, he has no known family on record at this time."

The courtroom falls silent. She then calls for a fifteen-minute recess.

I bow my head and shut my eyes. Everything turns black. The room seems to rotate around me. For over eight years I'd suppressed those feelings from that fateful day in the back of my mind. Now they have re-emerged. I can distinctly see James's face and that vacant look in his eyes. I try and push the memories away, but I can't.

***

"I hate you!" the boy viciously screamed from the top of the stairs. He held a voluminous hard cover book in his hand. "I. Hate. You!" he screamed once more before tossing it down the flight of stairs. I attempted to duck but my response time was too slow. It whizzed sharply past my face, leaving a cut under my eye before it slammed down on the hardwood floors. He then charged down the stairs at full speed with both fists balled up causing us to crash down on the floor. He landed on top of me and I didn't move as his heavy fist pounded my chest over and over again. The tears flowed uninterrupted as he continued to scream ferociously "I. Hate. You!"

***

"All rise," the bailiff announces, introducing the judge once more. I promptly stand up, still shaken from those memories.

"The State of Michigan Versus Jayson Lee Jackson II," the judge announces with a bit of hostility in her voice. The incident had clearly left her disturbed, causing a shift in her mood.

Shorty stands next to Jeffery Scott. "Mr. Jackson, can you please raise your right hand?" Her voice is direct and firm. Shorty does as instructed. Once he's sworn in, she doesn't hold back and goes straight for the jugular.

"After reading over your file, I am impressed but not totally convinced." She looks up through her reading glasses and says, "You do understand why I addressed you as Mr. Jayson Lee Jackson II?"

He takes a deep breath and says, "Yes, ma'am, I believe so."

"Can you tell me why?" she asks Shorty with a piercing look on her face.

Beads of sweat form over my forehead, and I start to feel dizzy. Mrs. Scott squeezes my hand very tight. It looks as if Shorty is trying his best to hold it together as he answers.

"Well, ma'am, I believe it's because I am an adult and no longer a juvenile."

The judge remains stern as she responds, "That is correct! And now that you are officially an adult, you have no more room for juvenile mistakes. Whatever you do from this day forward will have adult consequences. You can no longer hide behind your youth, young man, because there is no youth left! Happy birthday, and welcome to the real world."

She starts to come down really hard on Shorty, and I can sense that he is about to break. "Mr. Jackson, if I decide to let you walk out of my courtroom a free man, how can I be sure that you will become a productive citizen in our society? How can I be sure that you will not pick up another gun and shoot someone else? How can I be sure that I won't be making the biggest mistake of my life?"

Jeffery Scott raises his hand to speak, but she cuts him off. "No! Mr. Scott, I've been hearing from you for the past two years. I think it is now time for me to hear from Mr. Jackson." Jeffery steps back and nods his head in agreement.

Shorty stands alone and his body language reads of fear. He slowly turns to look at Mrs. Scott, but his eyes land on me. I want to reach out and grab him but I cannot. I want to tell the judge to punish me. I want to tell her that I was a selfish person who put himself before his kid. I want her to know how sorry I am for not being a better parent.

Shorty notices me and suddenly things go awry and he starts to cry. I bow my head and it's as if I can see the devil laughing at me. I can't take it anymore so I start to cry on the inside, wishing I could trade places with both my sons.

The judge shows no mercy. "Mr. Jackson, if you're here to gain sympathy, then you'd better think again. I have never been moved by tears."

Jeffery Scott throws his hand up and practically begs the judge for a recess. She looks at her watch and agrees to a one-hour recess, promising to pick right up where she left off.

The entire courtroom breathes a sigh of relief, because she was really tough. The bailiff then escorts Shorty to the small holding cell.

I bow my head inside my hands and think about my own father, Mr. James Jackson. He had not been a perfect man, but he tried his best to lay a strong foundation for our family. He entrusted me with all of the ingredients to continue that success, and I altered them. This would be the end result.

Twenty Years Earlier...

Fishing and Failure

"No! Not this time, Big Man. I'm afraid that I'm not going to do it."

Pops' voice was firm as he stood behind the bar stacking an assortment of beers inside the cooler.

"No?" I answered, confused. "Pops, are you kidding me? This is serious. I really need the five hundred dollars to pay for a tutor. If I don't come up with the money, I will fail the two courses I need to graduate on time."

He immediately stopped what he was doing and turned in my direction. He placed his hand up to his chin and appeared to be in deep thought.

His behavior left me baffled. For the first time ever, he made me explain myself. It felt foreign. It was almost as if he wanted to see me beg. I became quiet. Begging or asking twice for something was beneath my dignity and I decided that I wasn't going to do it.

When Pops noticed the bewildered look on my face, he grabbed two beers and took a seat at the bar. He opened his and slid the other to me. I stared at it not sure if I should drink it. Although I had drunk plenty of beer and alcohol at college, I never drank in front of him, out of respect. I didn't want it to seem as though my priorities were misaligned.

He waited for me to open the bottle. "Big Man, you're twenty-one years old and a junior in college. There's no way you're going to convince me that you don't drink."

There was no need to argue. I accepted the beer as Pops was starting to preach.

"Big Man, do you realize that you've been going to that university for three years and every semester it's the same damn song?"

I offered no response as he continued to speak.

"Why is it that every year I'm out of thousands and thousands of dollars, paying for tutors, books, housing, cars, and extracurricular activities, when you had a full scholarship?"

A lump formed in my throat. I couldn't believe he brought that up.

I tried as best as I could to defend myself. "Pops you know I didn't purposely lose that scholarship. It wasn't my fault that I got hurt my sophomore year. The pain of not being able to play the game caused me to slip into a deep depression, so my grades faltered." I responded.

Pops looked displeased and he wouldn't let me finish.

"Big Man, that's an excuse. When you fall down, you have to get up and get back into the game. The reason I've worked so hard all these years was to try and build a legacy for our family. I didn't want you and my future grandkids to have to face the financial burdens I had as a child. I'm afraid that giving you handouts and not making you earn your way has done more harm than good. I regret the fact that I have never taught you how to fish."

I looked at him from out the corner of my eye. "Pops, you don't have to feel bad about that. I don't want to learn how to fish. The thought of touching a worm makes me sick, I'm allergic to bees, and I've never been into all that nature stuff."

Pops looked alarmed. He responded, "Oh my goodness! What

have I done to you? You sound just like my brother, your Uncle Buddy. You have an excuse for everything. *Excuses are the nails used to build a house of failure.*"

He then stopped talking for a few moments so that I could let that absorb.

I was angry and disappointed at the fact that he was insinuating I was going to be a failure. We'd had many disagreements in the past, but we always respected each other's feelings. That day was different. He'd crossed the line.

I slammed my beer on the counter and it erupted like a volcano. I never bothered to clean up the mess. I snatched my keys off the counter in an attempt to leave. I didn't want to say anything that I would later regret.

"Pops, you sure know how to kick a dog when it's down. If I had known that asking for five hundred dollars would lead to me being labeled a failure, then I wouldn't have asked."

He sat in the chair with his arms folded and he stared me up and down. I was really bothered because he seemed unnerved.

When Pops noticed how infuriated I was, he issued me a direct order.

"Jayson Jackson, have a seat!" My eyes became small, my nose flared, and my chest heaved in and out.

Pops remained calm as he pulled out my chair. "Big Man, I don't give a damn about you being mad. You came asking me for money. I didn't come to you. Therefore you will sit and listen to everything that I have to say. Besides, this conversation should have taken place years ago. It's long overdue."

I grabbed the seat and focused on the beer so that I didn't have to look at Pops. That didn't last long before he started.

"Big Man, did you pass the classes you needed to graduate?" I was still angry, so I shook my head no. Satisfied with my response Pops continued.

"Well, if you didn't pass those classes, then that means that you failed! Am I correct?" I offered no comment at his facetious statement.

"Big Man, can you tell me the difference between this failure and the last three failures?"

Again I said nothing because he seemed to have all of the answers.

"Big Man, the reason why you can't answer that is because you haven't learned anything from the previous failures. The reason that you haven't learned anything is because you continued to make excuses and I continued to feed you fish.

"When I was a young boy I failed many times. The reason that I was able to learn and grow from my failures is because I had no one that would feed me fish. If I wanted to eat, then I had to learn how to catch my own. That's the beauty of failure. It teaches more than success. When you throw excuses into the mix, it changes the entire ballgame and only leads to more failure.

"Your Uncle Buddy, on the other hand, never learned how to fish. Our momma sat there and fed him fish every day. And when Momma died, Buddy remained on this earth a hungry man. If it hadn't been for me, he'd still be hungry."

Pops went on to talk about his beginnings.

Pops and Uncle Buddy

Pops began his story…

Big Man, I was born toward the end of the Great Depression in 1938 in a small town outside of Tunica, Mississippi. My parents and I lived in a little two-bedroom shack on a farm. It was a piece of property that my grandfather owned free and clear and he passed it down to my daddy. I can remember playing on the farm while my daddy worked hard to keep it up. He was proud of that land.

The Great Depression was caused when the stock market crashed in 1929. It lasted a little over ten years. It wiped out millions of investors, causing half of the country's banks to fold. Many businesses were forced to close, and it left over 15 million people unemployed. It was the worst economic calamity in our history.

When those rich folks lost all their money in the banks, they couldn't handle being poor, so many of them took their own lives. They'd rather be dead and buried six feet underground than to live on this earth poor and penniless. My momma and daddy never did feel the wrath of the Great Depression, because they never had much money to begin with. That's why my daddy treasured that piece of land. He was a farmer who grew his own crops, and he sold them for money. I was his little helper. He'd let me feed the chickens, water the plants and pick the fruits and vegetables.

When I turned five years old, my daddy received his orders to serve in World War II. My mother was pregnant with Buddy at the time. They both were afraid, but they knew nothing could be done so they made the best of every moment. I can remember how my daddy and I would come inside from working hard on that farm all day and Momma having us a hot meal ready. Daddy was affectionate when it came to his wife. He'd come in and rub her belly and sing to their unborn child every evening.

He was a tall yellow man with light eyes and a slim nose. Momma was a petite woman who was a few shades darker than Daddy, with long thick hair that she kept in cornrows.

One of my fondest memories of him was how he made beautiful music playing his saxophone. We would gather around every night and he'd pull out that beautiful brass instrument from the black case. First, he'd shine it up until it looked like gold. He'd then play it for Momma, their unborn child, and me. I loved to hear my daddy play that instrument because he made beautiful music and took pride in the fact that the instrument was an heirloom that had been in his family for generations.

When the time came for my daddy to leave for that war, he sat me down on the couch and kneeled directly in front of me so that we were eye level. The grave expression on his face had me afraid. He sensed it, so he picked me up and sat me on his lap as a way of comforting me. I wrapped my arms around his big broad shoulders and he softly rubbed my back.

"Son, I'm going away to the war for a while and I'm gonna need for you to take care of things until I make it back. Your momma will have the baby while I'm away, so I need for you to step in and be the man around this place until I return."

I can remember feeling scared when he said that. I planted my head inside his shoulder and cried.

"Daddy, I can't be a man, look how small I am." When he heard my cries, he sternly removed me from his lap and once again we were eye level. He then issued a stark warning I'll never forget.

"James, you can be or do whatever you put yo' mind to. Yes, son, you are small, but don't ever use that as an excuse. You are a Jackson, and Jacksons don't make excuses or blame circumstances ever! Life is full of roadblocks. When you hit a roadblock, learn how to go around it. Just don't ever give up."

I remember wiping the tears from my eyes and saying, "Okay, Daddy. I'll take care of the family."

The next day he was gone off to the war. I remember how I had to care for Momma and do little things around the shack like empty the trash, sweep the floor and stack the dishes. I also worked out on the farm. I fetched the water, picked the fruits and vegetables, and fed the chickens and collected the eggs. Sometimes I had to walk several miles to the town store to get little supplies that we needed, all while staying out of the white man's way.

The day that Momma's water had broken, I remember running down the road to get the midwife Mrs. Smith. When the midwife and I made it to the house, the baby was already in position and on its way out. She quickly set up her equipment and told Momma to push. Suddenly the midwife stopped and said, "Oh my, this isn't good. The baby is breeched."

When Momma was told that his feet were coming out first, she started screaming. This frightened me, so I cried right along wit' my momma. The midwife remained calm but that didn't do Momma any good. She knew that it was a chance that the baby wouldn't make it because it happened to Mrs. Johnson up the road. Her baby was breeched, and the poor child died. Well, that midwife must have had some magic powers, because she stuck her hand inside of Momma and about fifteen minutes later, she managed to turn the baby around.

When the baby came out, he wasn't crying. When Momma didn't hear his voice I remembered how she started calling on the Lord. "Sweet Jesus, please put some air into my baby's lungs. Sweet Jesus, please let my child live." Almost instantaneously he started screaming.

I remember that cry, because the midwife said that he had some of the strongest lungs she'd ever heard for a baby. Momma was certain that it was Daddy's way of showing her that he was present, because Daddy had those same lungs.

The midwife was so happy for Momma. She cleaned the baby off and sat him in her arms. The midwife looked at me and said, "Looks like you have a little buddy to play with."

I remember how Momma cradled him and said, "Herbert Samuel Jackson, you are one special little boy. Jesus heard my cries and the way that I will repay Him is by protecting you forever." And that's just what Momma did.

***

The tone of Pops' voice became calm and he had a faraway look in his eyes. I had no idea the pain that he encountered as a child, because he kept that part of his life private.

That day in the bar he put it all out on the table. He wanted me to know just how he became the strong man that he was.

He let out a long heavy sigh and said, "Big Man, although I was only six years old at that time, it's something that I'll never forget."

***

Pops continued his story...

My father never made it home from that war. About two months later we received a telegram informing us that he'd been killed in combat. It felt like someone had ripped out the insides of my body. I wanted my daddy because I was tired of being a man. I knew with him being gone there was no hope for any relief.

My poor momma cried for what seemed like an entire year. She never really got out of the bed and when she did, she was on her knees praying and holding on to that baby. I had just turned seven years old and I can remember feeling jealous and alone.

I soon had to learn to pick up the pieces. With my daddy being gone I felt as though he was watching over me and I didn't want to let him down. I took being a man as serious as any seven year-old could.

The midwife's husband, Mr. Smith, owned a barbershop and a pool hall. Mr. Smith was a short, round jolly old black man who liked to drink homemade corn liquor and crack jokes. He'd pick me up every day after I'd leave the little schoolhouse that was up the road so that I could earn some money to help care for Momma and Buddy.

There I learned how to shine shoes, rack the balls for the pool table, and I was also the water boy. Those old men knew my circumstances so they always put nickels and dimes inside my tip jar. I enjoyed hanging out with those old men because I obtained a lot of wisdom and I also learned how to count and save money.

As the years went by, Momma had finally started to get stronger. She had to actually get a job since the savings that Daddy had left us were starting to run thin. She worked as a seamstress and she did it right from the little shack that we lived in. She also cleaned houses a few days out of the week, for the white folks in town. Those were the days when I had to stay home and care for Buddy. She didn't like leaving him because he was her pride and joy and a spitting image of Daddy.

When Buddy turned six years old, I felt that it was time to teach him how to do little things around the house. Momma was off in the city cleaning houses and I was left at home with Buddy. I tried waking him up.

"Come on, Buddy, there's work to be done around here. You're six years old and it's time that you start learning how to care for this place."

I remember how he peeked up from under them covers and said, "I'm too little. I can't do any work."

I remember how I pulled those covers back and made him sit up. Momma had coddled that boy so much that he didn't even know how to brush his own teeth. With her being out of the house, this was my chance to teach him how to work. I looked at Buddy and tried to give him the speech that Daddy had given me about not making excuses, when I was six. Buddy wasn't trying to hear any of that.

He looked at me and said, "Oh, shut up, I'm not making up excuses. I really am too little." He then snatched the covers back and plopped back down on the bed.

This made me angry. I snatched the covers off him and drug him through the house. He was kicking and screaming and crying the entire time. His words were "Wait 'til Momma gets home--you're gonna' get it." I knew that Momma wouldn't like it, but I knew she'd thank me later.

It was very hot that day, and I had that boy out in the yard picking fruits and vegetables, and feeding the chickens. He complained all while doing it, but he knew if he ran back in the house, I was gonna give him a whipping. Momma walked up the road about an hour later. When Buddy saw her, he dropped all the fruits and vegetables right there on that grass and ran up to her and started crying.

"Momma, James has been beating on me and he made me come out here and do all of this hard work while he sat on the back porch drinking tea with Monica from down the road."

My mouth hit the floor--*That little lying son of a gun*. Momma had a few bags in her hands and she put them down and swooped Buddy up while giving me a mean glare. She held him like a newborn child and said, "I'm sorry baby, now run along. You don't have to do any more work." She then handed him a beautiful red apple that was inside one of those bags.

Buddy ran off smiling, but not before sticking his tongue out at me when she turned her head.

Momma didn't give me a chance to explain myself. She was angry. "James Jackson, what in the heck is wrong wit' you? Buddy is too young and too little to be out here working."

I looked at Momma in disappointment and said, "I was only trying to teach him what Daddy taught me."

This made Momma even angrier. "James Jackson, shame on you for bringing the dead into this! You are just lazy and trying to push your work off on my poor lil' Buddy. Now this discussion is over. I'm going to need for you to hurry up and pick those vegetables, and wash those greens so I can get dinner started."

I remember the hurt that I felt. I'd been helping to care for our family ever since I was six years old. She never once stopped to say thank you, or son, I'm proud of you. The only word that she could manage to find was *lazy*.

"James, did you hear what I just said?" Momma screamed when I didn't respond fast enough.

"Yes ma'am," was all I could say.

***

As the years passed, I continued to work around the house, and when I became old enough I started cutting hair at the barbershop and was practically running the pool hall.

Big Man, I was making decent money for my age and throughout all those years, I managed to save up about one hundred and fifty dollars. Back in those days, that was a whole lot of money. I had a jar that I'd kept hidden inside of the wall and when Momma found me counting all of my money I had no choice but to tell her what I'd been doing.

As far as Buddy, Momma continued to let him do nothing but eat, sleep, and play my daddy's saxophone. She had given him that horn after he'd completed high school. I must admit he did have Daddy's lungs, because he was a natural at it. I guess he heard the sound from Momma's womb when our daddy was around and it stuck.

Buddy looked an awful lot like Daddy, so I really believe that's who Momma saw when she looked at him. Momma waited on Buddy hand and foot, and she never made him clean up after himself. If she asked him to do something for her, he'd just pull out that saxophone and play her a sweet tune and she'd forget all about whatever it was that she asked. Most of the time she just did it herself if I wasn't around.

Buddy soon had started hanging out at the bars, pool halls and juke joints playing that saxophone. He considered this work. When he did make money, he'd spend it all on himself, because Momma and I had never seen any of it. All of the other young boys in the area had to work on the farms or they went to the towns to work as busboys or waiters. The neighbors up the road told Momma that they were sure they could find Buddy some real work. The only thing that he had to do was be ready and in front of the house by six a.m.

I thought it was a great idea. Momma didn't think so. President John F. Kennedy had recently been assassinated in Dallas, Texas while riding in a motorcade and Momma said that she didn't trust those white folks. If they'd killed one of their own kinds, then they sure as heck wouldn't give a care about her Buddy. She also said that she didn't want him doing any hard labor on those farms. Besides, he was making good money playing that saxophone. She claimed that we had enough money in that house to live off, so Buddy didn't need to work a job like that. He was going to be a successful musician.

When she said that, I knew that she was referring to the hard-earned money that I had saved. I had made up my mind that I was going to move out of that little shack so her and Buddy could live happily ever after.

That day I understood my father more than I ever had. I appreciated how he taught me how to be a man. He knew that there was a great chance that he wouldn't make it back from that war and he wanted to make sure that I knew how to make in this world on my own.

***

When Pops finished with that story, I had gulped the entire beer down. I understood what he meant by learning how to fish. I also understood the reason that he was sharing this story. He felt that he was doing to me what his mother had done to Buddy. Pops just didn't realize that times had changed; I didn't expect for him to take care of me forever.

I stared at Pops and told him how I really felt. "Pops, Uncle Buddy was still a kid and I believe that you were being a little hard on him."

"Big Man, back in those days I wasn't hard enough on Buddy. When I think about what Momma did to him, I felt like I didn't keep up my end of the deal with my daddy. It really took a lot to run a household and it was only fair that everyone did their share. It makes it a little easier on everyone living in the home. I only wanted Buddy to learn and develop a strong work ethic so he'd be able to provide for himself. I didn't expect for him to do everything that I had done, but at least he would have known how. You can't expect to go through life with folks propping you up along the way. Eventually you have to help yourself.

"My mother just didn't know how to let go and I believe that she didn't want to let go. Buddy never complained because everything always seemed to work in his favor."

***

I was starting to loosen up, so I got up and went inside the beer cooler and grabbed two more beers as I asked my next question. "So Pops, how did you end up moving to the Motor City?"

He took a deep breath and said, "After my girlfriend Monica had the baby, I had to get out of Mississippi."

I nearly choked on the beer? "Pops, you have another child in Mississippi?" He didn't answer that question right away and began to stare off into space.

The Wedding

Pops told me about Monica…

I had been going out steady with Monica Washington for many years. I was in love with her even though Momma didn't care for her. She said something about her eyes. Momma said the best way to tell if a person was really sincere was to look them in the eyes.

The eyes are the windows to a person's soul. When a person is sincere, they have soft eyes and you can look straight into their soul. Momma said that Monica had those sneaky eyes. She said that they always looked as if she was up to something. Momma also hated the way that she dressed. She said that her skirts were too short and her shirts were too tight. I thought that she looked nice.

Well anyhow, Monica became pregnant. I was scared, but I didn't question it because she was my woman, and we were having sex. I worked even harder once I found out that she was going to have my child. I cut more hair at Mr. Smith's Barbershop, I waited more tables as a busboy, and I managed to save another fifteen dollars.

I became excited and so did Mr. Smith and his wife. They gave me their children's old furniture, toys, and clothes for the baby. I figured that once she had the baby, I'd have enough saved to get us our own place.

I remembered how I was at the small kitchen table packing up all of the stuff for the baby when Buddy walked in and noticed what I was doing.

"James, you really serious about Monica and this baby?"

I gave him a dumb look because I'd never expect for him to understand. He stared right back at me leaning against the kitchen sink wearing those silly clothes. He had on one of those fedora hats, a tight three-piece suit, and was smoking a cigarette.

"James. I wasn't going to mention anything, but I almost had to let redhead Freckle Face Frank have it. The only reason that I didn't knock him out was because he had too much to drink and it wouldn't have been a fair fight, so I just let it go."

I managed to laugh when he told that part. Buddy was a tall, slender, high yellow, pretty boy who'd never had a fight in his life. Many folks wanted to kick his behind but Buddy was a slick, fast talker, who always managed to outsmart his opponent. He'd make peace by buying them a drink, cracking a joke, or he'd let 'em beat him in craps. He didn't worry about losing because he'd buy them a few more drinks, and swap the dice for a pair of loaded dice, and he'd get all of his money back plus all of theirs.

I knew that Buddy had probably backed down because he wouldn't have stood a chance. Freckle Face Frank was also known as Big Red because of his red hair, his freckles, and he could box.

I just played into Buddy's story because he wasn't exactly what you'd call a liar. He'd just tell you a story and you had to listen closely because the truth was buried somewhere in between all of the hoopla.

"Wow, Buddy, I'm sure glad that Frank backed down, because I know that it wouldn't have been pretty."

Buddy turned around and squashed his cigarette into the ashtray that sat on top of the sink and said, "You damn right he backed down," and he threw a few jabs out into the air. "He may be big, but I'm fast and quick."

I just shook my head and let out a nervous laugh because I had no idea what he was about to say. "Buddy, what did you say was the problem with you and Frank anyway?"

Buddy became upset and fired up another cigarette. "He said something 'bout you being a big fool for falling in love with Monica, because everyone knew that she was a loose cannon. He also said that Monica named you as the father because you had all of those jobs. I told Frank to shut the hell up but he just wouldn't let it go. Frank just went on and on. James, I know that you and I may have our differences at times, but I'm just not gonna sit around and let somebody talk about you like that."

I found Buddy humorous. I'd been taking care of Buddy all of his life now he felt as though I needed protection.

"Buddy, let's be clear. Daddy raised a man, not a boy. I've never had the privilege of being that. I've been with that woman for a long time and we've been getting it on quite a bit. I believe that's my child and I'm going to be there to provide for the baby until proven otherwise. I couldn't walk out on the woman knowing that there's a great possibility that a part of me is inside of her. Your little pool hall band buddies have no clue what it's like to stand up and take care of responsibility. I don't worry about foolishness and you shouldn't either."

Buddy looked and said, "All right, James, I guess you have this all figured out. I'm going to let Freckle Face Frank off the hook this time. Now if you find out that the child isn't yours, you can't say that I didn't warn you."

Buddy left the kitchen scratching his head. On the inside I was disturbed by the allegations, but on the outside I put on a brave face. I'd bought Monica a gold-plated band and we'd planned to get married before the baby arrived. After all, I was a man like my father. I was going to make an honest woman out of Monica. I didn't want to bring no child into this world without being married to its mother. I was able to push what Buddy had told me to the back of my mind and continued packing things for the baby.

A month before Monica's due date, I finally had everything completed for the baby's arrival. We had a small wooden crib, plenty of cloth diapers and T-shirts, and I had even managed to buy the baby a beautiful blanket.

When I finished setting everything up, her mother barged into the small bedroom waving a white piece of paper. Mrs. Washington was a tall woman with a large frame, a loud voice and a controlling demeanor. "Now Monica and James, we need to have a talk."

Monica and I both turned in her direction because when she spoke you'd better listen. "This here letter is from Henry. He's found us a place and is working steady at that factory up in Flint, Michigan. He'll be back here by the end of next month to pack up this little ole shack so we can move with him."

Henry was her husband and Monica's father. Mr. Washington was a passive, soft-spoken, skinny little man who loved his wife. He didn't have a problem with her bossiness because he never complained. He was really content with living in their little shack. When Mrs. Washington's sister and her sister's husband told her that they were going up north, she sent Mr. Washington with them. She wasn't going to let anyone have more than she had.

She then directed all her attention towards me and chastened, "Now James, if you have no plans on marrying our Monica, then she's coming with us. That baby will be here in less than a month and I need to know--what's your plan?"

Monica looked at me, waiting for me to rescue her. She loved

Mississippi and I'm sure she didn't want to move up to the cold north, but she never would have told her controlling mother that.

Monica knew that I'd planned to get the ring and that Pastor Gray wasn't due back from the civil rights march in Alabama until the following week. He promised to give us a little ceremony when he returned. But with the news that Buddy had sprung on me, I wasn't sure if I could do it. I had so many things to consider. I knew that I hadn't been the only guy she'd ever been with. I did meet her at the pool hall. I also thought about how on occasion, she tended to overindulge on her liquor.

I looked over at her mother. Monica bore a striking resemblance to her, except she was a more tender, youthful-looking version. I wondered if I married her, would she boss me around like that? Would I be as foolish as her father? Would Monica look like that in twenty years? All of this raced through my mind as I felt a sharp nudge on my arm from Monica. I caved in to the pressure. After all, I was a man of integrity who had a lot invested in the relationship. That baby deserved a father and I just had to trust and believe that I was the father.

I looked at Mrs. Washington with confidence and said, "Pastor Gray will be back next week and he plans to marry us then."

Monica was ecstatic. "James, I'm so happy that you got the ring. I was afraid that you were not going to go through with it."

When she said that, it had me on edge. I became suspicious and asked in a paranoid voice. "Now Monica, what would make me do something like that? Is there something I should know?" I thought about how silly I sounded. Was this going to be my new life, questioning everything that this woman said?

Monica had a nervous look on her face. "Everything is fine, James--I just know that this is such a big commitment." I had to let it go and relax, so I wrapped my arms around her and my unborn child.

This satisfied Mrs. Washington. "Well, since you two are getting married, me and Henry have decided to give you this little ole shack as a starter home. Now it ain't much, but it's paid for. It has a lot of land out back in which you could add on to if you'd like. If Henry didn't have that job up north, I'd make him do it. Oh well--no sense in talkin' bout that. James, you're a pretty strong young man and you should have no problem fixin' this place up for yo' family." She smiled at us both and walked away.

That week went by fast. Pastor Gray had set the wedding for the following Thursday at four p.m. A day before the wedding, Momma sat me down and told me that she was proud of me and that she'd only wished that my daddy were here to see the man that I'd become. She then looked me in the eye and grabbed both my hands and said, "James, you're making the right decision."

When Momma said that, I became paranoid once again. My eyes were huge as quarters as I asked in a frenzied voice, "Why did you say that, Momma? Did Buddy tell you something? What did you hear?"

Momma giggled. "Wedding jitters, James--it's to be expected."

That evening, I waited around the house for Buddy. I wanted him to have a drink with me to celebrate my last day as a single man. He never showed up. I decided to go to the pool hall to look for him, but he wasn't there either. Instead Mr. Smith was there.

I sat at the bar as he poured me a shot of corn liquor. He looked at my face and said, "James, I'm familiar with that look. I had the same look twenty-five years ago. It just takes some getting accustomed to, but I promise that it'll all work out."

I wanted to ask if he'd heard something, but I decided against it. I had made a commitment and I was going to honor it. If it wasn't meant to happen, then I was sure that the Creator would intervene.

The day of the wedding I woke up at five a.m. because I couldn't sleep. I went into the kitchen to fix a pot of coffee when I realized that Buddy hadn't come in. I felt disappointed. I had been there for him on the most important day of his life, which was his birth, and he couldn't be there for mine.

An hour went by when he finally stepped through the front door. His clothes smelled like smoke, he was sloppy drunk and he was in no shape to be my best man. I was so frustrated when I asked, "Buddy, where have you been? Do you realize what today is?"

"He answered in a drunken state. "James, I've been out doing what you should be doing... hanging out with a bunch of pretty women. As far as what day it is, I believe today is the day that you make the biggest mistake of your life. I plan to take no part in that." He then headed to the room and slammed the door. He meant it, too, because he never came back out.

Momma and I both were dressed and ready by three o'clock. Mr. and Mrs. Smith were at the house ready to take us to the church. When they asked about Buddy, I told them that he wasn't feeling well.

When we pulled up to the church, I began to sweat. It was a beautiful day and not a cloud in sight. I remember looking up and asking whoever was up there for some sort of sign to stop this wedding if it wasn't the right thing to do. Nothing happened.

The church was very small and only had enough seating for about sixty people. The church nurse and six other church members showed up. The pastor was up front reading the Bible as the pianist sat in the corner ready to play the wedding song. Momma held my hand the entire time.

Pastor Gray came over and congratulated me one last time and shook my hand. We then took our positions because the ceremony was about to begin. The pianist played the music and the congregation stood. Monica, being escorted in by her mother stood at the end of the aisle. Although Monica was pregnant, she looked beautiful. She wore a long, simple white dress, trimmed in lace, and it fit perfect around her large belly. She had her hair pinned up, with a few flowers in it that matched her bouquet. Mrs. Washington stood next to Monica wearing a floral print dress with a large hat. She wore a huge smile on her face, but it still didn't mask her overbearing nature.

As the pianist played "Here Comes the Bride," I let out a staged smile, as uncertainty filled my entire insides.

Monica and her mother slowly two-stepped down the aisle when at the halfway mark, Monica dropped her bouquet and let out a loud piercing scream that penetrated the walls of the church. "Arrrrrrgh!!!" The music abruptly stopped. She then dropped to her knees and said, "My water just broke!" Everyone ran to assist her.

"Step back and give her some air." Mrs. Washington barked in her loud boisterous voice. I kneeled down next to my soon-to-be bride and held her hand. Mrs. Washington then said, "A lil' water ain't never hurt nobody. C'mon Pastor, let's hurry up and marry these two so that this baby doesn't come into this world born a bastard."

He grabbed his Bible, but Monica let out that scream again. "Arrrrrgh!!! It hurts so badly! I can feel this baby slipping out of me. Help me!!!"

Before Mrs. Bossy could say another word, Momma stepped in. "Hold on now, Mary. God is merciful. I'm pretty sure that He understands what's going on here. There must be a reason that He chose to bring this child into this world at this very moment. We're not going to have no bastard talk either. We're all of His chil'ren and he loves us all the same. Now go grab some towels and some water and let's get yo' grandchild into this world safely." Momma looked at me after she said that and nodded her head.

The baby was born rather quickly. Monica gave two hard pushes and out he came. The nurse immediately put the baby in my arms as she proceeded to cut the umbilical cord. I held the bloody baby, feeling so proud. All doubts were erased as I held that beautiful innocent child. Once the nurse cut the umbilical cord she took the baby out of my arms and began to clean the baby. I was staring at Monica smiling, hating the fact that I ever had any doubts. A few seconds later, the nurse handed the baby back to me and I was able to get a good look at him. I bowed my head and tried to hold back tears. It was no use. I let out a loud cry.

Monica, who was in excruciating pain reached for the baby. She took one look at him and her cries suddenly matched my own. The baby came out with fair skin and red hair.

Momma walked over to me and put her arms around my waist and guided me toward the door. I heard Mrs. Bossy yelling something vulgar, but her sounds became muffled because my mind was somewhere else.

***

Pops stopped talking for a few seconds and somberly shook his head. I felt so bad for Pops because I had no idea that he went through something so traumatic.

I then asked, "So what did Buddy have to say about the entire situation?"

Pops shrugged his shoulders and said, "Humph. He did just as I expected."

***

When we made it back to the house, Buddy was up, dressed, and on his way out the door. I swear I don't know how he did it. His body seemed to operate on naps alone, because I don't ever recall him getting a full night's rest.

Once he saw Momma and me standing there, he peeked down at his watch. He appeared surprised that we were back so soon. "James, where's your beautiful blushing bride?" he said, flashing that gold tooth.

It would only be a matter of time before word traveled around, so I figured that it was best that he heard it from me.

He sat down on the sofa with one hand on his chin and remained silent as I told the story. When I finished telling him what happened, he was astounded. Buddy jumped off the couch and slapped his knee as he screamed in disbelief. "What? You have got to be kidding me!" he said. When he realized how serious I was, he laughed. He tried to contain it, but he just couldn't help it.

Momma looked at Buddy with great scorn and said, "Buddy, this is no laughing matter. James is hurting and he doesn't need you making fun of him."

Buddy tried to contain the laughter. He then said, "I'm sorry Momma, but I wasn't laughing at James. I'm laughing at Freckle Face Frank. He talked about that woman like she was the scum of the earth, and he's the one who actually got caught with his hand in the cookie jar." Buddy laughed another big hearty laugh as I walked away into the kitchen.

His impassive behavior led me to believe that he never realized I had feelings. He had assumed that I was stronger than I really was, because he never bothered to ask if I was okay. Instead he kept at it.

"Whew--James, you sure need to get on your knees and thank whoever it was up there looking out for you, because you sure as hell dodged a bullet that time. I say we go out and have a party. Now I'll definitely drink to that!"

I stepped back into the room and said, "Buddy, there's really nothing to celebrate, because there are no winners. An innocent child has been born and he never asked for what happened today. He deserves to have a mother and a father and I can only hope that Frank steps up like a man and takes care of his child."

Buddy looked at me, still unable to comprehend. I walked off and that became the end of the discussion.

For the next few weeks, I drowned myself in my work hoping that it would assuage my desire to reach out to Monica. It really didn't help very much. I thought about it every day, and sometimes I begin to feel sorry for myself.

One evening, I'd decided that there would be no more sadness. I had to pick myself up and move forward. I knew that it wasn't going to get any better if I didn't face the situation head on. I had to stop running away from it and go to her. I'd been humiliated in front of the entire town and I wanted to know why.

I went into the cupboard where Buddy kept his stash of corn liquor and poured myself a shot. It seemed that it always made Buddy feel better. Come to think of it, anything that didn't have to do with physical labor always fulfilled him. I turned up a glass of that stuff and said, "Yuck, what the hell is it made out of?" But moments later, I was a bit more relaxed and it really didn't matter what was in it, because it seemed to work. I grabbed a light jacket and walked the two miles over to Monica's house.

I took my time, rehearsing my speech along the way. Less than an hour later I made it to her little shack. I had to get my nerves in check, so I stood outside the door for a few minutes before I knocked.

Nostalgia set in as I looked at the wooden swing set that was hanging from the tree in front of the place. I remembered how she would feed me grapes and we'd drink sweet homemade wine as we tried counting the stars. That swing was the very place where she told me that she was expecting. I recalled how I rubbed her belly and promised her that I was going to protect them both from all the troubles of the world. I really meant that. I thought about the day when I laid eyes on her pretty face in the pool hall. She seemed so sweet and innocent.

I was wishing that we could somehow go back to that happy place. She was a wonderful friend, a great listener, and she didn't mind getting her hands dirty when she helped me on that farm. She would take just about every vegetable we would pick out of the garden and make delicious vegetable soup, and after a hard day's work she'd give me a full-body massage. I hated the fact that we'd been together for years, and shared many dreams, goals, and aspirations, and without warning it was all gone.

I stood outside her door, and it was as if the beating of my heart was heard from the inside, because I didn't have to knock. The door swung open before I could even raise my knuckles. Monica was attempting to exit the door with the baby wrapped securely in her arms. She was taken aback when she saw me and immediately turned around to slam the door. I forcefully stuck my arm out, preventing her from doing so. I needed closure and I had planned to get it.

Her eyes were suddenly drowning in deep waters. She then buried her head inside of the baby's blanket. I wasn't there to bring her comfort. I'd rather see her drown than to offer a life preserver.

After a few moments, I asked the burning question. "Why, Monica?" I wasn't so sure if I was prepared for the answer, but I was a man who deserved to know the truth.

"James, I'm so sorry." I closed my eyes and threw my hand up to silence her. I got angry at hearing that word. I always believed that the word sorry is oftentimes thrown around too loosely. People tend to use that word because it's convenient and easy to say. Monica had cut me so deep that the wound was beyond repair. That word had no value and was meaningless. The time for her to say that she was sorry was immediately after she'd slept with Frank. As far as I was concerned, she was only sorry that I'd found out.

I dropped my hand and told her that I didn't want her to waste any time on an apology because I wasn't there for that. I just wanted the truth.

"It only happened once," she said through tears.

I clenched my jaw really tight and said, "I guess that's all it takes."

She sniffled and replied, "James, I understand your anger, but this baby being Frank's caught me by surprise also."

She was hardly able to control her sobs as she continued with the story. "James, I was at the bar and I had too much to drink and Frank offered to take me home. He used that opportunity to make vile and derogatory comments about you. He told me that you were a fool and an Uncle Tom for going down to the city working for the white man. He said that there was enough work to be done in our own small town. He also said that any man who had a woman as fine as I was wouldn't let me out of his sight."

I stopped Monica right there. I had heard enough. I found it to be disgusting that a man would stoop so low in order to have his way with another man's woman. What made matters even worse was the fact that my woman fell for it. She knew me better than anyone.

Monica claimed that the liquor made her weak and vulnerable. She said that she became lonely because I was hardly around. I guess it never occurred to her that I was working hard so that we could have a better life. I was done listening to any more rhetoric about how Freckle Face Frank, a wanna-be boxer, seduced my woman. He knew nothing about the value of hard work. He and my brother were one and the same.

I asked her why she let me believe that it was my child. She said that she just didn't think that it was a possibility it was Frank's, since it only happened that one time. She and I had been together for so long, and we were intimate every free chance that we had, so she was positive that I was the father. She said that although she loved the child, she was really disappointed when she realized that Frank and not me was the father.

After their evening, Monica claimed that she'd cut him off. She told him that it had been a big mistake and that it should have never happened. Frank was very angry that he had lost a woman that was never his, so he went around telling everyone that Monica was loose. He thought that word would get back to me and that I would leave her. She ended with, "James, I despise the father of my child."

When she finished speaking, I sat there silent. My eyes were soon filled with more tears than the Mississippi River. She wasn't worth my tears, so I bowed my head so that she wouldn't see them. Sadly, I still loved her and as crazy as it sounded, part of me still wanted to be with her and the child. I just couldn't make my feelings go away overnight.

Monica spoke again. "James, we can get past this. We can't just throw away all that we've had for one mistake. You really mean the world to me. Please take as much time as you need. This baby needs you. You're the only father that he knows."

That statement tugged at my heartstrings and like a running faucet, the tears began to flow. I had been a fool for at least nine months too long. Me singing and reading to her belly did not make me that baby's father, although I wished it had. I knew that I could not raise that child because every time that I laid eyes on him would be like looking at the aftermath of Monica and Frank's deception.

I looked at her for one last time and said, "All the time I will need is forever. Goodbye, Monica."

***

Pops stopped talking again. He sat at the bar and held on to that beer as he rocked his head back and forth. I remember looking at him and wondering if traveling back down that road was worth it. It seemed as if the pain of that entire situation was still there.

Pops admitted that it was still difficult to talk about even after all those years had gone by. He said that Monica was his first heartbreak. After he left Mississippi, he moved forward without ever allowing himself to heal. He tried pushing it to the back of his mind and on occasion, the pain would resurface.

He said that because of Monica, and his inability to heal, he sabotaged many relationships by carrying excess baggage.

"Big Man, after I left Monica's, I knew that my days were numbered in Mississippi. If I stayed, there was a great chance that I would have run into Freckle Face Frank and there's no telling what I may have done had I saw him.

"Luckily that never happened. A couple of days later while I was working in the barbershop, a few guys came in talking about how the job opportunities were much better up here in Detroit. They said that segregation was much more tolerable there. They talked about how the jobs were plentiful in the auto industry and they paid good money. The men mentioned a train that would be leaving in a few days and I'd made up my mind right then on the spot. I didn't even think twice, because I'd had enough. I knew that as long as I stayed in the South, there was a great possibility of me taking care of Buddy and Momma forever. I didn't mind taking care of my momma--Buddy was whom I had the problem with. I also thought about Monica's father who had found a good job in Michigan, and as far as I knew, he seemed to be adjusting quite well. I figured that I'd give it a shot because I had nothing to lose.

"I made it home and packed up my few belongings and told Momma that I was leaving. She cried because she hated to see me go, but Buddy on the other hand was happy. He wanted me out of the way so that he could have free reign with Momma. I knew that he'd been hanging out and gambling away all the money that Momma was giving him, but I never said a word to her about it. She would have just defended him or made up some excuse. I knew that I was out of there so she would just have to sit back and deal with the mess that she had created.

"When it was time for me to leave, I kept one hundred and fifty dollars of my savings and gave the rest to Momma. She was so happy that she actually cried. I was good at making and saving money, so it was no big deal for me. I knew that she needed it far more than I did. I kissed her on the cheek, and told her to tell my brother goodbye. I headed for the train to Detroit with a light overnight bag and the clothes on my back."

The Motor City

Pops told me about how he came to Detroit...

"Welcome to the Motor City and the home of Motown," the bus driver yelled excitedly into the microphone.

I opened my eyes to bright lights, beeping horns, and lots of noise. The only thing that went through my mind was a beautiful new city, endless possibilities, and no chance of running into Frank and Monica.

What a great way to start a new life--or so I thought....

The year was 1966 and Detroit was a beautiful sight to see. This city was fast and busy, lit up, and jumping. I remember seeing the Ambassador Bridge, and the Detroit River as I exited outside of the bus station. They had numerous café's, donut houses and coffee shops all around the city. The air was filled with the wonderful sounds of Motown. I remembered hearing The Supremes' "Stop in the Name of Love" playing in the background. This music seemed to play all throughout the day on the radio. If you didn't have a radio, you still heard music. Folks played instruments on the street corners, you could hear sounds coming out the jukeboxes at the local bars, and you could even hear it coming from folks' apartments when you walked past their windows.

The shopping was awesome. Hudson's and Crowley's were downtown's higher-end department stores. Woolworth's and Kresge's were the lower end stores, and if you wanted to get a nice hat, you could find that at Henry the Hatter.

After taking in the beautiful scenery of my new hometown, I finally rented a cheap motel room so that I could get a good night's rest. The next day I got a map and caught the bus down to Chrysler's employment office, which was located on Lynch Road. I still remember the big help wanted sign at the front door. Back in those days, anyone could get a job. If you worked at Chrysler and didn't like it, you could go to Ford and get a job. The same went for General Motors. There really was no reason for any man to be unemployed back in those days.

I walked into that employment office with the intentions of finding a job. But I left that place with a revived spirit, a fluttering heartbeat, and the realization that you can't run from love.

Her name was Blanche Callahan. She was the clerk at the employment office. Her beautiful face demanded my attention. When I set eyes on her, it was love at first sight. Her skin tone was a deep beautiful chocolate brown, with a light touch of cream. Her thick eyelashes and eyebrows made her brown eyes dreamy and she had a beautiful black mole above her perfect heart-shaped lips. When she opened her mouth, her words seemed to flow like a sweet melody.

"How can I assist you today, sir?" she softly said.

Now Big Man, you must remember that I was from the South, and being a young black boy from down there, you just didn't hear that word sir. I either heard my given name James Jackson by the people who knew me, or Nigger by those who didn't. So being called sir made me remove my hat and take a bow right there at that desk. She smelled so good. I was so enamored by her beauty that I never answered her question. She finally cleared her throat. I then snapped back into reality.

"Pardon my manners, ma'am, but your kind words and pleasant nature caught me by surprise. Could you please be so kind and assist me with the application process?" Flattered by my response, she flashed a radiant smile before turning around and heading to the file cabinets.

When she stepped away from the counter and I was able to get a good look at her entire frame...oh my goodness! That woman's slender top half was deceiving. It served the bottom half no justice because she was built like a brick house. She had a lot of meat on those bones! She wasn't fat, either. I'd like to call it well-proportioned in all the right places. She wore a full plaid A-line skirt that snugged at her large rear end and it caused the rest of the skirt to dance freely on its own. She sent an electrical charge running through my body and it was about to blow a fuse. I not only wanted her, I needed her and had to have her.

I continued to admire her backside as she reached over in the lower file cabinet searching for the application. She retrieved it and headed back in my direction cupping the few stacks of paper. Just watching her invigorated the juices that were flowing through my mind and I began to undress her with my eyes. When she caught me staring, I shifted my eyes back down to the dancing skirt.

She sat the application on the counter and we both leaned forward, softly bumping heads as she put X's on the lines where I needed to sign. As she straightened her posture, my face stopped short of touching her pillow-soft-looking D cups. She cleared her throat once more and put her left hand over her chest in an attempt to cover her chest. That's when I saw that she was wearing a small diamond on her left ring finger. I died inside. It felt as though I had found and lost love all in a matter of minutes. I felt silly and immediately apologized.

"I'm sorry for staring, it's just that I can't seem to read that nametag."

She quickly put my mind at ease by offering a pleasant smile while she fixed the nametag. "It's Blanche Callahan."

I grabbed the paperwork and took one last look at my lost love.

"Thanks for all of your help, Mrs. Callahan," and I headed toward the chairs to fill out the application.

She soon stopped me. "It's Miss, I'm not married. And if you need any help filling that paperwork out, I'll be happy to assist you."

The warm look in her eyes when she said that she wasn't married told it all. We both were vibrating to the same beat. Big Man, I didn't need any help. I'm sure she was accustomed to helping men fill out paperwork, but not this country boy. I knew how to read and comprehend perfectly fine.

When I returned to the counter, she was impressed. Her face had a glow as she said, "Report to the gate at three-thirty p.m. because your shift starts at four." I gladly accepted my assignment and I left.

***

Pops took another swig of beer and folded his arms and said, "I sure showed her."

Pops sat quiet and smiled after that last statement.

I wasn't impressed with how that story ended, so I stared at Pops and raised my eyebrows.

"You mean to tell me that you went through all that foaming at the mouth, longing, and undressing her with your eyes, and all that you did was show her that you could read and write? Did you even get her phone number?"

He laughed. "Big Man, that's not the end of the story. It's just that I still get butterflies thinking about that beautiful woman. I had to be honest with myself. If that woman had me losing my mind and I had just met her, then what would happen if I really got to know her? I guess I needed to prove to myself that I could walk away."

"Pops, that makes no sense whatsoever."

"Big Man, maybe it doesn't make sense to you, but with everything that Monica had sent me through, I was just happy to know that my heart could still skip a beat. Besides, I had nothing to offer that sophisticated woman at that time. I'd definitely planned to pursue her, but it was all about timing."

***

That afternoon I started working at the factory and I adapted rather quickly. If you didn't know why Detroit was called the Motor City, you knew once you stepped inside that place. It was like a small city and it was hotter and steamier than Mississippi in the summertime. That place smelled like a mixture of oil, smoke, and dirty money.

It was hard work back in those days. Your entire body would ache. That metal was so heavy that it took two or more people to lift it. There were hundreds of welders going off at the same time, and those welding machines sent off sparks that you wouldn't believe. If you weren't careful, you could get severely burned, or badly bruised.

Since folks were hired in right off the streets, so you had many different characters working there. You could get just about whatever you wanted in that place. You could play your numbers, bet on the horse races, and buy pills. If it was cold outside, you could even buy a pair of boots and a fur coat.

My southern accent caused me to stand out right away and I soon became known as Mississippi James to some of the guys in that place. I'd also realized that just when you thought that you've had it bad, there's always someone who's got it much worse.

I heard so many sob stories. The men complained about their wives, how they weren't being able to make ends meet, their hungry children, and utility shutoff notices. Before I knew it, I had become a petty loan shark.

I was one of the very few men who didn't have a family, and so my little nest egg that I'd saved up made this all possible. I was familiar with how it worked because I had collected plenty of times for Mr. Smith. My interest rate was twenty five percent and I always followed the golden rule: "Never loan more than you can afford to lose." I stuck to that rule and capped out at fifteen dollars. If you needed more than that, then you had to go to Black Jack.

Black Jack was the old man and the original owner of this topless bar. I met him the second week I started working. I asked a few guys about housing and they said that Black Jack was my guy.

When I came into this establishment, he sat in this exact spot. He was a big, tall, dark, old man with silver hair and a gold tooth in the front of his mouth. He had a southern accent, and the moment he spoke, I knew that he was from the South. When I introduced myself, as James Jackson, he gave a friendly smile.

"Well, James, that just happens to be my son's name, and you surely don't want to be mistaken for him. So do you mind if I called you Jimmy?"

I returned the smile. "I don't mind if you do."

Black Jack and I both were from Mississippi. He too was a veteran of World War II just like my daddy, but he made it out alive. He moved his family north shortly after he returned from the war for better job opportunities. His wife had passed away a few years earlier and he knew that he would never remarry. This bar was just a form of entertainment for him and it kept him from feeling lonely.

I sat down and told Black Jack about what life was like in Mississippi. I also talked about the job skills I acquired while growing up. When I told him about the down payment that I had, Black Jack couldn't believe it. He said that most men came to him needing a loan or some credit, and here I was, much younger than most of them and much more disciplined.

He told me about a duplex that he had and if I wanted to purchase it, he could talk to his son who was a banker and he could make it happen. I wasn't ready to purchase anything yet, but I did rent out one of the units. Black Jack said that the offer would remain open if I ever changed my mind. He said that he was getting old and tired of the business.

That day, Black Jack and I became a team. He had a lot of respect for me because he deemed me an honest man. He wished that his own son, James Vernon, would take over the establishment, but that wasn't likely to happen because his son had much bigger goals. I agreed to help Black Jack out because I had the experience, and needed the extra money. It also kept me from thinking about home.

Black Jack gave me a tour of the small watering hole. It had a small kitchen with a room attached to the back where the go-go dancers changed into their attire. It had a long bar with a dance floor and a stage surrounded by several tables and chairs for patrons to sit.

Black Jack was proud of his establishment. "Jimmy, it ain't much, but at least our people have somewhere that they can come to after a hard day's work."

The next stop was The Black Jack Room. It was a small, damp room with pale green walls and a cement floor, located in the basement of the building. It had a pool table, a craps table and a couple of card tables. There was also a small bar with a jukebox that sat off in the corner. Another small room with lots of boxes, and a few broken tables and chairs attached to it. The place was not very big, but it did have lots of room for expansion.

Black Jack told me that was he was the king of Black Jack and that he had been called that name since he was a teenage boy. Every Friday, he had a few loyal customers that would stay there all night, playing cards, poker and listening to the blues on the jukebox.

Once I finished with his tour, I asked Black Jack if he knew Blanche Callahan.

Black Jack looked at me and said, "I sure do know that pretty young lady. I also know her father, Dr. Callahan, too. Jimmy, I'm going to be honest with you. Dr. Callahan has three girls and all of them are well-educated. I heard Dr. Callahan say with my own ears that his girls are not going to marry any factory workers, or grease monkeys as he'd called 'em. He treats them girls like queens. Jimmy, you wouldn't stand a chance. If you don't believe me, well then asks my son James Vernon. He's married to his oldest daughter Nancy. My son does pretty well in the banking business, but he's a workaholic. He's trying extra hard to impress that doctor. This bar, along with working in the factory, is what put him through college. Now all of a sudden he says that this neighborhood is not safe and that's why he doesn't come around much." Black Jack let out a long sigh and said, "Humph. The nerve of that son of mine."

Black Jack stood his ground. He told his son that he loved his establishment and the customers did too. They were more family to him than a son who only dropped in to complain.

I didn't mention any more about Blanche to Black Jack. I knew what I saw and felt when I laid eyes on that beautiful woman. There definitely was some sort of chemistry between the two of us. I was also glad that Black Jack had given me this piece of information about Dr. Callahan. But I wasn't going to let her father's perception of what he considered a real man get in my way of asking her out.

I worked hard in that factory every day, and on the weekends I worked at the bar with Black Jack. I loved my new city and my new life. I was also proud of the fact that every Friday when I got paid, I was able to send twenty dollars home to Momma. I knew that she was still taking care of Buddy, who was then a grown man, but at least I didn't have to see it.

Momma did send letters thanking me for the money. She also told me how proud of me Daddy would have been. When she didn't mention Buddy, I knew that things probably hadn't changed. A few months later, Momma wrote me a letter stating that Buddy had finally gotten a job. She said that I didn't have to send any more money because he was making enough to take care of his own basic needs.

I wrote her back stating how proud of Buddy I was, but my congratulations came too little too late. Buddy had lost his job. Of course Momma said that it wasn't his fault. She couldn't believe that the job expected him to come to work even though he was sick. When Buddy didn't show up, they'd fired him. I inquired no further. I just started sending the twenty dollars home again.

After about six months, I had a hefty savings, and a comfortable duplex that I was renting. I bought some wood and made a swing that I hung on the tree, and I also planted a vegetable garden. The place was really starting to look and feel like home. I was finally ready to purchase a car. Black Jack thought it was a great idea and he knew just who to call. But before he contacted his son, he issued me a stern warning.

"Jimmy, my son is well-educated and he has a pretty good position at the bank. Sometimes he tends to look down on folk. I don't believe that the boy means any harm. That money has just gone to his head. Sometimes people tend to forget where they come from when they get a good job and a few dollars in their pocket. My son happens to be one of them."

The next day I met up with James Vernon, who was a few years older than I was. He was a tall, fair-skinned man with broad shoulders, and a confident demeanor. He was very articulate and his professionalism could easily be mistaken for an "uppity Negro." I understood the misconception that Black Jack had of his son, but I also knew that it was all a part of this game called…doing what you have to do to get ahead in life.

James Vernon seemed genuinely pleased to meet me because he said that his father spoke very highly of me. That moment felt awkward because unfortunately I couldn't say the same. James Vernon laughed and said, "I didn't expect you'd be able to say the same thing because my father is old, and set in his antiquated ways. He's upset that I won't put my career aside and help run his bar. It's unfortunate, but that bar is his dream, not mine."

James Vernon then pulled out the application and proceeded to read it to me. I stopped him before he could read the first sentence. "Can I take a look at that, sir?"

He gave me a strange look and stumbled over the words. "Why, sure."

I nodded at him and read it out loud. Once I finished reading it, I asked for a pen. I then gave James Vernon a quick wink and signed on the dotted line. He had a look of embarrassment on his face, but he did his best to contain it. That was the day that we had become friends. I drove away in a 1957 Chrysler Imperial. It was in immaculate shape for an eight-year-old car.

I was proud of all that I'd accomplished in the past six months, so I felt that it was time to go and claim my prize. The beautiful Blanche Callahan.

***

Pops wore that big wide smile again and I thought, *She must have been one special lady.*

He continued with the story...

***

I knew that she still worked at the employment office because I'd been keeping a close eye on her. I tried to convince myself that

I'd forget all about her and move on once I was situated. But I just couldn't shake her from my mind. I dreamed about that woman every night and day.

One morning, I put on my best clothes and hung around that employment office. I remembered how I kept peeking through the window staring at her. Around noon I watched as she grabbed her sweater and headed for the door. I admired her from a short distance. She looked very elegant, wearing a beautiful flowered skirt with a nice ruffled blouse. I looked down at my nice black slacks and button-down shirt topped off with black dress shoes and a black hat. I said to myself, "Just because I work in the factory, doesn't mean that I have to look like I work there."

I began to follow her. She stopped at a small café around the corner from her job. I followed her inside. She stepped up to the counter and took a seat. I paused by the door and removed my hat and sat right next to her. "Ms. Callahan. What a surprise I should find you here." She turned and looked at me and I could see the stars in her eyes.

"James Jackson, what a surprise. I thought that I would never see you again." Once she said my name I knew that I'd left some sort of impression on her.

I asked her if she wanted to sit in a booth. She smiled as I led the way. We moved over to the small booth and I couldn't help but to stare at the beautiful mole that was just above the right side of her lips. It gave her an exotic look and I couldn't seem to take my eyes off of that woman's face.

Blanche knew that I was staring at her mole, which she hated. So she picked up her menu and put it above her lip, only exposing her eyes. I knew that she was trying to hide behind the menu so I said to her, "I love that beauty mark above your lip."

She blushed and said, "As a child I got teased about it all the time, but now I guess I've just grown accustomed to it." She then removed the menu.

We sat there like two long-lost friends playing catch-up.

Blanche came from a prestigious white-collar family. Her father was a doctor and her mother was a schoolteacher. She was the youngest of three girls. Her older sister Nancy was a part-time nurse and happily married to James Vernon. Her middle sister was single and a schoolteacher in Chicago. Blanche was only twenty-three years old and had a degree in human resources. She had been working at the employment office for about a year.

Hearing this woman's background made me feel a bit insecure and I soon felt as if I wasn't good enough. I'd had only heard, or read about black families like hers, so being in her presence was an honor in itself. There wasn't anything that I could say that would bring my family even close to hers. I did tell her how proud of the fact that my daddy was a great saxophone player and that he died a war hero. I really didn't know if the government classified him as such, but I sure did.

I told her that I was raised in the South and it wasn't easy. "I've had to earn my way since I was a small child."

When I said that, Blanche seemed to become fascinated. She wanted to know more. "Wow! What was that like?" I told her about the talk that my daddy and me had before he went to war and the promise that I made to him. I respected and looked up to my daddy and I was going to honor his wishes. I talked about how I had gotten a job at a young age and have worked hard my entire life to take care of my mother and younger brother Buddy.

Blanche was really turned on. "James, you're such a handsome fellow, why on earth haven't any of those southern women snatched you up?"

I paused because I didn't know how to answer that question. I'd been so busy with moving, working, and saving money that I didn't have time to even think about Monica.

Blanche noticed how hesitant I became. She put her hand over her mouth and said, "Oh my! Are you married, James? I shouldn't be having lunch with a married man."

I knew that I had to clear that up. Blanche was a beautiful woman and the day that I set eyes on her was the day that Monica had become a distant memory. I needed Blanche. Even if it was just to keep my mind off of Monica.

I looked into her beautiful eyes and said, "Blanche, I'm not married." I tried to contain the pain in my voice, but it was no use. I clasped my hands together and slightly bowed my head. It was then that I realized how much hurt I still harbored from my failed relationship with Monica.

I thought that by moving to Detroit, the hurt and pain would go away. But once the last box was unpacked, the dust settled and the mere mentioning of her name, the pain had resurfaced. I guessed that it never really left. Moving was only a temporary distraction.

As I stared at Blanche, I knew that I needed to talk about what happened with Monica. Although I had just formally met her, I trusted her. I really wanted a fresh start and in order to get that, I had to rid myself of the excess baggage. I figured that was the only way to make the pain go away.

"I told Blanche everything about my relationship with Monica. I talked about her being kind, loving, a great cook and friend. Blanche held my hand and listened attentively as I told her about the baby.

"Blanche, I loved that baby when I felt him move in her belly. I was really looking forward to becoming a father. I had to leave Mississippi because there's no way that I could have stayed there after what happened. I was ashamed and felt inadequate. I also knew that I would have never been able to look at Monica and her baby and not wish that they were my family.'"

Blanche appeared sympathetic and kind, and even became teary-eyed. She couldn't believe that a woman could be so cruel. It felt good talking to her. Although I hadn't known her long, just being in her presence alleviated most of the pain from my past.

I didn't want to sound as if I was throwing a pity party, so I changed the subject and told her about Buddy. I shared the story about his birth.

"Blanche I have a brother who is five years younger than me. He was born shortly after my father went off to the war. I was there for his birth and it was really scary. My brother Buddy started to come out breeched until the midwife turned him around. When he came into this world he wasn't breathing. Momma prayed over that boy and a few seconds later he started screaming. Momma felt that her prayers were answered. She believed that he was a special child because God let him live. When she looked at his fair skin and he opened up those green eyes she saw Daddy. She made up in her mind that God had took Daddy away and brought her Buddy in his place. She promised God that she'd protect him from harm and she kept that promise literally. She held on to that baby and now over twenty years later, she's still holding on. Buddy has Momma wrapped around his finger. He's charming, flashy, and cares only about himself."

Blanche was so tickled that she started laughing. "Your brother sounds like a real character."

I shook my head and said, "You've got that right. He came into this world ass-backwards and he's been living his life that way ever since."

We both had a big laugh at that one.

"I was having such a good time with her that the time was flying so fast. I looked down at my watch and it was twenty minutes until her lunch hour was up. I had learned that her father was in his late sixties and he talked about grandchildren. He wanted for one of his daughters to get married and have some children before he was too old to enjoy them. He set aside a huge trust fund just for grandchildren.

She talked about how her sister Nancy and James Vernon were both happy. They were too busy with trying to get his business ventures off the ground to settle down and have children. Her middle sister Marie loved her job and traveling so she didn't see kids in her near future. I looked at her wondering if she was the one who was perceived to have the first grandchild. I couldn't help but to stare at the small chip of diamond on her finger and wanted to know so desperately what that was all about.

"Blanche I can't help but notice that you're wearing that beautiful ring on your left hand." She looked down at the ring in distress and twirled it around on her finger.

"Winston gave me this before he took off for medical school in California." she said. This caught my attention. I didn't have to ask who Winston was because she willingly volunteered.

"We've been together since junior high, and we are all the other knows." She wore a smug look on her face as she continued to talk. "Mother says that I shouldn't have accepted the ring since we were both still very young and haven't had a chance to experience other people. Father thinks differently. He absolutely adores Winston. He loves the fact that he comes from a wealthy family and is studying to become a doctor. My father believes in marrying your own kind. He wouldn't approve of me dating someone who doesn't have an education."

My palms became sweaty. I then looked at Blanche, who seemed to have mixed emotions. "Well, Blanche, what do you think?"

When I asked that, her face seemed to relax and she had a sparkle in her eye.

"James, no one has ever asked me how I felt. When I tried explaining to Winston that maybe we shouldn't think about marriage and that he should just focus on becoming a great doctor, he wasn't listening and he forced me to take the ring. When Mother saw the ring, she said to give it back. Father said that was nonsense, and for me to keep the ring and marry that good man before he finds another good girl to marry. Everyone made such a fuss over my life, that I don't know what to feel."

Blanche said that she felt a sense of obligation to accept the ring because she was in a very bad car accident her freshman year in college and that she was in pretty bad shape. She had to have several reconstructive surgeries and had to learn how to walk all over again. Winston was there and never left her side.

I looked at her and said, "Well, that's what a good man does."

Blanche smiled and said, "Yes, he is a gentleman and a very nice man." She wore a soft smile as she played with the ring and repeated herself once again. "Yes, he is a very nice man."

When I heard her say the word "nice," that threw up a red flag for me. I'd learned throughout my lifetime that women tended to take them for granted. When I thought about my relationship with Monica, I remembered how she often referred to me as a nice guy or a good man. In the end, I came out on the bottom.

I secretly despised that phrase.

I'd decided to end the talk about Winston and focus on what was in front of me.

"Blanche, since he's going to be away in medical school for at least a few years, why don't you just do what feels natural? You are a beautiful woman, who has a job. Your parents can't speak on your personal business if they don't know any of it."

She looked me and smiled. "I knew that there was something special about you."

From that day forward we became really close friends. I took my time and coasted throughout the friendship for the next few weeks. I didn't want to rush my feelings because I knew that the pain from having your feelings hurt was too difficult to recover from.

I took her to lunch a few times a week. On the weekends we would meet downtown where she would give me a tour of this great city. This went on for several months, with no mention of her parents or Winston. Around that time, I was no longer able to control my feelings.

I woke up with Blanche on my mind, and went to bed with her on my mind. I envisioned having a family with her. I wanted children--lots of them. I sensed that she felt the same, by the way that she grabbed my hand while we strolled down the street, and the way she would bury her face in my chest when we watched a movie in the theatre. She'd also let me grab her face and thumb my finger across the mole that she once felt so insecure about. After about a month our relationship suddenly took flight. I was in love with Blanche and I couldn't seem to get enough of her.

At that time I understood what Freckle Face Frank meant when he told Monica that a man with a woman this fine shouldn't leave her side. I felt the same thing about Winston. That man was foolish for leaving this beautiful woman behind.

I'd given Blanche a key to my duplex, and on some days when I'd get off of work, she'd be waiting for me. She helped me turn my duplex into a home by helping to decorate it. We painted the entire house an eggshell white and I chose a soft blue color for the spare bedroom. Blanche added her own personal touch by adding candles and flowers. She spent a lot of time at my place. I had no idea what she told her parents, and didn't care. I was just happy to be with her.

I thought that Blanche was perfect. She'd helped me with my vegetable garden and I taught her how to make vegetable soup. On Sunday evenings, we would sit in the backyard on the swing and count the stars or I would lay a blanket across the grass where she would give me a full-body massage.

I continued working long hours at the factory and at the bar on the weekends with Black Jack. Every free moment after that had been spent with Blanche. Many women in that bar had approached me and some even tried to seduce me, but I wouldn't fall for it. No other woman in the city of Detroit could measure up to Blanche. I wanted a family and lots of children, and Blanche was the one that I wanted that with. I even bought a rocking chair to put inside of the spare bedroom.

Our relationship had been going strong for almost a year when I received a letter from Momma. She stated how she really appreciated the money, but she'd appreciate it even more if my lady friend and me would come home to pay her a visit.

Blanche was stacking dishes in his kitchen as I read the letter to her. She suddenly dropped a glass plate on the floor and shot me a troubled look. "James, you told your mother about us?" she asked in a disturbed voice.

I became still. "Yes Blanche. She knew about you the day I laid eyes on you."

Blanche became nervous. "I can't. There's just no way that I could account for being gone that amount of time."

I suddenly felt ill. I'd been so busy working two jobs, saving money, and loving a woman who had to keep me a secret. I soon realized that once again, I'd played the fool. My mother knew all about Blanche, but her parents knew nothing about me. I was disappointed because Blanche was a grown woman who was still afraid of her father.

I re-evaluated my life and soon realized that it was like running on a treadmill--moving fast, but going nowhere.

That was the moment that I wished that I could be more like Buddy. But it seemed as if Buddy and I were cut from two different cloths. I couldn't manage to control my feelings, whereas Buddy didn't seem to have any feelings. I can never recall Buddy ever being hurt.

"When it came to Blanche, I could no longer ignore the elephant in the room. We could no longer tap-dance around her family, me not having a college education, and Winston. Ignoring these issues did not mean that they didn't exist, and it certainly wouldn't make them go away. I couldn't handle being hidden. I wanted to be accepted. I may not have had a college education, or came from a prestigious family but I was not ashamed of who I was. I was proud of being a hard worker and a good man who learned to put away money in the bank. That surely had to count for something.

Blanche was bent over with the broom and dustpan, picking up the glass when I tapped her on her shoulder.

"Please have a seat, Blanche. I'll clean the glass up." She was still shaking as she moved over to the small sofa. She played with her hands as I tried to get her to look at me. I needed to see her eyes. I remembered what Momma had said about a woman's eyes. I was wondering what I'd see when I looked into hers. I wanted Momma to meet her. If I couldn't see anything, Momma surely could.

Blanche finally looked up and the only things that I could see were misty eyes, and a lot of sadness. She took her hands and started rubbing her eyes. I reached behind her and grabbed the box of Kleenex. She took a couple and started blowing her nose.

I kneeled down next to her and said, "I am in love with you and I want to spend the rest of my life with you. I want a family. A great big family and I want that with you. I promise that as long as you're with me, you won't ever have to worry about anything."

Blanche was quiet. You could hear more sound in a mausoleum than you could with her. She sat there with her mouth open, her eyes wide, and yet and still, she couldn't come up with any words. I wondered how long did she think that we could play part-time house?

I didn't know what to make of it. I didn't know if it was too soon to be talking like that, and I didn't know if I was rushing her. I then started to question if she felt the same.

"James, this is just too much for me to handle right now. I'm afraid that my father would never approve of us. I'm so sorry, James, but I knew that this day was going to come. I'm not the woman for you. I can't give you what you want."

I stopped her and practically begged. "Blanche, I won't let you face this alone. I will go to your father and Winston. I'm not afraid. You and I were made for each other."

Blanche jumped up and started crying while still trying to hold it all together. "It's over, James! Find someone who can give you what you deserve. I can't be your family or even give you a family."

I begged her to stop saying that, but she wouldn't.

"James, you just said that you want a family and lots of children. That's all you seem to talk about. Well, James, I can't have children." Those words came as a shock. I didn't know what to say. Blanche continued speaking while holding back tears. "James, because of my accident, the doctor said that there's a great possibility that I won't be able to have children."

I took a deep breath and grabbed both her hands as a way of soothing her. "Blanche, you said that the doctor said that it's a great chance you won't be able to have children, he didn't say there was zero chance."

Blanche started shaking her head. "James, it's been validated! I can't give you a family!"

"Blanche, how do you know that? We've never tried to have children." I said desperately.

She grabbed her purse and headed for the door still in tears. "James, we've been together for almost a year and we're intimate every time that we're together and I've never gotten pregnant. It's not like I was trying to have kids, but I wasn't doing anything to prevent having them. I can't help but to ask myself--is this a punishment for betraying Winston? I see the longing in your eyes every time we're together and a couple walks by with a baby. You stop and stare. I wanted to give you that. I wanted to give you the child that Monica didn't give you."

Blanche then pointed into the spare bedroom. "James, look at that bedroom. You even bought a rocking chair. The only thing that is missing is a crib and the baby. I told myself that I wouldn't mention this, but I feel that I have to. When you came to bed last night, you were so tired. I started massaging your back and you called me Monica."

I stood there and dropped my head. I was completely embarrassed.

Blanche then said, "James, when I was unpacking the boxes that you asked me to a while back, this fell out."

She reached into her purse and held up a photo of Monica and me sitting on the swing in Mississippi. I remembered that photo. Mr. Washington had taken it before he left for Michigan.

She handed me the photo. "James, who are you really seeing when you look at me?" I studied the picture. I never realized how much Blanche and Monica looked alike. Blanche was a little fuller than Monica and she had a mole above her lip, but other than that, they looked very similar.

"James, all of the memories that we have are the same memories that you and Monica created. You ran away from a life in Mississippi only to recreate that life here." Blanche then stepped over to the window and pointed to the backyard. "The swing outside, the garden, and the vegetable soup that you have me make." she said somberly.

My mouth hung wide open but I didn't speak. I'd told her all these things about Monica at the beginning of our relationship and now my words were coming back to haunt me. I wanted to say something, but I was afraid of saying the wrong thing.

Blanche continued to speak through soggy tears. "James, I wanted to tell my parents about us but I felt that there was a great chance I'd get hurt. I've lost a big part of myself in this romance by trying to fill another woman's shoes only to find out that I can't. James, I can never come close to that woman because I can't have children."

I tried to reach out and grab Blanche, but she moved closer to the door.

She took the Kleenex and started to dry her eyes. She then regained her composure and said, "Winston will be back in two weeks. I've been avoiding all of his calls. He's expecting an answer about our future. I thought long and hard about it for the past few weeks and I believe that it's best that I go and be with him."

I was floored. "Blanche, you just said that you were willing to have my baby. How can you possibly be with Winston?"

She sniffled once more and straightened her posture almost convincing herself that this was what she wanted. "Winston knows me and he loves me and I won't have to compete for his love. He accepts the fact that we will never have kids. He just wants me to be Mrs. Winston Baker. He's even willing to leave school in California and attend school here if that's what it takes to make me happy. My father loves him. If I decide to be with you, I could risk my father's love, and I won't let that happen."

Blanche then gathered up all of her strength and said, "James, I choose Winston Baker. He's a safe bet and I'd be a fool to gamble all of that away."

I was disappointed and heartbroken at hearing those words. I knew that Blanche's decision to be with Winston had everything to do with

LOST SOUL

Pops continued his story about going home to Mississippi...

When I made it to the tiny shack in Tunica Mississippi, it was unrecognizable. Buddy had let the place go to crap. The lawn was brown, the porch seemed to be cracking, and the aluminum awning had several dents and part of it hung down like a branch on a weeping willow tree. I walked around to the back and was sad to see that the vegetable garden was gone and so were all of those chickens.

I wasn't upset, nor surprised. I just shook my head and said, *This is was what Momma created.*

I stepped onto the back porch, which looked worse than the front and tapped on the door. Buddy opened the door barefoot, wearing a pair of pajama bottoms, and a plain white t-shirt. It was well after noon, and by the look of him, he had just woken up.

Before I could step in, Buddy gave me a big celebratory hug and said, "James Jackson, look at you! You must be living really good up there in Detroit, because you're as clean as a whistle.' I really didn't have time for my brother's foolishness so I hugged him back and said, 'It's good to see you too, Buddy. Now where's Momma?"

His body language weakened and his demeanor became sobering when I didn't give in to all of the hokum.

pleasing her father rather than herself because she never confessed her love for Winston.

"Wow, Blanche! I guess that I can't top that! I really want you to know that I'm sorry for calling you Monica and that I really do love you."

Blanche held on to the door and closed her eyes. "James, it was fun while it lasted. Now go and find someone who can give you a family. I would never be able to live with myself for taking that away from you."

Blanche then opened the door and softly closed it behind herself.

I wanted to chase after her, but the paralysis from my spirit wouldn't allow me to move. Blanche had somebody who really cared for her and I had no business getting involved. I didn't like the pain that Freckle Face Frank caused by stealing my woman. What right did I have to inflict that exact pain on someone else?

***

Big Man, that day I can remember sitting on that floor for hours, thinking, drinking, and evaluating the last few years of my life. It was then that I decided to open Buddy's letter that had been sitting on the table for a few days.

His letter said that I needed to get home as soon as possible because Momma's health was really failing her. I thought about the letter that Momma had recently sent. I soon realized that she didn't want to alarm me, but her asking to see me was her way of saying that something was wrong.

Big Man, I didn't hesitate. I took a week off of work and hopped into my Chrysler Imperial and headed south.

"She's in the back and she's not doing well at all." He then wiped a few tears from his eyes and said, "I don't know what we're going to do without Momma!"

I kind of felt bad for the poor boy. Although he was an adult according to age, he was nothing but a big ole kid. The clown-like behavior and all of the hype was nothing but a façade. He was a scared little boy on the inside.

I gave my brother one last hug and said, "It's going to be all right." I removed my black fedora hat and proceeded through the filthy house. Dishes were piled in the sink, the floor was dirty, and the flies seemed to have made a team huddle around the overflowing trash. I kept quiet. The small living area was worse than the kitchen. It seems as if Buddy had had a party. The ashtrays were full of cigarette butts, liquor bottles were scattered throughout the room, and articles of clothing were hanging over the couch. It was disgusting.

Before I entered Momma's room, a short dark-skinned young woman was leaving with a cigarette hanging from her mouth fixing her blouse. She yelled to Buddy, "Who's at the door?" After nearly running over me, she gave me a surprised look and boldly asked, "Who are you?" Before I could let this lady have it, Buddy ran up and nervously intervened.

"Lisa, this is my big brother James. James, this is Lisa, she stopped by to help me clean this place up. Since Momma has been down, I've been having a hard time keeping this place up." Lisa put her hand on her hip and appeared as if she was getting ready to let Buddy have it. But he gave her a look as if to say that she'd better not.

I was fed up with all of this so I asked, very direct, "Where the hell is my momma and why on earth is Lisa coming out of her room with a cigarette in her mouth?"

Buddy grew even more nervous because he didn't want to see my other side, so he started speaking fast. "Momma and I traded bedrooms." My eyes grew wide. Buddy sensed my anger, so he started talking faster. "James, it was her idea. She liked the smaller room because it was closer to the bathroom and the window was larger." I was upset, but I had no more time to waste. I walked in the direction of the smaller room, which was exactly three steps away from the bigger room and gave a light tap on the door before I entered.

Momma was resting quietly. The room was small, but at least Buddy had the decency to keep it tidy. I sat in the rocking chair that was next to her bed and I watched her sleep. Momma always had a strong sense of smell, so she soon opened her eyes and sat up.

She looked at me and smiled. "James, I'm so happy to see you." I stared at the beautiful, petite brown-skinned woman, with the dark brown eyes and thick black hair that was plaited in four braids. I realized just how much I looked like her.

"I'm so happy to see you too, Momma. Can I get you anything?"

She smiled at me and said, "James, I have all that I need right here. You have been taking care of me my entire life; and that, my son, is more than enough."

She reached over to the small dresser and grabbed a glass of water and took a sip. "The nurse just left here a few hours ago and she made sure that I was comfortable." Momma pointed to the pill bottles that were left there on the dresser for her to take. "James, I'm very ill. I have chronic heart disease and unfortunately there's nothing that they can do about it other than give me a bunch of pills to take. Son, they make me really tired and I can't get out of this bed. I never wanted to be a burden on anybody, so I decided to stop taking all of those pills and to let the good Lord's will be done."

I sat there and bowed my head; her words hurt. She was only fifty-five years old and her life was being cut short way too soon.

She looked at me and suddenly had a quick burst of energy. "James Jackson, didn't your father teach you to be strong? I don't want any sympathy. I'm ready to meet my Creator and I know that my husband will be standing there waiting on me. Oh, how I miss his handsome face. I can't wait to look into those green eyes, and touch his wavy hair."

Momma then reached over and picked up the small black and white wedding picture of her and Daddy, and she kissed it. She held the picture so that I could see it. "Buddy looks just like your father." I smiled because he really did. When I looked at the picture, I really understood why Buddy got away with so much. Momma really saw Daddy when she looked at Buddy.

She drifted off to sleep holding that photo. I kissed her head and quietly walked out of the room.

I took a seat in the living area when I noticed that someone had made an effort to clean up. Most of the bottles and trash were gone, but the tables were still dusty and a strong stale cigarette smell lingered throughout air. I also noticed that a pair of men's dress shoes and socks was kicked under the couch. I found it to be rather amusing that Buddy was supposedly a grown man and he still cleaned like a small child.

Buddy stepped out of the room alone looking as though he was on his way to a fool's convention. He wore a black three-piece sharkskin suit, with a white dress shirt, which he purposely left the first four buttons undone so that one could see that his neck was draped in gold. He sported a gold watch on each wrist and four gold rings dressed each finger on his right hand. My brother really knew how to stand out.

My initial response was to tell him how silly he looked, but I knew Momma wouldn't like that. There were more important things to discuss regarding Momma, the house, and the insurance policies. I didn't want to waste time on something so frivolous.

Buddy paced back and forth in the small living area looking for something. I reached under the couch and pulled out a pair of lizard shoes. Buddy gleamed as I held the shoes up. I then tossed them at him. He quickly erupted and said, "Whoa James. You just can't go tossing my stuff around. These ain't some cheap pair of shoes; they're Stacey Adams." He then swooped the shoes up and gently wiped them.

I shook my head in despair. I had to then get serious. "Buddy, you need to take a seat, there's some things that we need to discuss regarding Momma."

He looked at his watch and stormed for the door. "James, I can't talk about that stuff right now. I have a meeting with a few of the fellas. We're starting a new band and we have to talk about that. Sammy should have been here ten minutes ago. I'm running late."

Just like Buddy, I thought, *always on the go*. He never had time for anything important. To him life was nothing but all fun.

I stood and grabbed my keys. "Buddy, I'll take you. I've been looking forward to seeing Mr. Smith. We have a lot of catching up to do."

I went into the room to check on Momma before we left. She wasn't asleep. She sat in her rocking chair next to the window with her crochet hook and yarn, making something. She looked angelic as the light shined across her beautiful face.

She smiled at me as she patted the bed, inviting me to have a seat. "James, I may not have said it as often as I should have, but I've always been so proud of you. When I look at you, I see your father's strength. I've never had to do anything for you because you've always been so strong."

I smiled and gave my momma a big hug. I'd been waiting a long time to hear those words. It felt good to know that she saw a part of Daddy when she looked at me and that she appreciated all the sacrifices that I had made.

Momma then gave me a soft pat on my hand and whispered, "James, promise me that you'll take care of your brother. He's not strong like you and he's going to need a little help. All you two will have is each other."

I kissed Momma on the hand. I didn't like to think about her leaving this earth, but after hearing her speak, she was already gone. She was tired of the pain and she was ready to be with her husband. For me to want her to stay would have been selfish.

I made that promise to Momma, although I believe we had two different definitions of what *take care of* meant.

***

Buddy was standing outside admiring my car.

"OOOOWeeee James, this car sure is sharp! So this is how they do it up in Detroit, huh?" Buddy jumped in the passenger's side and continued to be in awe. "See, this is how I'm gonna be living in a few years." He smiled and bobbed his head up and down. I looked over at my brother, who would probably never be able to afford anything on his own if he didn't change his ways. I then used that as an opportunity to tell him about life.

"Buddy, you have to get a job and make some money in order to live like this. Momma won't be here forever. It's time that you grew up. You are going to have to stand on your own two feet."

This struck a nerve with Buddy. "Whoa, whoa, whoa James." He put up two fingers and said, "Peace on that!" I stopped talking after that. He didn't want to hear it. This was Buddy's way of diffusing any situation, so I returned the peace sign and let him talk.

He pulled out a roll of bills and began to fan himself with the money. "James, I've got money. I'm just not ready to buy a ride yet. I'm trying to put some things together. I got everything under control." he said.

When I saw those bills, I knew that he was just showing off. Buddy couldn't hold on to any money, and before night's end, he would squander it all away.

When we pulled up to the barbershop and pool hall, Buddy hurriedly jumped out of the car and headed toward the back door. "Hey Buddy, aren't you going to come in and say hello to Mr. Smith?"

Buddy was halfway around the back when he shouted, "You go right on ahead and play catch-up; I'll see him later." He then disappeared behind the building.

Mr. Smith was so happy to see me. Other than a few extra gray hairs, he looked the same. Once he spotted me, he stopped cutting hair and embraced me with a big hug.

"James Jackson, it sure is good to see you." I returned the embrace, because it really felt good to be home.

He then said, "Didn't I just see that Buddy get out of the car with you?"

I laughed and said, "Well, Mr. Smith, you know how he is, dying to get to that pool hall."

Mr. Smith slowly nodded his head and said, "That Buddy is something else. He's nothing like you, James. I could always count on you, and you were a man of your word. That damn brother of yours doesn't want to work. I tried giving him a job up here because I know that your momma could probably use the money. He shows up when he feels like it, he half works, and expects to be paid for doing nothing." He shook his head in disgust. "James, you are so much like yo' daddy, and I know that he would be proud."

I tried laughing. "Buddy can't be that bad." I knew that he probably was. I was just hoping that Mr. Smith would notice my discomfort and let it go. But he didn't.

"That damn Buddy is a jive turkey." I really laughed when Mr. Smith said that one. That was a phrase that the older, wiser men used when someone was being dishonest or trying to take advantage of someone. Now Mr. Smith liked everybody. I can't ever remember him speaking bad about any one. So if he called you a jive turkey, then that's probably what you were. He continued speaking about Buddy.

"He's owed me ten dollars for over a month. Instead of paying it back, he likes to duck and dodge me. Now since he has borrowed that money from me, he hasn't been in here. I heard about him flashing money around, but he just goes all out of his way to avoid paying me back my money. When he didn't pay me back when he promised, that taught me a lot about his character. He has none and I can't trust him."

Hearing folks talk about my brother like that really hurt me. I couldn't even defend Buddy because he did it to himself. Everything that he said about my brother was true.

Mr. Smith laughed as he talked more about Buddy. "I've learned throughout the years that the easiest way to get rid of a person is to loan them some money. Buddy actually thinks that he's hiding from me, when I'm the one hiding from him. I don't even want him to pay me back. If all it cost me was ten dollars to get rid of him, then I feel like I got off pretty cheap. With that being said, I consider that ten dollars well spent."

Everyone in the shop laughed, except for me. Momma had damaged Buddy so bad, that he was actually running out of bridges to burn.

***

Momma died early the next day. The nurse said that she went quietly and there was hardly any suffering. I was sad deep down, but I felt good knowing that her pain was now over and that she could finally rest with Daddy. Buddy took it hard. He lay across her bed and cried like a baby. He knew that she was the backbone of his entire life and from that day forward he would have to stand up and be a man.

We buried her a few days later. I had taken care of all the arrangements, because Buddy was a total mess. The pain of losing Momma was too much for him to handle. His way of coping with her loss was to run. He busied himself every day with the band, booze, and the pool hall. He never sat down and actually grieved.

After Momma was laid to rest, it was time for me to head back home. I promised Momma that I'd take care of him, but I never said how.

Buddy and I had not had our discussion about the house and how he was going to make it without a job and Momma. He was clueless and short-sighted. He never looked past what was in front of him. He lived every day in the moment. I guess he figured it was working, because at the age of twenty-two, he was still standing.

I did love my brother, but he was going to have to stay behind and sit in his own mess. I knew that it would only be a matter of time before he would collapse. He would have to be completely torn down in order for me to build him back up. It was unfortunate, but it was also necessary.

I awoke early the next day after the funeral and gathered up the paperwork to the house. I sat everything on the table and knocked on Buddy's door. I could no longer prolong the inevitable. I warned him to get a good night's rest because in the morning, he was going to have to finally grow up.

I knocked on his door and his lady friend answered. She said that Buddy had left late the night before and hadn't returned. I told her to tell him that I was leaving for Detroit in a few hours and if he wanted to talk he could catch me at the barbershop. I grabbed the papers and left.

I contemplated Mr. Smith's proposal for the past few days and I'd decided to accept his offer. We met at his shop that morning and I handed him the deed to the house. In exchange, he handed me an envelope with eight hundred dollars in it. I looked at the bills and snatched ten dollars out and handed it to him. It was the first of many tabs that I would be taking care of for Buddy.

Mr. Smith and I had an agreement. After he took ownership of the house, he wouldn't mention anything to Buddy and he would let him stay rent-free for three months. I knew that within those three months, Buddy would fold. He believed that waking up was the only requirement we had in life. I guess he figured that things just somehow took care of themselves. So I knew that he wouldn't inquire about the house.

I felt terrible about selling my momma and daddy's house, but there really was no other alternative. I had no desire to move back south and I knew that Buddy wasn't capable of keeping the house up. I also knew that he was eventually going to have to leave the south and come north with me, because he could never make it on his own.

***

When I made it back home to Detroit, I went straight to the bank to see James Vernon. I put the seven hundred and ninety dollars in an account and told him that I was interested in purchasing the entire duplex. He was excited. That would be the first of many properties that I'd buy from him.

A few months after I'd purchased the duplex, was when I received a letter from Buddy and Mr. Smith. I opened Buddy's letter first. Buddy wrote to tell me that the stove stopped working and the electricity didn't work even though he changed all of the light bulbs. "James, this old house is really falling apart. I don't believe that I'll stay here much longer. Lisa said that I could move in with her and I believe that it's a good idea." I chuckled to myself after reading his letter. This lady Lisa was fooled by his charm, that pretty face and those green eyes, because she had no idea what she was in for.

Mr. Smith's letter was next. He asked if I was psychic or something because he said that Buddy had fallen flat on his face. As soon as I left, Buddy resurfaced and trashed the entire house. He let the band have practice at the house every day. They were drinking and partying and having a good ole time. The girl Lisa practically moved in, and that didn't sit too well with the other women that he'd been messing around with. One had come over and knocked out a few windows. He ended his letter with "James, it's really bad and I believe that if Buddy stays any longer, he will tear the house completely down."

I responded to both letters. I wrote Buddy and told him that he should think long and hard about moving in with a woman. "God blesses the child that has his own!" The letter came back return to sender, because he had already made up his mind. I told Mr. Smith to do what he had to do, because I understood.

Buddy and Lisa didn't last very long. Apparently he didn't realize that when you move in with someone, you had to help out and respect her rules. Buddy never had any rules, so he thought that he could just move in and carry on like he had done in the past.

When he didn't come home for two days, Lisa became angry. She then hit him where it hurt. She burned up all of his clothes. All of those nice suits, shirts, and those lizard shoes. He was devastated because this stuff defined him. He hid behind all of those fancy clothes. When he wore those things, his class of so-called friends never even noticed that he really had nothing going on underneath all of that stuff. So without that stuff, he had to stand on his own merit, which was something that he was incapable of doing. It was unfortunate because Buddy "knew the price of everything and the value of nothing."

After that happened, Lisa put him out. Buddy tried staying with the woman that he'd been messing around with, but she didn't want him. It's something about a man who has a woman that makes another woman attracted to him. He went to her house smelling like liquor, carrying that saxophone and telling her that he wanted to move in and date her exclusively. She was turned off because he sounded desperate, so she didn't let him in.

Buddy went back to Momma's house, but Mr. Smith had changed the locks. Buddy was officially homeless and destitute. He found himself at Mr. Smith's barbershop. The man that he had stepped on when he thought that things were looking up was the very same man that he needed when things had fallen down.

Mr. Smith didn't hold a grudge. He cared about Momma and me and believe it or not, he even cared about Buddy. He fed Buddy, gave him a few dollars to put in his pocket, bought him a train ticket, and sent him up to Detroit with only the clothes on his back and the gold saxophone that he cherished.

***

After Pops shared that story he seemed to be in a daze as he gripped the bottle and stared down at the bar countertop.

"Big Man, although my mother was not a perfect woman, I still loved and respected her dearly. If it weren't for the love that I had for her, I would have turned my back on my brother a long time ago."

***

Pops had started on his fourth beer and he didn't appear to be slowing down anytime soon. This was out of the ordinary for him. He had always been a serious businessman who remained sharp and poised at all times. I've never known him to let his guard down. The beers brought out a soft humble side of him that I never knew existed. I liked that side.

Pops looked at me and grinned. It was kind of a silly-looking grin and after about a minute it forced me to laugh. Pops went to apologize, "I'm so sorry, Big Man, and I shouldn't let you see me like this."

I wrapped my arms around him. "It's okay, you've earned that right. Please let it out."

He laughed. "It's a good thing that I'm closed today. I can't let folks see this side of me. They'd take advantage of me."

I looked at my old man and said, "I don't believe that for one second. Everybody loves you. I don't believe that you have an enemy in the world."

He grinned, "Big Man, you know that you're probably right. It's just that I don't trust very many people. When I want something done, I have to do it myself, or risk not having it done at all. Running this bar and those rental properties takes a lot out of a person. Sometimes I feel like walking away from it all, but I know how many people depend on me for employment and shelter."

I felt bad hearing Pops say that, knowing that I was a part of the problem.

He saw me hang my head low. "Big Man, no need to feel bad. You are one of the best things that have ever happened to me." Pops looked at me really proud while he nodded his head up and down. He murmured, "Yup, I wouldn't have it any other way."

He then said, "As far as everything else, I don't blame anyone but myself. I took all of this on because I thought that I would have help. I was wrong. I wanted more for your Uncle Buddy than he wanted for himself, and this is my reward. Long hours, long money, and no real social life.

"When Buddy came to Detroit I wanted to believe that a change of environment would give him a new lease on life. I had big plans for us. That experience taught me that relocating doesn't always constitute change. It first starts in your mind, then followed through by actions. Buddy was complacent in his life and he didn't feel the need to change.

"The very first day when I went to pick him up from train station, I remembered questioning myself. Would it have just been better for everyone if I had just taken care of the upkeep on the house in Mississippi and left him there?"

Same Buddy, Different City

Pops continued the story of what happened when Buddy came to Detroit...

    The traffic in downtown Detroit was congested and at a standstill. It was after midnight on a Saturday evening and the city seemed to be wide-awake. It was rather warm for the end of April, so I rolled my windows down. I was still unable to feel a breeze. Instead I felt the warm love that was in the air as the happy-go-lucky people laughed and danced and strolled along the streets.

    I tried to not let it bother me, but it was hard to ignore. I thought about the many times that Blanche and I had danced along those same streets. I soon realized how cold and lonely my life was without anyone to love. I missed her and my mother dearly.

    I eased my car over to the right and was able to slide right into a spot directly in front of the train station. I knew that my car couldn't stand there long, since the sign read no parking. After a few minutes, I became agitated as the motorcycles revved their engines, the taxicabs honked their horns, and the buses sped along the busy street forcing me to move my vehicle.

    I just wanted so badly for things to go as planned. Buddy's train was supposed to be in at midnight, and he was instructed to stand on the corner of the train station at 12:15 where I would swoop him up and take him back to the house. It was about thirty minutes after midnight and I knew that it would be difficult to find another parking spot without paying a fortune. I circled the block a few times and still no sign of Buddy.

I started to hop on the expressway and head back home, but I was really looking forward to seeing a familiar face from back home. I finally was able to find a spot on the street about three blocks away. I made it inside of the train station at exactly 12:50. It was deserted except for a few stray people sitting on the benches.

I walked up to the window where a white male clerk was sitting reading the newspaper. I was very polite. "Excuse me, sir, but did the train from Mississippi come in yet?"

"About an hour ago," he responded without looking up.

"He then raised his arm in an attempt to close the window when I asked, "Did you happen to see a rather tall gentleman with green eyes and very light skin?"

The clerk put his finger on his chin and hesitated as if he appeared to be thinking. "Hmnnnn. I believe so." I felt relieved, thinking at least Buddy hadn't missed the train. The clerk then said, "Was he a negro?" I nodded my head yes. Then the clerk said, "Hell, every negro male that got off of that train looked just like that, so I guess you could say that I saw about fifty people who fit that description." The clerk then crumbled up his face and slammed his window shut. The word "closed" soon took his place.

I paid his comments no mind. Big Man, that was the '60s, and although racism wasn't as bad as the South, it still existed. We had learned to live with it. Besides, I was tired, restless and I just wanted to go home. I'd been working long hours at the factory, and at the bar with Black Jack on the weekends in order to keep my mind off of Blanche and my momma.

It was close to 1 a.m. when I gave up. I figured that Buddy had probably missed the train. Knowing that he had some money in his pocket along with the address and the phone number brought me comfort.

Once I made it home I showered, shaved, and drank a cold can of beer and crashed across the sofa. Just as I had fallen into a deep sleep, the constant ringing of the doorbell forced me to jump up and grab my baseball bat. I eased over to the door. I then heard someone outside blowing their car horn, along with laughing, giggling, and a female voice shouting the words "hurry up." When I peeked out of the small window curtain, I wanted to pass out.

Buddy had a young beautiful girl propped up against the house where she unknowingly leaned on the doorbell. They had a heavy make-out session going on while another young lady sat in the car.

I startled Buddy when I snatched the door open. "Buddy, what in the hell do you think that you're doing causing all of this commotion in front of my house?"

He looked at me and with the same happy grin as always. "Hey James, peace on that!" He handed me his saxophone and his overnight bag and uttered, "Give me a few minutes, I need to walk Veronica back to her car."

She laughed. "It's Valerie, silly." They both giggled, appearing to be highly intoxicated, so I slammed the door in frustration. Buddy had a serious problem. Buddy sat outside about fifteen more minutes. It was close to three in the morning, and I could hardly hold my eyes open before Buddy came inside.

"James, why is it so dark in here? You need to cut some lights on." I cut the lights on, because in his mind, it was still early. Buddy then gave me a big hug. I wanted to ask what the hell happened at the train station, but the way the he hugged me made me remember why I still was crazy about him. He was just a funny man who made his own rules. There was no in between with Buddy. You either loved him or you hated him.

He looked around and said, "Man, this is some place. I could really get used to this. James, you just don't know how much it means to me that you've invited me up here to live with you. Don't worry, you won't have to take care of me for long, I already have a gig lined up."

Hearing him say that he had a gig lined up didn't really surprise me. Buddy was a man who wouldn't stay down for long. He knew how to make money, but what he did with it was a story within itself.

He walked into the kitchen and cracked open a beer. "James, I would offer to bring you a beer, but this is the last one."

"No problem, Buddy, just help yourself."

Buddy started to tell me about his new gig. "James, my train came in about a half an hour early. I retrieved my bag and waited for you on the corner just like you instructed. When I looked around this city I couldn't believe how beautiful it was. I'd never seen anything like it. Since it was still early, I figured I'd walk around for a few minutes just to take it all in. I ended up at a nice jazz bar that was a few blocks from the station. When the pretty woman who was collecting the money at the door, saw the saxophone around my neck, she figured that I was a part of the band. So she let me in with no questions asked. James, you know me. I ain't turning down nothing but my collar." he laughed.

"I walked in and it seemed like every woman in the club had her eyes on me. The band wasn't around so I grabbed a seat at the bar. The owner of the bar walked over to me and introduced himself as Douglas. He was a tall and dark man who smoked a cigar. 'Where's the rest of the band? They were supposed to be here at eight,' he asked.

"'James, I just went with the flow and said to the old man, 'Yeah, they had to cancel because of car trouble. I don't live very far away so I decided to show up anyway.'

" 'Damn, boy! What part of the South are you from?' he asked.

"I had to laugh at that. 'Mississippi sir, and my name is Buddy.'

"He laughed right back and said, 'Well Buddy, I guess the stage belongs to you, my daughter Valerie, and my niece Cheryl. Valerie is one of best singers around and Cheryl is a mean sister on that piano. Cheryl also sings, but she feels right at home on that piano. He then shook his head. It's just so hard to get people to show up. I'm so glad that you're here.'"

Buddy said that he eyed both of the sexy women and felt like the luckiest man on earth. Valerie was a beautiful dark-skinned sister, with large brown eyes, and extra-long eyelashes, a slim nose and full pouty red lips. Cheryl was a tall woman with fair skin a deep set of brown eyes and long lashes. They both wore short Afro's, with big hoop earrings short mini skirts and white go-go boots. They looked very unique.

Valerie appeared to be more outgoing than Cheryl. She laughed, smiled, and mingled with everyone inside the club. She kept a glass of liquor in her hand at all times. Cheryl seemed standoffish. She sat at the bar and sipped water as she surveyed the crowd.

Buddy said that he took his position and warmed the crowd up.

"James, I had that crowd feeling good. They couldn't get enough of me as they waved their hands up in the air and rocked back and forth. When Valerie and Cheryl both took to the stage, they brought down the house.

"Douglas was right about those women. Valerie had a deep powerful voice just like Etta James, and her cousin Cheryl played that piano and hummed along and before we knew it, the entire bar was on their feet dancing and clapping. The crowd started throwing money on that stage. James, those women were bad! I believe that it was by no accident that the band didn't show up, because those women were intimidating. They could steal anybody's thunder."

Buddy then laughed and said, "Of course they can't steal my thunder James," and he threw his hand up to slap me a high five.

Buddy continued to laugh and before I knew it, I was laughing right along with him. He lived for times like that.

Buddy said that when the set was over, the crowd gave them a standing ovation. Douglas said that was the best performance yet.

He split the tips between the three of them and gave Buddy twenty dollars. He told Buddy that he'd like to make him a part of their group. Buddy said to Douglas, "I bet that you didn't think that this Mississippi boy had that much soul."

Douglas looked at him and said, "I like that." Buddy took a bow. Then Douglas said, "It's set. We've got a name."

Buddy, Val and Cheryl all looked at each other and said, what's the name? Douglas responded, "Mississippi Soul, featuring Val White and Cheryl Crawford."

***

As Pops told that part of the story, I cleared my throat and looked away. He ignored my gesture and continued to speak when I rudely interrupted.

"Pops, can we please change the subject? I really don't care to hear anything about her."

When I was a small child, Pops tried as best he could to keep Cheryl relevant. I'd get goose bumps hearing him tell those tales about how my mother was a big superstar who was away working overseas. I can recall having her photos taped to the wall on the side of my bed while hoping and praying for her to return. When I'd ask when she was coming home, the only response that he could offer was "soon." I held on to that word for years, but "soon" never came. So as the years passed and the memories faded, my heart toughened and she eventually became just a person who carried me for nine months. I had no physical or emotional connection to that woman whatsoever.

Pops didn't seem surprised by my request. He still felt as though he had a sense of obligation to tell me the facts about my mother. What I did with the information was up to me.

"Big Man, you have every right to feel that way, but it still won't change the fact that she's the one who gave birth to you."

I closed my eyes to gather my thoughts. He'd made a valid point. I then looked over at Pops and asked earnestly, "Since you're going to tell me about her, can I ask that you leave the gloss behind? I'm now a grown man. There's no longer the need to make her out to be more than what she actually was."

He shook his head at me. "I promise I won't.

***

Pops continued his story…

The next morning I'd awakened early to find Buddy fully dressed, wearing my clothes, sitting in the kitchen sipping a cup of coffee and smoking a cigarette. His saxophone sat at the table as Buddy was attempting to clean it.

I stepped inside the kitchen and said, "I guess old habits are hard to break."

Buddy laughed. "James, I can't sleep in a city like this. It's too much action going on and I wouldn't be Buddy if I weren't a part of it. James, I hope you don't mind, but I borrowed some of your clothes."

I smiled. "I guess you wouldn't be Buddy if you had asked prior."

I quickly got dressed and grabbed the keys to the duplex unit that was adjacent to mine.

Buddy walked in and immediately fell in love with the place. He stood in the living room and put his hand on his chin. "James, is this really where I'm going to be staying?"

"It's all yours, Buddy."

His home looked just like my place. When I'd bought the place it was partially furnished. The living room was a nice size. It had an old cloth couch that was in decent shape, along with a chair and a coffee table. The kitchen had a stove and a refrigerator along with a small table and two chairs. There was also a door inside the kitchen. Buddy eyed the door and asked, "What's behind this door?" I pointed so that he could see for himself.

We both walked through the door where there was a set of stairs that led down to the basement.

"OOOOweee James, I have never seen a basement inside of a house before. I don't know what I'm going to do with myself and all of this room." We both eyed the big space.

"Buddy, I'm sure that you'll find plenty to do with it. Now let's go get some breakfast, and get you some things to get you all settled in. By next week, you should be ready for me to take you down to Chrysler's employment office so you can get a job."

I was really thinking about Blanche. I hadn't seen her since she'd left my house a few months back and I'd avoided going that way in order to not run into her. With Buddy being in town, I had a legitimate excuse to go to her.

When I mentioned a job doing physical labor, Buddy looked at me as if he'd been told that he had a terminal illness.

"Peace on that, James! I just made it into town." He then started talking really fast and making up excuses. "I can't work in the factory. I have a bad back, I can't stand on my feet for long, and that's just too many long hours. Besides, I told you last night that I had a job."

I knew that Buddy still didn't get it, so I tried my best to make him understand.

"Buddy, Momma is gone! She's dead!" Buddy eyed me, seeming as if he wanted to throw a punch because of my boldness. He also knew that it would be like signing his own death certificate.

"Buddy, I have no intention of taking up where she left off. You are an adult, not a child. You need to learn to take care of yourself. This house has a mortgage payment on it and I am not going to do it by myself."

Buddy cut me off right there. "James, I agreed to come here because I thought that you really wanted to help me out, not put me down. Just tell me how much I need to pay, give me a month, and I promise that you won't have to worry about taking care of me ever again."

I stuck my hand out and gave Buddy a firm handshake. "Deal!" we both said at the same time.

I told Buddy that he needed to have seventy-five dollars every month to cover his living expenses, and there would be no exceptions. I took Buddy to breakfast, and then to the shops downtown. I bought him a few pieces of clothing and the bare necessities for his house and I stayed out of his way.

It didn't take long for Buddy to become acclimated to the city. Within the first few weeks he knew his way around the city better than I did. He soon became one popular man.

The owner of that bar Douglas managed their group. Mississippi Soul was an overnight sensation. Douglas had a lot of connections and for three months straight, the group soared. They sold out at the local venues such as Baker's keyboard lounge, The Rooster Tail, and the 20 Grand.

Those were some of the hottest spots in Detroit back in the '60s. I am almost certain that if they had kept at it, they were going to be more than just an opening act; they were on their way to becoming show headliners.

I was so excited for Buddy, because he was doing what he loved and he made pretty good money at it. Not only did Buddy give me the seventy-five dollars, he even tacked on an extra twenty-five. I never spent the extra. Buddy's past behavior had taught me that he would soon come back for it.

Within a few weeks, Buddy had painted his duplex, cleaned up the basement and turned it into a small studio. When they weren't performing, the group held practice there. I wasn't really bothered by what Buddy had done with the place, because I had a really busy schedule and was hardly ever there.

That is, until one day when I came home and couldn't park in my own driveway. The block was full of cars and when I went to Buddy's door, a big fella was standing guard, charging people a quarter to enter. I was steaming mad as I heard the music playing, and people dancing and making out on the stairs. The big fella wouldn't let me enter unless I paid the fee. When I told him that I lived at the residence, he made me wait at the door until Buddy approved.

Buddy came up the stairs dressed in his usual fashion and said, "James, what are you doing home so early?"

I was so mad, but I remained calm. "Buddy if you don't get these people out of here right now, I'm going to call the cops." Buddy didn't want to cause a scene, so he told me to give him a few minutes.

I stepped outside and walked to his side of the house and that's when I saw Cheryl. She was angry, upset and crying. When I asked her what was wrong, she said that the group thing really wasn't working out. Valerie and Buddy both needed to take things more seriously. Her uncle had just given them the news that they would be opening up at the Fox Theatre for the Motown Revue and instead of practicing, like they had all agreed upon, Buddy decided to have a party. Cheryl said that she wasn't against having a party, it's just that they needed to make sure that they had their act together before they celebrated. Cheryl said that she really loved performing with Val and Buddy because of the great chemistry that they each brought to the table, but she didn't know how much longer she could take those two.

Buddy and Val bickered all the time and Cheryl said that she often found herself in the middle, trying to keep peace between the two. She said that they both had the exact same "pleasure before work" mindset. She didn't want to tell her uncle, because had he known what was really going on behind the scenes, he wouldn't have liked it one bit.

As I listened to Cheryl, I became worried because I knew that without her, their group wouldn't survive and Buddy would more than likely be jobless again.

Cheryl sat there squirming. She needed to use the bathroom and didn't feel like dealing with all of those folks in Buddy's place, so I invited her inside. I told her to make herself comfortable and that's just what she did. Cheryl spent most of the evening complaining about Buddy and Val.

I told her to deal with the two as best as she could. "Cream always rises to the top. If you continue to work hard and stay focused, it will pay off and you'll be shining on your own."

After we had that conversation, Cheryl walked into the kitchen to fix herself a glass of wine when Buddy barged inside the door. He'd just cleared the basement and he wasn't happy about it.

"James I have done more than paid my share of the bills around here. I work really hard and if it weren't for me, our group wouldn't even have made it this far. I feel as though I've earned the right to unwind at my own house. You should see how those girls bicker back and forth--I just needed a break from it all."

Buddy and I suddenly heard a loud crash inside the kitchen. Cheryl stormed into the room and stepped into Buddy's face as if she was challenging him to a fight. He looked surprised.

"Buddy, you are a goddamn liar. You and Val are full of it. I am the only stable fixture in this group and you both know it. I came here because we were supposed to be rehearsing for our big gig at the Fox Theatre, and instead of practicing you and Val call yourselves celebrating. How can we ever get ahead if you two don't want to get your acts together?"

Buddy was cold busted. I felt relieved because I didn't have to say a word to Buddy. Cheryl took care of it. She hadn't known Buddy but a few months, and she had him all figured out.

Cheryl continued, "After our gig at the Fox Theatre, I'm leaving the group. I'm sick of you, all your women and all these games you're playing. So Mr. Lover boy or Playboy or whatever those women call you. Let's see how far you and Val get when you're both on your own." Buddy didn't say anything. Cheryl kept going, "That is, if you two can leave the pills, the drugs, and the liquor bottle alone."

The room became still. Hearing her say that about Buddy took me by surprise. I really wanted to believe in him. I knew he was irresponsible, but just never wanted to believe that his behavior was that reckless.

Her harsh words brought out the worst in Buddy. He reached his arm back as if he was going to slap Cheryl, but he wasn't quick enough. She caught his arm and said, "If you even think about putting a hand on me, I'll rip it off and serve it to you for breakfast on a platter."

Buddy was infuriated. He dropped his arm and stormed out. His darkest secrets had been exposed.

***

After Pops shared that story, I let out a heavy breath. "Man, Pops, that's some story. So did Cheryl really quit the group after their performance at the Fox?"

Pops shook his head. "Big Man, that day really brings back some terrible memories. It was unfortunate, but The Fox Theatre never happened."

***

Pops told the next part of the story...

"Cheryl was so upset she was shaking. I made her have a seat and fixed us both a pot of coffee. She'd finally calmed down. She said that she was done. Buddy had really disappointed her because he acted as though he wanted their group to go all the way to the top. He claimed the reason that he left Mississippi was because his group down there didn't want to go anywhere. Cheryl soon realized that Buddy was more than likely the problem.

Cheryl then opened up to me. She was in her early twenties and had recently moved from Chicago with her mother's brother Douglas and his daughter Valerie, after her mother had died of a drug overdose. Both her and Val had no children and they shared a place that her uncle paid for. Cheryl said that after that night she was seriously considering getting a job and moving out on her own. She said that she'd never give up on her real passion, which was singing and playing the piano, but that would have to be put on the back-burner.

I told Cheryl a little about myself, but this time I was very careful with my words. I only mentioned how I wanted to be married and have children someday. I never mentioned what Blanche and Monica had sent me through.

Big Man, Cheryl was young and full of ambition. I liked the fact that she had a strong mind and stood up for herself. Cheryl said that she wished she'd met me before she dealt with Buddy because I could have warned her about his behavior.

"James, I hate wasting my time. I feel bad about all the money my uncle spent on the flyers, posters, and promotions, but I can no longer fulfill my obligation with the group. Buddy and Val will have to find a replacement because after our performance at the Fox Theatre, I'm leaving the group." Cheryl said.

I totally understood her frustration.

After Cheryl and I discussed Buddy, we stayed up until the wee hours enjoying each other's company. It was after 4 a.m. when Cheryl began to get restless. I grabbed my keys in an attempt to take her home.

Big Man, that was a day in Detroit's history that I would never forget.

Detroit Riots

Pops continued ...

That day was July 23, 1967. Both Cheryl and I exited the house and when we made it to the front porch, we heard loud sirens from police cars, fire trucks, and ambulances. People were standing on their porches trying to figure out what was happening. I knocked on Buddy's door but there was no answer. Cheryl and I hopped into my car, but we didn't make it very far. The cops had barricaded the streets and instructed us to go back home because there was a riot.

Big Man, at that time, it was known as one of the worst race riots in US history. It was called the Twelfth Street Riot, and it was less than a mile from the duplex.

It all happened because there was a police raid of an unlicensed after-hours club. We called them Blind Pigs. Cheryl and I parked the car and walked a few blocks up the street. We were astounded by what we saw. It looked like something out of a war zone. The street was in total chaos. Folks were screaming, fighting, breaking windows, flipping over cars, looting and burning down businesses. The cops were outnumbered. Black people were fed up with the racism and being harassed by a particularly white police force so they decided to take a strong stand.

It was about 3:45 a.m. Sunday when the riot started. The afterhours establishment was hosting a party for several veterans who'd recently returned from Vietnam. Everyone who was at the party was having a good time and they didn't want to leave, so the police were called. The police called in a paddy wagon to haul folks off to jail and that's when the ruckus broke out.

Cheryl and I went back into the house. I knocked on Buddy's door once again to tell him what was going on, but again he didn't answer. I went inside his place with my key and he wasn't there. I became worried because I knew that Buddy liked to frequent those types of establishments. There was nothing that I could do so I just had to sit back and wait.

Cheryl and I went back to my place and our eyes were glued to the television set. There was special programming on because of what was happening. Cheryl fell into my arms and cried at all the chaos that was going on.

That riot changed the face of Detroit for the worse. It was so out of control that Governor George W. Romney declared a state of emergency, and ordered the National Guard to Detroit. President Lyndon B. Johnson sent in the 82nd Airborne Division to help try and control the violence and vandalism.

Cheryl and I didn't leave my home. We watched as most of it unfolded right before our eyes. The riots lasted a few days, but it felt more like an eternity. It seemed as if the world was going to end. Cheryl and I were both scared, but I tried as best as I could to mask my fears. We held each other close and things between us just happened.

When the dust finally settled four days later, the aftermath was unimaginable. Many businesses were burned completely down, grocery stores had been looted, and some folks lost their lives just trying to protect their businesses.

Black Jack was one of them. He died right here in this bar of a heart attack, with a shotgun lying right next to him. Everyone knew and loved Black Jack and although some of the neighboring businesses were destroyed, most of his loyal customers stood in front of this building to make sure that it was safe. That pressure put too much of a strain on his heart and he died.

His son James Vernon was devastated. When Black Jack was alive, he gave him such a hard time about this building. He wanted him to get rid of it. When Black Jack died, James Vernon wanted nothing more but to hold on to the building in remembrance of his father.

It's strange how death makes you treat people better than when they were alive.

He spent so much money on Black Jack's home-going service. He laid that man out in a gold casket, an expensive tailor-made suit, some gold jewelry, and he had several limousines. It's a shame, because he really didn't know his father that well. Black Jack was a giver with a huge heart. He was never the flashy type. He'd rather have had his son feed the homeless or donate to the poor than to put all that money in the ground. I kept quiet though. It really wasn't my place to say anything.

At the service, James Vernon asked if I would sit up front with the family because he wasn't sure how well he'd hold up. I deeply cared about Black Jack, so I had no problem with it. James Vernon sat there with his head bowed the entire service. His wife Nancy looked very beautiful and poised and she held it together for the sake of her husband. Blanche sat next to her sister. It was the first time that I had seen her since the day at my place and I must say that she still took my breath away.

Judging by the number of people at that service, one could tell how much Black Jack was loved and respected.

When James Vernon got up to speak about his father, he could hardly get the words out. He was deeply hurt. He praised Black Jack and told him that he wished that he had been a better son. He said that if he had it to do all over again, he would hire an army to protect the thing that Black Jack held dear to him. He acknowledged how that bar fed him and sent him through school and that he would do everything in his power to keep the legacy going.

Hearing James Vernon say all of those kind things made me feel sadder for Black Jack. I wished that James Vernon had let it go. What good is an apology if it's not said when it matters the most?

After James Vernon made his speech, his wife began to weep. When the wife wept, it was a trickle-down effect and Blanche began to weep right along with her sister. Somehow Blanche's head ended up on my shoulder and I found my arm wrapped around her. For a millisecond I imagined that she was my wife. In those few seconds, my feelings for her resurfaced and I found myself wanting to protect her.

After the service, everyone embraced each other before we made it out into the front of the church. As we stood in front of the church, Blanche turned to me and said, "James, it's so good to see you."

I longingly looked at her and said, "I've never stopped missing you." We both stared at each other and for a second I thought that maybe there was a glimmer of hope for us.

Suddenly, I heard a male voice shout, "Blanche, darling. There you are. I've been looking all over for you."

He was a tall, slender man, with a long nose, wearing round glasses and he had a very stiff posture. He had a peculiar look about him, and I knew right away that it was Winston. It felt as if someone had just pulled the rug from under me. That's just how bad I was feeling. I had forgotten all about him. Blanche took a deep breath, squeezed my hand, and said apologetically, "I must go. Again. It was great seeing you."

Just like that she walked off with Winston, leaving me in a relapsed state of mind. James Vernon asked me to ride to the cemetery in the family vehicle, but I made up an excuse. There was no way that I could fully recover my equilibrium that fast.

James Vernon slipped a letter into my hand and whispered, "Please think long and hard about it before you respond." He headed off toward the limo and said he'd be in touch with me real soon.

Blanche was still heavy on my mind so I figured that it would be best if I just headed home.

***

I pulled up to the house just as Buddy was about to enter his place. He'd been avoiding me since the blow-up with Cheryl, and I hadn't seen him since the riot.

When I got out of my vehicle I walked toward him. He gave a wave and said dismissively, "Hey James, I'm kind of in a hurry, so I'll have to catch up with you later."

I knew that he was ashamed about what happened with Cheryl, so I wanted to put Buddy's mind at ease.

When I walked to his door, Buddy was holding the door as if he didn't want me to enter. He seemed to be hiding something. I started to walk away until my eyes managed to land inside his home. I nearly snapped my neck at what I had seen. Buddy tried shutting the door, but he wasn't quick enough. I stuck my arm out and pushed the door completely open. I was disappointed. His house looked like a storage facility with all the boxes.

I shoved my way inside and asked, "Buddy, do you plan on moving?" I looked around at the place in disgust. It was filled with all sorts of things like boxes of dress shirts, slacks, and shoes. He had brand-new sheets and towels and pillows, but what stood out the most was his brand-new saxophone.

"Buddy, where the heck did you get all of this stuff from?" I said explosively.

He gave me that look and said, "Mind your own business James! As long as I give you your money on the first, that's all that you need to be concerned with."

"Buddy, you stole all of these things during the riot?" I said angrily.

He answered back rather quickly. "I didn't steal anything, I just happen to know people."

His casual response infuriated me. I thought about Black Jack, who lost his life trying to keep folks from taking what didn't belong to them, and here I was living with a person who was just "morally bankrupt."

"Buddy, now I'm no saint, but I do know that by indulging in this type of behavior, you won't have any good luck. You will certainly block your blessings." I yelled.

Buddy let out a loud wicked laugh right in my face. "Ha! Well, maybe this is my blessing, James."

I looked over at my brother in disdain and shouted, "You ought to be ashamed of yourself. I know that Momma taught you better than that."

He quickly cut me off. "Well, I'll be damned! I guess you are the only one who gets to benefit from stealing." I was baffled. Buddy then stepped in my face and said, "Don't get to looking all crazy now, James. You stole Momma's house and sold it from right under me to Mr. Smith."

I couldn't take his absurd behavior any longer so I screamed, "What?"

Before I could even defend myself, Buddy pulled out an envelope from his back pocket. It was a letter from his ex-girlfriend Lisa in Mississippi.

"James, I received this letter in the mail today. It's from Lisa. She said that she needed to talk to me about an important matter so she went to the house looking for me. When she made it to the house, it had been painted, fresh flowers had been planted, new windows had been put in and it had a For Rent sign in the window. When she called the number, she found out that Mr. Smith was the owner of the house. He told Lisa that he had bought the house from you after Momma died."

I sat there with my arms folded and listened to everything that Buddy had to say without any interruptions. I had to calm myself down and select my words carefully, because I refused to argue with a fool.

Buddy took my silence as a sign of guilt. He jumped up in my face again and started yelling. "So, James--now you're just going to get all quiet because you're busted!"

I calmly stepped away from my brother before I did something that I wouldn't be able to take back.

I took a deep breath and calmly said, "Buddy, right after Momma died, I asked you several times to talk about the house, but you were too busy and didn't have time."

Before I could even finish my statement, he interrupted me. His anger was at the max.

"So, James, that just gave you a reason to steal Momma's house?" He wouldn't let me respond. He stomped his feet and took his fist and pounded on the wooden table and screamed. "Look James. I. Want. My. Money!!!" He yelled.

Buddy said that as if he was trying to instill fear inside me. I hadn't been that angry since I'd found out that I wasn't the father of Monica's baby.

I raised my voice louder than Buddy's and said, "Look, Buddy! You had your chance. I left you in the house when I moved up here. You trashed the place, didn't pay any bills, and you just left it to move in with Lisa."

He started flailing his arms, trying to state his case. "I was going to go back to the house. I just needed to sort some things out. I was putting together a plan when you let Mr. Smith change the locks. James, those bills weren't going anywhere."

I stopped him right there. I wasn't going to waste another second on trying to make a fool understand. He would have to get it on his own.

I took a deep breath, and pointed my finger straight in his face. "Buddy, the house is gone! I sold it for a little of nothing and put the down payment on this place. Had I done nothing with the house in Mississippi, the state would have taken the home for taxes. They really don't care about you and your problems, Buddy. Business is business. This is now your home."

He was mad and again he flailed his arms and started yelling. "Well, I don't wanna live here anymore. I hate this place!"

I did a double take. "Buddy, I thought that you liked it here? What happened with the band? You guys seemed to be on to something big. Seems as if you are just reverting back into your old ways."

"It's your entire fault, James. Everything was good until you went blabbing all of my business to Cheryl. She ruined everything."

"Buddy, what did Cheryl say that caused you to hate this place so much?"

Buddy repeated the incident from earlier.

"James, I'd just left the bar with Douglas and the ladies. The Fox Theatre was still a go, and after that performance Douglas said he was very confident that a record deal was in the makings. He then pulled out a contract that he wanted us all to sign. He was even willing to pay us an up-front allowance. Val and I were excited and prepared to sign."

Buddy pounded his fist on the table in anger and said, "James, that was the break that I'd been looking for my entire life. Cheryl suddenly threw her hand up and demanded that Douglas put a stiff practice clause in the agreement. She said that I needed to cut back on dating so many women, because they were a distraction. She also said that we needed to practice at least five times a week and that we should only consume alcohol on the weekends."

I felt no sympathy for Buddy, because I didn't think that those were unreasonable requests. When I didn't agree with what he was saying, Buddy became angrier.

"James, can you believe Douglas agreed with Cheryl? He said that most groups didn't have longevity because of sex, drugs, and alcohol."

Buddy said that he and Val lost their cool. They didn't think it was fair. Cheryl needed to lighten up and relax and stop taking everything so seriously.

When Doug asked if there was a problem, Cheryl blurted out that Val and Buddy were the problem. She went on and on about how they were heavy drinkers, did way too much partying and how they didn't like to practice.

Val became sick of Cheryl's saintly attitude, and then out of nowhere she shoved Cheryl really hard.

Buddy said, "James, once that happened, Douglas couldn't step in fast enough. Those two women started fighting. They were pulling clothes and hair, and tossing around on the floor. Douglas expected me to help break it up, but I wasn't gonna mess up my good shoes."

"After everything was all said and done, our group was dismantled, Cheryl and Val were no longer speaking, and Douglas called me a coward and said if I didn't willingly leave from his establishment, he was going to throw me out on my head."

Buddy then said, "James, I didn't want any trouble, so I just left. I really wanted that contract, though." He squeezed his two fingers together and held them close to my face. "I was this close. I could taste the fame. Now because of Cheryl and her unreasonable demands, it's all over. James, I want out of this stupid place."

He then held up Lisa's letter. "Maybe it all worked out for the best. I need to go back home and settle a few things. Lisa says that she is five months pregnant and she wants me to come back home so that we can work things out."

When Buddy told me that Lisa was pregnant, I paused. That statement alone took something out of me. I felt envy. I had lived my entire life working hard, being obedient, and doing all the right things and it didn't seem to be paying off. Buddy screwed up everything, burned bridges wherever he went, and if he didn't like something, he'd just walk away with no remorse. He seemed to get rewarded all the time. It wasn't fair that he was going to be a father and not me.

I didn't want to hear any more. I needed a break away from my brother. I reached inside my pocket and handed him my last two hundred dollars.

"Here you go, Buddy. It's all I have on hand. I'm sorry that things didn't turn out the way you had hoped they would, but one day you'll realize you have to give things a chance.

He quickly snatched the money out my hand and said, "James I've been here for four months, and this just isn't the place for me."

I knew that Buddy would be back. He didn't hate Detroit, he just hated the fact that he couldn't do what he wanted.

SUPERSTAR

Pops continued his story…

In Memoriam of Jesse Vernon (better known as Black Jack).

I must have read that letter a hundred times. It didn't seem real. James Vernon wanted me to take over his father's establishment. Now Big Man, when I tell you that I wanted no part of this bar whatsoever, I meant it. James Vernon just would not let it go. If he could have brought his father back from the dead, he would have. It's a darn shame how people live their lives doing good and helping others and they never get the proper accolades until they are dead and gone.

I set the letter aside. I just wasn't ready to deal with it at that time.

Later that evening, there was a knock at my door. When I looked out the window, it was Cheryl. She looked confused and disoriented. When I opened the door I noticed she had a few scratches across her face, and her eyes were red and swollen. I knew they'd come from the big fight with her cousin Val.

I welcomed her in and she just cried. Her life was a complete mess and she just needed a place to stay for a few days. Her uncle didn't put her out; Cheryl no longer wanted to stay with her cousin Val. So I offered to let her stay as long as she liked.

She accepted my proposal. I really didn't mind because Cheryl was great company and I knew that she'd keep my mind occupied. I invited her into the kitchen and offered to fix her something to eat. She wasn't hungry, but she did want a glass of wine.

As we sat at the table, she noticed the letter from James Vernon. I picked up the letter and I began reading it to her. I told her all about the circumstances surrounding James Vernon and Black Jack, and her response was "I think that you should go for it." Cheryl was very familiar with the entertainment business because her uncle had been in it for a long time. She said that running his bar gave his life so much meaning and it really brought him joy. In desperate times like the city was in, entertainment was at least an escape away from all of the pain, sadness and frustration that black folks were facing. If black folks couldn't do anything else; we knew how to entertain and have a good time.

That evening after talking to Cheryl, I'd decided to take James Vernon up on his offer.

***

I awoke early the next morning to find that Cheryl was not there. I had offered to sleep on the couch and let her have the bed, but she didn't want that. She wanted to sleep right next to me. As I adjusted my eyes, I heard voices downstairs. I grabbed my robe and went to check to see what was happening.

Buddy was there with his two suitcases and he wasn't pleased to find Cheryl at my home. I swear those two bickered like an old married couple. They couldn't stand to be in the same room together.

"Cheryl, why are you here? Haven't you caused enough trouble already?" Buddy said.

I was coming down the stairs just as Cheryl was saying, "Buddy you can kiss my…."

Before she got the chance to really let Buddy have it, I intervened. "Hey, you two, what's going on?"

Buddy looked at me and said, "James, this woman is nothing but bad luck. You shouldn't trust her. She shouldn't even be here."

I looked at Cheryl and said, "Could you please let me speak to my brother alone?" She rolled her eyes at Buddy and headed up the stairs.

"Buddy, I'm highly capable of running my home and I don't need your permission to have company. Now what do you need?"

"Well I hope that you know…."

I eyed Buddy and cut him off mid-sentence. What is it that I need to know?"

He then let out a deep huff and said, "Oh, never mind. I just came to tell you goodbye. I'm going to catch a ride with a friend who's going down south to visit his mother. I'm going to be a daddy, so I'm going to try and make it work with Lisa."

I smiled at my brother and said, "Buddy, it's good to hear that you're finally ready to take responsibility. Maybe this child is what you need. I just want you to know that I was on the phone with Mr. Smith last night and he told me that Lisa was looking at the place. She promised him that if he rented it out to her she'd take good care of it. Buddy, I vouched for you both. This is your last chance. I told Mr. Smith that I would pay half your rent until you got on your feet. According to Mr. Smith Lisa is a good, hard-working woman. If you have no intentions of doing right by her, I suggest you leave her alone and just provide for that child."

Buddy's eyes grew wide as he gave me a big hug and patted me on the back. "Thank you, James. This is just what I need. I promise that I am going to get it together."

I reached for the envelope that I had sealed the night before, and handed it to Buddy. He wore a huge smile when I said; "This should cover your expenses for a while. Buddy was overwhelmed. He gave me another big hug and said, "Thank you James, I'm going to make you proud." I smiled at my brother one last time and said, "Make Lisa and that baby proud. Goodbye, Buddy."

When Cheryl heard the door shut, she came down the stairs, dressed and refreshed. "James, did I hear Buddy say that he was moving back down south and that he was going to be a father?" she asked with skepticism.

I didn't want her to speak bad about my brother, so I said. "Buddy has been lost his entire life. Maybe this situation will add balance to his life."

Cheryl responded as if she almost felt bad. "Well, I hope I wasn't the cause of him leaving."

I laughed. "Buddy doesn't need a reason to run away."

***

On the ride to James Vernon's office later that morning, Cheryl said that she was excited for me and that she'd help me out as much as she could. She also said that she didn't plan on staying with me for long.

"Jimmy, I know how men love their space and I certainly need mine." I remember her saying that she just needed to save up a little more money until she could afford her own. Big Man, she really wasn't a bother and I was in no hurry for her to leave, but I didn't say anything. I didn't want to put my feelings on the line.

Cheryl sat down with me as I signed the agreement with James Vernon. I purchased the building on a land contract and he only charged me what Black Jack had owed on the building. He had many investments going on, so he needed the business for tax purposes.

James Vernon was overjoyed that I had agreed. He said that his father had died protecting that bar, so he felt a strong sense of obligation to keep his legacy going. He said that he owed him that.

He did whatever he could to make sure that the transition was smooth and that I was satisfied. Less than a month after Black Jack's death, we were back in business. He also introduced us to Black Jack's brother, Mr. Charlie. Mr. Charlie was married and had recently retired from the factory and he was happy to work as a security guard. Black Jack's death really seemed to soften James Vernon's heart.

My co-workers from the factory were so happy that I had taken over the bar. Although it wasn't a big fancy place, it was like their second home. They liked having somewhere that they could go to after work to look at some pretty woman and have a good time. It took their mind off of their troubles and the things that were going on in the city.

The first month, Cheryl was a great big help. Our relationship was special. I thought she was the greatest friend that a man could ask for. Although we had intimate relations, we never pressured each other. I paid Cheryl good money to open this place up and assist the girls in whatever they needed. She also kept up with the inventory and did some light bookkeeping. During that second month, I started noticing changes in her attitude. She'd have mood swings and became very irritable. I had finally seen what Buddy had seen all along. That bar didn't make her feel whole. She needed more. I didn't like that side of her, so I had learned to keep my distance until it passed, which was usually a day or two.

Then one day out of the blue she said that she had found herself a place. I was a little disappointed, because I didn't want her to go, but I knew that I had no right to stand in her way. She was passionate about becoming an artist and she would have never been fully satisfied with working in a bar. Without the hindrance of Valerie or Buddy, she planned to focus solely on her music career.

A few days before her move Cheryl asked me if I would take her to her uncle's home so that she could retrieve her belongings. She hadn't seen him or Valerie since the incident and she was afraid of what might transpire. I willingly agreed.

As I turned into her uncle's neighborhood I was moved. He lived in the upscale beautiful Boston Edison district in Detroit where every home had well-manicured lawns, gated backyards, and expensive cars in the driveways. I knew that's how I wanted to live.

Cheryl stood nervous as we rang the doorbell. When the door swung open a short, older black woman wearing an apron opened the door. She smiled once she saw Cheryl. She reached out and gave Cheryl a big welcoming hug and invited us both in.

She introduced me to Ms. Grace the housekeeper, and she lived up to that name. She had a pleasant smile, a friendly nature, and she walked with a lot of grace.

The inside of the home was even more captivating. It had very large windows accented with expensive drapery, polished wood floors, a long spiral staircase, and chandeliers throughout. Her uncle was well-off.

Ms. Grace escorted us to the living area while she went and called for Douglas.

Douglas stepped into the room dressed in a nice pair of slacks, wearing a button-down shirt and smoking a cigar. He was happy to see his niece. She introduced me as an acquaintance and I was pleased at the fact that she never mentioned my relationship to Buddy.

They made small talk when her uncle had told her that he had checked his daughter into a rehabilitation facility. She had a serious drug and alcohol problem. He then said, "That boy from Mississippi sure had a lot of talent, but he was just plain ole bad news."

Cheryl saw the blank expression on my face, and she quickly interrupted her uncle to spare my feelings. "Uncle Doug, let's just focus on Val. I don't believe in looking back."

Douglas looked a bit sad and said, "I guess you're right. Val should have had her own mind."

I thought that was a kind thing for Cheryl to do. I also thought about the money that I had given Buddy, and only hoped and prayed that he'd do the right thing.

Douglas sat at his desk and started writing Cheryl a check. He stood up and handed it to her. "Here you are, my beautiful niece. This is a token of my appreciation."

Cheryl didn't want to accept the money. "Uncle you don't owe me anything. You have been taking care of me since my mother died--I believe that I owe you."

Douglas started to get a little sentimental. He took a deep breath and looked at us both. "Cheryl, you have always had what it took to be a solo artist. I knew that the first time I heard you play and sing. You were so much better than Valerie. I just didn't want to let you go because I knew that she'd fall apart. You were strong, and always had your own mind. My Valerie was weak. I guess what I was doing was trying to fit a square peg inside of a round hole. I was proud at the way that you stepped in and tried to salvage Mississippi Soul. I knew that it wasn't going to work, but I was trying so hard to make it. That Val and Buddy have a lot to learn. I have no idea how that boy was raised, but it is evident that he missed the being responsible part. He's a slick one and I can recognize that from a mile away. My only concern now is to get my Valerie back healthy."

He shoved the check in her hand and told her that whenever she was ready to get back into music, he'd get her a contract. He also said that her things were neatly packed away and when she was ready, he'd hire some movers to take them to wherever she liked.

**

Cheryl was feeling good after we left her uncle's. She was in a great mood and wanted to take me out to eat to celebrate. I wasn't really in the mood to celebrate; Buddy was heavy on my mind. I knew that there was nothing that I could really do about it, but it still didn't stop me from worrying.

Cheryl tossed and turned all that night. I assumed that she was excited about her new place. She woke up early the next morning and ran to the bathroom. I heard her in there gagging. I knocked on the door to see what she needed and she asked for some tea. She thought that she was coming down with a virus.

The next day I took her to the free clinic and it wasn't a virus that she had. She was pregnant. I remember when the nurse walked out and told her that she was pregnant. Cheryl bowed her head and started crying. I cried too. The only difference between our tears was that mine were tears of joy and hers were tears of sorrow.

She wasn't ready to be a mother. She was scared. "What if I fail at being a mother?" she said.

I held her tight and said, "Cheryl, I won't let your fail. I will be right here to catch you."

She still wasn't so sure. "James, I don't know how to even take care of a baby."

I responded, "I do. I practically helped to raise Buddy."

Nothing that I said seemed to cheer Cheryl up. I remember how I stopped at the florist and bought her a bouquet of roses and some chocolates. That still didn't work. I went to the market and bought her every type of fruit that my arms could hold, and that didn't work.

She finally sat me down and said, "James, I'm confused. I was really looking forward to being on my own and getting my career started. A child would only complicate things. I'm afraid that I may hate myself if I don't at least attempt to follow my dream. Please give me a little time; maybe it will pass."

I remember how down I was feeling. *Why me?* I thought. I knew that I'd make a good father, husband and family man.

The next day when I went to work I couldn't focus. I left work and I went to the bar and I felt even worse.

I'd just hired Ms. Shirley, who I had met through James Vernon. She and I were the same age. She was a tall, big-boned woman with a loud mouth, great big boobs and a large behind. She knew how to run a bar because her aunt raised her. That aunt ran a brothel.

Ms. Shirley was strong, fierce, and no-nonsense. She ran that bar with an iron fist. Everyone loved and respected her because she had the perfect amount of balance. She knew how to make you feel good and put you in your place all at the same time. The older clients loved her and they'd give her half of their pay just to stare at them boobs. No one ever tried to touch them either, because they knew if they did, she'd cut their hands off. She and I got along great.

When Ms. Shirley took one look at me, she knew that something was wrong. I sat there and told her all about Cheryl and how I wanted so badly to be a father. Shirley looked at me and said, "Jimmy, you're a good man. Just give her some time; she'll come around."

Shirley and I talked for a while. That day she became more than just an employee--she became my friend. I learned about her situation with her ex-husband. He had left her for a much younger woman. He claimed that Ms. Shirley acted too much like his mother. Shirley said that she didn't think that asking him to work, take care of his responsibilities, and come home at a decent hour was too much to ask. She said that the younger woman let him do whatever he wanted to do without question. Ms. Shirley said that she was never going to let any man walk over her like that. So she filed for divorce and he moved on with that woman.

I left that bar feeling a little better. When I made it back to my place, it was dark. I turned the key in the lock and when I opened the door an empty feeling came over me. Cheryl would normally wait up for me, but that day she hadn't. I called her name, but there was no answer. I searched the entire house and she was gone. She didn't leave a note or a message-- she was just gone. I sat in that living room, heartbroken once again. I couldn't move. Two days had gone by and there still was no sign of her. I hadn't bothered to eat, shower, or call in to work.

On the third day, I heard a car pull into the driveway. Then seconds later there was heavy knocking. The voice through the door was Ms. Shirley. She had gotten in touch with James Vernon and told him that I was missing. I heard her yell my name. "Jimmy?" When I didn't answer she said, "I know you're in there."

I screamed through the door, "Go away."

She yelled to James Vernon, "He's in there."

I finally got up and opened the door because I knew that they weren't going away. Ms. Shirley wrapped her arms around me and said, "Jimmy, I was worried sick about you."

I looked at her and said, "I'm okay. Now please just leave me alone."

James Vernon got out the car and stepped inside. "Jimmy, I'm so happy to see that you're well. I was worried. It made me think of how I found my father dead a few days after the riot. That's not a good feeling."

I gave an empty smile and said, "Well as you can see, I'm alive and well."

Shirley asked, "Which way is the kitchen? I need to get you something to eat because you don't look so good."

James Vernon pointed Shirley toward the kitchen just as Cheryl was walking through the door. She looked worse than I did. Her make-up was smudged, her hair was matted, and her clothes were wrinkled. James Vernon and Shirley each looked at me. "Jimmy, we'll catch you later." Shirley didn't look happy as she gave Cheryl a grimacing look before she exited the door.

Once Cheryl and I were alone she sat down on the couch and started crying again. I sat there feeling helpless because I had no idea what she had done or what she was thinking.

"James, I'm sorry for leaving without telling you where I was. It's just that this is all too much. I'm scared and I really don't want to be a mother. I feel like a horrible person for saying that. I just don't think that I'm cut out for that. I watched how my own mother failed and how I spent most of my teenage years taking care of her. I don't want to be responsible for another person's life."

I sat there in a stupor. I had no idea what she meant by any of this. The pain that Monica had caused felt more like a sting; Cheryl's felt like a slow burn. I held my breath but didn't know how much longer I could sit there without actually passing out.

When she saw the strained look on my face, she grabbed both my hands and began to squeeze them tight. "James, for a second I thought about suicide, until I realized that I didn't want to die. I thought about going to one of those clinics and getting rid of the baby, but my heart just wouldn't let me. I thought about running away forever until I realized that I'd be even more lost. Then I thought about that gleaming look in your eyes when you found out I was pregnant. I remembered all that you've been through and how it all seems to have made you an even stronger person because of it. I believe that this child would only multiply your strength. James, this baby deserves a father like you."

Big Man, when she made that last statement I was able to exhale. I remembered how I hugged her and cried so hard. I was really going to be a father.

***

Pops noticed how silent I was. My knuckles were pressed up against my temples and my eyes were shut extremely tight. Hearing this really hurt. Pops had always protected Cheryl and refused to speak bad about her. Now he was spilling everything and I didn't understand why. Before that day I had never formed a real opinion of Cheryl--I just forgot about her. But hearing all of this was starting to make me hate this woman.

He patted my shoulder and said, "I know you're wondering why I am telling you all of this."

I never looked up. I continued to rub my throbbing temples. My feelings were hurt. I finally looked over at Pops. "Why do I need to know?"

His answer was simple. "To let you know that I am sorry."

I hunched my shoulders. "Pops, I won't accept that. You're not the one who's sorry!"

He knew where this was going so he stopped me from cutting deeper into Cheryl.

"Big Man, I don't fault Cheryl. She had so many other options that she could have taken, but she chose to give life to you. Every woman that has a child is not always fit to be a parent. It may sound ridiculous, but it's true. Cheryl fit that criteria."

***

A week after Cheryl came back, we went down to the courthouse and got married. I wanted to do everything in my power to make her feel secure. I made sure that she never had to work. Ms. Shirley practically ran the bar for me so that I could be with Cheryl.

Shortly after you were born, she went into a deep depression. She felt that sense of loneliness and the only thing that seemed to ease that pain was her music. I'd turned Buddy's half of the house into a mock studio. She had everything that she needed but it still seemed as if something was still missing although Ms. Shirley and I were right there.

Ms. Shirley was a mother who knew all about postpartum depression. That's what she believed Cheryl, was going through. She also admitted that she'd personally never seen a case so severe.

Big Man, although Cheryl loved you, she just didn't bond very well with you. Ms. Shirley managed to fill in. She and I took rotating shifts and we never really left her alone with you. Ms. Shirley was great and if it wasn't for her, I don't think that I could have made it.

After your second birthday, Cheryl wanted to get back out there and work. I really didn't want her to, but if it was going to make her happy then I was all for it. Ms. Shirley thought that was a good idea since we'd tried everything except for that. Cheryl called her uncle and he'd set her up to sing lead in a band. She was happy and I must admit that I enjoyed seeing her smile. Ms. Shirley and I were her biggest fans. Cheryl would leave early in the morning for practice, and return later on in the evening with a reinvigorated spirit. The music seemed to be the missing ingredient that had been deprived from her insatiable appetite.

The group was solid. Cheryl sang lead as they performed at the smaller venues all over the city and Ms. Shirley and I took turns cheering her on. That wouldn't last long, because after about a year with the group, the depression returned, but this time it was much deeper. Ms. Shirley and I were getting a little burned out but we both managed to suppress our frustrations in order to help Cheryl.

When you turned three years old, I was forced out of denial. Cheryl and I took you to the playground and you had fallen off the sliding board and scraped your knee. You screamed from the pain and instead of going to her, you ran straight into my arms. She stood there clueless. I tried to hand you to her so I could get some napkins out the car but she pushed you away and said, "James, that's blood. I don't want to get that stuff all over my clothes." That was my breaking point. I didn't get angry, but I did have to find a way out.

The drive home was quiet. She stared out the window looking as if she belonged out in the free world. I looked at her and softly said, "What is it going to take to make you happy?" She didn't even hear me because she was too busy daydreaming. I raised my pitch. "Cheryl?" She turned around with tears in her eyes. I rephrased the question. "What can I do to assist in your happiness? I'm willing to do whatever it takes, because we just can't go on like this anymore."

She answered excitedly, "Are you serious, James? I mean... whatever I want?" I nodded my head yes because it seemed as if she had been searching for her own way to make an exit.

"James, I want to travel the world and be a superstar. I'm tired of playing at those small venues. You remember what my uncle said about me those few years back, don't you?" She became even more excited as she thought back on that day. "He said that I have what it takes. I'm so much bigger and better than those small places--I know that now."

As Cheryl spoke, I thought about my momma, who was a real woman. When my daddy died, she didn't quit on her family to chase a dream. She stayed right there with us. I am a strong man because of my momma's love for our family. Cheryl was just the opposite. I knew that if my momma were alive she'd tell me to let that woman go.

Big Man, Cheryl's excitement had made you scream in the back seat. When I turned to look at you, you weren't actually screaming, but laughing and clapping your hands. I looked deep into your eyes and that's when I saw my momma talking to me. Your smile and eyes are just like hers. Big Man, you look just like your grandmother. Cheryl had never made you laugh or smile, so I knew it had to be my momma talking to me. *"Let that burden go."*

"When are you leaving?" I asked. Cheryl looked surprised.

"You mean that you don't have a problem with me leaving?" She jumped up and down in the car and it caused you to jump up and down too.

I eyed her and said, "I would never want to stand in the way of your happiness."

Cheryl was ecstatic as she responded, "My uncle already has the reservations. The bus leaves the day after tomorrow. We'll be on tour all over the United Sates for about a year, but I promise to write as much as I can, I'll send presents, and I will send for you two real soon."

Big Man, she had already planned to leave us. I guess her sadness came from wondering when and how she was going to break the news to us. We dropped your mother off on the designated date. She was in really good spirits. When it was time to leave her, I held you. I was so afraid that you were going to cry. That's when you grabbed my face and looked me in the eyes. I saw my momma again. This time she was saying, "*You're doing the right thing.*"

I waved as Cheryl stepped onto the bus and to my surprise you not only waved, but you said "Bye-bye. See you later, Cheryl." She was so excited about her new journey that I don't believe that she even heard what you called her. She gave a big wide grin and a big wave and she was out of our lives for good.

***

My jaws were clenched, and I placed one hand over my mouth in disappointment. I'd blocked that woman out of my mind years ago, but hearing this reaffirmed my belief that she had no heart.

"Pops, why did you just let her leave like that?" There was a long silence before he answered.

"Big, Man, you can't make a person want to be with you. The first few months she sent pictures, cards, and a few toys. I never responded because I figured that if she really wanted to be with her family, she'd come back. Your mother became a big star overseas. She hooked up with some big producer over there and the next thing I knew, I was sent divorce papers. I didn't contest. I signed the papers and that was the end of Cheryl."

***

"I guess things were meant to happen that way, because that was the same year that your Uncle Buddy returned to Detroit. Of course it wasn't his fault. He blamed Lisa. According to him she nagged too much. Big Man, when Buddy returned I had decided to let him be. I had plenty of money and other investments so I didn't sweat him about paying me. I just let him live his life. After my relationship with Cheryl, I started to believe that maybe I was meant to be alone. As I looked back over all of the women in my life, Blanche was the only woman that I had ever truly longed for. No one could compare to the way that I felt about her."

Pops' face had a spark as he talked about Blanche, so I just had to say, "I guess that explains Ms. Shirley."

He gave a gracious smile when I mentioned her name.

"Big Man, I was very fond of that woman and I appreciated how she stepped in when Cheryl took off, but it wasn't enough to make me want to be exclusive with her. She deserved a man who could love her wholeheartedly. I wasn't that man. I respected her too much to lead her on and she respected herself too much to be led on so we parted ways on friendly terms.

"After Ms. Shirley left, it was hard looking at you without feeling like I'd failed you once again. So instead of just dealing with it, I made up for it by giving you money and things without ever making you work for it.

"I guess that's how my momma felt when Daddy died and Buddy came along. Since he never had Daddy she never made him pull his weight. She thought that giving him everything was compensation for Daddy. That was a big mistake. Momma left one big burden in this world."

Pops then looked at me and gave me a strong pat on the back.

"Big Man, I don't want to leave a burden in this world like my momma did. From this day forward, there will be no more free meal tickets. You will have to learn how to earn your own way."

I felt a bit nervous when Pops said that. The tone of his voice was calm and measured. I knew that he meant business. I still gave it one last shot.

"But Pops, what about my classes and the lease on my apartment?"

The tone in his voice never changed. "Big Man, it's been said, 'If you want something bad enough, you'll find a way. If you don't, then you'll find an excuse.' I guess that you'll just have to save up and pay for them with your own money."

My throat felt dry, so I swallowed. "But where will I find a job that will pay me enough money to take care of myself?

Pops stood and spread his arms out wide. "Welcome to your first day on the job."

I sat there confused. I didn't quite understand what he was trying to say, so I questioned him. "You're going to make me work for you?"

He let out a huge smile. "Big Man, I'm going to let you work with me. It's time that I teach you this business." He then followed up with a facetious statement. "Unless you have something better in mind?"

I was taken aback. It was all so sudden. I then stood and walked around the small outdated bar stopping in the middle of the small dance floor. I put my hand under my chin when Pops walked over and joined me.

"Big Man, this bar is old and in need of some renovations, but it's built on a strong foundation. I've been here for many years, made a lot of money, and I've met some great people who have been loyal since I've been here. At times I think about spending the money to overhaul this place, but I'm not sure if this is what I really want to do anymore. I own plenty of rental properties, made some good investments, and it's time that I start thinking about my retirement. Who knows, maybe I'll be able to find me a wife and settle down and buy me a summer home on the West Coast, next to my buddy Vernon. I could follow his pattern and hire someone to manage my properties while I just pop into town a few times a month to make sure that everything is running smoothly."

I laughed on the inside at that statement because I knew that settling down would be hard for Pops to do. He had told me countless times how money was the most important thing in the world. If he settled down, there was a chance that he could lose it all if it didn't work.

He wrapped his arm around me. "Big Man, we'll take baby steps."

I couldn't help but to ask, "Do you think that I can really do this?"

He squeezed that arm tightly around my shoulders and said, "I know that you can."

CARLA

The very first assignment Pops gave me was to take care of the monthly payment on the bar. He handed me a check and instructed me to take it down to James Vernon and Associates.

"Big Man, hand the check to the office manager and make sure that you get a receipt."

That seemed easy enough. I figured there was no way I could mess that up.

About a half hour later I made it down to Vernon and Associates. When I knocked on the heavy, solid wood door I had no idea who was standing on the other side of it. After a brief pause, the door swung open and to my surprise there stood a short, brown-skinned woman, wearing a little black dress, tall stiletto heels, and bright red lipstick. She was gorgeous. I was immediately star struck.

I'd watched Carla Roberts hundreds of times on the morning news throughout my high school years. I'd even daydream about the sassy rookie reporter back in those days. I'm not sure if she even remembered, but she interviewed me when our school won the state championship.

"May I help you?" she said with the same familiar voice that I remembered from a few years ago. When I didn't respond, I noticed that a big oversized security guard opened the door a little wider.

"I'm sorry, it's just that I neve...."

She looked at me and smiled. "That's okay, I don't bite." The security guard went back to his post.

I handed her the check and said, "I'm here to make a payment." She looked at the check, then back up at me and said, "Aren't you Jayson Jackson?" I flashed her a smile, ecstatic that she actually remembered. Not wanting to appear foolish, I responded with a cool and casual "Yes" although it felt more like a million caterpillars morphed into butterflies right inside my stomach.

"Wow! Small world," she shot back. "Your father James Jackson said that he was showing his son the ropes of the business and that he was sending you down to drop off the payment. I had no idea that it was Eastside High school's Star Quarterback from 1986."

I started feeling giddy and couldn't control my smile as she actually remembered the details.

It was four years ago--the seemingly classy woman stuck the microphone in my face asking me how we pulled off the win, when we were considered the major underdogs. I don't remember what my answers were, or even if they made any sense because my teammates claimed that I was foaming at the mouth when she asked her questions. They never let me live that day down.

Carla led the way to her desk and I couldn't help but to stare in awe at the beautiful spacious office. The walls were lined with numerous journalism awards, framed newspaper articles, photos she'd taken with public figures and a few celebrities. My personal favorite picture was of her with then Detroit Mayor Coleman A. Young.

Carla continued making conversation, as she swiftly moved through the office.

"Jayson, I can remember doing that big story on your school winning the state championship a few years back. I thought that your future seemed pretty bright and that you'd be playing professional football by now. I really believed that you'd be the one to really make something of yourself. I never expected to see you running your dad's little bar."

Ouch! My stomach turned sour because the butterflies seemed to have dissipated one by one at her callous remark. I faintly responded, "Things happen that way somtimes."

Carla noticed the uncomfortable look on my face, so she tried to conciliate what she'd just said. "Oh well. I guess it's better than nothing. Some kids have nothing to fall back on and they end up in the streets trying to make a quick buck." She then pressed her lips together and forced a sympathetic smile as she grabbed a pen.

That only exacerbated the situation and without warning I snapped, "Who in the hell are you calling a kid? I'm far from being a kid and I'm definitely not a charity case and I certainly don't need your sympathy."

Her eyes widened and she was attempting to apologize when I rudely cut her off. "The receipt, please."

The room was soon filled with an awkward silence. Her hands shivered as she wrote out the receipt. At that moment my eyes became fixated on the 5 x 7 crystal framed photo of her and Mr. James Vernon displayed proudly on her desk. They wore formal attire and smiled happily for the camera. Carla looked like a beautiful showpiece with her dark hair swept neatly off of her face, accenting her big beautiful brown eyes. Mr. Vernon stood behind with his arms wrapped tightly around her waist, sporting a black and white tuxedo with a low-cut salt and pepper Afro with a freshly trimmed salt and pepper beard. They looked like an odd couple, since he was actually old enough to be her father.

When she noticed that I'd caught glimpse of the picture, the tension in the room became palpable. Carla hurriedly completed the receipt, ripped the paper from the book, and tried to shove it in my hand. I wasn't going away that easy.

I pointed at the picture and decided to poke some fun. "You and your father look really nice."

My specious comment caught her off guard. Her arm became limp and her look of vibrancy immediately changed to shame and displeasure as the flimsy piece paper that she was holding floated out of her hand and spiraled a few feet across the room.

"I guess having somebody is better than having nobody. Some girls don't have anybody," I taunted, throwing her words back in her face, along with the identical fake smile.

Her weak body language gave her away. She couldn't take what she had just dished out. She then turned her attention to the receipt that was on the floor. She stooped down to pick up the paper and I decided to follow her lead. Since I was going to be dealing with her, I wanted to make sure that there were no hard feelings.

Our bodies were in sync as we both reached for our target. Our eyes collided and I could clearly see the look of humiliation and embarrassment all over her face. I placed my hand on top of hers to try and ease some of the tension.

She spoke. "He's getting a divorce." The tone in her voice was now soft and meek. *How sad*, I thought. Her words were filled with such platitudes and I wondered if she really believed them. This game was no longer fun. I felt pity for this woman, because Pops had just attended Mr. Vernon's 30th wedding anniversary in Hawaii. Sparing her from further embarrassment, I took the slip, helped her to her feet, and said, "I wish you the best," and I made my way out the door.

When I left her office that day, I couldn't get what had happened out of my mind. Her condescending attitude toward me had left a bitter taste in my mouth. My entire life I had people looking up, not down, to me. I wasn't average, had never been average, and I wasn't going to succumb to being average.

That day I must've driven twice the speed limit to make it back to the bar. I was ready to reinvent myself. I whipped into the parking lot and ran inside the bar feeling like a ball of fire.

I screamed with enthusiasm as I entered the bar and headed toward the back. "Pops I'm ready." He exited the kitchen with a stack of magazines in his hand seeming perplexed at my sudden burst of energy.

"What are you ready to do?" I could hardly contain my breathing. "I'm really serious. I want to learn everything there is to know about this business. I know that you said we'll take baby steps, but I'm ready to run."

Pops dropped the stack of magazines on the counter, no longer confused. He knew what I had seen.

"Big Man, what transpired when you went down there?" I tried to hide my grin. I couldn't fool Pops, though. He knew me all too well.

"Big Man, don't even think about messing with that woman; she's out of your league."

I listened to what Pops had to say, but I wasn't actually hearing him. He sensed that and it bothered him, so he offered a stern piece of advice.

"Big Man, this isn't a game for little boys. You're in the big league now. I can assure you that you won't get very far in this business if you don't learn to control your hormones. The first thing that you must learn is that when you become the boss, women will throw themselves all over you. If you don't have self-control and discipline, you will lose every time!"

Pops gave me a wink. "Remember to keep your eyes on the prize, because money rules just about everything."

I really didn't believe that I could ever afford a woman such as Carla Roberts, but it sure didn't hurt to dream. I admired Mr. Vernon, and at that age my eyes were young. I believed that he had the best of both worlds…a dedicated wife at home, and a beautiful young trophy piece on the side. I just didn't believe it got any better than that.

I still had hunger in my heart and soul. I wanted what James Vernon had and was willing to sacrifice it all to make it happen.

Pops sat down at the bar and flipped opened one of the magazines as he wore a proud smile across his face. I peeked over at the magazine to see what the smile was all about. My jaw dropped when I noticed that they were the photos from Mr. Vernon's 30th wedding anniversary in Hawaii.

Pops turned over the glossy magazine and there stood a photo of him and Mr. Vernon decked out in linen suits and leather sandals. They looked good for their ages. The layout was very nice. The crystal-blue waters off Hawaii accented by the sandy beaches made me long to be just like that even more.

I flipped to the beginning of the article, which was titled "Celebrating thirty years of marriage." The subtitle read "Detroit business mogul Mr. & Mrs. James Vernon renew their wedding vows on the beautiful Island of Hawaii." Mr. Vernon's beautiful older wife wore a long flowing white summer dress, with a large colorful flower in her hair and was holding a giant bouquet of red roses. The island was lined with lots of rose petals and a small cake that read "Happy 30th Anniversary."

I closed the magazine. I had seen enough. "Pops, where did you get this from?"

He smiled. "Not bad for men our age, huh?" I was dismayed that I couldn't respond. Pops answered, "That's the new magazine company that James Vernon just purchased. It's still in the pilot stage. This trial issue doesn't come out until next month."

I shook my head, thinking about Carla. How on earth was Mr. Vernon ever going to talk his way out of this one?

Pops must have read my mind. "Big Man, remember when I told you that money rules just about everything?" I nodded my head yes. Pops threw his hands in the air and said, "I rest my case."

***

After that day, Pops introduced me to the business little by little. As the weeks went on he still insisted that I wasn't fully ready because I was always late.

"You have to be on time, Big Man. If you're late, folks will never take you serious. That's one of the reasons your Uncle Buddy can't keep a job."

That first month flew by really fast and James Vernon's magazine was finally released. Pops had about fifty complimentary copies stacked by the door ready for the customers to take home with them. It was also time for me to drop the check off to Carla Roberts.

I was anxious about seeing her again and I was prepared for whatever shade she had to throw at me. I wore a nice pair of khaki pants, a button-down shirt, and black loafers. I sprayed on some cologne and was ready to go.

I stopped by the car wash and had my Mustang detailed inside and out. I wanted it to shine.

***

The parking lot at Vernon and Associates was deserted except for a black convertible BMW. I pulled next to the car and headed to the door.

I knocked several times, but there was no answer. I waited a few more minutes and when I didn't get a response, I headed to my car. Just as I was getting ready to hop inside, I heard someone call my name. I turned around and the door was half cracked. I walked back to the door and there stood Carla inside the building with the blinds closed, the lights out, and she was wearing dark sunglasses. The only problem, there was no sun.

She opened the door just enough to let me enter and when I was finally able to see her-- she looked terrible. Her hair was disheveled, her face was red and puffy, her clothes were stretched, and she smelled as though she'd been drinking. I kept quiet.

She closed the door behind me and before I knew it, she removed her glasses and started crying really hard. I didn't know what to do so I just stood there.

Carla grabbed several copies of the magazine articles and threw them at me. "Can you believe this shit?" she yelled. I didn't say a word. "I helped this bastard take his business to the next level and this is the thanks that I get. He's a freaking liar, and a user." She made two fists with her hands and started shaking them. "I swear to God I'm going to make his old ass pay for this. That damn wife of his is so stupid. She doesn't even know what's going on right under her nose. She doesn't give a damn about James Vernon. All she cares about is getting spa treatments, traveling with her social club, and spending up all his money that I helped him make."

Carla was slurring her words and she really looked and sounded pathetic. I offered no comment. "Do you know that she doesn't even have sex with the poor man? They don't even sleep in the same bed. And do you know what else?" I shook my head no. "She doesn't even work. I fucking hate her!" Carla then turned up her nose and wore a look of disgust on her face.

It felt kind of strange hearing such a classy lady use such harsh language. Her behavior was most uncouth and it left me confused, because she accepted none of the blame. If it weren't so sad, it would've been considered comical, because she sounded foolish. Did it ever occur to her that "stupid is not when you don't know, it's when you do know"? Mrs. Vernon didn't know. Carla did. I kept those thoughts to myself because she really believed what Mr. Vernon had told her, and I doubted very seriously if any of it were true. Carla wasn't the true victim that she had made herself out to be--his unsuspecting wife was.

She went over to her desk and grabbed the bottle of wine, turned it up and poured it down her throat. When she put the half-empty bottle down, she took the sleeve of her blouse and used it as a napkin. She wiped her entire face with that sleeve. Her eyes were smudged with black liner, and lipstick was smeared all across her face. I watched in shame, feeling very little sympathy for her. She allowed herself to be used. She had a good career, no children, and was well-respected. I had no idea why she needed more.

She walked over to a rolling file cabinet and snatched it open. "Look at all of these fucking contracts, business deals, bank statements, and everything else. I run this motherfucker, not him."

She was really losing her mind. She stumbled backwards catching her balance before she fell. "Can you believe that bastard actually told me that he purchased that magazine?"

I still didn't respond but continued to listen.

She then began to talk in a drunken whiney voice, mimicking what Mr. Vernon had said to her.

"Carla, it's not what you think," she sobbed. "If I divorce Nancy now, she would take everything." Carla started making these crazy funny-looking faces. She was really bugging out. She then fell to her knees and began crying again.

I tried consoling her. I put my arm around her shoulder and said the only thing that I could think of. "Carla, I've never been married, but I'm sure that he has the best lawyers. Maybe they advised him that it isn't a good time for a divorce right now."

She lifted her head and looked at me. "How stupid is that?" she slurred. "Is there ever really a good time for a divorce?" She had that same condescending attitude from our first encounter. This time I gave her a free pass because she was really going through a lot.

She then said, "You're just still a kid, the hired help! What do you know about anything? You're probably still a damn virgin, too." Those last words did it! Carla was really crazy.

I stood up, leaving her right there on that floor. She was going to have to pick her own self up and figure her own way out of this mangled mess that she'd created.

I walked toward the door and before I could turn the knob, she sobbed very loud and pleaded. "I'm sorry. Please don't go. I can't be by myself."

I stopped and turned around. I counted to five before I let out a heavy sigh and walked over to her. I picked her up off of the floor and gently laid her across the leather sofa. I found the bathroom and retrieved a towel. I wet it with steaming hot water, kneeled down next to her, and rubbed it across her forehead.

It was then that I unexpectedly became the therapist and she the patient.

* * *

Carla whimpered. "I came from nothing, and I'm not ever going back there. My mother migrated here from Haiti when she was a young woman in hopes of finding the American dream. She then married my 'handsome' American father who was a traveling musician and I guess in my mother's eyes, my father was that dream. He had a twin brother who was the opposite of him. His brother Carl opted for an education instead. I was born a short time after my parents married, and that's when their struggles began. With an extra mouth to feed, my mother was unable to travel with him and he often left her behind to chase after that one big gig that he claimed would solve all of their money problems. She believed in him and she did whatever she had to do in order to hold our family together. My mother also suffered from depression. Some days she'd be up and the other days she'd be down. I'd watch her work odd jobs as a way of making up for my father's shortcomings while he continued to drink and party away the rent money."

She hesitated for a few seconds as tears raced down her face. She then became quite melancholic as she continued to talk about her parents.

"Although my father was always around, mentally, he was never there. He was too busy dreaming and making promises that he couldn't fulfill. As a little girl I was his biggest fan and too young to see his flaws. My senior year in high school, that all changed. The biggest devastation of my life happened when my father was found in the bathroom at one of those parties with a needle in his arm, slumped over the toilet. He had overdosed."

***

As I sat there and listened to Carla, I began to feel pity for her. I didn't want her to sober up and have any regrets about telling me her business, so I looked her in the eyes and said, "You don't have to tell me this." She pretended as if she didn't hear me. She spoke as if I wasn't there. She was relaxed in a sedated mindset as she stared blankly at the ceiling.

***

Carla continued to go back in time. "That calamity sent my mother into an even deeper depression. She became reclusive and six months after my father's death, she gave up. She proudly watched me walk across the stage to receive my high school diploma knowing that I had a full scholarship to Wayne State University and that I was on my way to a better life. When I returned home that evening from my graduation celebration, she was laying there peacefully with an empty bottle of sleeping pills. I was officially alone. My father's twin brother Carl Roberts stepped in and paid my mother's funeral expenses and offered me support. I was grateful, but I didn't accept it. I was not his responsibility and I wanted to make it on my own. "

My views about Carla soon changed. I admired her tenacity and moxie because I could have never made it without Pops. I guess I was starting to understand her reasoning behind her relationship with Mr. Vernon.

"Jayson, do you know what I learned from my parents?" she asked through a sniffle as she was starting to pull herself together.

"What is that, Carla?"

"That I never want a love like theirs, because love don't pay any goddamn bills!" she blustered.

Her anger resurfaced and she began castigating her mentally ill mother as she relived her past. "I believe that she used depression as an excuse. She was just a weak woman with a small mind. She was satisfied with living in a small home and driving a small car because she never chased after anything bigger. She was beautiful and probably could have had any man that she wanted. She spent her entire life chasing after something that was never within her reach."

Although I didn't know Carla's mother or anything about her mental illness, she sounded like a wonderful, loyal woman to me.

Seconds later the office phone rang, releasing her from her fury. She abruptly sat up like she had forgotten where she was. It rang about three times when she picked it up and slammed it back down. It immediately rang again but this time she let the answering machine pick it up. A deep male voice called out with urgency. "Carla. Carla." Before he could leave a full message, Carla went into a rage and snatched the phone out of the wall.

She then grabbed her purse, put on a sexy red fedora, and said, "Let's go. Get me the hell out of here."

I followed behind her, although I had no idea where we were headed. A small fraction of me knew that I shouldn't have gotten involved, but the greater part trumped it all. In spite of everything that had happened between us, I still found her fascinating; therefore I felt the need to mollify her anger.

Once we were outside, she said with a slight frown, "Is that your little car over there?" I lightly shook my head and chuckled on the inside. She meant no harm by her insults. They were just a part of who she was.

My Mustang was only three years old. I loved that car and had begged Pops to buy it for me. But at that moment, I somehow felt that it wasn't good enough, so the word "No" rolled off of my tongue faster than I could catch it. I had no choice but to follow it up with another lie. "I tore up the Mercedes that my Pops gave me so he's making me drive this thing." It was a really stupid lie and little did I know that lie would only be the beginning of many more to come.

She hopped in and pulled down the sun visor and applied some bright red lipstick, put on a pair of big designer shades and said aggressively, "Drive!"

I started driving down the street when I asked, "Where are we going?"

She looked at me and said, "I need to get away. Let's go to your place?" My heart sank.

"Uhmmmmm, I'm still in the process of fixing my place up--you really don't want to go there." The lies became easier. She looked at me and grinned and pointed in the direction of the expressway.

About twenty minutes later, we were in front of a nice quiet restaurant tucked away in the suburbs. I parked the car and we headed to the door. The lunch menu was displayed on a chalkboard outside of the restaurant and my heart began to race at the expensive prices. I only had about one hundred and fifty bucks on me and I silently prayed that I'd have enough.

Carla was a regular customer at the restaurant; the female greeter called her by name. We were quickly seated in a small cozy booth near the back of the restaurant. I looked around at the fancy place and it was definitely nice, low-key and upscale. I then spotted Donna. She was one of the ladies that danced at Pops' bar. She was with a much older gentleman and he seemed to be really into her. I tried my best to relax but I was really nervous. If this got back to Pops, he would kill me.

Carla reached under the table and grabbed my leg. I jumped. "Loosen up, Jayson; I don't bite." I laughed. I had never been on a date at a place so nice and elegant before.

My heart began to thump when the waitress brought the wine list over and there weren't any prices behind them. Carla looked at her and said, "The usual, but this time I'm going to need the entire bottle."

The waitress smiled and then turned her attention to me. I played it safe. "Bring me whatever you have on tap."

The drinks came fast and it was soon time to order our food. I can remember feeling relieved when Carla ordered a salad. Although it was no ordinary salad, and was well overpriced, it wouldn't break the bank. I ordered what they called a gourmet burger and steak fries.

When Carla was on her third glass of wine she started to loosen up. Her relationship with James Vernon had then become an open book.

Carla was engaged to her college sweetheart when she started working at the news station. She met James Vernon when she interviewed him for becoming the first black vice president of Detroit National Bank. He liked her drive and tenacity and within a year she became his publicist.

Mr. Vernon left the bank and started his own consulting firm. Carla worked for him part-time. Her fiancé at the time was overseas playing professional basketball and he wanted Carla to drop everything and fly over to Europe to join him. She refused. Living overseas was not how she envisioned her life and her fiancé had no plans for what he wanted to do after basketball ended. That engagement soon fizzled and Carla poured herself into her work.

Carla left the news station and became a part-time journalist so that she could work full time for James Vernon. She was actually the brain behind Vernon and Associates. She was smart and savvy and had a lot of passion for what she did. James Vernon trusted her, so he put up the capital and she did the rest. He was so happy with the work that she was doing, that he started showering her with expensive gifts and lavish vacations, and he also bought her a home. She made him a lot of money.

Because of James Vernon, Carla had traveled to some amazing places and met some of the most famous people. He had given her an open checkbook so that she could travel and have the resources to cover some of the most sought-after public figures. It was a lifestyle that many women could only dream of.

We sat in the bar for a few hours as she talked, cried, and reminisced, all while polishing off two bottles of wine. Her stories were fascinating so I didn't bother to interrupt.

The check finally arrived and I grew nervous as the waitress slid it directly in front of me. I crossed my fingers as I turned it over. Carla reached across the table and slapped my hand away. "Don't be silly, this is on James Vernon," she said sternly.

I was relieved. I doubted if I even had enough money to pay for it anyway. But I still was a man with a lot of pride. So I at least had to offer. "Please don't insult me like that, Carla. I have money."

She laughed once more and tilted her head to the side and squinted her eyes like women do when they mean business and said, "Jayson, I need to make myself clear. This thing between James Vernon and me has just become personal. I wouldn't even let the proprietor of this establishment give us this meal for free. When I said that he was going to pay, I meant it!" She then closed the discussion.

That bill was over two hundred dollars and she handed the waitress a gold credit card without batting an eyelash. She even left her a hundred-dollar tip. When it was time to leave, Carla stood up and stumbled out of her chair into my arms. She knocked over a few glasses that were on our table and it caused all eyes to focus on us.

Donna looked at me and winked. That caused me to become agitated because I knew that I'd been caught. Carla started laughing. I whispered in her ear, "Please hold it together; I don't want you to make a fool out of yourself."

She stood up straight as she possibly could and said, "Oh shut up and let's go."

I found her behavior amusing. All the money in the world couldn't suppress the true person that one tries to bury deep down inside.

It was still early and Carla wasn't ready to be alone. We ended up at her home, which was in the quiet upscale suburb of Bloomfield Hills, Michigan. I was apprehensive about being there until she put my mind to rest by saying that James Vernon was out of town on a business trip and wasn't expected back for a few days. She claimed that she needed to take that time to sort some things out.

She gave me a tour of the home and I was very impressed. The two-story home wasn't very big, but it was elegant and tastefully done.

She had a beautiful African art collection along the walls and in the back of the house was a large family room that had a state of the art surround sound system with a huge television built into the wall. A fully stocked bar sat in the back corner with all top-shelf liquor.

She offered me a drink. I wasn't a big drinker, so I asked for a beer. She laughed and said, "Look, I'm going to make me a drink, and it's no fun drinking by myself."

I cut her off. "I'll have whatever you're having." She became excited and reached on the top shelf and grabbed a big bottle of cognac. She kissed the bottle. After she poured the glasses, she made a toast: "Courtesy of Vernon."

I put the glass up to my lips and before I could gulp it down, she stopped me. "This isn't your ordinary cognac. This is Louis XIII and it cost over fifteen hundred dollars. You're supposed to sip it and enjoy the taste."

After the brief history lesson, I did as I was instructed. I liked the taste. It went down very smooth and there was no after burn like the cheap stuff I drank in college.

She walked over to a cabinet and slid it open and there were hundreds of CDs to choose from. She then opened the blinds so that her spacious backyard was fully exposed. Big tall trees lined the private yard and it was equipped with a swimming pool, a deck with a hot tub, and next to it sat beautiful, expensive-looking patio furniture. She was really living the good life. She told me to make myself comfortable as she disappeared upstairs.

I looked through her music selection and I was surprised at the variety that she had. She had a variety of music, which inclued Sam Cooke, Sammy Davis, Nat King Cole, to the latest R and B. I knew that the older material had to have been for James Vernon.

Although I really wanted to hear some rap music, I settled for

Stevie Wonder. I was sitting there sipping, listening to the music, imagining that this was my home.

Carla came down the stairs about fifteen minutes later, refreshed and smelling good, wearing a long flowing yellow sundress and with freshly painted red lips.

She grabbed the bottle of cognac and led the way outside to the patio. We both continued to drink and I started to really become relaxed. Carla then looked at me very seriously and said, "Ask me." I grinned because I had no idea what I was supposed to ask her.

"Ask me whatever questions you want; I'm sure you have plenty."

Since she started it, I figured I'd go for it. "So is it all worth it?" She kept a straight face and hesitated before she answered. She looked around at her beautiful home and said "yes." I guess that I couldn't argue with her because she did have a lovely home.

"Exactly how old are you Carla?"

She started blushing and said, "How old do I look?"

I let out a laugh because I wasn't going to fall for that old trick. I learned years ago that women never liked to look their age. So I decided to make her feel good. "You look to be about eighteen." She did have a younger-looking face, but the way that she handled herself was that more like a 35-year-old woman. I knew that would get me slapped across the face if I reached that high.

She giggled. "Eighteen, huh? I'll take it. I'm twenty- seven."

"Wow, you look great," was all that I could say before I moved on to my next question. "Carla, you're twenty-seven years old and he is close to sixty. That's such a huge age gap. Don't you ever worry about getting bored with him?"

Again she looked around at her home and said, "I love what I do and plus I have a few projects that I'm working on outside of this business. I'm too busy to even think about getting bored. Besides, I don't believe that I know any woman who will ever get bored with spending money."

My next question was a tough one, but I just had to know, "What about marriage and a family?"

She seemed a bit uncomfortable with the question and before she responded, she carefully selected her words. "Jayson, it's a great big world out there and I plan to see every bit of it. Kids will only get in the way."

Before I even digested her answer, I said, "So do you still think that you and James Vernon will get married?" She suddenly looked away and started picking at something on her dress. I felt like such a jerk for asking her that question. I then said, "Please don't answer that."

She gave an earnest smile and patted my hand and said in an upbeat voice. "Let's talk about you." I smiled back and agreed.

She then became personal. "So if I'm doing my math correctly, you have to be about twenty-two?" I smiled because she was right on the money. "So tell me, Jayson, what's your girlfriend like?" I didn't hesitate in answering that one. "I haven't had a real girlfriend since my sophomore year in high school."

Carla looked at me and said, "I don't believe that. You're such a handsome kid." She quickly put her hand over her mouth in an attempt to apologize for calling me a kid. I smiled and told her about my very first girlfriend Mandy.

***

Her name was Amanda Clark but everyone called her Mandy. She and I first encountered one another in the sixth grade. Mandy was tall with long legs, bright skin, and huge light-brown eyes with very thick eyelashes. She was the new girl in our class and every boy liked her, including me.

Her first day of class my two classmates Ron and Aaron made a secret three-dollar bet on which one of them she'd choose. They put the money in an envelope and the winner was supposed to keep all the money and take her out to the arcade. I can remember telling them to include me in on the bet. They both looked at me and laughed, because I was a fat kid. They thought it was highly unlikely she'd even give me the time of day. I can remember Ron saying, "Oh well, that's more money for me to take her out with."

That evening we all wrote her a letter and sealed it up. We put it in her notebook the very next morning. We all patiently waited until lunchtime to see whom she'd choose.

I wore my best clothes that day and when she walked into the cafeteria all our eyes were on her. Aaron and Ron both stood up, just knowing that they were the chosen ones. She stepped over to our table wearing a huge smile as she pointed and winked at me. They both looked at each other with a puzzled look. "Jayson, would you like to sit with me?"

I proudly stood up, sucked my protruding belly in and said, "I most certainly will." As I walked away with my new girlfriend, I heard the words "I can't believe it." I didn't bother to entertain them. I stuck my hand behind my back and Ron slapped me the envelope with my small fortune in it.

***

Carla smiled at that story. "How cute. Well, I guess that taught you a very important lesson. Size doesn't really matter."

I laughed when Carla said that. "That's bullshit, Carla. I cheated."

She was sort of confused when she asked, "How did you cheat?"

"That evening when I made it home I started writing her the letter. My Uncle Buddy stopped by to grab something to eat when I told him about Mandy and the letter. He and my Pops don't actually see eye to eye on a lot of things, but in my eyes my uncle is one cool cat. Women seemed to love him. He pulled out a ten-dollar bill and told me to add it to my letter. 'Jayson, you must always learn to stay one step ahead of your opponent.'

Carla was bent over laughing. "Jayson, you mean to tell me that you bought your very first girlfriend?" I shook my head yes and laughed along with Carla, thinking about how foolish I was at that time.

"Carla, as I look back over that relationship, I really wished that I hadn't. Since she was my first girlfriend, I was a complete fool for her. Amanda spent up all my money, bossed me around, damaged my self-esteem, made fun of my size, and I wouldn't build up the confidence to break up with her until high school."

Carla was enjoying hearing me talk about myself. It seemed to take her mind off Vernon.

"So Jayson, how did you get the name Big Man?" I laughed again when she asked that question.

***

I'd played in football leagues throughout my youth and I had a pretty good arm. My only problem was that I was overweight and I couldn't run very fast.

When I made it to high school, I had decided to hang my hat with football. That is, until Coach Grier spotted me walking down the hall and asked me my name. He gave my shoulder a tight squeeze and smiled at me exposing a wide gap between his teeth, stating, "Jayson, we sure could use a man of your size on our football team." I looked at him and tried to turn him down nicely. High school football was much more serious than little league football because you had to actually produce. My father paid for me to be in the league so I didn't have to try out. I wasn't so sure if I could make the high school team on my own so I said to the coach, "Well, I'm not really interested in playing football."

Coach Grier sized me up once more and said, "I'm not taking no for an answer. I've been coaching for a long time and I can spot talent from a mile away. Jayson I'll see you in try-outs."

I looked at Carla and said, "Since Coach Grier was so persistent on me being on the football team, I took his invitation as an endorsement and actually tried out."

I told Carla how those were the toughest two weeks of my life. The guys on the field all looked like well-trained professional athletes fighting hard to secure their positions--and I, on the other hand, just couldn't keep up. I was too slow. I didn't stand a chance competing with any of those guys. I looked terrible out on that field.

On the last day of try-outs, Coach Grier finally had enough. He blew the whistle for what seemed like an eternity. Everyone on the field stopped. I was slumped over, coughing hard, while trying to catch my breath. He screamed. "Hey you!" I managed to look up. He crumbled his face as he pointed in my direction. "Yes you. The Big Man over there." My heart dropped. I was so pitiful that he didn't even bother to remember my name. He ran over to me and kneeled down in my face and said, "Get off of my damn field!" The guys on the team all fell out laughing.

Embarrassed by his cruel attack, I managed to straighten my prostrated body to try and appear unfazed. He needed to say no more. I knew that I didn't have the skills to be on that team. Refusing to be castigated any longer, I grabbed my helmet and swiftly headed toward the locker room.

When everyone made it back inside the locker room, they all had jokes. I was even badgered about being called Big Man. Since they wouldn't let up, I joined in on the laugher because it seemed to ease the embarrassment.

Carla had a mortified look on her face as I shared that story.

"Oh no, Jayson! I have never heard of anything so humiliating."

I looked at her and said, "I got through it. Coach Grier humiliated me on purpose. He knew that I had potential I wasn't living up to. He said that sometimes in life you have to break people all the way down in order to build them back up, and that's just what he did.

"When the team left the locker room he made me stay. I assumed that he was going to chastise me even more but he didn't. He told me that I was on the team. I was surprised because I thought that the man hated me."

Carla smiled as I shared what Coach had said: "Big Man, I spot something inside of you and I am rarely ever wrong. I know that you have what it takes to be a great player." I smiled. It felt good to hear that. Coach then said, "I'm placing you on a strict diet, you're going to hit the gym every day, and you will weigh in every week." We shook on it and just like that I was on the team.

I can remember how pissed off Mandy was.

She whined, "Jayson, it's stupid that we can't go out to eat anymore because of some dumb football team. What about our relationship? We haven't been to the mall, the movies, or even out to eat since you've been on that stupid team."

That was the moment when I realized that she was just plain ole selfish. I was noticeably smaller, I felt healthier, and I was actually happier. She never mentioned those things. It was all about her and her needs.

When I still hadn't played after our fourth game, she stood outside the locker and issued me an ultimatum.

"Jayson, this is so stupid. I feel embarrassed for you. I'm not coming to another game just to sit here and watch you keep the bench warm. You're going to have to make a choice. Either you're going to be committed to me or to this football team, but you can't have both.

Mandy didn't wait for a response. She walked off assuming that I would chase behind her like I had done the entire relationship. In the back of my mind I was thinking, *Good riddance*. But that wouldn't be the end of her. She had a plan that I wasn't prepared for.

Late the next evening while Pops was at work, there was a knock on my door. I peeked out of the window to find Mandy standing there. She opened her coat and revealed a skimpy little panty and bra set. I got very excited. I opened the door and she barged in.

She looked beautiful. Her hair was pinned up, she had on fire-red lipstick and she smelled divine. She opened her coat to tease me once more. I was weak. She had me and she knew it. When I threw my arms around her, she pushed me backwards and I fell onto the couch. She slowly bent over, being sure to wiggle her butt from side to side, and exposed all of her goodies. She then turned the radio on, and the smooth sounds of Marvin Gaye's "Sexual Healing" crooned throughout the house as she did that stripper dance, like the women did at Pops' bar. Mandy then dropped her coat and lifted her leg high above her head and did a ballerina spin. I began to salivate. When I reached out to touch her, she pushed me away. I was going insane. She did this dance for a few more minutes when I realized that she wasn't going to let me touch her. She wanted to retrain me into the boyfriend that I had been all those years back, and sadly, it was working.

Unable to take any more of this torture, I stood up and reached inside of my pockets. I had the two hundred dollars that Pops had given me for some football equipment. I had ten twenty-dollar bills, and Mandy was about to get them all.

When she saw what I was doing, she moved in closer and bent over in front of me and touched her toes. I slid a bill into the back of her underwear. She then seductively extended her left arm, and then her right arm, back and forth across her body and slowly snaked her way back up. I was going crazy. She looked really good, as she exposed both of her perky breasts. Before she would let me touch them, she made sure that I put a bill in each one. I tucked them both under her wet sticky breast. I had never experienced anything like this before. I had seen the women in Pops' bar, but I was never allowed to touch them. Having Mandy there was like a dream turned reality.

We played that game until all of my money was hers. Before she would let me go any further, she wanted to use the bathroom. She took her purse with her, so I knew that she was putting her money away. I didn't care about that money; this was definitely worth it.

She came out minutes later, with nothing on, and three condoms in her hand. "Which color do you want to use first?" she said in a salacious voice. My eyes grew wide. I was shocked. The Mandy that I knew barely let me go all the way and now she was saying that we were going to go three rounds.

I don't know what color I picked first. I was so worked up and ready, I snatched the foil wrapper out of her hands, clicked off the light, and we went at it. We went at it for a long time. Mandy was moving, humping and grinding and doing things I never even knew existed. This girl was a pro. I was so excited that I must have told her that I loved her a hundred times.

Once she saw that she had me right where she wanted me, she stopped right in the middle of the second session and pushed me off of her.

"That's enough, I'm tired!" she snapped, sounding like the old Mandy. I was disappointed, but I tried not to show it. I wouldn't dare force myself on her. "No means no" is what Pops instilled in me. I then understood why he had to do that. I kept my cool.

"What do you mean you're tired? I'm not."

Mandy then said, "Well, I'm sorry but I should be asleep right now because I have to work in the morning. My mom is not loaded like your dad."

That statement alone let me know that her visit wasn't about me being on the football team but actually about money. At that point I really didn't care, because I wanted to finish. I looked down at my friend who was standing at full attention and said, "Listen Mandy. Don't worry about money. I've got plenty more."

Her mood quickly changed as I reached inside my dresser drawer and pulled out my last fifty dollars. She snatched the last condom off of the floor and let me finish.

I didn't last very long after that. Her taking all my money must have pissed my friend off down there, because he had dropped his salute.

Fifteen minutes after we were done, she looked at her watch and started putting on her clothes. A horn blew a few minutes later. "I have to go--my sister's here. Get up and walk me out to the car." She was still overbearing.

I was repulsed by her attitude. She came there with the motive of taking my money, because she never mentioned the football team.

There was no way that I was going to walk her to any car. I looked at Mandy and shot her exact words right back at her: "I'm tired." She looked at me and pretended to be mad. I knew that she really wasn't. After all, she was leaving my house two hundred and fifty dollars richer.

That was my last physical encounter with Mandy. I ignored her and focused on football.

After I stopped seeing her, my game improved. I had lost a lot of weight, I was in great shape, and I actually picked up speed. I think she was the one who was holding me back all that time, so I never had any regrets.

Before the season ended, I was awarded the position of second-string quarterback and I'd actually helped our team make it to the playoffs when our starting quarterback sustained an injury. That game was the beginning of my popularity. Almost every girl in the school wanted to go out with me. I dated several of them just to get back at Mandy. She couldn't take it so she begged me to take her back. I didn't. Instead I went out with her ex- best friend. That caused her to hate me. Her last words to me were, "Big Man you're going to pay for this. I really didn't care. I just wanted her out of my life for good. Mandy was actually the last real girlfriend that I had, because I just didn't know if I could trust anyone again after what she'd put me through.

College was pretty much like a meat market. There was lots of drinking and partying and I knew that I couldn't take any of those girls seriously. When I did find one that I kind of liked, I found out that she had slept with one of my teammates. I really couldn't tell if the girls liked me for me or because I played football.

After I finished the story, Carla stared at me and said, "Wow! You sure had an interesting childhood."

***

After I shared part of my life story with Carla, I realized we both were buzzed. I soon excused myself to go the restroom. When I returned several minutes later I was surprised to find her in a two-piece bathing suit relaxing in the hot tub. It had started to get dark and it seemed as though a billion stars illuminated off the beautiful waters. She was so relaxed that I didn't know if I should hop in or sit back down.

She soon called out, "Jayson, please join me." I looked down at myself and she started laughing. "Take your pants off--your briefs will be fine." I didn't hesitate. I hurriedly removed my pants and hopped into the hot water.

We both relaxed and it felt really good being in her presence. I found it hard to believe that just a few weeks prior, I looked up to this woman and felt extremely intimidated by her. As I lay there in her arms, I realized that without all of the cameras, the make-up and the attitude, she was no different than me. Our hearts beat the same and they hurt the same. We were both human.

That evening at Carla's house I was able to get a glimpse inside her head.

When Carla opened up to me, I had a better understanding of how the mind of a woman of her status really worked. She was a visionary who was determined to have it all even if it came at the expense of causing pain to others.

She continuously talked about how her mother was weak and foolish for waiting on a man who constantly let her down and could offer her nothing. She was never going to take that route. I felt as though she was competing with the dead. It was as if she wanted to show her mother what "living your dreams" really meant. Life was all about Carla Roberts.

It had started to get late and I was highly intoxicated. I stumbled my way out of the hot tub and was starting to put on my clothes, when Carla suddenly burst out, "You can't leave!" I gave her a strange look because it sounded more like an order. When she looked at my face, she rephrased the statement and said in a softer voice, "I won't let you." That last statement had me, although I had no idea what I was up against.

Her bedroom was like a big love nest. The walls were painted with dark earth tone colors, she had candles everywhere, there was a king-sized four-poster bed with curtains draped around it, and soft jazz music played in the background.

She stretched her beautiful body across the bed and asked me to join her. I was hesitant at first because I wasn't sure if she really wanted me or it was just the liquor talking. When she noticed that I didn't move she said in a very sexy voice, "Jayson, have you ever made love to a woman before?"

When she said that, she had my full attention. I'd had it with her insults and if she wanted me to make love to her, then that's just what I was going to do. I had to make sure it was what she really wanted.

"Carla, I don't want to take advantage of this situation because we both have been drinking."

She came back with a quick response. "Jayson, I know what I want and need. I need to be satisfied, and I want you to do it." She then rubbed her hands over her entire body.

"Where's the protection?" I asked. My manhood was rock-solid. "I'm on the pill." She said that casually, like protection was only for preventing pregnancy.

***

Hearing her dismiss using a condom took me back to my freshman year in college. My college roommate Brandon once failed to use protection with a girl and he paid the price for it. He ran out the locker room stalls screaming and holding his crotch. He said that it felt as if he was peeing fire. I believe that every member of our team felt his pain. Coach took him to the clinic that evening. Brandon came back telling us that he had to get a shot in his butt with a long needle. I believe that experience taught us all a valuable lesson. From that point on, our Coach always made sure that we all had condoms.

***

"Well, I guess we can never be too careful." I quickly reached inside my wallet and found two condoms. They'd been there for a while but I was sure they worked.

I rolled the latex over my manhood and jumped up in that bed and went to work. She felt so good. Her skin was soft, her butt was nice and round, and her breasts were full which made her irresistible. I was going so hard and fast that she started screaming my name. I ignored her screams because I wanted her to know that I knew how to satisfy a woman. I may not have had James Vernon's money, but I knew his old ass didn't have my energy.

I pounded and pounded for about fifteen minutes. She continued to scream my name and that only made me reach my sexual peak even quicker. I wanted to hold back but I figured that she couldn't take anymore so I let go and released it all.

When I finally finished I lay on top of her. I needed to catch my breath.

She suddenly used all of her energy to push me off of her.

"What the hell was that?" she said very harshly.

I thought that she was probably upset because it didn't last that long, so I responded, "I'm sorry. I just got so excited and I couldn't hold it. Let me catch my breath, I have another condom--the second round is always longer."

Her follow-up to that response was a direct blow to my ego.

"Jayson, that was not love, that felt more like war."

I was humiliated and I came back with, "I've never had any complaints before." She knew that she'd had hurt my feelings, so she explained it to me as gently as she possibly could.

"Jayson, slow and steady wins the race. The music is playing in the background for a reason. If we're making love and I can't hear the music, then you're doing it wrong."

I felt foolish. "Carla, I heard you call my name, so I thought that you liked it."

She giggled. "Jayson, that's locker room talk. You guys think that the louder us women scream the more satisfied we are. That couldn't be further from the truth. I yelled your name because it hurt."

She abruptly got up and said, "I need to go and soak."

I was mortified. "Sorry" was the only thing that I could say.

She went into her bathroom and lit a few candles and started to fill her tub. About five minutes later she called my name. I really wanted to leave because I doubted if I'd be able to have another erection after that.

I slowly walked into her bathroom and I was surprised to find that she had a Jacuzzi tub filled with bubbles. She stood inside the tub naked. I tried to approach, but she told me to stop, and stand there and enjoy the view.

Her body was beautiful. After a few minutes, she asked me to join her. This time I was in no rush. I had never taken a bath with a woman before so I wanted to savor every moment of this. She handed me some soap and told me to wash her from head to toe. My manhood was starting to come back to life as I lathered the soap in my hands and cleansed her body from top to bottom. She did the same thing to me.

After the bath, she asked me to carry her back into the bedroom. I did just as I was asked. I gently laid her down and she told me to get the oil out of her top drawer. I massaged every inch of her body with that oil and it felt as though my manhood was ready to explode, but I'd learned to control it.

The soft music continued to play in the background and I made sure that I could hear it at all times. She then had me lie on my back and she massaged my entire body with the oil. Once she was done, she led the way. She moved slow and seductive and instructed me to do the same.

We made sweet beautiful love, and not one time was the music drowned out. She was actually humming to the music. I'd never forget that day because for the first time ever, I had finally made love to a woman. I was so lost in Carla that I'd forgotten to use protection. She claimed to be on the pill and I hoped that she was. Besides, why would she want to have a baby by me; I was broke and had nothing to offer. As far as the burning that my friend had… that day I took my chance.

I stayed wrapped under Carla the entire night. I even dreamed about her although she was right there. I really hoped and prayed that James Vernon was a thing of the past. I knew that I didn't have his wealth, but with time and patience she would fall in love with me and the material things wouldn't matter. She'd realize that together we would build our own wealth.

***

The alarm clock beeped loudly. I opened my eyes and it read 5:00 a.m. I extended my arms wide when I noticed that the bed was empty. I jumped up thinking that maybe I had imagined last night. I looked around the room and realized it wasn't a dream.

The bathroom door was cracked and I heard sniffling. I tiptoed over to the door. I started to knock when I suddenly heard her whispering. I assumed she was on the phone until she sniffled once more. Her words were clear. "Shit…what have I done….he's the damn help!"

My heart plummeted! It really was the liquor talking last night.

I softly knocked on the door and when she didn't say anything, I let myself in. As I entered, she was sitting on the toilet seat fully clothed and crying.

"Carla, are you all right? Can I get you anything?" She grabbed some tissue to make it out like she was blowing her nose, but I knew better. Something was wrong.

"Jayson, I'm okay. Periodically, I have these crying spells and I don't know why. I think that you should just leave." I was stunned when she said that, because I didn't want to go.

"Maybe I could get you some aspirin or something, I just don't want to leave you this way." I noticed that a bottle of pills were next to the sink and I didn't know what they were for.

She pointed at the bottle and said "I took something already." Her words were cold so I left her alone.

My feelings were hurt. I really wanted to believe that Carla was different and not like the other girls that I had in the past.

Just as I was fully dressed, she came out of the bathroom a totally different person. She smiled at me and said, "I'm sorry for snapping at you like that; I just get emotional at times." I wanted to ask her about *the help* comment but I didn't. I was just glad that she wasn't upset anymore.

She then said, "I really enjoyed myself last night--hopefully we can hook up real soon." I looked at her, realizing that she was really dismissing me. I smiled. She grabbed my face and kissed me softly on the lips. "I promise to call you soon."

I smiled again and said, "I'll be waiting."

It was 5:30 a.m. when I got into my car. I pulled out of her subdivision and realized that she didn't have my phone number. That left me in a dense fog and I didn't know what to make of it.

When I finally made it home around six a.m. Pops was sitting at the kitchen table sipping coffee and reading the day's newspaper. I went straight for the fridge to grab the orange juice when Pops chimed in. "Can you at least call me the next time you plan on disappearing for the entire evening? I assumed that you were coming back to the bar. I was worried about you."

I looked at Pops and apologized. "I had to help a friend out."

Pops then said, "Would that friend happen to be the one that Donna saw you out with yesterday?"

I stopped and looked at Pops and said, "She told you that she saw me?"

Pops laughed and said, "No. I overheard her and the other girls giggling and talking about how you sure have grown up to be a fine young man. She mentioned something about seeing you at a restaurant."

I grew nervous. "Did she say who I was with?"

Pops laughed. "Big Man, I didn't entertain those silly women. Please know that when they see that you're running the bar, they're going to be on you like vultures. Stay away from those kinds of women. They will try to take you for everything that you have. Heck, they'll even try and come after me."

Pops and I both laughed.

He grabbed his keys and headed for the door. "See you later, son; I'm headed out to meet the liquor distributor." When he said that, I knew I wanted to be there. I needed to show that I was serious, because I really wanted to be co-owner of the bar.

"I'll hop in the shower and meet you at the bar in about forty-five minutes." Pops nodded his head. "Good. I'm glad to see that you're really taking this business serious."

I made it to the bar before the distributor made it there. I had on a brand new sweat suit with matching tennis shoes.

Pops looked at me and said, "I know it's early, but when you're running a business at your age, it's best that you wear a pair of slacks and maybe a polo shirt. You're a young black man, and you want to be taken seriously. Try not to ever leave any room for doubt."

Pops reached inside of his pocket and gave me a roll of bills. "Go and buy yourself a couple pair of slacks and a few white shirts. That should hold you over for a while."

I took his words to heart. I was so proud as I accepted the money.

* * *

The liquor distributor came and everything went smoothly. I started having knots in my stomach once I realized that half of the day had gone by and I hadn't received a call from Carla. I continued to push on even though I wanted to call just to check up on her.

Later that evening, I went to the mall to get a few pairs of slacks. I went inside the men's store and I had the salesman pick me out a few outfits. I was comfortable with wearing jeans and T-shirts so I had no idea what I was looking for. He brought out three pairs of slacks, which cost a hundred and twenty five dollars each. He assured me that they were nice and would last a nice long time.

They were too long, so they had to be tailored. He told me to come back later that evening or the next day to pick them up. I left out of that store about five hundred dollars lighter in the pockets, but it felt good that my life finally had some direction. "*Boss,*" I said to myself. I liked the way that sounded.

A few more days went by and still no call from Carla. I worked really hard at the bar trying to keep my mind occupied, but it wasn't working. Pops asked was something bothering me, but I lied and said, "Just trying to make you proud." He was satisfied with that answer so he gave me a roll of bills and insisted that I take the day off.

I really didn't want the day off because I knew that it only left room for me to think of Carla. It wasn't optional. Pops stood holding the door open motioning for me to exit.

***

I rode around the city in circles contemplating whether I should ride past her house or office when I ended up in front of Uncle Buddy's duplex.

I knocked on his door and it quickly swung open. He had an overnight bag and his saxophone sitting by the door. "Big Man, what a surprise to see you here. I thought that you were my partner Skip. We're doing a big gig in Ohio and he was supposed to be here over an hour ago." He looked down at his watch. "He's late. I'll tell ya. You just can't depend on folks to show up on time."

I laughed at Uncle Buddy, because people often said the same thing about him.

"So tell me, Big Man, what brings you over this way?"

I was sort of nervous and I wasn't sure if I should talk to him about it so I said. "Oh nothing, Uncle, I was just in the neighborhood."

Uncle Buddy shook his head and said, "I know better." You sure couldn't fool him easily. "No, Big Man, I'm not buying that one. I've seen that look too many times. So tell me--what's her name?" I let out a nervous laugh. I then sat on Uncle Buddy's couch and told him the most basic elements of the story without telling him her name.

"She's a special lady who happens to be a little older than me. She'd just broken up with her boyfriend and I was there to offer support. She invited me back to her place and I spent the entire evening with her. I really thought that we had something going on except that it's been three days and I haven't heard anything from her."

Uncle Buddy sat on the arm of the couch looking up, scratching his chin as if he was thinking of something. He then asked the question. "Did you leave the next morning on your own, or did she ask you to leave?"

I thought about it for a second and said, "Well, the next morning she did say that she enjoyed my company and hopefully she'll see me soon."

Uncle Buddy shook his head and said "Umph, umph, umph. Big Man, I'm afraid that you are going to have to let this woman go."

I looked at him alarmed and said, "Huhhh?"

He stepped away from the couch and looked me square in the eyes. "Whenever you meet a woman for the first time, you must take the lead. Women like strong, secure, and confident men. When she was having problems with her man, it was all right to help her out. But once you made it to her place and got her all settled in, you were supposed to get up and leave. You blew it by spending the night. She sees you just as weak and vulnerable as her. No woman wants a man who she can just dance around like a puppet on a string."

I was just as confused as ever. "Uncle Buddy, that just doesn't make any sense. She asked me to stay."

He laughed a little bit. "No, Big Man, it doesn't make any sense. Nature just set it up that way. Good guys finish last while bad boys have all the fun. People always want what feels good to them, and not good for them. They're always looking for a challenge. Now if you had told that woman that you couldn't stay long because you had somebody, that woman would still have you lying up at her place. The thrill of the chasing something that you can't have far outweighs a person who's easily available. Finding that perfect balance is plain ole difficult."

I thought long and hard about what Uncle Buddy was saying and wondered if it was really true.

"So Uncle Buddy if you're such a specialist on all of this, then how come you're not settled down?"

He let out another little laugh. "The only woman that I have ever loved is my son's mother Lisa and she's still down in Mississippi. Her and I had some great times, and I will admit that I really messed that up. I took her for granted. She was a tough woman who didn't take a lot of mess. I pushed the envelope too many times and she finally had enough. When I left from down there I told that woman that she was going to be sorry that she let me go and that I was never coming back there. I thought that she was going to chase me down here, but she didn't."

Uncle Buddy let out a sad kind of laugh. "It didn't take long for that woman to move on. She married her a good old man. Ohhhhhhhh, my soul still aches for that woman. I sure do miss her. The last time I went down to Mississippi to see my son Byron she made me wait outside in the car. Her and that old man is living in the house that my momma and daddy owned. I was raised in that house. Her old man fixed that house up so nice that you can't even recognize it. They even had a couple of kids."

Uncle Buddy then bowed his head and whispered. "Yup, I messed that up real bad."

***

I left Uncle Buddy's feeling worse than when I had arrived. I didn't know what to do.

Another day went by and she still hadn't called. I'd lost sleep, wasn't able to eat, and I couldn't think straight. I thought about my conversation with Uncle Buddy and I came up with my own reasoning. Maybe she wasn't able to get in touch with me because she didn't know how. Maybe she was afraid of calling the bar for fear of Pops finding out. Maybe she was sitting there waiting for me to come to her. Maybe Uncle Buddy meant that only Southern women feel that way.

I got out of bed early and decided that I was going to go to Carla's office.

First, I went to the bar and did some cleaning and restocked all the liquor. When I finished up it was a little after 10:00 a.m. I knew that she had to be at her office.

I left the bar and headed toward Vernon and Associates.

When I pulled in the parking lot, I didn't see her car. Instead there was a red and shiny two-seater convertible Mercedes with a new car sticker in the window. It was nice. I took a few deep breaths before I got out of my car. When I walked by the car, I noticed that there was luggage in the back seat.

I tapped on the door a few times and seconds later I heard footsteps approaching. My breathing suddenly became shallow, as I had no idea what I was going to say.

Carla opened the door, wearing another sexy dress with tall black heels, looking beautiful as ever. She was holding the cordless phone to her ear. The burning in my heart was even stronger. She was deep into her conversation. She took one look at me and put her hand over the receiver and whispered in her professional voice, "Have a seat; I'll be right with you." She then stepped away to continue the call. I sat there and stared at the floor feeling like a child left in time-out.

After she completed her call, she headed in my direction. She was gorgeous and I couldn't take my eyes off of her. Her beauty, radiant smile, and that sexy black dress gave me an intense euphoric high. I stood and without hesitation I reached for her. She didn't return the gesture as she continued to speak in her professional voice.

"Jayson, how can I help you?" It was as if she had taken a sharp blade and cut me deep. Those painful words felt like all the blood had been obliterated from my body.

I hadn't slept or eaten in days. I was literally going insane and she spoke to me as if I was a client that she was meeting for the very first time.

When she noticed the desperate look on my face, she put her left hand over her heart and said, "Why did you come here?" Feeling like I was a child being reprimanded for wetting his pants, I stuck my hands inside of my pockets and stared down at the ground. I couldn't answer her because I was blinded. Not only by her beauty, but the huge rock that she wore on her left ring finger. I'd never noticed it before. James Vernon had won her back.

I couldn't hide the fact that I was hurt and Carla couldn't help but sense it. She tried to alleviate the pain by saying, "I'm sorry." I shook my head and didn't utter a word. I turned toward the door but she wouldn't let me leave without trying to explain.

I must admit I was too weak to walk away. I had a minuscule amount of hope that she would say we were going to be together. Instead she let me down just as easy as she possibly could.

"Jayson, you're so young, and handsome, and talented--and you deserve to be with someone your own age. I'm not a good fit for you, and besides Vernon needs me. I can't leave him. We have too much at stake and to be honest, I'm not ready to give all of this up. You couldn't possibly take care of me and I don't want to settle."

When she said that, there was no need for me to let her continue. No, she was not Mandy; she was far worse.

I turned to leave, but before I walked out the door I asked the question, "Didn't the other day mean anything to you? Did you feel anything for me, or is that just normal practice for you?"

She looked at me with a deep sincerity and said, "Jayson, it was just sex."

She then tried to caress my face, but I forcefully pushed her hands away. She tried to say that she was sorry, but I wouldn't let her. I ran out of that office a damaged man.

I can remember feeling sick. I didn't think that I would ever pick myself up from that one. I can remember going to the beach and throwing pebbles into the water. I don't remember shedding tears on the outside, but on the inside, I cried hard. I swore that I'd never love another woman again.

I vowed from that moment on, women would be the one loving, lusting and crying over me. I had to be foolish to think that I could even come close to a man like James Vernon. He was rich, powerful, and handsome. Hell, if I was a woman I guess I'd pick him also.

I kept to myself for a couple days. I still couldn't eat and I didn't want to get out of bed. I told Pops that I was really sick. It wasn't a complete lie. I was indeed lovesick.

On the third day I was lying on the couch wrapped in a blanket when I heard music playing, a horn blowing, and a car door slam. I knew it was Uncle Buddy. Whenever he'd come around he always made a grand entrance.

He did his signature five short knocks. I opened the door and resumed my position stretched across the couch. He entered the house looking sharp as ever, smoking a cigarette. He thumped it into the bushes before he closed the door. He was in good spirits. In fact, I can't ever recall a time when he wasn't in a good mood.

"Hey Big Man, I've been looking all over for you. I stopped by the bar and your father told me you were home, sick."

I looked up from the couch trying to put on a strong face. Uncle Buddy could always tell by my body language if something was wrong.

He didn't really look at me before he started to speak.

"I want you to ride to the bus station with me to pick up my son Byron. He called a few days ago and said that he had to get out of Mississippi fast."

When Uncle Buddy said that, I quickly sat up as he talked about Byron.

'That son of mine has messed around and gotten himself into some trouble. He's about to become a dad. When his fiancée's father found out, he went over to Byron's mother's house with a shotgun, threatening to kill him."

I looked at Uncle Buddy and said, "That doesn't make sense. Their wedding is only a few months away. It's not uncommon for a bride to get pregnant before her big day."

Uncle Buddy shook his head.

"Well Big Man, I told that boy the same thing. The only problem is, the woman he's having a baby with is not the woman he's set to marry. His fiancée's father claims that he's going to make Byron pay, for breaking his daughter's heart. I told him to hop on the next bus and come on up here, cause if I go down to Mississippi, somebody's gonna get hurt."

Uncle Buddy then instructed me to hurry up and get dressed.

I stood and immediately felt weak, so I sat back down. Uncle Buddy took a good look at me and said, "Damn, Big Man, what in the hell has that woman done to you? I was so busy worrying about Byron, I hadn't even paid you any mind."

He opened the curtains and walked inside the kitchen and came out with a glass of orange juice and a bowl of cereal. "Big Man, you don't even have to tell me. You went to that woman and you got your feelings hurt all over again."

I bowed my head in shame. Uncle Buddy sat next to me and patted me on the back.

"It's okay. I know the feeling. You and my son have a lot to learn about women. I've been on both sides of the coin. I've been the one hurt and I've been the one doing the hurting. I must have cried over Byron's mother Lisa many days and nights, but I soon realized that the show had to go on."

He shook his head once more. "That's sometimes how life works. We always want what we can't have and we can't have what we always want. You'll be okay, Big Man. It gets easier with time."

He stood up and headed to the door. "I'm going to the bus station to pick up your cousin. I'll show him around a little bit and maybe in a few days you'll be back to your normal self and you guys can get reacquainted."

He then offered one last piece of advice. "The best way over somebody is under somebody else." That really made me laugh. In fact, I couldn't even remember the last time that I had actually laughed.

Uncle Buddy then threw up two fingers and said, "Peace on that!" I returned the gesture still wearing the huge smile across my face.

As he walked out the door, I felt slightly embarrassed by my behavior. I knew that it would be a long time, if ever, before I got over Carla.

I thought about what he said, *"The show must still go on."*

I slipped on a pair of sweats and a baseball cap and headed to the mall to pick up my new attire. I decided that I was going to be a man of substance. My goal was to stay focused and build my own legacy, one dancer at a time.

JACKIE

My convertible was clean and I had the music blasting in an attempt to drown out all thoughts of Carla.

The parking lot was full. I spotted an empty space and just as I was turning into the spot a blue Chrysler came out of nowhere and whipped into it first. My bumper accidentally hit hers. *Damn! I don't need this today.*

This strikingly beautiful young woman got out the car cursing and screaming. I quickly surveyed the damage. There was nothing but a scratch on her car. As she continued her rage I realized who it was. *Jackie Scott.*

Her brother Jeff and I were friends in high school. We played football together and their mother was an active volunteer at our school. Wow, had she grown into a stunning young woman--although I was a bit blown away by the foul language she used. I knew that Mrs. Scott hadn't raised her like that. It was as if she was angry at the entire world. She had no idea who I was. In fact she called me sir when I tried to apologize.

I reached inside my pocket and gave her three hundred dollars and a business card to my friend's collision shop. "Here's for your trouble."

Her mood quickly changed as she pocketed the money. She started smiling and blushing. "Oh my goodness, Big Man. I didn't realize who you were."

I responded, "I could never forget your pretty face. You've grown into a beautiful young woman."

Jackie continued to smile. We made small talk and before we parted ways she had given me a ticket to her gymnastics competition in appreciation for paying for her car to get repaired. I accepted the ticket thinking maybe she was the "somebody" I needed to take my mind off Carla.

***

The arena was filled with hundreds of people. I had never been to an event like that so I stood in amazement at all the young women jumping around in leotards hoping to win a title.

An usher took my ticket and pointed to the direction of my seat. It was close to the main floor. I had no intention of sitting in my assigned seat, so I found an empty seat a few rows over. My eyes were glued to the main floor looking for Jackie. All the women looked beautiful. Jackie seemed to stand out. She was the darkest of them all and she looked like a beautiful swan, as she stood tall and stretched her flexible lean body in an upward motion.

When she completed her stretches, she gave a full smile and excitedly waved her arms back and forth. *She spotted me*, I thought. I smiled and extended my arms and blew her a kiss. Suddenly I heard someone calling her name a few rows over. I turned in that direction. There sat her mom, dad, her brother Jeff, and another older lady. Feeling embarrassed, I dropped my arms. I didn't want to be seen.

I suddenly felt like a mannish boy peeking through a young a girl's window as she undressed. I had no business being there. I'd watched her grow up throughout the years. She was seventeen, which made her five years my junior. It left me feeling uncomfortable.

I knew that I should have gotten up and left, but something inside of me made me stay. I began to reason with myself. *Big Man, it's harmless. You can walk away after this performance.* I sat, hoping that I would go unnoticed.

An usher walked by with a bucket full of roses. I caught her attention and bought a dozen. Being able to hide behind them relieved some of the tension.

The performances lasted for a few hours. I wasn't bored and I actually enjoyed watching the beautiful women do flips. Jackie was the personification of fine arts when she took the floor. Her craft was mastered and perfected as she floated through the air like a beautiful butterfly. Her smile lit up the entire arena and I couldn't think of any place that I'd rather have been at that place and time.

I turned in the direction of her family. Jeff, Mr. Scott, and the other lady all stood with their mouths open and their hands clasped together, appearing to be mesmerized by her performance. Mrs. Scott looked different. She stayed seated, with her jaws tight and her lips firmly pressed together as if she were a judge who wasn't allowed to show emotion.

Jackie lost the competition, but she didn't seem upset. When the judges introduced the winners, Jackie clapped, did flips and cartwheels, and began cheering. I thought that maybe I'd missed something. I didn't. She was just that good of a sport. She should have won an award for sportsmanship alone.

Her brother and father and the other lady all wore big proud smiles. They all were waving at Jackie, with the exception of Mrs. Scott. Her arms were folded and she didn't look happy as they made their way down to the main floor. I stood back as they all embraced her. After several minutes, Jackie took off toward the locker room.

I stood in limbo waiting for her to exit. She was laughing and joking with a few girls when she came out. I still couldn't believe how amazing she looked.

Before she could walk any farther, I placed the flowers in her hand and told her that she was a winner in my book. Her vibrant smile and bubbly demeanor said it all. She couldn't believe that I had made it. She threw her arms around me and although the hug was much needed, it felt so wrong.

I tried to end it before it had even gotten started.

"Jackie, you were spectacular. I wanted to tell you that earlier, but I know that your family wouldn't approve of me being here."

Before I could finish my thoughts, she cut me off.

"Don't worry about my family. I'm seventeen and I make my own rules. I'll see you tomorrow, the same place where we met." She said as if she was really in control.

I left the arena that day feeling excited and guilty at the same time. She was too young and I knew that I'd more than likely would have regrets afterwards.

When the next day arrived, I'd decided to meet Jackie with the intent of telling her that a relationship between the two of us just wouldn't work.

I purposely pulled up to the mall ten minutes late. Jackie stood outside her car patiently waiting like a schoolgirl at the bus stop. I pulled my car next to hers and before I could shut my engine off, she was pulling on my door handle. She wore a short skirt that accented her long legs, a ribbed tank top that enhanced her perfectly toned arms, and she let her long hair flow down her back. She still looked like the pretty chocolate girl that I remembered from long ago. I unlocked the door and she hopped inside.

"What's up, Big Man? I thought that you were going to stand me up," she said in a mischievous tone while undressing me with her eyes.

I was tongue-tied because I wasn't expecting that.

"Jackie, I really think that you're an attractive young lady, it's just that...."

When she realized what I was about to say, she became aggressive.

"Oh, hell no! I didn't come all the way to this mall only to be rejected. What's the problem Big Man, are you scared? You know that big things do come in small packages?" She then ran her hands down her elongated legs.

Again, I was left scratching my head. Her look of innocence mixed with the edginess turned me on. I still continued to fight the urge.

"Jackie, I practically grew up with your family and your brother and I were friends."

Jackie exhaled. "Look, don't worry about my family. I told you that I am my own woman." She pulled out a cigarette and a lighter and fired it up inside my car. She took a few long drags off the cigarette and thumped it outside the window. She then popped a fresh mint into her mouth. "I've been trying to quit for the longest, but it seems as if cigarettes calm my nerves."

I was speechless. The little Jackie that I knew was raised by her mother to be prim and proper at all times, but the minute that she was out of her mother's presence, another person took her place.

Jackie was all over me in that parking lot. I failed miserably at attempting to keep her hands off of me. She whispered in my ear, "Let's go to your place." she demanded. *She won.* I put the car in gear and headed to my house.

She kissed my neck the entire ride. There was so much that I wanted to know, but she wasn't really interested in talking. I looked at the clock and I knew that Pops wasn't home. Even if he were, he would have never said anything. We lived in a spacious home and I always used the back entrance.

When we made it to my room, Jackie quickly undressed and lay across my bed. My head was so twisted until I wasn't able to think straight. I hurriedly removed my shirt, socks, shoes, and just as I was getting ready to unbuckle my pants, I stopped. My conscience had kicked in.

"Jackie, what are we doing?"

When I said that, Jackie quickly sat up. "Shit! Not this again." She started to explain. "Look! I've been perfect all my life. I've been the smartest, most popular girl in school, the perfect daughter, sister, and friend and guess what?" She yelled with frustration in her voice, "I'm sick of this perfect shit. I want to see what it feels like to live life on the edge before I'm too old."

I touched her soft cheek and removed the hair from her beautiful face. "Jackie, this makes no sense. You're still so young and you have your entire life ahead of you."

She pulled her head away. "I'm not young, I'm a woman." She then reached between my legs and grabbed my hardening manhood and gave it a gentle squeeze. "Does this thing work, or do I need to lay here and satisfy myself?"

Jackie was bold and I couldn't help but to be turned on. If I hadn't witnessed it with my own eyes I would have never believed it.

I reached inside my nightstand to get a condom. She grabbed my hand and said, "No. This is my first time and I want to feel the real deal." I was hesitant at first, but the way she'd challenged my manhood, I felt forced to comply with her demands.

The little girl from all those years ago no longer existed. Jackie was out to prove that she was a woman and she did a damn good job of stating her case.

She was energetic and very easy to please. She needed no music, candles, or rhythms. Jackie was on a mission to fulfill her sexual desires and I was happy to play the part.

When we were done, she stood and pranced into the bathroom without any clothes on. She wasn't shy at all. Her slender frame was beautiful but her small breasts and buttocks seemed as if was they were still developing.

The guilty feeling from earlier returned. I thought about Carla. Her full body, curves, and demeanor weren't questionable. She had woman written all over her. I missed her.

As I sat on the edge of my bed, Jackie stuck her head out and said, "Hey Big Man, what time is it?"

I looked at the clock on my nightstand. "It's six o'clock. What time you have to be there?" I joked.

"I have to have my mom's car back by eleven tonight," she casually replied.

Once she mentioned her curfew I couldn't dismiss the fact that Jackie really wasn't her own woman.

I'd decided to take her out to eat and buy her something from the mall before I took her back to her car. I had no plans of seeing her again. She was much too young, but she deserved to be compensated for what she'd just given up.

I chose the upscale Somerset mall. She couldn't contain her excitement as we stood inside the department store and I told her get whatever she liked. Since I frequented that store often, a few of the saleswomen walked by and addressed me by name. "Big Man, is there anything that we can help you find today?"

Jackie was flattered when I responded, "Help this pretty lady find something nice."

They handed Jackie several items and she'd given me my own personal fashion show. She looked good in everything but the skintight jeans and fitted sweater looked the best.

She was shocked at the three hundred dollar total. I didn't sweat it. The look of delight and admiration she wore on her face did far more for my ego than I could ever do for her. I'd spent plenty of money on my ex-girlfriend Mandy and she'd never expressed gratitude. She often claimed that I didn't spend enough. I overlooked it back then because I felt lucky to have a pretty girl like her. But with Jackie things were just the opposite. She was young and vulnerable and easy to impress. For once I was in control and I liked the feeling. I imagined this was the way James Vernon made Carla feel.

I leaned in close and whispered in Jackie's ear, "Baby this is how a king is supposed to take care of his queen." She just couldn't stop smiling. I'd dismissed the advice that Pops had given me about being the boss and women throwing themselves at me. *"Big Man, you will lose every time."* I didn't feel like I could lose, because with money came power, and as long as I supplied the money, the women would give me all the power.

We grabbed something to eat and finally made it back to her car around nine o'clock. She couldn't keep her hands to herself. The thought of not seeing her again quickly faded away. I liked her. I only wished that she weren't so young. Being with her took my mind off Carla.

We sat in that parking lot talking and holding hands. I told her everything about me and Pops and the reason I had to leave school. She was interested in everything I had to say and she was even more fascinated about me being prepped to become co-owner of his bar.

As the evening came to an end, Jackie had a longing look in her eyes. She didn't want to leave. "Big Man, this date was awesome."

I reached over and gave her a hug and said, "Sweet dreams, princess." That statement changed the mood. She pushed me away and forced herself from my embrace. She jumped out the car and slammed my door. I had no idea where the sudden anger came from. I rolled down my window. "Jackie, what did you do that for?"

She twisted her face as she fumbled in her purse, searching for her keys. "I'm not a goddamn child." I held my wrist up and checked my watch to see how much time we had left. That only insulted her more. She hopped in her mother's car and sped off.

After Jackie left, thoughts of Carla resumed. I really wanted to see her. I'd decided to take a ride in hopes of clearing my head. I rode around through downtown Detroit for about thirty minutes when I couldn't resist the urge to hop on the expressway to ride past Carla's house.

I knew that she'd said that it was nothing but sex between her and me, but I still couldn't stop thinking of her. I parked across the street and cut my lights off. Her house was dark and looked deserted. I imagined myself walking up to the front door and letting myself in. I then laughed at myself thinking how strange life really was. The more you couldn't have a person, the more you wanted to be with them. That was the case with Carla.

After a few minutes I started my engine and headed home.

I pulled into the back of my house and walked up to the door and before I could stick my key in the lock someone ran up behind me. I turned around in a panic. I was surprised to see who it was.

"I'm sorry. I know that I shouldn't be here--it's just that I missed you." My heart rate finally slowed down as we headed inside. Before I could speak, she grabbed me and started passionately kissing me. I led the way to my bedroom and within seconds we were undressed and between the sheets. She held me tight and continued to apologize. She really wanted to be with me and she'd do whatever she had to do to please me.

I couldn't resist her. I was hurting inside but the pain temporarily went away when I was with her. We fell asleep in each other's arms until I was awakened by footsteps. It was Pops. He was home from the bar.

I looked at the clock and it was 3:45 a.m. "Damn," I whispered.

She awoke and turned her head toward the clock. "Shit," she retorted. "I didn't mean to stay this long."

I started reaching for her clothes. "Jackie, where did you tell your parents you were going?"

She started hurriedly putting her clothes on and said, "I didn't tell them anything." My mouth dropped.

She then said, "When I made it home, they turned the television off and went to bed. I went to my room and changed into my pajamas and I just couldn't sleep after the way our night ended so I grabbed the keys and left. I'd been sitting outside of your house for about thirty minutes. I was afraid that you weren't going to come home."

My eyes were big. "Jackie, you have to be more careful. Your parents will kill me if they find out about us."

Jackie didn't seem to care, because from that day forward she continued to take risks.

Jackie managed to temporarily take my mind off Carla because she was young, full of energy, easy to please and fun to be around. Whenever she was around, there was never a dull moment.

Moving Up

"Pops, tomorrow is the first. Would you like for me to drop the check off today?" I tried sounding unenthusiastic, although I was yearning on the inside. It had been weeks since I'd last saw Carla and I was eager to be near her.

Pops stopped counting the roll of coins and gave a proud smile. "Big Man, I'm really impressed with you. It's as if you did a 180-degree turn overnight."

I remained composed. I didn't want to draw any suspicion. I put on a businesslike face and said in a nonchalant manner, "Well, it has to be done, so I might as well get it out of the way."

He beamed with pride as he wrote out the check, while my insides became jittery at the mere thought of her name.

Just as I was leaving, Pops stopped me. "Big Man, you have to stop at the information desk to get the suite number."

I hesitated and turned around. "I've been to the office before."

He shook his head. "Oh no son, James Vernon has expanded his business. He's now located inside the Renaissance Center downtown. He's leased an entire floor."

My mouth became dry. I tried to swallow, but nothing was there. I thought I would faint. I gave Pops a quick nod and started on my journey downtown.

***

The Renaissance Center was Detroit's crown jewel. The beautiful building stood tall off the river in the heart of downtown.

When I walked into the main entrance I couldn't help but to be overcome by size and opulence. The thought of Mr. Vernon leasing out an entire floor had awakened my sense of insecurities and once again I felt inadequate.

I tried pushing those feelings aside as I headed over to the information desk where an older white lady sat. I smiled and used my professional voice as I read her nametag. "Good afternoon Ms. McDowell, I'm looking for Vernon and Associates, please."

She returned the smile. "Can I have your name, please?"

I cleared my scratchy throat and said, "Mr. Jayson Jackson."

She scanned the piece of paper in front of her. When she made it to the bottom of the list she scanned it again. "I'm sorry but I don't see your name, sir."

I cleared my throat once more and leaned in close and spoke barely above a whisper. "Ms. McDowell, my company has been doing business with Vernon and Associates for a very long time. In the past we haven't needed an appointment."

She remained polite. "Well, sir, I'm sorry about the inconvenience, but Vernon and Associates have made a lot of changes to their policies. I've been instructed to take a message from anyone who doesn't have an appointment."

I felt slighted. A few people had formed a line behind me and I didn't want to walk away embarrassed. I leaned in and whispered once more. "Could you please call up to their office? I really need to drop something off."

She gave a stern smirk, her politeness turned annoyance and she whispered, "Now Mr. Jackson, if I made that exception for everyone, I'd be out of a job. You can leave your package with me and I'll make sure that they receive it."

She offered a closing smile and said, "May I help you sir?" to the man behind me." I left the envelope on the counter feeling humiliated.

***

It was still early when I made it back to the bar. We had about an hour before we opened. I pulled into the lot and was surprised to find that Jackie's car along with a few others was parked in front of the building.

I became uptight because I'd never officially taken her there. *Why isn't she in school?* I thought. She had been bugging me about meeting Pops and I told her that I would introduce them when the time was right. It angered me to know that she'd show up unannounced.

I hurried and jumped out of my car. Donna was exiting just as I was about to enter. I hadn't seen her since I was at the restaurant with Carla. "Hey Big Man, you sure know how to pick 'em."

I gave her an odd look and responded, "What's that supposed to mean?"

She laughed. "A drunk news reporter and an exotic dancer. What a combination." She laughed again, "When will I get my turn?"

She then stuck her nasty tongue out and ran it across her big fat lips. *Never in your wildest dreams* is what went through my mind.

I reached in my pocket and slid Donna a hundred-dollar bill. "Please don't ever mention what you saw at that restaurant. Pops wouldn't like that."

She looked at the money and said, "This sure isn't a lot of money, but your secret is safe with me. I need my job." She continued to laugh as I turned away. Then all of a sudden she pinched my butt. "I'm not through with you, Big Man."

I felt violated. Donna wasn't a bad-looking woman, it's just that she stood for absolutely nothing. She was the top moneymaker in this bar-- and she should have been, because she had been there the longest. She also did moonlighting on the side. For the right price, you could have your way with her. I guess she did what she had to do, but she certainly wasn't my type.

When I walked into the building the music was blasting. Rick James "Super Freak" was playing and there were four girls around the stage laughing and chanting the words, "Go, go, go." I looked at Pops and said, "What's going on?" He was so engrossed in what was taking place that he didn't answer me.

I looked up at the stage as the woman did a backwards flip and wrapped her legs around the pole and lifted her body up as she bounced up and down. I stood still. I couldn't move. She then started spinning around on the pole super fast, and then suddenly she let go of the pole, jumped up in the air and landed in a split. She then bounced up and down several times and did what looked like a breakdance move. Those women loved her moves. They continued to clap, wishing that they could be as flexible as she was.

I ran over to the jukebox and cut the music off. I then ran to the stage and grabbed Jackie's arm.

"What in the hell do you think you're doing?"

All the ladies gasped. They then went on the attack. "Leave her alone, Big Man. We all need to learn how to tighten up our skills."

I pushed them off of me. I was upset. No woman of mine was going to behave like that.

Pops walked over to me. "Big Man, you can't control people. You don't own that woman. Jackie here was just showing these girls some moves."

I looked at Pops in anger. "Stay out of it."

I escorted Jackie outside by her arm. "What are you doing here? Why aren't you at school?"

Jackie snatched her arm away. "Goddammit--your father was right, you can't control me. I didn't have school today because I had an interview for an internship at a law office."

I felt really bad. I was still upset from what happened earlier that I took my anger and dumped it all over Jackie. I apologized. "I'm so sorry. This job has me under a lot of stress. I meant to call you back last night, but this place was just so busy and I forgot."

She wiped a few tears from her eyes. "I needed you last night. When I woke up this morning, I tried calling your house but I didn't get an answer. I thought you were purposely ignoring me, so I came here directly after my interview. I introduced myself to your father as only your friend. It kind of hurt my feelings that he knew nothing about me. I saw those stiff ladies up there practicing and I thought that it'd be fun to show them some moves. They sure as heck needed it. I'm sorry if I offended you."

I gave Jackie a hug and I apologized over and over. I had no business losing my cool. I reached inside my pocket and gave her a hundred-dollar bill. "I'll call you later. I promise." She grabbed the money, gave me a kiss, and left.

Pops wasn't pleased with my behavior. I apologized to him and the ladies that were in the bar. They all seemed to have liked Jackie and they made me promise to have her come back and work with them.

"Big Man, that lady friend of yours is something special. She's a smart lady too. She came here looking for you, all the while scoping out her competition. 'Keep your enemies close.' That's just what she did. She won just about all of her enemies over except for that damn Donna."

I laughed. "Yes Pops, she's a special friend. I just don't think that she and I will make it."

I quickly changed the subject. "Pops, how come you didn't tell me that I needed an appointment to go and drop the payment off?"

Pops' face was brittle and he was unimpressed. "That's James Vernon for you. He always manages to outdo himself." He took a long breath. "Son, I've been in this business for too many years and I'm afraid that it might just be time for me to hang up my hat."

"What are you talking about, Pops? I was serious when I said that I was going to help you."

He patted my shoulder. "If it were only that simple. James Vernon has started purchasing land all over the city and he plans to branch out across other cities. He's taking his business global and he wants me to be a part of it right here in Detroit."

I followed Pops to the door and around to the back of the building. "Do you see all this land back here, Big Man?" The field behind Pops' bar was huge. One couldn't miss it. "Well, Vernon owns all of this land. He's offering it to me first. He's going to sell it to me for pennies on a dollar. It's all a part of helping to rebuild Detroit." Pops then became quiet as if he were having doubts.

I stood there with my hand on my chin as I surveyed the land. I thought of James Vernon, who had purchased an entire floor in the Renaissance building, and envisioned Pops and I having just the same. Although I had only come into contact with him a few times, he was definitely a man I aspired to be like.

I spread my arms wide and started turning in circles. "Pops, you have to be crazy not to take him up on this. That man is filthy rich. He's offering to take you right along with him, and now you want to just quit in the middle of the game. Pops, weren't you the one who told me that nothing is more important than money?"

Pops kind of laughed. "Yes I did, son. But when James Vernon called me with this a few days ago, my attitude began to change. I have been working hard my entire life. I have made really good investments, and I like this shabby little place just the way it is. I'm really just ready to sit back and travel and spend some of the money that I've already made. James Vernon is different. He eats, sleeps, and breathes for this type of thing. I'm not sure that I have that type of energy."

My heart rate began to go up just by listening to all of this. "Pops, please don't turn this down. This is big. I mean huge. I want this bad! I promise to work hard and pretty soon you won't have to do a thing. You can retire and travel to wherever you want. Just please don't turn this down."

Pops, laughed once more. "Big Man, I promise to give it more thought." He then walked back to the front and into the bar.

Precious Gift

"Pregnant? Jackie, you can't be serious." She wore what appeared to be a sly smile as she waved the little white stick. The plus sign was as clear as water. I became dizzy and fell onto my bed. I put my head in my hands.

She sat next to me and coddled my head. "Big Man, it's not the end of the world. This baby is a precious gift from God."

Her calmness annoyed me. My angry expression made her shake.

"Don't stare at me like that--I didn't do this all by myself."

I hopped off the bed and yelled at her. "Did you do this on purpose?"

She slapped my face. "Kiss my ass, Big Man. My baby and I will be fine without you." She then ran out the door with tears streaming down her face, never answering the question.

I chased after her. I couldn't let her drive upset like that. She fumbled through her purse searching for her keys. "I'm sorry, Jackie; please don't go." I then held her as she began to wail. I had to be strong although I was afraid. I was in no position to become someone's father. My own father was still financially providing for me. Jackie listened, but she had no plans of getting rid of the baby.

"Big Man, sometimes things happen without any rhyme or reason. It's how you deal with it that matters the most. I'm having this child. We will find a way." she said.

Jackie's response alone led me to believe that she had planned the entire pregnancy. I fell into her trap so I blamed myself.

"Jackie, what about your parents?"

She gave a brazen response, "What about them?"

Jackie didn't appear to be in her right state of mind so I said, "In case you've forgot, we've been together for a little less than six months and they don't even know about me."

Her response was even bolder, "So! It's my life and I can do what I want."

I then said, "What about school and the scholarships that you've been offered?"

She stopped me before I could go any further. "Big Man, if this is a ploy to talk me out of having this baby, then you're wasting your time. I can handle my parents. I can still go to school, while keeping my precious gift from God. Now are you going to come along for the ride or do you get off right here?" I sat there helpless. Who could argue with God? Her decision was final and I didn't have any say in the matter.

***

Jackie's pregnancy caused a lot of friction and turmoil in her household. Her mother felt betrayed because she trusted Jackie when she said that she was working evenings at the mall. She found out about the pregnancy when she took Jackie to have her physical exam. Jackie was left with no choice but to tell her mother who the father of the child was.

Mrs. Scott was hurt beyond measure when she found out I was the child's father. She felt that I was too old for her daughter and that I'd taken advantage of her innocent child. Jackie set her mother straight. "Big Man didn't do anything to me that I didn't want to happen."

Pops wasn't proud of what Jackie and I had done, but he was very understanding. He took it upon himself to come with me when I went to speak with Jackie's father because her mother shut completely down. She wanted nothing to do with me.

Mr. Scott was more diplomatic than I thought he'd be. Of course he wasn't happy about his baby girl having a child right out of high school, but he understood that things sometimes happened. Of course every parent wanted more for their child than what they had--and he felt that Jackie did. She had accomplished things that he and his wife could only dream of. For that, he was still proud. He wanted to make sure that I was going to step up and take responsibility as a father. He still wanted Jackie to pursue her college education. He didn't think that was asking too much. He assured us that in time Mrs. Scott would come around.

Pops loved Jackie. He admired her strength and courage to stand firm on what she believed in.

"Big Man, whether you realize it or not, that is a very brave young woman. She isn't afraid to go after what she wants. When I see the way she looks at you, it put me in the mind of Blanche. She was the only woman who'd ever looked at me that way. Her only problem was that she was afraid of her father and not being able to have children. She played life too safe, whereas Jackie doesn't care what anyone thinks. She loves you and she isn't going to let anything stand in her way. Big Man, I'll do whatever I can to support you and Jackie."

Pops then handed me an appointment card. He'd decided to take James Vernon up on his offer. We had an appointment and it was exactly one week away. This baby thing was working out, after all.

The Boss

"Slow down, Big Man--you know I can't walk that fast."

I came to a complete halt and turned toward Jackie. She was several feet away. I never realized how far ahead of her I was. My mind was all over the place. I was operating on autopilot. I hadn't seen or heard from Carla in months so I'd been anticipating this meeting ever since the day my father had given me the appointment card.

Jackie finally caught up to me. She was free of make-up and she wore a simple pair of black slacks, a white button down shirt, some black leather flat shoes, and her hair was pinned up in a bun. She looked very pretty.

"Does this outfit make me look fat?" I hated when she asked me that stupid question. She was only a couple of weeks pregnant, and it seemed she was anxious about having a bulging belly.

"Jackie, of course not. You're not even showing. You look like a beautiful princess." She hated when I called her that, so she rolled her eyes and pouted.

Jackie and I stopped at the information desk, and this time I had an appointment. The older lady smiled as she gave us the all clear to head up to the floor which was now the new home of Vernon and Associates.

I could barely contain myself on the elevator. I looked at my watch every few seconds, I fixed my nice suit numerous times, and I played with my thumbs. "Big Man, why are you so jumpy? Your father has taken care of everything. All that you need to do is sign on the dotted line."

I couldn't tell Jackie the real reason I was nervous so I said, "Jackie, this is one of the most important things that I've ever done. I think it's perfectly normal to be nervous."

I really wished that I could have left her behind.

Pops said it'd be a good experience for the both of us....

"Big Man, Jackie is the reason that I decided to buy the land."

My cousin Byron even convinced me to take Jackie....

"Of course you should take Jackie with you. After the way that damn woman toyed with your head, she needs to see how well you rebounded after the way her cold-hearted ass treated you."

The elevator stopped. We both stepped off. The entire floor seemed to be made of glass and we were surrounded by the city of Detroit's waterfront. The view was spectacular.

An older black lady who looked as though she could have been someone's grandmother sat at a desk. The gold nameplate read Agnes Roberts. She offered a warm smile as she brought us a fresh cup of coffee.

Jackie beamed as she looked around the big glass office. "Big Man, I have never seen an office so beautiful."

I felt slightly embarrassed at Jackie's giddiness. "Sit down, Jackie," I whispered.

She looked at me and pouted. "It's not my fault that you don't like to dream."

Carla was about twenty feet away. She strutted in our direction looking and smelling like a boss. Her bouncy hair was cut in a fresh bob;

she wore a black pantsuit, with the matching jacket and really expensive-looking high heels. She was confident and undeniably gorgeous.

She flashed a perfect professional smile and extended her hand, being sure the huge diamond on her left hand was visible. "Mr. Jackson?" she called as if we'd never met.

I did my best to remain in control, although I wanted to scream, *"You know who in the hell I am."* I grabbed her soft perfume-scented hand and said, "Yes."

She looked over at Jackie, whose mouth was wide open and unable to hide her excitement. "And this is?" Carla continued to smile as she waited for me to introduce Jackie. I was confused as to what to call Jackie. Girlfriend sounded so childish, and lady friend didn't seem appropriate.

"My fiancée, Jacqueline Scott," I blurted. Jackie snapped out of the star-struck state and proudly grabbed and squeezed my hand.

Carla appeared to be the least bit jealous. She turned toward Jackie and said, "Isn't she just the cutest thing? You guys make such a lovely young couple." Her comments made Jackie smile. I knew better. That was a direct insult to me.

She led us back to a big round table where a man sat with a stack of papers. Carla introduced us to John. "Sorry I can't stay. I have to catch a flight out in the morning. We're opening up a new office in Boston, so I have to take care of some things before my flight leaves. You're in really good hands, and please tell your father that we're happy he's decided to purchase the land." She flashed those pearly whites once more. "John will take great care of you two." She then looked at Jackie. "It was so nice meeting you and I wish you two the very best on your upcoming nuptials."

Jackie and I were in with John for less than an hour. Pops had already signed his papers, so my signature was the only one missing.

Jackie was so excited at what was happening. I on the other hand was thinking of nothing but Carla.

When we made it down to the front of the building, Jackie nearly exploded. "Wow, that Carla lady was hot! She looks even better in person than she did on TV."

I eyed Jackie. "She was all right, I guess."

Jackie carried on. "That's just how I'm going to live, 'Like a boss.' That woman was so well-polished, in control and she made sure that she let us know that she was running things. I have mad respect for her and after we get married, and get this business off of the ground, that's just how I'm going to look."

When Jackie said the *married* word I started to get cold feet. I had only called her my fiancée out of courtesy. I knew that I couldn't take it back.

***

There was a message for me when I returned to the bar. It was marked urgent with only a phone number and no name.

I dialed the number and the woman answered on the first ring. "Hey, Jayson. It's been a while. I almost forgot just how good you looked." My body went into total shock. I put my hand over the mouthpiece of the phone because I didn't want anyone to hear the call.

"What's wrong, you can't talk?" she said. I cleared my throat. "I'm here. I just can't believe that I'm actually talking to you." There was laughter on her end of the phone. "It's urgent that I see you. "I need to talk to you about something very important." I held the phone. I wanted to tell her where she could go, but I really wouldn't have meant it. I couldn't resist that woman even if I had tried.

"Give me about an hour."

***

I made it there in less than an hour. I sat in front of her house for a few minutes and tried to talk myself out of going inside. I had moved on. I was going to have a child and a beautiful wife. I shouldn't have come.

I then reasoned with myself, *I need closure.* Yes, that's why I needed to be there. I wanted to know what I had done so bad that caused her to abruptly cut me off.

The front door opened wide. She smiled and waved for me to come in. The inside of her house looked like a storage facility. My heart pitter-pattered as I stepped over the suitcases and all the boxes. I felt sad on the inside because I didn't want her to leave the state. Even though she wasn't mine, at least she was at a distance where I could easily ride by and see how she was doing.

She poured me a shot of cognac. I refused. I didn't want to fall into that trap again. She poured herself a glass of wine.

"Carla, why did you call me here?" She sipped on her glass of wine as she moved in closer to me. Her silk house robe exposed her full breast and her entire bare leg. She let her soft lips brush up against mine. I was getting excited. I grabbed the shot of liquor and gulped it down.

"Jayson, I'm so sorry for hurting you. I wanted to reach out to you, but I was afraid that you couldn't handle what I needed." She then kissed my lips and I couldn't manage to pull away. "What makes you think that I can handle you now?" I said, returning her soft kisses.

Carla unfastened her robe and exposed her nude body. "Well the playing field is leveled now. It seems as if you have a little more experience under your belt. Let's just have a little fun and afterwards we both can go back to our lives. I'll make it well worth your while. You just name the amount." She dropped her robe and stroked her hands up and down her bare skin. "You did enjoy it Jayson, didn't you?"

I was blown away. She only wanted me for one thing and was willing to pay me. *A sugar mama? Wasn't this every young man's dream?* I felt cheap. I felt confused. And it seemed quite ridiculous. But it didn't matter. At that very moment I wanted her bad, even though I knew it was wrong.

Carla started unbuttoning my shirt. I softly placed my hands over hers as I looked down. The chemistry burned strong and I became weaker by the millisecond. I was losing the battle to stop her advances.

I tried pleading.

"I have a fiancée. This wouldn't be fair to her."

Carla had my shirt off and kissed my chest.

"Jayson, that beautiful young girl is fascinated by you. I could tell by the way her eyes gleamed when you called her your fiancée. She wouldn't leave you even if she walked through that door this very moment. She would attack and blame me. That's the thing about a lot of young women. They love dominant men with money. Once you give them that number one spot, most of them will remain loyal for life!"

I stopped and looked at Carla.

"You're much younger than James Vernon--why doesn't this apply to you?"

She huffed. "I am loyal. But I still have needs."

Carla and I had gone all the way. We were on top of the boxes, suitcases, and ultimately the floor. There was no more talking. She was more like a hungry animal that wanted to be satisfied without any strings attached. I accepted my role at that moment although I knew it was wrong. The desire to be inside her outweighed any good judgment that I may have had.

She was in complete control and seemed to enjoy herself much more than I had, which caused my guilt to return. I couldn't really get into it. Once we were done, she grabbed her robe and asked me to follow her up the stairs so we could finish up and take one last shower together before she moved.

I was no longer interested. I grabbed my things and declined her offer. "No thank you. I really have to get going."

She turned around to make sure that she'd heard me correctly. She looked embarrassed when she noticed I was getting dressed.

"It's fine. I still have lots of packing to do anyway." She reached inside her purse and pulled out a roll of bills and an ink pen. She hurriedly scribbled down her number, which she hadn't done before. I felt even cheaper.

She pleaded, "Please take this. I really would like to see you again." I looked at her and the money. My heart started to ache. I pushed her hand away.

"Carla, you broke my heart once and I came here because I wanted to know why. Then when I come here to find out why, you break my heart again." I let out a half laugh. "Shame on me, I guess."

She folded her arms, bowed her head, and looked away.

"Carla, you've taught me a valuable lesson about chasing after something that's not mine. It's a dangerous game and you're almost guaranteed to get hurt." I gave her one last earnest smile. "You can't put a price tag on that." I gathered the rest of my things and whispered, "Enjoy your new life, Carla."

Marriage and the Baby

"Big Man, which dress do you like the best?" Jackie held three seemingly identical dresses across her bulging belly. Saying that they all looked the same would only extend our time in the department store, so I chose the one in the middle.

"I love that one, Jackie--now can we please just pay for the dress and go?" She looked at the dress with uncertainty and I began to feel irritated. "Let's just take them all."

She and I had been in the same store for over an hour trying to find her the right dress. Her graduation was nearing and she had to look perfect. She wanted to silence all the teachers and school staff that made her the topic of their morning discussion. She was not a waste, or another black teenage pregnancy statistic that they made her out to be. Unlike her mother, Jackie wanted them to know that she was not ashamed of being pregnant and she wasn't going to hide it.

Mrs. Scott never could get over the pregnancy. She was disappointed and embarrassed so she quit working at the school in order to avoid all of the gossip. She and Jackie bickered all the time about what was Jackie going to do with her life.

Jackie told her mother, "I'm going to graduate and Big Man and I will get married."

Mrs. Scott cried. "No! Please Jackie, don't ruin your life by getting married so young."

Suddenly a baby didn't sound so bad to Mrs. Scott.

Jackie knew she could never please her mother, so she quit trying altogether. After she graduated from high school, she and I went to the Justice of the Peace in Ohio and eloped. It was her idea. I wanted to tell my father about it, but Jackie made me promise I wouldn't. She didn't want anyone trying to talk us out of it.

Life was moving so fast. I wasn't really ready for marriage, but since she was having my child, I felt that I had no choice. I then swallowed my fears and went along with it.

After we returned from Ohio, Jackie felt liberated. She went straight to her parents' house and packed her bags and moved in with my father and me.

Mrs. Scott cried even more. She told Jackie that she didn't care if she had a baby and got married--just please don't move out. Jackie kissed her mother on the cheek and told her that she loved her and that she needed to find her own way.

***

Jackie and I had been married for only a few months when the time came. It was a Friday evening and Pops had just stepped into the bar from working at the factory. He hadn't even removed his coat when the phone rang. It was Mrs. Scott and Jackie was in labor.

"Big Man, get your things, your wife is in labor. Mrs. Scott says they're on their way down to the hospital." I remember feeling scared. I had rehearsed that day in my mind over a thousand times, but nothing could compare to the actual moment.

"Pops, can you come with me?"

He looked around at the crowded bar and said, "I guess we can shut down early." I knew that wasn't possible. I thought of Byron, and then I soon realized he was at work and of course Uncle Buddy was never around when you needed him. I scrambled around the bar lost. I couldn't find my keys, my jacket, or my wallet.

Pops went inside the office and grabbed my things. He touched my shoulders and noticed that I was soaking wet from sweat. "Big Man, relax. It's okay."

As I was heading out the door, I'd bumped into Olivia, who was wearing a big cowboy hat and a long trench coat. That was one of her many disguises. She was the new girl and had been there for only a few weeks. Jackie really liked her because she was the only dancer who was taking college classes, appeared to be focused, and actually had attainable goals in life.

Olivia was tall and beautiful and a showstopper. She could have had any man that she wanted, but she kept it as professional as she possibly could in that environment. Her main goal was to make it through nursing school.

"Big Man, what's wrong?" Olivia said. "You look like you just saw a ghost."

I tried to catch my breath. "Jackie is in labor. I need to get to the hospital."

She snatched the keys out of my hand and said, "Let's go, I'll take you."

We made it to the hospital in record time. Olivia parked my car and we both ran to the reception desk. I was out of breath and could hardly speak. "I'm looking for my wife, who is in labor."

The receptionist gave a friendly smile. "It's okay, sir. May I have her name?"

I began to stutter and I couldn't think of her name. Olivia stepped in and took over the conversation. "It's Jacqueline Jackson, ma'am." The receptionist handed us a pass and directed us toward elevator.

Jackie was being wheeled to her room when we stepped off the elevator. She was nauseated and in pain. Mrs. Scott's eyes were as big as ping-pong balls once she saw me. I ran and grabbed my wife's hand. Jackie managed to smile and said, "I was hoping that the baby could have held off into the morning so that you wouldn't have to leave the bar."

When she said that, Mrs. Scott's face turned beet-red. "Jackie dear, you can't apologize for God's timing."

I stared at my beautiful wife and said, "Your mother's right, baby, I would have crossed many oceans to get here."

Mrs. Scott then stared at Olivia. She remained polite, but her tone was a bit sarcastic. "Jayson, I didn't know that you had a sister." I was oblivious as to what she was trying to say until I looked over at Olivia. I had been so worried about getting to the hospital that I didn't even think twice about what she was wearing.

Olivia realized what Mrs. Scott was insinuating, so she tried her best to clear up any misunderstanding. "I work at the bar…I mean, Big Man was in no condition to drive…."

Mrs. Scott's eyebrows shot straight up in the air. Jackie looked at her mother and said, "Please stop it, Mother! Olivia is my friend. I don't care how my husband got here, I'm just so happy that he made it."

Jackie looked at Olivia and blew her a kiss and whispered the words thank you. Olivia reached in and gave Jackie a kiss on her forehead and walked away with her head bowed.

I called out to Olivia. "I'll have Pops come down and pick me up, and I'll get my car later. Thanks again."

Mrs. Scott didn't say another word; instead she tightened her jaws and looked away.

***

After our son Jayson Jackson II was born, Jackie went to her parents' house, as our home was under construction. Pops had given us his old duplex as a wedding present. Mrs. Scott was so happy to have Jackie home with her that she refrained from saying anything negative about our marriage or how Jackie was living her life.

Things were beginning to look up for us as we settled into our new life. I worked tirelessly at the bar trying to attract a younger clientele while Jackie attended Wayne County Community College. She was extremely smart, so school came very easy for her. In less than two years she had an associate's degree in business. Jackie had no desire to go any further in school. She said that she had all the tools that she needed to make our business a success.

Jackie's relationship with her mother had started to improve. Her parents had bonded with our son, so they agreed to keep him full time since we both had busy schedules.

Jackie was a go-getter and had a greater vision for the bar. She knew that in order for the business to thrive it would need a major facelift. She sketched out a design, along with a business plan and the cost, and presented it to Pops. She even included Byron in the plan. Since he worked in security, she helped him to start his own small business and she put him in charge of the security detail at the bar. Pops couldn't deny Jackie because he trusted her and loved the fact that she had made me a better man. Pops hired the contractors and moved out of Jackie's way.

It didn't take long. Within three years our business was strong and solid. The entire establishment had been remodeled, including the basement. The atmosphere inside the bar was bright and inviting. We had solid wood floors, custom-made booths, shiny stripper poles, and glass and mirrors throughout the establishment.

Jackie also overhauled all of the dancers. She choreographed their routines, made the costumes. and helped with their hair and make-up.

The basement had been painted white, along with a new floor, a custom bar, pool table, and a few card tables. I made pretty good money on the card games, but I saw potential for so much more. I knew just the person who could make it happen.

***

"Big Man, I don't think your father is going to agree to something like that. The type of set-up that you're looking for is serious business." Uncle Buddy said.

I eyed Uncle Buddy and said, "Let me handle Pops. Just tell me how I can get the stuff." He put his hand on his chin as he sat on his sofa staring out into space. I started to head for the door because I needed to find someone who was really going to help me. Uncle Buddy stopped me.

"Where you going, Big Man? I'm still thinking."

I looked at him and said, "I don't want Pops coming after you, so I'll just go and try and get the stuff on my own."

Uncle Buddy hopped up. "Big Man, I see that you're going to make it happen with or without me. You have a strong mind, just like me." I nodded my head yes. "Well, the only reason I'm going to agree to this is because I don't want you to go out there and get yourself caught up in some trouble. I know a lot of people. Some good ones and some bad ones and believe me, sometimes you can't tell them apart. Give me a few days. I'll make it happen."

In less than a week, I had a few slot machines, a poker table, and a blackjack table. Uncle Buddy sat me down and gave me the unwritten rules of the business.

"Big Man, you need to charge at least twenty dollars per head. People will pay the money to have a good time. Think of the fee as an insurance policy. If the police bust up the place, you can cash the policy in to get yourself out of trouble. Make sure that you have good security, don't deal in drugs and weapons, and try to deal with only the people you know. If the police come in here, the most that you'll receive is a citation. I'll help you out from time to time, but I don't do commitments."

***

Pops was nervous when I told him what I was doing. "Big Man, that's not a very good idea. You're playing a very dangerous game and I don't like it."

He never gave his approval. Instead he had the papers drawn up and turned the bar solely over to Jackie and me. Jackie didn't actually agree with it either, but she stayed out of it. I went ahead with my plan and as promised, I only opened up on the weekends.

Our business was booming and Jackie was the mastermind behind it all. Other than my after-hours, Pops was proud of what we had accomplished. Jackie and I didn't have the fortune of Vernon and Associates, but we were able to live a comfortable life. We had more than enough.

APEX

You Are Cordially Invited
To Attend a Black Tie Event Hosted by Vernon and Associates
Celebrating the Development of Small Businesses in the City of Detroit
Your Host Will Be Ms. Carla Roberts
This Event Will Be Held at the Beautiful Renaissance Center in Downtown Detroit
Live Entertainment; Dinner and Drinks Will Be Served

Pops handed me the invitation along with four V.I.P. tickets worth five hundred dollars apiece.

"Big Man, Vernon and Associates are moving their headquarters back to Detroit. They're having a big black tie gala to celebrate the new development that they have planned for downtown. Everybody who is somebody will be in the building and unfortunately I can't make it. Big Man, this is an event that you and Jackie can't afford to miss."

I stared at the tickets thinking that the world would have to collapse in order for me to miss that one. I hadn't seen or heard from Carla since we parted ways at her home over six years ago. Once she moved to Boston, Vernon and Associates business soared and their stock seemed to go through the roof. His company invested in commercial real estate across several major cities including, Boston, Philadelphia, Chicago, and now Detroit was on that list. James Vernon was now a very rich and well-known business mogul who received all of the praise and accolades even though Carla was really the brain behind his entire operation. He was interviewed in several business magazines, but Carla was never at the forefront. She always remained in the shadow.

I remembered the look of excitement on Jackie's face once I gave her the invitation. Her mouth and eyes became wide and she seemed mesmerized as she held the invitation. She soon jumped into my arms and before I knew it we were swinging around in circles like two small children. One would have thought that we were being invited to the White House.

"Big Man, this is huge," she screamed. I must admit that I was excited, but it couldn't compare to the way that Jackie was feeling.

Once I released her, she started running around in circles. "Big Man, this is in less than a month." She patted her hair. "How am I going to wear my hair? What type of dress will I wear? Who's going to do my make-up?"

She went on and on for a few minutes when I finally said, "Jackie, calm down, baby! It's okay."

She did an abrupt halt and put her hand on her hip. "Big Man, you don't understand. I need to be really ready!"

I laughed. "Don't worry about that--I'm going to make sure that you're ready. In fact, you're going to be more than ready," I positively assured her.

"We're going all out. I plan to break the bank for this one. I know what I want my wife to look like. I'm picking your attire."

Jackie didn't argue. She threw her arms around my neck and stared straight into my eyes wearing a huge grin. "Big Man, you just don't know how good you make me feel."

I kissed her lips and said, "That's how kings are supposed to make queens feel."

Once the excitement subsided, she held the other two tickets in my face. "Since your father isn't going, what will you do with these?"

I hunched my shoulders. "I was thinking of giving them to Byron."

Jackie didn't like that idea. She liked Byron but she didn't like his ways. He had too many women and she didn't trust us together. She really hated how I'd cover for him when his women couldn't find him. It was just a man thing and Jackie would never understand that.

Jackie handed me his ticket and said, "I don't like his taste in women, so I'll hold on to this one." She had some nerve. Her tastes in friends were no better.

"So Jackie, are you going to invite your drunk friend Debbie?"

That struck a nerve with her and she softly punched me in my arm. "Big Man, that was low."

Jackie was sensitive about her friend because they grew up next door to each other and they were once as close as sisters. When Debbie went off to college, she got messed up with drugs and alcohol immediately after she set foot on campus and hadn't been the same since. She has a wonderful son named Michael whom her mother adopted because she had signed him over to the state immediately after he was born.

The disappointed look on Jackie's face forced me to apologize.

"I'm sorry, Jackie. Do what you want with the ticket." Her mood was once again upbeat.

"I'm going to take Olivia. This will be the perfect graduation present for her."

I couldn't argue with that choice. Olivia had come a long way throughout the years. Her mother was a secretary at a high school who couldn't afford to send her to college, so she started working at the bar to pay for it on her own. Jackie stayed on her and helped her get a scholarship so that she could finish nursing school. Olivia made the most money in the bar because she kept it strictly professional. She wore a different costume every night so no patron ever really knew what she looked like. She was also a loyal friend to Jackie. She never smiled or laughed in my face like the other girls and if someone got too close to me, she'd straighten them out, and she never mentioned anything to Jackie.

It was settled. Olivia and Byron were going to be our invited guests.

Since Jackie and I never had a formal wedding, I wanted her to feel special. I called the Bloomfield Hills Boutique and arranged to have a sales associate come out to our home to take Jackie's measurements. My objective was to make her look and feel like a beautiful bride.

***

Danny was sent out to the house. He was tall and slim and a proud gay white guy. His jet-black hair was tapered better than any woman's I'd ever seen. His attire was preppy and the designer bag that he wore across his shoulder had diva written all over it.

Jackie fell in love with him the minute she laid eyes on him. He knew style and he spoke the girlfriend language. He became her assistant throughout the entire process.

I went to the boutique alone to pick out Jackie's dress. I wanted her to be surprised. Danny had set out ten evening gowns. As I circled the dresses, I noticed a sales associate putting the finishing touches on a mannequin. My eyes zeroed in on the shiny silver dress.

"That's it, Danny." The top half of the dress was made of small crystals, with a plunging neckline that rested slightly off of the shoulders and the bottom half was fitted with a slit that would reach Jackie's mid-thigh. I knew that she'd look beautiful in the dress.

Danny looked over at the dress and frowned while smacking his lips. He twirled his wrist and spoke in a soft feminine voice. "That is a beautiful dress, but it's much too busy." He threw both arms up in the air and went into full drama mode. "It just screams attention. Ms. Jackie is a classy lady."

I stared at him wondering how much more of him I could take. He then pointed his skinny finger at me and said, "You know what they say about class: 'It doesn't have to holler.'" He then held up a black strapless gown. "I was thinking more on the line of this. It's subtle, elegant, and it's chic. I believe that it's perfect for the occasion."

Danny talked about the designer, the material, and before I let him go any further with the history lesson on that plain dress, I cut him off in a firm voice.

"Danny, it's boring!" He put his hand over his heart as if he had gotten shot. He was insulted.

"Look, I want Jackie to be seen from miles away. If you have any Christmas lights you can add those too. Now do you understand?" I said.

He was still in shock at my boldness, so I threatened.

"If you don't want my business, then I can go elsewhere."

Danny quickly changed his attitude. He pursed his lips and forced a smile. "That silver dress is the perfect choice. Do you want to know how much it costs?"

I shook my head. "Cost isn't a factor. Just make sure that she has all the necessary accessories, including handbag and shoes. I need this dress packaged and hand-delivered to her the morning of the event."

He grabbed a receipt book and scribbled down the total thinking that I was going to change my mind. I casually pulled out my gold American Express card and paid the fifteen hundred dollar total and slid two hundred bucks in his hand.

"Danny, I want you there to assist my beautiful lady with whatever she needs. I'll pay you your fee when this is all taken care of."

***

The night before the event, Jackie stayed at her parents' house. She dialed my phone around eight o'clock the morning of. She was crying and excited all at the same time.

"Big Man, I'm speechless. You really outdid yourself this time. The five dozen roses, the chocolates, the wine, and this dress and shoes…." I could hear her sniffle. "I'm afraid to touch them."

I smiled. "Jackie, you don't have to touch it. That's Danny's job. I want you to relax. He'll be there around four to help you get dressed." I could actually feel her tears through the phone.

***

The limo arrived around seven o'clock that evening. I was all decked out in my custom-made black and silver tuxedo that matched perfectly with Jackie's dress.

Before I headed to the limo Byron rang the doorbell. He looked sharp in a black tuxedo. We looked each other over and smiled. I gave him his ticket and said, "Jackie and I will be there around eight o'clock. Olivia is her invited guest, so can you please be nice to her?"

Byron couldn't deny that Olivia was beautiful. He just didn't like the fact that she was a dancer. Olivia, on the other hand, didn't care what he thought about her. She knew what she was after and it was certainly better than sitting around waiting on a man who couldn't control his hormones.

Byron smiled. "It'll be so many fine-ass women in that place, I doubt that I'll even notice her."

I made it to Jackie's parents' house around seven-thirty. Although the Scotts were my in-laws, my blood pressure always seemed to elevate whenever I had to go there. Mrs. Scott didn't really care for our business and she often complained that we didn't spend enough time with our son, who Jackie had nicknamed Shorty.

The driver opened my door and I grabbed the huge bag and proceeded to the door.

Shorty's big eyes peeped out of the window as I rang the bell. His scream was loud enough to wake the entire neighborhood.

"Nana, it's Big Man, and he has presents." I never went there empty-handed. Since I couldn't be there as often as I should have, I made up for it with presents.

Shorty wrapped his small body around my legs. I bent over and gave him a hug. His interest in me was brief as he hurriedly snatched the bag out of my hand and threw all the toys on the floor. He was so engrossed in his own little world that I believe he forgot I was there.

I couldn't fool Mrs. Scott. She could see right through the façade. I offered her some money but as usual she wouldn't accept it.

"You and Jackie need to put that money away for this child's college education." Mr. Scott stepped into the room from the kitchen just in time. He had a beer in his hand. I liked when Mr. Scott was around; he was easy to get along with and he always made me feel comfortable. He wasn't formal like Mrs. Scott either, because he addressed me as Big Man.

"Hey, Big Man, would you like a beer?"

I thought about it for a second. "I better not, Mr. Scott; we really need to get going."

He then said, "I understand. You really make my princess happy and as long as she's happy, I'm happy.

Mrs. Scott gave a fixed smile. "Jackie will be down in a minute. She really looks beautiful. That Danny did a wonderful job." I started to relax when she said that, I felt as though I had finally done something right.

Danny came down the stairs first. He introduced Jackie. Mr. Scott ran and grabbed his camera.

Jackie was stunning. The back of her hair was pinned up and the front of it was full of curls. The sparkling dress made her mocha-colored skin glow, the tall heels made her look like a supermodel and her smile lit up the entire room. She was drop-dead gorgeous.

***

The searchlights and red carpet made the Renaissance Center look like a miniature Hollywood event. There were countless public figures, local celebrities, and business owners all waiting around to be interviewed, photographed or some just to be seen. Jackie couldn't believe that we were actually taking part in something so big.

The driver opened our door. It was the middle of August and the weather was perfect. Jackie stepped out of the limo and she could hardly contain herself. My feelings matched hers. I could really get used to this lifestyle.

I thought of James Vernon, who started as a banker and worked his way up to all of this. He was definitely the man that I aspired to be like.

Before Jackie and I could take our first step, a waitress walked over and handed both of us a glass of wine. We made a toast to our establishment: "The Lady."

As we worked our way through the crowd, Olivia spotted us. She dashed over to Jackie. Jackie turned around and Olivia's mouth dropped. "Oh my goodness Jackie, look at you!" She grabbed Jackie's hand and started spinning her around. "You belong on the red carpet in Hollywood. I'm embarrassed at what I'm wearing."

Jackie laughed at her facetiousness. "Olivia, you would look good in a paper bag." Olivia really did look nice, but she blended in with everyone else.

I could hardly focus as we entered the event. The ballroom was huge with decorative lights, large crystal chandeliers, and lots of fresh flowers. There were a variety of stages set up that stemmed from jazz to Motown, to R and B and even classical. It was one big networking affair. It seemed as if everyone who was starting a new business in Detroit was in the building.

Jackie tapped my arm. "Big Man, Olivia and I are going to the ladies' room." I leaned over to give her a kiss. I soon spotted Carla, who was laughing and smiling, walking in our direction. It had been a number of years since I'd last saw her.

Carla's beauty and poise remained intact. She still caused me to have a shortness of breath. Her dress was long, black, and simple. The huge diamond-encrusted necklace, bracelet, and earrings made a bold statement. But her left ring finger was bare. The visible earpiece and the security detail that trailed her made her look and seem of great importance.

She stopped directly in front of us and said, "Oh my, don't you two look fabulous?"

Jackie was bursting over with excitement.

My response was a casual "Thank you!"

Carla immediately went into amnesia mode. "Please forgive me, but I deal with hundreds of clients each year. Let me see if I can get your name right."

It was hard trying to contain myself, but I managed quite well.

"Oh I remember now. It's Jayson Jackson. You guys owned that bar called The Lady. How's that working out for you?"

That woman should have been an actress, because she was good.

Jackie was clueless as to what was happening, so she eagerly responded, "Ms. Roberts, it's going really well. We've overhauled the entire business…." Before Jackie could finish bragging about our accomplishments, Carla cut her off.

She smiled at Jackie and said, "Oh, and it shows." She then eyed Jackie up and down. "That dress and those shoes…" She lifted Jackie's arm up so that she could get a full view. Jackie was overjoyed and did a fashion pose. "I know my fashion. That's an original piece and it's not cheap. It looks simply stunning on you." Carla said.

Jackie's face glowed. It was obvious that she was flattered at having Carla's stamp of approval. Olivia stood back with her arms folded, seeming unimpressed with Carla.

Carla remained professional. "Well, I really hope that you guys enjoy yourselves. Vernon and Associates really worked hard on putting this event together. We're so proud of all the small businesses in the Detroit Metropolitan area that we were able to help. We wanted everyone under one roof so that they could get the exposure in hopes of giving their business a jumpstart. So please relax, make yourselves comfortable, make wonderful connections, and enjoy the many vendors and entertainment, along with the food and drinks."

She then pointed to the corner in the back of the building. "I'd love for you to join me over at the rhythm and blues stage in about an hour where I will be launching my Detroit magazine and children's book series."

Jackie's face continued to glow and she responded as if she'd just had a personal invite from Oprah Winfrey herself. "Ms. Roberts, we wouldn't miss that for the world. I am inspired by you."

Carla gave Jackie a big smile and said, "Why thank you, that's such an honor."

I was slightly embarrassed at Jackie's behavior. She had no clue as to what kind of woman Carla really was. Carla seemed to take it all in. She offered me a sly smile.

"Mr. Jackson, your wife is so charming, maybe I can teach her a thing or two about this business."

I cut in. "She's managing quite well. Ms. Roberts. Will Mr. Vernon be joining us? He seems to be the man that the city of Detroit can't get enough of." I then offered my own devious smile as I twirled my ring finger.

Carla's tried as best as she could to keep a straight face. She knew what I was insinuating. Although she was the brain behind this entire operation, it really meant nothing because he still hadn't married her. She stuttered as she motioned for her detail to lead the way. "Well, of course. He should be here any minute."

As Carla disappeared through the crowd, Jackie turned to me, more enthused than I had ever seen her before. "Oh! My! God! I love that woman." She and Olivia then headed for the restroom.

I walked through the huge ballroom in amazement. Everyone was drinking, socializing, networking, and having a great time. James Vernon was a clever man to have a woman like Carla on his team. She was an organizational genius. The vendors were strategically placed around the perimeter of the entire ballroom. You could find almost everything including fur, high-end clothing, art, fine jewelry, costume jewelry--but the one that grabbed my attention was the mini massage salon.

It was encased in glass, there were serenity fountains, soft flowers, candles, and two young beautiful ladies dressed in white scrubs were giving complimentary back massages.

The receptionist, who looked to be a little older than the girls, was sitting at the table wearing all black, with her hair pulled into a sleek ponytail with huge diamonds in her ears and around her neck. She was taking names for the appointments.

I patiently waited in line behind three older gentlemen to add my name to the list. I soon turned my back to the crowded ballroom floor when Byron suddenly appeared out of nowhere. He held a drink in his hand and it was obvious that he was having a good time. He stood next to me as we both took it all in when suddenly a voice behind blustered with a bit of irony.

"Well if it isn't the infamous Jayson Jackson." Shockwaves went right through me. I was taken all the way back to our high school days. I could never forget her voice. Aside from my mother, she was the first girl who had ever stolen my heart. I was speechless because it had been over ten years since I'd last seen her.

"Turn around, Big Man," Mandy demanded with that same bossy attitude from the past. "You did come here for service, didn't you?"

Byron looked perplexed at her boldness. I took a deep breath. Her intimidation tactics couldn't work anymore. I soon turned around and she was standing tall and looked gorgeous as ever. Time had definitely been good to her. Everything inside of me softened and I realized just how weak I still was.

"Hi Mandy, I would like to get a complimentary massage." I tried to sound cool and calm, but my voice was a bit shaky.

She hesitated for a second before responding to my request. She leaned in close and whispered in a nice nasty voice, "They're not taking any more appointments…but since I owe you how about you come back in about an hour." She then let out a soft laugh.

I followed her lead and laughed along. The ice was broken. I became friendly and let my guard down. "Mandy, you can't still be mad after all these years." After I said that I wished that I hadn't. The cocky, egotistical Mandy resurfaced.

"I got over it! I'm still standing! Had you not broken up with me, I might have married you and we'd probably be struggling with a couple of bratty kids." She spread her arms out wide and said, "This business here is all mine. I'm doing quite well for myself."

I shook my head and smiled. "That's good to hear, Mandy. You had always been a pretty good hustler."

Mandy smiled and grabbed her briefcase and said, "I'll see you in an hour." She walked off with her head held high.

Byron looked over at me and asked, "Damn, Big Man, what in the hell was that all about?"

I let out a long sigh and responded, "My bitter ex-girlfriend from high school."

Byron looked confused. "Big Man, that's a long time for anyone to hold a grudge." I told Byron about the three-dollar bet and how instead of winning I actually lost because that girl was mean and cruel and took my pockets to the cleaners.

Byron responded, "Well, it seems that things haven't changed."

We both had a good laugh. I then said, "You're right and I feel sorry for whatever sucker that has to deal with her ass. She comes with a really steep price tag."

I walked away from Mandy's business with no intention of returning for a free massage ever.

Since Jackie and Olivia had yet to surface, Byron and I wandered freely through the ballroom listening to the variety of music, looking at the beautiful women, and we sampled all types of food and alcohol. We were having a great time until I looked down at my watch.

"Damn! Jackie is going to kill me because I'm late."

Byron responded, "Late for what?" I started walking as Byron followed. "I was supposed to meet her over at the R and B stage over fifteen minutes ago. Carla Roberts is launching a new magazine and children's book series and she gave Jackie and me a personal invitation."

He stopped. "Hold up! Isn't that the woman who made a complete ass out of you some time ago?"

I ignored his statement and continued walking in the direction of the stage.

"I have no idea who you're talking about, Byron." He stayed behind.

"Well, I remember what you and I discussed some time ago and I don't want to be a part of that. I'll catch up to you later."

Within minutes I had arrived at the very far end of the ballroom. It was sectioned off with a sign that said VIP Launch Party along with posters of a new cognac and wine called "Assuage." There was also a beautiful large poster of Carla and a young boy. They held up her children's book series called "Truly Special Kids" and her Detroit magazine.

An older black woman sat at the long table checking off names and handing out gift bags as people entered the private room. There was a bit of a line but it moved swiftly. As folks held their badges, I realized that Carla hadn't given me a badge. I was afraid to step to the table because I didn't want to get turned away. I waited until everyone entered.

When the last person entered, I noticed the woman that was sitting behind the table turned her back and started talking to someone. I eased up to the table and that's when I saw the young boy from the poster on floor. I was startled. His complexion was dark, he was husky and he had big brown eyes. He was wearing a black tuxedo but it made no difference; he was comfortable on the floor. His shoes were off, his shirt wasn't tucked in, and he lay flat on his stomach surrounded by coloring books, drawing paper, colored pencils, and crayons.

I stared at the boy as the woman tried reasoning with him. "James, please get up off the floor. Can you just try to behave for your mommy? This day really means a lot to her." When I heard his name, it gave me chills and I became even more confused. That couldn't be Carla's son.

The boy acted as though he didn't hear the woman and continued to color. I was fascinated as I watched him swiftly move his hand back and forth on the paper. He never went outside the lines and his work looked like that of an artist. Although he was a little bigger than Shorty, he couldn't have been that much older.

The lady picked up one of the many drawing pads when I tapped her on the shoulder. "Can I see that?"

She jumped and said, "I'm sorry, I didn't see you standing there. I thought that everyone had gone into the event." I continued to point at the drawing pad. "Can I see that?" She was hesitant and seemed very protective over the little boy, but she gave in.

I studied the drawings and they were simply amazing. He had drawn a beach and a sunset with castles. The colors all blended so well.

"Did he do these?" She modestly nodded her head yes. "How old is he?"

She turned to face the little boy who was still engrossed in coloring as if we weren't even there. "He's five."

I said, "Wow! He's a truly special kid."

I looked at the poster and I understood the title of her series. I wanted to ask more questions but I couldn't. Jackie and Olivia had come outside the room to look for me.

"Big Man, I have been looking all over for you." Olivia stood next to Jackie and it seemed as if she was propping Jackie up. Jackie's eyes were glassy and she giggled a little.

I responded, "I was on my way in, but you had the passes."

Jackie looked at the lady and pointed. "He's with us."

The woman smiled at us all and said, "Enjoy yourselves." Olivia held Jackie's arm and led her back inside. I, on the other hand, remained in a state of confusion about the little boy.

The exclusive room was where all the big shots were. The decorative round tables with place cards on them let you know who was who. There I saw Detroit city council members, doctors, lawyers, Congressmen, bar owners, and I even recognized a couple of owners from the local car dealerships. The drinks were flowing, cameras were flashing, and everyone seemed to be having a great time.

I walked the entire room looking for Carla but she wasn't there. Forty-five minutes had gone by and she was still nowhere around. Neither was James Vernon. Our table sat directly next to his and his chair was the only empty seat at the eight-person table. The band continued to play and I guess no one even took notice that Carla wasn't there. I looked around for Jackie, but she and Olivia were outside on the balcony.

I walked outside and stepped to Jackie. "I need to go back out and look for Byron. I'll be back in a few." Jackie threw her arm around me and gave me a drunken kiss. "I am having such a good time. I've made so many connections and I have collected lots of business cards. This is just the motivation that we need to take The Lady to the next level."

I returned the kiss. "Well, Jackie--work your magic, baby. I'm ready." She continued to laugh as she swapped her empty glass for a full glass of champagne from the waitress' tray as she walked by.

My mind couldn't focus on the event. I had to find Carla. I needed to know about the little boy.

I reached inside my pocket and tried to slip Olivia a hundred-dollar bill. She didn't accept it. She eyed me very closely and whispered, "Don't worry, I'll take care of her." She then grabbed Jackie's half empty glass and said to her, "Let's go and grab some water."

I left that room as quick as I could. The lady and the boy had packed up and left.

I walked around the ballroom looking for Byron.

I somehow ended up in the lobby. I then eyed the elevators. There was no security guarding that post, so I made my way to the elevator and pressed the button. I had no idea what I would find once I reached the floor of Vernon and Associates, but that didn't stop me.

The elevator chimed letting me know that I'd reached my destination.

The entire floor was dark except for a few floodlights. I walked up to the glass door expecting for it to be locked, but it wasn't. The lights were out, but the skyline of the city illuminated the spacious room. I quietly walked around the office and I stopped once I heard yelling voices coming from an office in the back. I stepped closer to the door and crouched down.

***

"You heard what the hell I just said," a woman's voice roared. "Nancy, you're out of your fucking mind? I can't be out of here in seventy-two hours. I've spent years helping to build Vernon and Associates. You can't just waltz in here and tell me that I have to go. James won't let that happen."

My eyes bulged out of my head. It was Mrs. Vernon and Carla.

When Carla called Mr. Vernon "James," that sent Mrs. Vernon over the top. There was a brief silence. I peeked my head inside of the door.

Mrs. Vernon wore a long black pantsuit with high heels, her salt and pepper hair was in a short-cropped style, and she was a very attractive older woman.

She stepped right in Carla's face and pointed at her. Her voice was low and firm. "Listen here, I've been with that man for over thirty-five years, and all of this shit belongs to me. You started out as his assistant but you became consumed by greed. So you fell for that dumb ass line… *'Nancy and I haven't been happy for years'* so you decided to sleep your way up to the top."

After hearing that Carla's voice began to weaken. "What are you talking about?"

Nancy laughed and said, "That man has been a whore throughout our entire marriage. If you think that you're his one and only, then you're more foolish than I thought. The only reason that I hadn't left him was because I figured it was just a phase that he was going through. I thought that he would change. That couldn't be further from the truth. Men like my husband will never be satisfied with just one woman. My husband is selfish, a user, and doesn't give a damn about anyone but himself. It took me a long time to accept that. Carla sweetie, my husband was right. We haven't been happy for years. I started to leave him five years ago, but I knew what type of empire you were foolishly and unknowingly helping him build and I would have been stupid to leave with so little. So now that we're multimillionaires ten times over, I've decided that now is the perfect time to break this shit up."

After Mrs. Vernon said that, I was just short of passing out from holding my breath so long.

Carla's eyes welled up with tears. She began yelling. "You don't know what you're talking about." She then frantically reached for the phone. Mrs. Vernon stood there proud and confident with her arms folded. "Please do call that coward. He won't answer. The little puppet secretary that you and he hired warned him just as soon as I walked into that launch party." Carla continued to let the phone ring, and just as Mrs. Vernon said, he never answered.

Carla then screamed, "Get out! Get out of here right now!" Carla then threw the phone across the room.

Mrs. Vernon was still calm. "Oh, don't worry, I'm leaving. And please don't think that I'm doing it because you asked me to. I'm giving you a chance to pack your shit before the seventy-two hours are up."

She then pulled out a court order.

"If you're not out of here by then, I'm afraid that it's going to get really ugly because your name isn't on any of Vernon and Associates' properties. That means that you're entitled to nothing but that funky-ass magazine that he bought you. Now if you're still here after your time has expired, I'll throw your ass out and then go to court and take that magazine from you. I'm sure it was purchased with our money."

Mrs. Vernon then turned toward the door.

Carla grabbed her purse and a few belongings before shouting at Mrs. Vernon, "You can go to hell with your court papers. That doesn't mean a damn thing to me. I have more rights than you think I have."

Mrs. Vernon stopped and slowly turned toward Carla and spoke in a venomous tone.

"I gave you much more credit than you deserved. You can't be that fucking stupid. Using a kid as an insurance policy." She reached inside her purse and pulled out a little baggie with a toothbrush inside of it and threw it on the table. "That poor little boy. He deserves so much more than this."

Carla threw her purse down and raised her arm in an attempt to attack Mrs. Vernon while screaming, "Leave our son out of this."

Mrs. Vernon caught her arm and she began to twist and squeeze it.

"That's not his goddamn kid. If he could have had children don't you think that I'd have a boatload of them?" Mrs. Vernon then screamed in Carla's face. "Vernon can't have kids! That selfish, lowdown bastard snuck off and had a vasectomy a few years after we got married."

When Mrs. Vernon said that I don't know who felt worse, Carla or me. Carla took a deep breath. Then she took another. Suddenly it was as if she couldn't catch her breath because she was breathing really fast and heavy. Mrs. Vernon stepped back as Carla continued to struggle with her breathing. She gave Carla a pity sort of a laugh. "You really thought that you were outsmarting Mr. James Vernon but you managed to outsmart yourself. Like I said earlier, James doesn't give a damn about anyone but himself. He didn't even give a damn about his own father. He knew that wasn't his child but he couldn't afford to get rid of you. You were a great asset to that man."

Mrs. Vernon began to get upset as the pitch in her voice became louder. She screamed at Carla once more, "My husband is a liar, Carla! When you had that child, he told me that you named the little boy after him because you admired him. He even had a blood test done to prove it. He played daddy to that little boy because he needed you. He was even too damn selfish and greedy to divorce me. He didn't want me to take half." Carla was now bent over on the floor crying really hard. Mrs. Vernon continued. "I wish that I could feel sorry for you, but I don't! You are an attractive woman who had a lucrative career on your own, but you were greedy. You should be ashamed of yourself. The only person that I feel sorry for is that young boy. You and my husband are the lowest form of life on earth and as far as I'm concerned you two can rot in hell."

Mrs. Vernon then clutched her purse and headed to the door. She turned around and said, "Oh, better get packing. The clock is ticking."

I was balled up in a knot as Mrs. Vernon walked out of the office. I was in worse shape than Carla. If it wasn't Vernon's child, then whose was it?

Mrs. Vernon was gone. Carla sat on the floor crying. She grabbed the phone and dialed a number. No one answered. She then threw the phone across the room smashing it into pieces. She stood up and started searching through her purse. She pulled out a bottle of pills. I sat there nervous. What was she about to do? Her hands shook as she tried to open the bottle. Once she opened it, she poured the entire bottle of pills into her hands. On instinct, I hopped up and ran into the room. I yelled, "Don't do it!" I startled Carla and she dropped all of the pills on the floor. I ran over and grabbed her. She couldn't speak. She just cried and shook right there in my arms. I was at a loss. I didn't know what to do.

She continued to sob and mumble the words "I made a mess. I made a mess. I made a mess."

As time went by I was still holding Carla in silence. I knew that I was probably in trouble, but my hands were tied. I patted Carla on the back and said, "I have to get out of here, but I don't want to leave you in this condition.

She finally spoke. "Jayson, when did you get here?"

I knew that she really wanted to know how much I had heard. "Right after Mrs. Vernon arrived."

Carla began to sob all over again. She knew what I had heard. "Jayson, I need my pills. I won't be able to sleep without my pills."

I carried her over to the sofa and sat next to her. My entire tuxedo jacket was wet and smudged with make-up. There was no way that I could explain this. I grabbed the bottle of pills. Prozac was the name of the medication. I looked over at Carla who was still fragile and weak. I thought back to the time that I was at her home and she sat in the bathroom and cried after we had sex. It all made sense now. She suffered from some type of mental condition--probably the same one that her mother suffered from.

I grabbed the last pill that didn't manage to fall out of the bottle and handed it to her. I dropped to my hands and knees and searched for the pills that fell out of her hand. I managed to find eight of them. I put them back inside of the bottle and put the bottle inside of my pocket.

I went to the bathroom inside of the office and wet some paper towels. I laughed a sad kind of laugh because I remember doing the exact thing six years earlier. I cleaned Carla's face. I whispered to her, as she could barely keep her eyes opened. "I have to go. I promise that I'll be back." She waved a weakened goodbye.

***

I stepped to the elevator and was able to get a good look at myself in the glass mirror. My jacket was wrinkled, my bowtie was crooked and lipstick and mascara was smudged all over my white shirt. I ran over to the water fountain and splashed water all over myself. It was the best that I could do.

The elevator reached the lobby. I had no idea what would happen. When the doors opened, the lobby was packed with people drinking, laughing, and still having a good time.

When I stepped off of the elevator, Byron spotted me. He pushed his way through the crowd. He took one look at me and froze. "What in the hell have you been doing?" He grabbed me and hurriedly led me to the men's room.

"Shit! That was really close," he said, out of breath. He then asked, "What the hell happened to your clothes?"

I hunched my shoulders because I didn't know how to explain it. "Someone spilled a drink on me and I tried to clean myself up."

He shook his head. "Nice try, my brother, but that's a lot more than a drink. Oh well, if you say so." He concluded.

I looked at him and said, "Where's my wife?"

Byron responded. "You owe Olivia your life. She has been saving your ass all night. Jackie is drunk and Olivia has been doing everything in her power to keep her from making a complete fool out of herself. She sent me to go and find you over an hour ago. They're sitting in the lounge area waiting on you. Big Man, you need to get Jackie out of here."

Hearing that Jackie was drunk felt like I had been thrown a lifeline. She was never one to hold her liquor.

Byron led the way. We walked through the crowd headed toward the lounge area. Olivia and Jackie were sitting on a couch. Jackie's head rested lightly on her shoulder. She was asleep. Under any other circumstances, I would have been ashamed, but that day I wasn't. I viewed it as a blessing.

When I stepped to the table, Olivia wore a look of disgust as she stared at my clothes. Me holding a drink across my body couldn't fool her. She cut her eyes at me and spoke with irritation in her voice. "Please help me get your wife out of here."

I grabbed Jackie's arm and pulled her up and just as planned, my drink spilled. "Jackie, get it together," I said with a firm tone in my voice. "Look what you just did! You made me spill my drink and mess up my clothes." Olivia's mouth dropped to the floor. She then looked over at Byron and shook her head. He hunched his shoulders. Jackie stood and I wrapped my arms around her.

As we walked through the lobby, I spotted Mandy at the front desk. She was crying, and pleading for help. Byron and I both looked at each other quizzically. Security then yelled through the crowd, "Please step away from the elevators--we have the paramedics coming through." Everyone in the ballroom gasped as they separated from the elevators. No one knew what was happening.

Mandy rushed behind the paramedics. Her hair was messy, her make-up was smeared, and she was pleading, "Please hurry."

I wanted so desperately to know what was happening, but I couldn't. Jackie was too intoxicated and there was no way that I could leave her.

Byron and Olivia helped me get Jackie settled into the limo. I gave Byron a hug and whispered, "Thanks, bro. We have so much to talk about." I tried to give Olivia a hug but she refused. I sensed her disdain.

On the ride home I couldn't help but think of Carla and the little boy. I wouldn't be able to sleep until I had answers. I looked over at Jackie, who was passed out with a smile on her face. At least somebody had a good time.

It was a quarter past midnight when the limo pulled in front of our duplex. I wished that I didn't have to wake Jackie, but I had no choice. I tapped her. "Jackie, we're home. Can you at least make it out of the car?" She didn't move. I wrapped her heavy arm around my neck and carried her limp body up to the door. Uncle Buddy was on his way out when he saw me. I don't think that I had ever been so happy to see him.

"Big Man, what in the heck is wrong with your wife?"

"She had a little too much to drink."

He laughed. "Well, at least she's not afraid to have a good time." He helped me to get Jackie inside the house. We carried her up the stairs and laid her across the bed with all her clothes on. I removed her shoes, kissed her on the cheek, and proceeded to change my clothes.

I went downstairs grabbed my keys off the table and just as I was about to turn the knob, Uncle Buddy said, "Damn, boy, where are you headed in such a hurry?"

I paused. "Damn," I said under my breath. I just wanted to get out of there in one piece.

He'd exited the kitchen with two glasses and my good bottle of cognac in his hand. Whenever he came over he had a habit of helping himself to my good liquor. I didn't mind, though. I enjoyed his company and he was much easier-going than Pops.

"Uncle Buddy, I'm going to need a rain check. I have to go and help out a friend who's in trouble."

He looked at me with worry, and said, "You look frightened. Are you sure it's something you can handle alone?"

I let out a long sigh. "I have no choice."

***

It didn't take me long to make it back downtown. The party was wrapping up and folks were outside waiting for their cars and whispering amongst themselves. It was evident that something had happened, because several police cars and a white van with the words "Wayne County Coroners Office" were parked out front. I kept thinking of Carla, hoping that she hadn't done the unthinkable.

I zipped my car around the corner and found a spot that was about a block away. I locked the doors and jogged up to the building.

The crowd was thick around the door. I was able to force my way through to the front lobby. A security guard stood by the door asking anyone who didn't have a room or reservation at the hotel to please steer clear of the lobby.

I claimed to have a room at the hotel so I was able to slip my way inside.

There were very few people in the lobby. Two police officers were at the front desk speaking with the clerk behind the counter. Another set of officers was over in the corner speaking with two older silver-haired women and an older gentleman. Suddenly, one of the women let out a loud scream. "Dead! He can't be dead. No!" The entire lobby fell silent. The woman suddenly dropped to her knees. The gentleman and the other woman tried to catch her but they were too late. The couple then fell to their knees in an attempt to console her.

I walked over in their direction and that's when I noticed that the grieving woman was Mrs. Vernon. I caught a glimpse of the other woman who looked almost identical to Mrs. Vernon, except she had a mole above her lip. I knew right away it was her sister Blanche. I immediately thought about Pops.

Blanche was very gentle as she cradled Mrs. Vernon's head and offered some comforting words. "Nancy, I'm so sorry."

Her words fell flat because Mrs. Vernon continued to scream. "Blanche, he's my husband. I've been with that man for over thirty years. I want to see him. I want to touch him. I want to hold him."

Both officers remained calm, but anyone could feel the pain that this poor woman had. She sounded nothing like the woman from earlier. She really did love her husband despite all the things he'd put her through. At that moment, all was forgotten. Death is final; any unfinished business would have to be left that way and Mrs. Vernon wasn't ready to accept it.

One officer crouched down next to her and tried asking her questions. She was too distraught to speak. The gentleman intervened. "Officer, my name is Dr. Winston Baker and Mrs. Vernon is my sister-in-law. Can you please give us a little more detail?"

The officer gave a sympathetic smile and said, "Sir, our officers should be wrapping up their investigation shortly. We have to make sure that there wasn't any foul play before anyone can go near the body. We have questioned the woman who was with him at the time and she said that he'd stopped breathing as she was giving him a massage."

I was floored when the officer mentioned the woman and the massage. I walked away stunned but not necessarily surprised.

I headed to the elevator. I had no idea how I was going to break this news to Carla.

***

She wasn't where I'd left her. She sat on top of the huge windowsill, with her knees locked up to her chest, staring out into the Detroit River. She was shaking. The office was a mess. She had knocked over everything and the phone was in pieces.

I inched my way close to her. I softly called her name. "Carla, are you all right?" She said nothing. I sat next to her feet. "I'm ready to listen whenever you're ready to talk." Carla never looked at me. She continued to stare out into the river as she spoke.

She played the victim role and refused to accept any of the blame. She claimed that James Vernon had used her for years and she was going to make him pay. She felt so foolish for not putting anything in her name. She claimed that in order for her to go away quietly, he was going to have to pay her off or she was going to go public and smear the Vernon and Associates brand.

"Jayson, I can take this bastard down with a few phone calls. He messed with the wrong one this time." She clutched her knees tighter while rocking. She looked desperate and insane. I didn't have the guts to tell her that someone much bigger than us all had already taken him down. I was there to learn about the child, which she had failed to mention at that time.

At least another hour had gone by before I was able to talk her down from that windowsill and onto the sofa. She just lay there with her eyes wide, focusing on the ceiling. Tears followed the path of the previous ones down each corner of her eyes. It was my turn to question. I was afraid of what I might find out, but I had to know.

"The child, Carla? Who is the father of that little boy?" She looked scared. She shook as she stared me directly into the eyes. Her silence said more than any words could say.

"I found out that I was pregnant shortly after we relocated. Vernon never questioned it and he pretended to be ecstatic. He smothered me. He hired my aunt who lived alone in a senior citizens place to be my live-in assistant and nanny. She was happy to be with family, she loved to travel, and she became like a grandmother to my son. I never wanted for anything and I didn't have to lift a finger unless it was to pick up the phone and make a business transaction. All of my needs were met. I was indeed his greatest asset and he knew it. Over the past several years he accomplished a great deal and it was all because of me. James Vernon gave that boy everything but his time. Now I understand why."

She hesitated for a second and began to process her own words.

She had no idea when James Vernon was going to reveal the dark secret that he had known about since the beginning. He made sure that he milked everything that was inside of her until she became useless.

She actually wondered if he was the one who sent his wife up to confront her. It made no difference then; he was at the apex of his game and according to the document sitting on the table, she was entitled to nothing but a magazine that she demanded be put in her name.

"Carla, is that child mine?"

She put her hand over her throbbing head and tried to apologize. "Jayson, if I had thought for one second that the child was yours, I would have never given birth to it."

I closed my eyes and shook my head because her callousness was still intact. "Jayson, sorry to sound so harsh, but it's the truth. You were engaged and quite frankly you had nothing to offer either one of us. Vernon, on the other hand, was a clever man. He needed for me to have that child and had no problems leading me to believe that he was the father. It bought him plenty of time, and it kept me right under his thumb.

"I had a complicated pregnancy so it was impossible to do the math. I stayed on bed rest throughout the pregnancy and the doctors actually had to do an emergency C-section because of the many complications that I had.

"Jayson, the brief encounter that you and I had never crossed my mind until Nancy Vernon presented me with that. She then pointed over to the table where the toothbrush and a white piece of paper sat in a bag." Carla then rolled over and cried once again and continued to murmur, "That bastard is going to pay this time--and I mean it."

I had heard more than enough. It was time that she was brought up to speed.

"Carla, I'm sorry to be the one to break this news to you, but Mr. Vernon has paid. He's dead!"

The look on her face was one that I had never seen before. It was mixed with confusion, anger, sickness, and fury.

I continued. "It's true. He had a heart attack while he was having a massage."

***

We slipped out the back of the hotel around 4:30 a.m. in order to avoid the media.

Carla's tears dried up the moment that I told her about James Vernon. She was an emotional wreck and hadn't said a word since I told her of his death.

I drove her home and walked her up to the door. Her hand shook so bad that she couldn't manage to get the key inside the door. It suddenly opened. It was Ms. Agnes, wearing a strained look across her face. She'd been crying. Carla stepped through the door and didn't look back. Ms. Agnes closed the door as if I weren't even standing there.

***

Jackie was still asleep when I made it home. I had peeled off her clothes and snuggled up tightly against her. I was almost shell-shocked. I knew that our lives would never be the same.

Solitude

Vernon's death made national headlines. Many people formed their own opinion about what happened in that hotel room, but nothing was ever substantiated. The only two people who really knew what happened that fateful evening were Mandy and James Vernon. He was dead and Mandy never wavered from her original story.

As for Mrs. Vernon, she still loved her husband. She had hired top attorneys in the state of Michigan to protect his image. Not one negative thing was reported about James Vernon. He died as he lived, a philanthropist and a hero who had a huge heart.

The funeral was scheduled for the following week and it was set to be a private memorial with the exclusion of Carla.

Mrs. Vernon's attorney hand delivered her a letter along with a two hundred and fifty thousand dollar severance package. This meant that she had agreed to terminate her position at Vernon and Associates. If she refused to accept the package, then Mrs. Vernon claimed that she would take Carla to court. She said that she would sue her for embezzlement from her company and she had the proof to back up those claims.

I sat at Carla's kitchen table as she read the letter over and over again. She called me over to her house because she needed someone that she could talk to.

It was the first time that I'd seen her since his death. She hadn't left the house or taken any calls. Ms. Agnes accepted the letter and left it on the kitchen table for Carla right before she and the boy caught their flight back to Boston. Carla was going to join them after the funeral.

"So what are you going to do?" I asked.

She just stared at the letter. "This bitch is so cruel." Carla didn't look like her normal self. She wore a long thick bathrobe and she had a scarf wrapped around her head and her eyes were swollen from crying.

She wouldn't look at me; instead she found comfort in staring at the red coffee mug. She took both hands and twirled the mug as she answered.

"Take the money and run, I guess. I do own this home. Instead of relocating here, I could just sell it and stay in Boston. I have a townhouse that I'm leasing. Vernon paid the rent up for two years. I guess I'll just have to take my books and magazines and try and rebuild there."

I sat their quietly thinking about our son. There was a picture of him on the refrigerator and I couldn't take my eyes off of it.

I stood and walked over to the refrigerator and grabbed the photo. He was a husky kid whose dark skin tone, nose and lips matched Carla's. I really didn't see any resemblance to Shorty or me, but when I looked at his eyes, they were big and wide just like mine.

"How did he handle the news?"

She still refused to look up. "I haven't told him. I don't even know where to begin. We weren't scheduled to go back to Boston to pack up all of our things for our big move here until next week. I sent him and my aunt back early to protect him from this madness. He thinks that were coming back here to live."

"Carla, you can't run forever; sooner or later you will have to stop and face the music. Besides, I'm ready to meet my son."

That was the moment that she finally looked at me "Jayson, you don't have to do this. I know that you have a family; I don't want to come between that."

I looked at Carla and said, "I want to do this."

She reached in and gave me a tight hug. "Jayson, once the smoke blows over, I'll let you meet him. I'm not making any promises and just to warn you, my son James is like no other child that you've ever met. We'll hold off on the father part also. Just try and be his friend."

She handed me the picture. "Here, you can have this." I put the photo in the back of my wallet.

* * *

"Big Man, is you out of your damn mind?" Uncle Buddy yelled. "You can't just go around claiming kids without having them tested. If I went along with every woman who had told me that I was her kid's father, do you know how many children I would probably have?"

I shook my head at Uncle Buddy and answered, "I don't know."

He threw his hands up and said, "Hell, I don't know either. The only reason that I claimed Byron was because I couldn't deny him even if I had wanted to."

Uncle Buddy and I both laughed. He loved Byron right down to the core. He still loved Byron's mother also. Uncle Buddy knew that he had messed that relationship up, so he refrained from saying anything negative about Byron's mother. He then held his hand out.

"Let me see that photo." I gave him the photo. "Hot damn," he shouted. "This boy sure does have you and my momma's eyes. I can spot those eyes from anywhere."

I was thinking the same thing, but I didn't mention it.

"Big Man, what do your father and your wife have to say about this child?" When I didn't answer, he knew that I hadn't told them.

He sat me down on his couch. "Big Man, I know you mean well, but please hear me out. Just a couple of days ago James Vernon was the boy's daddy. Now that the poor man has died, that woman is trying to pawn that boy off on you. I bet she doesn't know who that boy's father really is. Don't fall for that! If you mention this to your father, you can kiss that business goodbye. He's no longer going to trust you and he's going to make you get a real nine to five job. That beautiful wife of yours is not going to like it one bit that you conceived a child out of wedlock. There's too much at stake and I wouldn't take that chance if I were you."

Uncle Buddy had really given me a lot to think about. I never really thought about the consequences or how I was going to tell my father or Jackie.

I looked at Uncle Buddy and said, "I'm going to meet the child. If I'm his father, then I'm going to step up and do the right thing. I'll get to know him first before I tell Pops and my wife."

I gave him a hug. "Thanks, Uncle Buddy. I really have a lot to take into consideration."

* * *

It was the day of Vernon's funeral. I had no plans to attend. I awoke early that day thinking and feeling sorry for Carla, who was probably alone.

Jackie lay asleep in the bed. The corners of her mouth were curled, forming the perfect smile. She had been on cloud nine since that party. She'd met a lot of professional people and bar owners who all promised to show her the ropes. I pretended to be happy, but my mind was too preoccupied to care. She was too overjoyed to notice the change in my behavior.

As far as Shorty, I hadn't seen him in a few days. I felt slightly guilty that he had a brother he knew nothing about. I wished that I could take him to meet the boy, but I hadn't formally met him.

I got dressed because I needed to meet the liquor distributor at the bar by nine o'clock. I didn't want to wake Jackie. I really wanted to be alone.

The liquor distributor came and went. I was finally by myself. I stacked the beers, wiped down all the liquor bottles, and swept the entire bar. I then ran a pail of water so that I could mop the ladies' dressing room.

When I went into the dressing room I was surprised to find that there was a huge scale sitting over by the small refrigerator. I had no idea where that came from.

Once I finished cleaning, I sat at the bar to have a cold beer. I then pulled the little boy's photo out of my wallet along with Shorty's. I stared at them both. I couldn't help but compare the very opposite photos. I sat them down next to each other and covered both of their noses and mouth with my hand leaving their eyes exposed. My heart beat heavy. They looked like the same set of eyes.

When I removed my hands, they looked different. Shorty looked like the happy kid that he was. James had a lost look about himself. His expression was just blank. He didn't smile nor frown and his wide beautiful eyes looked lost. I closed my eyes and envisioned both of my sons playing together. It brought a smile to my face.

A few minutes later I heard voices. When I opened my eyes, I saw Pops and Jackie. They had just entered the bar and were walking in my direction. I calmly picked the photos up and placed them inside my wallet.

"Wow, look at you two!" Pops was wearing a nice black tailored suit, with a matching fedora and some nice leather dress shoes. Jackie was a knockout. She wore a black hat with a wide brim and some oversized Jackie O frames along with a nice fitted black suit that hugged her hips and accented her small waistline. The small clutch purse and the stiletto heels she wore definitely made her stand out.

"Big Man, why aren't you dressed? I came by the house to pick up you and Jackie and she told me that you were here."

I knew that Pops was looking forward to me attending the funeral with him, but I just didn't want to go. I actually felt as though I were betraying Carla by attending. After that party, my perception of James Vernon changed, and I really didn't care to take part of his home-going celebration.

"Pops, I still have a lot of work to do around here. I just cleaned up this place and I still haven't made it down to the basement. I'm going to have to sit this one out. Please give his family my condolences."

Pops looked a little disappointed. Jackie didn't. She didn't give a damn about James Vernon; she knew that the funeral was going to be full of big shots and she planned to use that as an opportunity to make even more connections. I watched as she went through that closet and tried on every suit that she had until she found the perfect one.

Jackie walked over to me and gave me a peck on the cheek. She never liked ruining her lipstick. "Okay, Big Man, hold down the fort. We'll stand in your place. Let's go, Pops; nobody likes to be late for a funeral."

They walked out hand in hand and I sat and finished my beer.

Around three beers and an hour later, Donna and another one of the dancers barged through the door.

"Big Man, we've been looking for you," Donna yelled in her sassy voice.

I sat at the bar smiling. "Well, Donna, it seems like you have found me. Now what's the problem?"

Donna pointed to the refrigerator behind the bar and said, "We need a bottle of wine first, because this may take a minute."

I found Donna to be amusing. Since she had the most seniority of anyone at the bar, I had to give her whatever she wanted and I had no choice but to listen.

"That goddamn skinny-ass wife of yours has gone bonkers."

I spit my beer out laughing at Donna. "Hold up, can you at least be respectful?" I tried to contain my laughter but it was true. "What did she do?"

Donna gulped down her glass of wine and poured another and pointed to the back room. "She called us all fat!"

I looked at Donna and said "Nooooo. Jackie wouldn't say that."

Donna cut her eyes and replied, "Hmmmmp. Her exact words were that we were overweight. Quite frankly, Big Man, I don't see the difference. Fat, overweight, it means the same damn thing. She went out and bought that damn scale and said that we were going to have to weigh in every two weeks. If we didn't meet her quota then we were going to be on probation. She even threw all of our juices out the refrigerator and replaced them with water. Who in the hell does she think she is? Nobody wants to be with a bag of bones."

Donna then stood up and spread her arms out wide so that I could get a good look at her thick frame. She did look really good. She slapped her own huge butt and said, "Big Man, I ain't never had any complaints. I started to tell Jackie's ass, she wasn't all that. That news lady I saw you with a few years ago didn't look like a skeleton to me, so she'd better be careful."

When Donna mentioned Carla, I got the message loud and clear. She would forever hold that over my head.

"Hold on, Donna. No need to go mentioning that. That was such a long time ago. Jackie has been on a euphoric high since we left the black tie affair a few days ago. I'll make sure that I speak with her about her behavior."

Donna held out her hand and I slid a fifty in it. I was silently thinking that this was extortion. Donna didn't view it that way; she saw it as a hustle.

***

Jackie walked in the door a little after three. I had just come up from the basement. She flopped her exasperated body down at the bar. "Big Man, can you please get me a glass of wine?" I poured the glass.

"How was the service?" I asked with anticipation.

"The service was beautiful. The entire sanctuary was filled with nothing but prominent people. That James Vernon sure did have friends in mighty high places and everyone had nothing but wonderful things to say about him."

"That's nice," I said. "How was his wife?" Jackie made a very sad expression.

"That poor woman couldn't stop crying. I felt really bad for her. According to his obituary they had been married for thirty-five years and they didn't have any children. It was just terrible to watch her stand over that casket and mourn."

I nodded my head. "Yes, that's such a shame." Since I had that out of the way I was just going to mention the scale. "Jackie, I need to discuss something with you."

She took a sip from her glass and said, "Big Man, not now. I'm really worried about your father."

That statement caught my attention. "What's wrong with Pops?"

Jackie hesitated for a second. "Big Man, I really don't know how to put it into words, but as soon as we sat down behind the family he started acting strange. I believe that he saw something or someone that caused him to break down."

I gave Jackie a puzzled look. "You mean to tell me that Pops cried?"

Jackie looked at me and said, "I didn't actually see tears, but he bowed his head and it stayed that way throughout the entire service. After it was over he gave Mrs. Vernon a quick hug and he rushed out of there. We didn't even go to the burial or the repast. He hasn't spoken a word since we left the church. He dropped me off here and said that he'd catch up with us later."

I replayed James Vernon's death in my head and I could still see that beautiful Blanche lady holding her sister. The gentleman introduced himself as Winston Baker, Mrs. Vernon's brother in-law. That meant that Blanche had married Winston and after twenty-plus years, they were still together. Pops claimed that he hadn't seen her in over twenty years. I bet that being in the same room with that woman brought back painful memories. He really loved her, from what I could tell.

"Jackie, don't worry about Pops; he'll be fine. I will make sure that I go and check on him just as soon as I leave."

She lit a cigarette and took a long drag. "Thank you, honey. I hate seeing him like that."

I then cleared my throat and tried to sound casual as I asked my next question. "Hey Jackie, I noticed you bought a scale. What's that all about?"

She smashed her cigarette into the ashtray and said in a snobbish voice, "Have you seen those girls lately?"

I hunched my shoulders and said, "They look fine to me."

Jackie laughed before she snapped at me, "What about Donna?"

When she called Donna's name I knew what this was all about. She didn't like Donna because Donna was the only one who stood up to her.

"Jackie, Donna has been here for a long time. I've never heard any of the men complain about her. Besides--leave her alone, she brings a different type of spice to the club."

Jackie soon raised her voice. "Big Man, have you been talking to that big-mouthed ass Donna?"

I didn't want to throw Donna under the bus so I responded, "What makes you think that I've been talking to her?"

Jackie's voice became louder, "Because no one else had a problem with the scale and being weighed. Just like the old saying goes, 'Throw a rock into a pack of dogs and the only one that will holler is the one who got hit.'"

I looked at Jackie and said "What?"

She cut her eyes at me. "Well, she must have gotten hit."

Jackie left me speechless and she was just getting started.

"Big Man, what's really up with you and Donna? Every time I make a decision around here, all she says is, 'Does Big Man know about this? Does Big Man know about that? Wait till I tell Big Man.' I'm sick her of attitude and lack of respect for me."

Jackie continued, "She's been here too damn long anyway. Isn't she like thirty or something? What's she going to do, retire as a pole dancer?"

I looked at Jackie and couldn't take her arrogance any longer. She was my wife and I loved her, but that past week had indeed turned her into a real bitch.

I raised my voice louder than hers. "Can someone please send the woman I married back down to earth so I can communicate with her? I don't know who this foreign lady is."

Jackie's face was balled up. She didn't like what I was saying at all. She tried to cut me off. I wouldn't let her.

"Donna stays, and that's final! She's been here for a long time and if she want to shake her ass on that stage in a wheelchair or with a walker, then that's her damn business. When this bar had nothing, we had her. She always brought Pops plenty of business. Leave. Her. Alone!" I then snatched my keys from the counter and I stormed out the door with no explanation.

I had never seen Jackie look so angry. I hated to go there with her, but she had really started turning into a monster. The days were long gone when she would do whatever I asked of her without question. Whenever I asked her to do something, she did the exact opposite. It was as if her opinion was the only one that mattered. She had taken her leadership role a little too far.

***

I sat inside Jackie's Jeep Grand Cherokee debating whether I should go over to Carla's. Since that was the day that Vernon had been laid to rest, I knew that she wasn't holding up well. I had been thinking about her nonstop. I wanted to know how she was feeling, what was she thinking, and if she had changed her mind about remaining in Boston.

It didn't take long for me to pull up to her block. My hands began to sweat as I gripped the steering wheel. I felt a little guilt because I was in my wife's vehicle. I reasoned with myself. *It's harmless, Big Man; you're only going to see about a friend.*

As I pulled closer to her house, I noticed a black, shiny Cadillac with dark tinted windows in her driveway. I wondered who that could have been.

I parked across the street and waited for her visitor to leave. Ten minutes had gone by and the visitor was still there. I left and went to grab a bite to eat and when I returned the car was still there. I decided to park the Jeep and wait. When I looked at the clock, an hour had gone by and the car was still there. I wanted desperately to knock on the door and interrupt, but I didn't have any rights.

I cranked up the engine just as her door opened when a tall, older black gentleman wearing a nice dark suit and hat stepped out the door. Carla followed behind him wearing jeans and a t-shirt. They held a brief conversation in front of the house. I couldn't make out what they were saying. He reached in to give her a hug. She reciprocated. I can remember counting the seconds. It was seven long seconds that they embraced each other. I was boiling on the inside with jealously. When they unlocked from each other's arms he headed to his vehicle. Carla gave a big wave and the gentleman said "I'll call you soon." He pulled off and she went back into her house.

I felt so stupid. Why did I even go there? Uncle Buddy was a smart man. That woman probably didn't know who the father of that child was. I was going to forget that the past week had even existed. My primary focus would be my family and The Lady. I left. I was done with Carla for good.

I had thought about returning to the bar and apologizing to Jackie for the argument that we had until I remembered what she had said about Pops.

***

Pops' car was parked in his driveway so I knew he'd made it home.

I sensed that something was wrong when his doors and windows were shut, his newspaper lay on the porch untouched and his mailbox was full.

I used my key to let myself in.

Once inside I panicked. Pops was on his knees, with his back turned away from the door and his body leaned forward. I called his name but he didn't answer.

I braced myself as I slowly walked over to him, praying that he hadn't had a heart attack. I put my hand on his shoulder. He flinched but he never looked up.

My eyes widened when I saw the empty liquor bottle along with a box of photos. He had most of them scattered all over the floor. He seemed to be making a timeline of his life because he meticulously sorted each photo by year.

My eyes soon landed on an old worn black and white photo of Pops' mother and father. They were standing outside their tiny shack in Mississippi, smiling as they held Pops as an infant.

When I lifted the photo he began to speak. "I love that photo."

I nodded my head and said, "It's a beautiful photo, Pops."

He then said, "Momma and Daddy really loved each other."

I smiled and said, "I can tell."

He then held up an old photo of a man and a woman smiling as they stood in front of what looked like a barbershop.

Pops said, "These folks were the Smiths. They got married 'round the same time as my parents and they really loved each other too. They were really good folks."

I smiled at Pops and said, "I bet."

"Big Man, my entire life all I wanted was a wife that I could grow old with and have lots of children and grandchildren. As I look at these old photos of my parents and the Smiths, I realize that they really don't make that kind of love anymore. It seems as if everyone is out for themselves or they're living their lives to please everyone else."

When he said those words, I knew that he was referring to Blanche. I rubbed his shoulder and said, "Do you want to talk about the funeral?"

He shrugged, and said the word "no."

That's when I decided to tell him what I saw the day that James Vernon died inside the hotel lobby.

"I saw her, Pops." I never mentioned the fact that I also saw her husband, because I didn't want to upset him. When he gave me a strange look I asked, "Is that the reason that you didn't want to go to the black tie affair? You knew that there was a great chance you'd run into her after twenty-plus years and you wouldn't be able to handle it."

He bowed his head and at that moment. I could smell the liquor on him. He then looked at me with red-stained eyes and whispered, "She has a family." Pops was broken up inside. His body became limp and it was as if he wanted to cry.

I looked at Pops and said, "Jackie, Shorty, and I are your family." I knew that we could never fill a woman's shoes, but it was more than Blanche could have ever given him. Her husband was her only family because she couldn't have children.

He then looked at me and said, "You just don't understand."

Pops had no idea. I did understand. Carla gave me those same vibes.

Time and distance don't always change feelings. Love is an emotion that's beyond our control, I whispered inside my head.

Pops rummaged through the photos and pulled out some of Cheryl, Uncle Buddy, and the band Mississippi Soul. They really looked like they were having a fun time with all the exotic costumes and hairstyles. He smiled as he saw how happy Cheryl was, doing what she loved.

He then pulled out a postcard with Cheryl's last known address on it. He ran his hand along the address. That really bothered me, because I hated her.

"Pops what do you plan on doing with that postcard?"

He pressed his lips together and nodded his head. I had no idea what that meant.

"I know you don't plan to contact her after all these years?"

Pops looked at me and said, "There's so many unanswered questions. I need to know why."

I tried to contain myself but I couldn't. So I yelled, "I can answer the questions for you. She's a selfish bitch, that's why."

Pops' eyes seemed to have doubled in size. He wanted to say something, but I didn't give him a chance.

I grabbed my keys and said, "Pops, you've had way too much to drink. Liquor has a way of making us say and do things that we'll later regret. I don't like Cheryl and I probably never will. So if you plan on contacting her, please leave me out of it."

"I'll talk to you later."

I left Pops there in his solitude. I don't believe that he even heard me walk out the door. After that day he never mentioned Cheryl's name to me again.

GAMES

There was a bit of a crowd at the bar. Jackie was managing things quite well. I tried apologizing to her but she wouldn't hear of it. She'd become pretty good at holding grudges.

I remember how I went down to my office and sat in the oversize chair and drank and thought about how my world had changed seemingly overnight.

A few hours had gone by when the security guard awakened me. Everyone had left, including Jackie. I wasn't surprised. When I looked around for my house keys, they were gone. I knew that meant Jackie had locked me out of the house. I was going to have to beg my way back in like I'd done in the past.

I locked up the bar and asked Mr. Charlie to take me home.

Mr. Charlie was an alcoholic and I have no idea how he managed to drive under those conditions, but it wasn't my business. I could either take the ride or take my chances by waiting for a cab that might or might not show up.

When we made it to my house it looked deserted. Jackie's Jeep was not in the driveway and neither was Byron's nor Uncle Buddy's car. I was locked out. I thought about going to Pops' house but I felt as though I shouldn't have to. I had my own home and that's where I wanted to be.

Mr. Charlie pulled in front of the Scotts' house, and there was her Jeep. It was three fifteen in the morning and I really didn't want to ring their doorbell. I was beginning to get sick and tired of Jackie and her childish games.

I found a rock and threw it up to her bedroom window. "Psssst. Jackie, I know that you're up there. Come down." No response. I threw a few more rocks and still nothing.

I got up the nerve to ring the doorbell. After a few minutes the front porch light came on. Mr. Scott peeked through the window wearing his pajamas. Mrs. Scott stood behind him in a house robe.

"Jayson, what's going on? Is my daughter all right?" His face looked worried.

"Yes sir. Jackie left the bar a few hours ago and she told me that she's staying over here because she had to take Shorty to school in the morning. I'm locked out of our house because she must have taken my key by mistake."

Mr. Scott wasn't angry. "I see, son. Let me go wake her."

As he was turning to walk away Jackie appeared wearing an angry expression. "Mom, Dad--you can go back to bed. I'll handle this."

She stepped onto the porch wearing pajamas and a housecoat. She closed the door.

"What is it, Big Man?" she yelled.

I looked at my watch. "Are you kidding me, Jackie? It's after three o'clock in the morning and you still have an attitude. You have my keys. Now get your shit and let's go home. We can talk about this when we get there."

Jackie didn't budge. She rolled her eyes and snapped her neck. "Oh! Now your ass wants to talk. Well, I wanted to talk earlier, but you left so I guess that you'll have to wait until I feel like talking."

When she turned to walk in the house, I grabbed her arm. "That's bullshit, Jackie. You have my keys and I am not going to sleep out on the streets because you're mad."

She yelled, "Let my arm go."

Mr. Scott opened the door and saw our little tussle. He grabbed my collar and said, "Why in the hell are you grabbing on my daughter?" I tried to talk but I couldn't breathe.

Jackie grabbed her father's arm. "Daddy, let him go. He was just leaving."

Mr. Scott let my collar go. "I'm sorry, Mr. Scott. I didn't mean to grab her. I was just trying to get my house keys back from Jackie."

He looked at his daughter and said, "Princess please hand this man his keys so that he can get the hell off my property." That hurt.

Jackie still refused to give up my keys. Instead she made matters so much worse.

She stood behind her father and shouted. "I ain't giving him shit. Tell him to go and stay with that fat heifer Donna. The one that he put ahead of me."

Mr. Scott gave me the worst look. I couldn't believe that Jackie was putting our business out there like that.

"Jackie, you are so wrong for this!" I shouted back.

"Well, as long as she's still in the picture, then you and I really don't have much to talk about," she shouted back.

Mrs. Scott stood inside the door telling Jackie to calm down. I could see Shorty coming down the stairs wearing pajamas, rubbing his eyes. When he saw Jackie yelling he started crying.

I tried to reach inside the door to grab him but Jackie got to him first. "Leave us alone, Big Man--go attend to that bitch Donna." And she slammed the door.

I could faintly hear Mrs. Scott's voice through the door. "Jackie, watch your filthy mouth. You and Jayson need to just call it quits."

***

My relationship with her parents was irreparably damaged from that point on. Jackie and I would constantly argue all the time and instead of keeping it between us, she'd run back to her parent's house causing them to dislike me even more.

Jackie and I never learned how to communicate with each other. Arguing, yelling, and disrespect seemed to be the new standard set for our marriage. We never had a physical fight, however, the verbal was just as bad.

So many thoughts went through my head. *Maybe we really were too young to have gotten married. I guess we both still had a lot more growing to do. Maybe I should have taken Jackie's side over Donna's. She was my wife and that meant that in my eyes she was supposed to be right even though I felt she was wrong. It was hard to tell who drew first blood. Maybe it was her for hooking up with me so soon and getting pregnant, or maybe it was me for lying and being deceitful.* It really didn't matter. We were in too deep to turn around.

In the back of my mind I was thinking that Jackie would purposely break up with me because she liked the make-up. The make-up meant that I would have to buy my way back in, and that always cost me a fortune.

As far as Donna, she stayed at The Lady a few more weeks just to taunt Jackie. When she was satisfied with what she had done, she quit. She didn't quit empty-handed either; I paid her close to a grand just to walk away.

After a while our marriage and life had become a game for the both of us. Since she was constantly throwing me out into the streets, I'd turn it into a mini vacation. Whenever I wanted a three-day break from the marriage, I'd just pick an argument and then hand over my wallet. I knew that she wouldn't leave me. She loved that bar just as much as I did, so we learned to deal with our imperfect marriage. We both seemed to live separate lives.

I guess that's what made it so easy for me to accept Carla's proposal.

Roller Coaster

James Vernon had been gone close to a year when I finally heard from Carla. She'd been in Boston the entire time. She phoned and asked me to meet her in Orlando, Florida. It was time that I met our son. I didn't hesitate. I booked the first flight out and the only people who knew where I was going were Uncle Buddy and Byron.

I had stayed at a hotel a few miles from Disney World. We had plans to meet at two o'clock sharp inside a restaurant in the theme park. It was only 1:15 and I couldn't manage to keep my nerves in check. I sat at the bar inside my hotel and ordered two shots of cognac. I went to the bathroom and checked myself in the mirror for the third time. I looked closely at myself and wondered if the boy would see himself in my eyes. I also wondered if he'd even like me--and I also wondered what he would call me.

My shuttle had arrived. I made it inside the theme park with a few minutes to spare. I stopped at the gift shop and bought a big coloring book and crayons, since I remembered that he liked to color. I followed the map around to the restaurant and there was Carla in a beautiful green sundress with matching hat. She held a folder along with some magazines in her hand. The boy was nowhere in sight.

Carla's smile was warm after she took the presents out of my hands. "Hello, Jayson. I'm so glad that you were able to make it. James will love the gifts."

I looked around for the boy while saying, "Where is he?" She gave a kind of nervous smile. She then pointed over to the water sprinkler where there were several kids running, jumping, and laughing--and he wasn't one of them. He stood there frightened as the water covered his body. Ms. Agnes stood next to him cheering him on, but it wasn't working. He started to scream as she let go of his hand. I thought about my rambunctious Shorty, who loved the water park. Jackie and I would have had to drag him away from the water.

I took a step in his direction when Carla stopped me. "Jayson, no! I haven't told him about you yet. I just want you to sit back and observe."

I turned around and grabbed Carla's arm and led her over to the bench. I needed to know what was going on with this child. My voice was soft and sincere when I asked, "What type of kid is he?"

Her eyes focused in on him and she staged a huge smile. "One doctor seems to think that he may have autism or maybe Asperger's syndrome because he has difficulty communicating and forming relationships with other people. Another doctor said that he could have Select Mutism, which is a complex childhood anxiety disorder characterized by a child's inability to speak and communicate effectively in select social settings. Another doctor said that he's too young and that maybe he's still developing."

When she said these things I felt really bad. I immediately reached in to embrace her but she pushed me away. "No Jayson, we don't need any sympathy. He's okay. I don't care about those damn doctors and their labels. He's a smart kid and I believe he's still young and developing. No, he may not run around or be outgoing like other kids, but that doesn't mean he deserves to be ostracized. He's moving along at his own pace."

Carla went on to speak. "Did you know that Albert Einstein didn't speak until he was four years old? They put labels on him and look what type of man he turned out to be. He was the most influential physicist and philosopher of science of all time. James is a very special kid. That's the only label that I'm going to put on my son."

Carla opened the folder. She had several beautiful drawings by the child. I was in awe of his talents.

"Jayson, my son inspires me. He's the inspiration behind all of my books. If it weren't for him, I don't believe that I'd have any reason to live."

I sat and observed him for the rest of the afternoon. Ms. Agnes and Carla escorted him around the entire amusement park. It was heartbreaking to watch the women struggle with the boy as he would yell and scream at the many attractions. The only place that he really enjoyed was the gift shop. He loved the bright lights and all of the colorful books, balls, and the abstract art.

Later that evening I met Carla and James for dinner at the restaurant inside of the theme park. I arrived ten minutes early and was surprised to find that Carla and James were already there. As Carla waited to be seated, James had his frightened body wrapped completely around her leg. I walked over to Carla and offered her a hug. She bent down and tried to comfort the scared child.

"James, this is mommy's friend Big Man." She then gave me a wink. "He's the one that's having dinner with us." James never responded or looked up. His face remained plastered to her leg.

The hostess walked over to us and introduced us to Minnie and Mickey Mouse. Both characters put their arms around James as the hostess snapped several group photos before we were escorted to our seats.

We were seated in an extra-large booth. Carla pulled out a big drawing pad and crayons for James. He began to relax. I wanted to find a way to reach the boy, so I flipped over my paper placemat and begin to color. "Hey little fella, why don't you tell Big Man what you are coloring." The boy never responded. He was in his own little world.

Carla put her hand on my knee and whispered, "Relax. Give him some time."

I let out a disappointed sigh. I'd decided against forcing myself on the child. At least he was calm.

Carla and I moved down to the far end of the booth. She wanted to talk. "Jayson, I'm a new woman and I don't want to play any more games. James isn't the real reason that I called you here." I furrowed my eyebrows together because she had my undivided attention.

"I hate it in Boston. That's not my home. Detroit is my home and I'm going back there to rebuild. That bitch Nancy took everything. All the blood, sweat, and tears that I put into that company is gone. Nancy sold it all for a little of nothing." I sat there with my hands clasped together because everyone in Detroit knew what Mrs. Vernon had done.

"Jayson, I can't do it all by myself. I'm teaming up with a group of investors for new construction in downtown Detroit and I'm offering you the chance to get in on the deal. You have my word that this will strictly be between you and me. No strings attached."

I looked at Carla and said, "What is it that I need to do?" She pulled out the blueprint for the construction site. She drew a circle around part of the print. "Jayson, for seventy-five thousand dollars, this would be the new location for your bar, in the heart of downtown Detroit."

My jaw dropped and my head began to pound once she mentioned the amount of money it would take.

She took one look at my facial expression and said, "Listen--I know that you're thinking it's a lot of money, but it's really not. It's an investment. You'll get your money back. Once you give me the capital, that business that you own right now will have no choice but to expand because I have all of the connections and hundreds of clients and I plan to send them all your way. The Lady will have more business than you could possibly handle."

She was talking so fast that I could hardly process it all. "Carla, I really need to think about this."

She shook her head no. "Jayson, I need an answer before you leave here tomorrow. I have big plans and if you don't want to get in, then move out the way so I can find someone else."

My mind flashed back to the man that was at her house in the Cadillac and I knew it wouldn't be hard. She had a proven track record. After all this was the woman who'd help take James Vernon all the way to the top.

Carla was smart, beautiful, charming, a great negotiator, and she knew the business like the back of her hand. She was a visionary that could make things happen. I thought about The Lady, which was doing quite well, but I knew that with Carla, we could do so much better. My eyes saw dollar signs and I felt that I would have been foolish to pass up an opportunity like that.

Carla eyed me and said, "Jayson, are you ready to be a very rich man, or do I need to move on?"

Carla and I shook and the deal was final.

***

When I made it back to Detroit things took off pretty fast. Carla made good on her promise and the business at The Lady was booming.

She set me up with some contractors and we were able to expand The Lady.

In the beginning most of the residents in the neighborhood surrounding our business opposed the expansion. They quickly embraced the idea once we fixed up the surrounding properties in the area. We added more streetlights, put up new fences around their homes, planted flowers, and beefed up security. After the project was completed a vast majority of the residents were pleased because crime had decreased and their property values went up.

The Lady also fed the homeless on a monthly basis, gave away free toys to the kids at Christmas, and we bought new playground equipment for the local park that was in the area.

I believed it was the best investment that I had ever made. It didn't take long for me to become the talk of the town. My face graced many local magazines and newspapers and everyone knew who Big Man was. I was praised for being one of the youngest and fastest growing entrepreneurs in the city of Detroit and I loved it. Although our establishment The Lady was an adult entertainment bar, it was upscale and it brought a lot of life and revenue to the city.

Carla moved back to the city and started a new, smaller consulting firm and her magazine and children's books were selling well. Byron had expanded his security business and Jackie was able to travel, and shop, take sewing classes, and do whatever she liked. Uncle Buddy had also started with a brand-new band and they were doing well and he still continued to help with my after-hours club.

Pops finally retired and he did a lot of traveling. He also worried about all the attention, because he was a simple man. He thought that things were moving a little too fast. He was uncomfortable with the changes.

He warned, "Big Man, too much attention is never a good thing." I laughed because he'd been comfortable in the same spot for years. He had the potential to be so much more, but he was content with what he had.

I remember saying to him, "Sit back and enjoy your retirement. I got this! I will never run away from free publicity. I don't care if it's good or bad, because in the end, it will only add up to more dollars."

His response was "Son, the media will love you when you're hot, and turn on you when you're not. All they're interested in is a good headline."

***

Carla and I were a few months away from closing on the downtown development. We were sitting at her kitchen table toasting over a glass of wine. We were celebrating all that we'd accomplished in such short time when she said, "Big Man, this arrangement is not working for me anymore."

I can remember dropping my glass, shattering it all over her marble table.

"Carla, what are you saying?" She held her glass up to her mouth never taking her eyes off me before she took a swallow. "I'm changing the rules. I want more."

I began to feel sick.

"Carla you can't just change the rules in the middle of the game. You were the one who made up these arrangements. You've gained more than anyone else throughout this entire ordeal. You have control over just about everything. I give you most of my free time, we travel, we have fun, and I don't question anything that you do. How much more do you need?"

She finished up the entire glass of wine and eased over to my lap and threw her arms around me and kissed me on my neck. "I want all of you." She then sat the plane tickets on the table that I had purchased for Jackie and Shorty and me to go to California.

In the past I could never have resisted Carla's advances, but that day was different. I was completely turned off by her.

I jumped up and she fell backwards. I snatched the tickets up. "Where did you get these from?" Her feelings were hurt as she stumbled over her words.

"They fell out of your bag." She had told a bold-faced lie. I knew that they couldn't have fallen out my bag because they were securely tucked away.

"Carla, I'm so sorry, but I thought that a deal was a deal. We're friends. That's the way that you wanted it. You haven't let me develop a bond with James because you're afraid of what it might do to him. I accepted that. I kept up my end of the bargain and there's no way in hell that I'm leaving my wife."

She gave that familiar look when she was about to lose it. Normally I would try and appease her, but not that time. I wasn't going to leave Jackie, and that was final.

I stormed out of her house, not knowing what her next move might be. I heard a glass break as I closed the door.

I decided to steer clear of her for a few days. I was hoping that she'd calm down and come to her senses because we both needed each other.

For the next couple of days I let all of her calls go to voicemail. I wanted her to realize just how much of an asset I was.

The first few messages were calm. "Jayson, please call me." I ignored them. The next few messages sounded desperate. "Look, Jayson, I need for you to call me." I ignored those also. On the third day she sent a very disturbing message. Her words were slurred like she'd been drinking and crying at the same time. "Look here, you motherfucker. You better call me or else!" I knew from that point on, I had a big problem on my hands.

I sat inside my office and poured myself a drink before I finally answered her call. She didn't say hello, instead she screamed into the phone.

"Jayson, how long do you think that you can keep me and this son of ours a secret? If it weren't for me, you wouldn't be who you are! I made you! I own you! You owe me!"

Irritated with her threats, and demands, I pulled the phone away from my ear just as Jackie poked her head inside my office. I panicked. "You have the wrong number," I said, and I quickly closed the phone shut.

Jackie had a suspicious look on her face, but she didn't question me. Instead she said with sarcasm in her voice, "Big Man, I'm so glad that you finally decided to show up. I've only been calling your phone all afternoon." Before I could offer her an explanation, she threw her hand up and said, "Save it! Now can you get me some cranberry juice, and some change for this cash register out here."

She didn't wait for a response as she slammed the door. I could tell by the way that she pursed her lips together and cut her eyes at me that she was upset.

My phone rang again. "What?" I screamed into it. "What?"

Carla exploded back. "I'm going to show you what! I'm on my way down there and I'm going to blow the cover off this charade that you've been pulling for far too long. I've waited long enough!" I tried to respond, but she'd hung up.

I hastily pushed myself away from my desk and rolled the chair toward the locker with the safe inside. I could hardly open it because I couldn't seem to steady my hands. I grabbed a stack of ones, fives, tens, and twenties along with several rolls of coins and I stuffed it inside a bag. I grabbed two large bottles of cranberry juice and decided to pour myself a tall glass. I opened the door up to my office and headed to the bar.

The place was packed with mostly male patrons. Their tongues wagged like hungry animals as the beautiful, half-naked women slid up and down the poles and strutted their stuff across the runway stage. Jackie was behind the bar laughing and joking as she made drinks and directed orders. Once she spotted me, her expression hardened. I handed her the bag and she quickly snatched it away, never missing a beat as she continued smiling, and waiting on patrons. Pops sat in his usual spot at the end of the bar having a beer and enjoying the beautiful women and scenery at our establishment. Byron stood guard at the front door, making sure that things were running smoothly. I couldn't have asked for a better team. My stomach suddenly did flip-flops as I realized that in a matter of minutes, Carla was on her way down to wreak havoc on my life.

I was going to have to make a choice. That choice would never have been Carla. Even if Jackie had left me and took Shorty away, I still wouldn't have chosen Carla.

I walked to the front door of the bar where Byron, wearing full security gear, took one look at me and knew that something was wrong. "What's going on?" he said attentively with his hand on his holster that housed his baton. He looked as if he was ready to go on the attack.

"It's over," I hollered strongly over the music and I threw my hands up. "I can't take her anymore. The joyride is over!"

Byron, caught completely off guard by my response, leaned over to the young security guard that was standing next to him and said, "Hold it down, this will take a few." He then grabbed my arm and hurriedly whisked me away into my office.

Once inside of the office, he grabbed the remote and cut the big 36" television on. He sat on my desk with his arms folded and his head bowed toward the ground and sharply said the word, "Speak!"

"I can't live this lie any longer. It's not worth it. It's been too long and I've had enough. The threats, the blackmail, and the uncertainty of not knowing what she will try and pull next. It's just not worth it anymore. I just don't see but one way out, and that is to come clean," I yelled, as if I hadn't played a big hand in this. "This entire establishment, and all of its successes were built on nothing but one big lie."

Byron angrily rose from the table knocking over an entire stack of papers. "Cut it out!" he screamed. The bass from his voice pierced my ears. "Uncle Jimmy had this place long before Carla Roberts even stepped into the picture. Sure, she gave you some inside connections to help augment this establishment, but you didn't ask for it. She came to you. I call it being at the right place at the right time." He then ferociously stomped out of the office.

Byron was upset and I guess I couldn't blame him. His security business was latched to my business, and if Carla took me down, he wouldn't be too far behind, so he took her threats personally.

***

I stared at the plane tickets on the desk. Jackie and Shorty were on their way to visit her brother in California. They were going to be there for two weeks. I was going to join them the second week, where we were going to take a family vacation. Their flight was scheduled to leave the next day.

Carla had known about Jackie and Shorty, but Jackie didn't know about my relationship with Carla and James. Carla never felt threatened by my relationship with Jackie because she believed that Jackie was young and that I didn't take my marriage seriously.

Carla considered Jackie to be foolish for doing the so-called "dirty work." Through Carla's eyes, The Lady was a low-class establishment and she said that she'd never be caught dead in a place like that.

Everything seemed to be beneath Carla, including myself. Carla had a fixation with powerful men, money, and prestige. Since I didn't have either, she slowly molded me into the man that fit her criteria and I foolishly fell for it.

I did everything that Carla asked of me because I wanted it all. I saw and heard nothing but what was in front of me. I was moving at full speed and never considered the price I'd have to pay.

Carla really believed that she had me under her control and when she saw that I had no plans of leaving Jackie, she lost it.

That was the moment when I realized that my life had been more like a roller coaster. Everyone seemed to be enjoying the ride. Money was rolling in faster than I could count it. I had women that were throwing themselves at me. And it was nearly impossible for me to keep up with all the untruths I had to tell. I had soon lost control over my own life and I couldn't even begin to tell anyone when or how it happened.

I had gotten sloppy with my relationship with Carla. We'd been spotted out a few times by a couple of ladies that worked at the bar. They soon begin to spread rumors about me and Carla having a child together. I'm sure that Jackie heard them all, but she never mentioned anything.

Jackie loved running that bar, and the power that was attached to it caused her to become totally myopic. She had put her heart and soul into that place. She refused to let anyone or anything come between us, and what she'd thought we solely created. "Those people are just jealous" were her words.

***

The music thumped loud in the club as I sat there in a daze thinking back about how this mess all began. It was nearing midnight when I realized that an entire hour had gone by since Carla had hung up on me. I decided against calling her back or running to her house. There was no need to prolong the inevitable. I took a deep breath, poured a shot of cognac, and chased it down with the cranberry juice. I then lit up a cigarette and said, "Let the fireworks begin."

After the third shot of liquor, I was calm, mellow, and at ease.

Fifteen more minutes slowly went by, and there still wasn't any noise. I began to wonder if she was only bluffing like she had done in the past. After all, she had just as much to lose as I had.

Once the alcohol settled into my system, I suddenly didn't give a damn. *Maybe I'll call her bluff, and put myself out of all of this misery. It's long overdue.* I then decided to take a coin out of my pocket. "Heads, I tell Jackie first. Tails, I break the news to Pops first."

I tossed the coin into the air and before it could hit the ground the young security guard, who was at the door, burst into my office. He stuck his head in and was leaning on the door with one hand on the knob with very wide and alarming eyes. "Big Man, quick! Take this call." He threw his cell phone to me. Before I even put the phone up to my ear, I could hear the words "Damn. Damn. Damn!" along with heavy panting and breathing, and what sounded like a painful howl.

I looked at the security guard, and I pointed to his phone because I couldn't recognize the voice. "It's Byron," the security guard said in a frenzy.

I became alarmed. I put the phone up to my ear. "She's...crazy." He panted. "A goddamn lunatic." He panted even harder. "Damn!" he shouted back into the phone while trying to catch his breath.

"Byron! Byron!" I screamed back. "What in the hell is happening?"

He made that howling sound before he spoke. "I. I.... went to her house." He stuttered. "She. She...pulled out a gun." He continued with the stutter. When I heard the word gun, that really had my attention. He continued to breathe heavily into the phone, talking extremely fast through painful tears.

I couldn't wrap my head around what was happening. So I yelled into the phone "Slow the hell down and please tell me what is happening!"

He couldn't get the words out fast enough. I heard horns blowing in the background and he screamed the words "Her car just went up in flames!" The line went dead.

I dropped the cell phone and for a second everything turned black. I felt a little motion sickness coming on and my knees began to buckle. The young security guard caught me just before I fell, and he helped me to the chair. I looked at him quizzically and asked, "What in the hell just happened?" The young guy looked horror-stricken. He had only been working with Byron for about a week and he really had no clue as to what was going on.

As he spoke, he unfastened his vest. "Byron left out of here about an hour ago very upset. He told me to keep an eye on the place, and the next thing I know, he was ringing my cell phone, yelling and screaming telling me to hurry up and put you on the phone."

The guard freed himself from his vest. "I'm sorry, Big Man, but I really didn't sign up for anything like this. I just needed some extra money to pay for diapers and milk for my newborn baby. I'm going to have to find another job because something just doesn't feel right." He set the vest and baton on the table, snatched his phone, and took off. I followed out right behind him.

Jackie walked from behind the bar in a panic. "Big Man, what's going on and where's Byron? There's no security guarding the front door, we are just about at capacity, and we still have a few hours before we close."

"Tell Pops to get the door--I'm not feeling too well." She gave a suspicious look and did as instructed.

I knew that I had to find a way to get her out of there and on that plane the next morning before she heard the news. I went back inside my office, knowing that in a couple of minutes, she'd be walking in. I grabbed the half glass of cranberry juice and poured it all into the small wastebasket that sat next to my desk. Jackie was yelling to someone outside the door saying, "I'll be right back." As she turned the knob, I crouched down over the basket and stuck my finger in my mouth. She ran over to me in terror and started rubbing my back.

"Oh Big Man, are you all right?" She glimpsed down into the bucket and when she saw the red juice, she screamed. "Oh my God, you're throwing up blood! I have to get you out of here, and down to emergency."

I continued to cough. "No, Jackie! I hate the doctor. I'll be okay. I just need to lie down."

She dropped everything and said, "Sit here while I go and get my things. Your father can shut this place down and lock up. I have to take care of you, because Shorty and I need you."

Jackie grabbed the two-way radio and called for the parking attendant to pull her Jeep around to the door.

Once Jackie and I settled into her vehicle, she headed to the hotel. I'd booked a suite for the day since she and Shorty had an early-morning flight. We'd hired a sitter to stay with Shorty at the hotel. He loved the hotel because he viewed them as mini-vacations since they were equipped with a pool, an arcade, and 24-hour room service.

On our way to the room, I had forgotten to turn my cell phone on silent and it rang. I looked at the phone, contemplating my next move. I felt Jackie stare at me from the corner of her eye. She didn't have to say it, because I knew what she was thinking. I so desperately wanted to know what had transpired earlier, but I knew that I couldn't take the call. After the third ring, I turned the phone completely off. I knew that was a bad move and it was getting ready to cost me dearly. Considering the circumstances, I was prepared to pay.

Jackie cleared her throat and took a deep breath.

"I guess that explains why I can never seem to get through to you." She was still seething mad from earlier. I had so much on my mind--the last thing that I needed was for Jackie to be angry with me, so I tried my best to smooth things over.

"Look, baby, I tried to apologize earlier but you told me to save it. I was in a really important meeting and I couldn't talk." She got ready to say something but before she could, I pulled out a roll of bills. She suddenly got quiet. "Jackie, I don't think that I gave you enough spending money; here's an extra grand." I placed the roll of bills inside her bra. She didn't smile or say thank you, and she didn't give it back either.

Jackie then reached down to turn on the radio but I stopped her. "Baby, please, can we just have silence. I'm really not feeling well." She let it go and we drove the next fifteen minutes without a sound.

I didn't get a wink of sleep that night. I can remember lying in that bed watching Jackie and Shorty sleep. I went into the hallway and dialed Byron's cell phone several times but he never answered. The only thing that I could do was stare at the muted television screen and watch as firefighters extinguished a burning car along the highway.

I wasn't able to exhale until Jackie and Shorty were safely at the airport. I checked my phone and I hadn't received any calls and there weren't any messages.

Fallacies

Going to Carla's house was one of the hardest things that I ever had to do in my life. Since I could not find Byron, I went alone.

Ms. Agnes answered the door and she had been crying. Carla was dead and she and the boy were alone. I sat in the kitchen and held Ms. Agnes. I was broken up on the inside. There wasn't anything that I could possibly say that would make this terrible nightmare go away.

Ms. Agnes poured us both a cup of coffee.

"Jayson, I knew the day would come, when I wouldn't be able to save her. My niece suffered from bipolar disorder. It was the same disorder that her mother suffered from. She has been battling this for a very long time and I've always been there to calm her down. I really wanted to believe that she was getting better, but the last few days I was unsure. She'd stopped taking her medicine. Last night was the worst I'd ever seen her. She was yelling and screaming and throwing things. I couldn't get her to calm down. James was so frightened that he hid under the bed. She then grabbed her keys and ran out the door. I tried to stop her but she wouldn't listen. Then a man pulled up and she started yelling at him. Suddenly she jumped in her car and sped off."

Ms. Agnes then let out a loud cry and said, "That's the last that I heard from her. An officer knocked on the door early this morning and said that she had been in a head-on collision and that her car went up in flames." Ms. Agnes continued to cry.

I became choked up as I held her. There simply were no words.

I gathered all of my strength because I needed to be strong for James. I was all that he had. I exited out the kitchen when Ms. Agnes grabbed my arm. "He knows and he's not doing well."

When I saw him standing on the stairs he went on the attack. "I hate you!" he screamed from the top of the stairs. He held a voluminous hard cover book in his hand. "I. Hate. You."

He screamed once more before tossing it down the flight of stairs. I attempted to duck, but my response time was too slow. It sharply whizzed past my face, leaving a cut under my eye before it slammed down on the hardwood floors. He then charged down the stairs at full speed with both fists balled up. We crashed down on the floor. He landed on top of me and I didn't move as his heavy fist pounded my chest over and over again. The tears flowed uninterrupted as he continued to scream ferociously, "I. Hate. You!"

James had never really talked. I could never seem to reach him, although I tried for years. I didn't understand him. Most people didn't understand him, and the only person who did understand him was his mother Carla, and she was dead.

I lied there on the floor and let him have his way with me. Blood splattered everywhere and he didn't seem to take notice. He needed someone to blame and he had every right to blame me.

That was the last time that I would lay eyes on James. Ms. Agnes begged and pleaded for him to stop and after several moments of the abuse he let up and ran to her arms. I had never witnessed so much rage and anger in a child so young. It was almost as if he were possessed. Carla was his rock and now that rock was gone. I tried reaching for him once more when he started kicking and screaming again. Ms. Agnes used all of her strength to control the boy. She pleaded with me,

"Jayson, please just go. I need for him to calm down before he has a seizure."

It was difficult to leave, but I knew that I was only making matters worse. James really didn't want me around. He hated me.

***

Ms. Agnes was left in charge of Carla's estate. She along with Carla's uncle gave her a memorial and afterwards they'd planned to take the remains back to Haiti where she would be buried next to her parents'.

I respected Ms. Agnes' wishes and didn't attend the memorial. We met up at a café where she handed me a big box of photos and keepsakes that Carla had stashed away. When I asked about James, she looked sad and tired as she responded, "Give it some time."

Byron never did resurface. Seeing Carla's death took a lot out of him. He dropped everything and moved back to Mississippi without any warning.

The only person that I had left to talk to was Uncle Buddy. For the first time ever, he didn't have any answers. I wished that I could have gone to Pops, but I was ashamed of the lies and the deception that I had perpetrated. I didn't want to interfere with his life also. James Vernon's death had changed him. It made him want to live a little more, so he was always on the go. He deserved it. He'd been taking care of people his entire life; it wasn't fair for me to expect him to stop his life and fix my mess.

***

A week after Carla's death was when I was scheduled to close the bar and fly out to California to be with Jackie and Shorty. I couldn't bring myself to get on that plane or close the bar.

I hadn't slept a wink since the accident and I looked nothing like myself. I spent every waking moment at the bar. It had become a place of refuge for me. I didn't want to be alone. I was so afraid of having to face what I had created.

Jackie called the bar a day before my scheduled flight out. "Big Man, it's so beautiful out here. We miss you so much and can't wait until you get here. It's about time you shut that place down for a week." My voice was somber when I spoke.

"Jackie, I'm sorry to have to disappoint you and Shorty, but I can't make it."

Jackie went from happy to irate in a matter of seconds. "What in the hell do you mean you can't make it? This trip has been scheduled for quite some time. If your ass isn't on that plane tomorrow, we are going to have major problems!" Suddenly the line went dead.

She never even asked why, what happened, or "Is there anything that I can do?" Nope. It was all about her. At that point I didn't even care. I had grown accustomed to her threats.

***

Jackie didn't return from California until a month later. When she returned to the city, she went straight to her parents' home. Our marriage was on the brink of failure and the only thing that held it together was The Lady. It didn't matter how mad Jackie would get, she would never walk away from that bar. She loved it just as much as I did. I really loved my wife, but I was clueless as to how to repair the damage. I wished that I could have waved a magic wand and things would go back to the way they once were, but I knew that wasn't the case. Instead of dealing with our troubles, we both found it easier to run away from them.

We both came up with a mutual agreement. She'd run the top half and I ran the bottom. She lived her life and I lived mine.

Pops was hurt by our relationship, but he remained neutral. He loved us both and he was hoping that we would reconcile for the sake of Shorty.

***

As promised Ms. Agnes sent me monthly reports on James and I sent money. They had settled into Carla's home in Bloomfield Hills, Michigan and he was enrolled in a special school. He was adjusting well since he was around children who were more like him. I looked forward to her letters and the pictures although James never mentioned me in any of them. I still found joy knowing that he was going to be okay.

The letters went on for a few years until they suddenly stopped. I then checked my bank account and the last check that I'd mailed hadn't been cashed. I dialed Ms. Agnes' phone number and it went straight to voicemail. I'd decided that I would drop by the house when I thought that James was in school to check things out. That's when I found a letter in my mail from Michigan department of human services regarding James Jackson. I needed to contact a Mrs. Hunt as soon as possible.

I made the appointment and went to Mrs. Hunt's office. That's when I found out that James Lee Jackson had been in foster care for over a month.

***

I stared at the birth certificate that was on her desk. The child's name was listed as James Lee Jackson and Carla Roberts was the mother and Jayson Lee Jackson Sr. was the father.

Mrs. Hunt was an older African-American lady with white hair and round glasses, and she didn't smile.

"Mr. Jackson I brought you in here today because James Jackson's guardian suddenly passed away in her sleep last month."

I was speechless when I heard the terrible news. How much more could the poor child take?

I asked Mrs. Hunt about James. She looked up and said, "He's doing as well as can be expected considering the circumstances. He's with a lovely foster family where he will remain until we can locate his closest relative."

I looked at Mrs. Hunt and said, "Can I see him?"

She took a long pause. "Mr. Jackson, I'm going to cut right to the chase. Are you really this child's father?"

That question shocked me. I tried to answer as best as I knew how.

"Well, yes--my name's right there on the birth certificate."

She then said, "Well, I noticed that you never signed your name on the birth certificate and when we asked the child who his father was, he said that his father was dead. When we asked him if he knew who Jayson Jackson was, he got very upset and said that you weren't his father and that he hated you."

I felt a huge lump in my throat. I sat there not knowing how to explain this mess. I thought back to the day that Carla had changed the boy's name from James Vernon to James Lee Jackson. She wanted me to sign the birth certificate, but I never did. She never pressured me. She just wanted the child to know who he really was in the event that something ever happened to her.

When I told this to Mrs. Hunt she said, "Well, Mr. Jackson, we are going to need for you to establish paternity before we can move forward with your case."

I didn't say anything; I drifted off to another place. I knew that once I established paternity, there would be no turning back. I couldn't leave James in foster care. I decided that I was going to establish paternity and just deal with the consequences.

She must have called my name a few times before I snapped back into reality.

"Mrs. Hunt, I'm prepared. Now can I please see him before I go?"

She stood up and handed me a card with an address along with directions on it so that I could take the test. She then looked at me very sternly and said, "Mr. Jackson, in my thirty-two years of being a social worker, I have never seen a case as strange as this one. This child wants absolutely nothing to do with you; however, he's too young to make that decision. Once we establish that you are the father; that's only half the battle. We are going to have to stand before a judge so that he can force the little boy to live with you."

She gave me a firm handshake along with an awkward smile and concluded, "Have a nice day. We'll be in touch."

I felt sick when I left that office. There was no way I would want to put that child through any more hardships. I looked at the paper with the address on it and held it tight and I balled it up. It was then that I severed all ties.

***

I can remember going to the bar and drinking. I didn't tell anyone about what I had done. Not even Uncle Buddy, who no longer seemed to have any answers for his own life. I'd decided to live my life and let the chips fall where they may.

I extended the hours at my after-hours club. As long as people paid money and were buying drinks, I didn't care what time they left. I also hired more ladies to serve. If they looked nice and were willing to work, they had a job.

I can remember Pops trying to talk to me. I didn't want to hear it. He had no idea about my struggles, and I wasn't going to tell him.

This behavior went on for several months until the police raided the bar. Luckily, everyone had just cleared out and they didn't search my spot. They really didn't find anything except for a few marijuana cigarettes. I was issued a fine. They promised that they'd be back and that I had better clean up my act.

I couldn't afford for that to happen again, so I decided to close my spot for several weeks to let things cool off and to make some changes. I hired a contractor to come out and build me a new security door and a safe inside the wall. No one was allowed unless they were invited.

The week that I shut the bar down, Jackie's father died of a heart attack. She was torn up and his death actually brought us closer. We became friends again. Yes, the love was always there. We both were just too damn stubborn to apologize. His death helped us to realize just how short life really was.

We both sat at the empty bar. "Big Man, how did we get here?"

She looked so soft and sweet when she asked that question. It had been a while since I'd seen that side of her.

I humbly responded. "Lack of maturity, I guess."

She stared down at the bar and said, "So much has happened between us these past couple of years and I want to try and be friends again. Our son needs the both of us." I nodded my head and agreed.

"Big Man, there's something important that we need to discuss, but I need to be completely certain before I get into the details."

When she said that I closed my eyes and bowed my head. I knew that she wanted a divorce. I didn't want one, but I knew that the ultimate decision would be hers.

"Jackie, take all the time you need. Please don't rush with any hasty decisions. I'm confident that we can fix this. "

She stood up and kissed me on the forehead. "I promise I won't rush." Her cell phone rang and out the door she went.

THE DEVIL'S DUE

Jackie was very quiet for the next several weeks. I started to feel as though our past troubles would be left in the past and we were headed for some much-needed relief. The growth was evident in both of us. We'd learned to get along without bickering and Jackie actually let me touch her again. I started to feel a deeper love for her.

A few days before I was set to open up my new spot, Jackie was ready to talk.

"Big Man, I think I'm ready to come back home." My heart was filled with joy upon hearing this.

She looked at me and said, "Hold on with the excitement. Before we can move forward, I think that we need to be honest and lay everything on the table."

My outer disposition was calm, but the inside was the total opposite.

She grabbed my hand. "To put your mind at ease, I'll go first." I silently took a deep breath as she continued. "What I'm about to say will hurt, but if we are ever going to move ahead I must clear my conscience." Her face was serious, her words were sincere, and she looked like a pillar of strength. "Do you think that you will be able to handle what I am about to say because it will hurt?"

I cleared my throat and thought, *No, I probably can't handle what you are about to say, but it's too late. I am a man and I have to hear it!* "Go ahead and speak, Jackie," I answered, sounding as if a family of frogs were stuck in my throat.

"Big Man, when we hooked up at the mall all those years ago; I used you." She paused for a few seconds, waiting to see what my reaction would be.

I said nothing, although my jaws tightened, and both of my legs shook.

She continued to speak. "My mother raised me to be this perfect and proper child who wasn't allowed to make mistakes. Everyone from my teachers to my friends at school and my dance class all assumed that I had the perfect life." She let out a short laugh "Ha! Maybe I did have the perfect life, but I hated it. That's not who I wanted to be. When you and I got together I saw you as my way out. Your good looks, charm, and generosity made it that much easier. "

When Jackie said that, it hurt badly, but I had no room to judge. I cleared the frogs from my throat and asked the question. "So is it fair to say that you didn't really love me?"

Jackie bowed her head as if she had to think about her answer. "Big Man, I was too fascinated by all these things to know what love really was. I equated the money, the sex, and the freedom to love. I loved our life, our son, this business, and all of the perks that came along with these things. I never had time to stop and listen to my heart."

The conversation was much more than I could handle, but I needed to know what she was trying to say.

"So, Jackie, how do you feel about us now?"

Tears rolled down her face. "Seeing my father lying in that casket and my mother never wanting to leave his side made me realize just what love really is. I watched my mother and pretended that I was she. I believe the way one can tell if they really love a person is to imagine how they would feel if that person suddenly went away forever.

Although you and I have been fussing and fighting and bickering for the past several years, it's hard to imagine my life without you."

I exhaled at her words.

"Jackie, you just don't know how good it feels to hear you say that. No one is perfect. We were so young when we got married. I don't believe that we really knew what the depth of marriage really was. I don't care about what happened in the beginning, or the middle, of our relationship. All I care about is now. I took care of you and gave you things because I wanted to see you happy. If I had to do it all over again, I'd give you even more. The past is behind us and I'm ready to move forward."

Jackie let out a half smile. "Do you really mean that, Big Man?"

The sarcasm in her voice caused me discomfort. "Jackie, there's no need for me to look backwards--I don't plan to go that way."

Her smile disappeared and she became serious. "Big Man, let's not play games. I told you everything, and now I need to know your truth."

I threw my hands up just as Pops' words came to my mind--women always asked for the truth when in fact they really didn't want it. I thought of what Uncle Buddy would say-- are you out of your goddamn mind volunteering that type of information? I knew that I couldn't give in.

"Jackie, I don't know which truth that you're talking about. The only thing that I have to add is that we were both young, foolish, and made plenty of mistakes. I can't really offer you anything other than that."

Jackie stared at me for a while and said, "Is that it?"

I nodded my head and said "yes." I tried to sound convincing but she didn't seem to buy it.

She asked one last time, "So there's nothing else?"

I stood my ground "No, there's nothing else."

She was silent and closed her eyes for a few seconds. When she realized I wasn't going to volunteer any further, she gave a full smile and switched gears.

"Since you have told me everything, let's pop the champagne and move forward."

She then retrieved a business card from her purse and handed it to me. The name on the card read Robert Kendall. I stared at her quizzically. He was one of the investors with Carla.

"Big Man, Mr. Robert Kendall left a message for you on the answering machine. He said that since the other deal fell through, he had another building that you may be interested in." She folded her arms. "When were you going to tell me that we weren't opening up our new establishment?

I began to stutter, "Ummm.... well.... So much had happened over the past few years and it all became so overwhelming. Since you and I weren't communicating, I didn't think that I could go it alone."

Jackie stopped me. "Well, that's all in the past now."

I smiled at her and said, "Absolutely."

She then said, "I called Mr. Kendall myself and I went to take a look at the building. It's beautiful, spacious, and has all of the amenities that we've been looking for. I've agreed to put it in my name and all we need is a hundred grand and he will hold the place. When it's completed within the next year or so, we can give him the remainder."

I stood there speechless and in shock. Jackie had really proven herself.

"Well, Big Man, what do you say? Shall I tell Mr. Kendall that we want the building or should I tell him that's okay?"

I picked Jackie up and we spun around the bar until we both were dizzy. "Jackie, I promise I won't mess this up."

I escorted her down to my spot, where I shared everything with her. There would be no more secrets. We opened my safe and counted out the money. I really believed that good days were ahead.

We worked tirelessly at that bar in order to raise the money that we needed for our new establishment. We got along great and our bond seemed to grow with each passing day.

Within a year we had raised the money we needed to buy the building. That was when Jackie began acting strangely. The bar was empty and it was just her and me. There was no long speech, introduction, or tears--she just blurted out the words, "I'm sick. I have breast cancer."

That caught me off guard. I looked at her and didn't know what to say. I was scared and the only thing that I could do was reach out and hold her. "Are you sure? We'll go and get a second opinion. We'll find the best doctors. I'll do whatever you need me to do."

She wanted no sympathy. "Big Man, I'm okay. I've had a second opinion, and Olivia is a nurse so I can assure you that I'm getting the best possible treatment. I haven't told anyone, because I'm going to beat this."

I held her tight and said, "If there's anything I can do, please don't hesitate to ask."

She took an exasperated breath and said, "The only thing that I need from you is the truth!"

I closed my eyes and bowed my head because I thought that we'd moved past this. "Jackie, what are you talking about?"

"Big Man, I can no longer act like the rumors about your son with Carla don't exist. I've known for years. I'd been trying to piece that relationship together for the longest, but every time I came up short. After her death all those years ago, I finally gave up." Jackie gave a little laugh. "I believed that you really loved her, which caused me to secretly celebrate her demise."

When Jackie said these things, I felt horrible that she felt that way. I really wanted her to know that I loved her and only her. I kept a straight face. "Jackie, I love you and have always loved only you. Carla and I did business together and that's it. She and I had no child together."

"Big Man, please!" The pitch in her voice became a little higher and she sniffled. "Maybe God gave me this awful sickness in retaliation for how I've lived my life and ignored this motherless child. Maybe this illness came into my life to teach me to slow down, right some of my wrongs, change my ways, and focus on what's really important. Which is my son."

"Jackie please stop talking like that. Cancer can happen to anyone. I see nothing wrong with your ways. I love you just the way you are."

Jackie had a chilling look in her eyes. Her always-smiling face was now expressionless. Her eyes were glassy and she wrapped her arms tightly around her body as if she was trying to keep herself from falling.

I had never seen her this way before and for the first time ever; I was afraid of losing her.

The trembling in my hands and voice were just the same. I could hardly look her in the eyes. I somehow managed to lift my right arm and put it over my heart and said, "I swear on my dead mother's grave that I don't have another child."

Jackie looked at me and snapped in an irritable tone, "So when did your mother die?"

I looked at her and said, "She left me when I was three or four years old. I guess you could say about thirty-four years ago." I knew that I shouldn't have said that, but I was desperate. I didn't give a damn about a woman who had abandoned her own child at such a young age and never came back. With Jackie I just wanted things to go back to the way they once were.

Jackie looked tired and lethargic. She took a seat and put one hand up to her forehead and massaged her temples with her fingers. I grabbed a chair and sat down next her, placing my hand on her leg. She shoved it away in disgust. I sat there cowardly, because I was at her mercy.

She stood and raised her hands and pranced around the bar. "Look at this place. Isn't it beautiful?" I nodded yes. She looked down at her attire and expensive handbag. "Look at me, don't I look good?" Once again I nodded yes.

She then let out a pathetic-sounding cry. "Big Man, I asked for this life. I wanted the money, the power and the fame because I wanted to look and feel important. I thought that having all of these things meant freedom and even respect. I believed that money could fix all of life's problems. Cancer has taught me otherwise. Money can't fix cancer and it seems as if it only creates more problems. Having this sickness makes me view life much differently now. All this glitz and glamour mean absolutely nothing to me anymore and I'd give it all back just to have my health and strength and peace of mind. This sickness has made me appreciate the simple things that I once took for granted, like taking a breath of fresh air, spending quality time with Shorty, and happiness…oh yes, happiness."

Jackie took a short pause. "Big Man, cancer has taught me that money and things can never create happiness. Happiness comes from within. Happiness to me is making my Shorty smile. He's been asking for a sibling for a long time. With this illness I may never get the chance to make that happen." She then let out a desperate cry.

"Big Man, I really didn't expect for you tell me the truth about your indiscretions and infidelities with Carla. I understand that I may never know the truth of when and how it happened. What I do know is that somewhere out there is a child. And I'm begging for our son's sake.

Tell me where I can find his brother?"

I closed my eyes and silently asked God for forgiveness when Jackie pleaded, because I just couldn't tell her. Telling the truth would do me more harm than good, because I wouldn't be able to produce. I willingly walked away. If I admitted that to Jackie, she'd probably see me as an evil monster and I didn't want to take that chance. She was a sick woman and James was a child with emotional issues. I found it best to let it go.

I opened my eyes and grabbed Jackie's hands and said with as much sincerity as I could muster, "Jackie, I have no son with Carla."

Jackie cried for several more minutes before she finally pulled herself together. She slowly lifted her head and stared directly into my eyes without saying a word. I continued to hold a straight face. Once she realized I wasn't going to break she spoke.

Her words were soft and convincing. "Big Man, I believe you. I'm so sorry for doubting you. This medicine sometimes makes me emotional. I guess I was having one of those moments. I'm tired and I really feel it's time for me to let it go. I will no longer let those awful lies that Donna spreads consume my thoughts another day. I promise to never mention it again."

I let out a sigh of relief after hearing those words.

Jackie then said, "Big Man, we need a clean slate. I want to start our relationship all over."

I kissed her face and said, "Whatever I have to do to make you happy, I'm willing."

Jackie smiled. "Big Man, I want to get divorced." I froze. She then gave a weak laugh and said, "Let's put this toxic marriage behind us. I want every girl's dream, the whole shebang! I want you to buy me a new ring and drop down on one knee and propose. I want a wedding with lots of flowers, a big dress, and even a church."

I thought Jackie's request was a bit extreme, but I agreed. I was desperate for the clean slate.

The next day we stopped by the jeweler to pick out a new engagement ring. Olivia then met us at the floral shop where I spent over forty thousand dollars on flowers that were to be flown in from different parts of the country. We then upgraded her Jeep for the latest model and I followed her down to the attorney's office where we filed for a divorce.

A few months had passed before the divorce was finalized. Jackie said that she was putting the finishing touches on the ceremony. She claimed that she didn't need my help, only my money.

"Big Man, the only thing I need you to do is just show up." I gave her whatever amount of money she asked for, because it seemed to make her happy and take her mind off the cancer.

Since Jackie was handling all the wedding stuff, I'd decided to surprise her with a new condo. I was elated. After everything she and I had been through, we were still standing stronger than ever. I was happy that my family and I were finally going to be under one roof.

***

The day had finally come for Jackie and me to close on the property downtown. I had a huge celebration planned because it was also the day that we were set to move into our new place. Everything seemed perfect. We'd hired two new managers to open and close the bar so that we could spend more time with each other and focus on our new endeavors.

Jackie had the keys to the condo and all the money that she needed to close the deal. I was at home listening to the radio and packing up the last of my things when the phone rang.

"Hello, may I speak with Mr. or Mrs. Jayson Jackson?"

An uneasy feeling came over me when I heard the familiar voice. "This is Mr. Jayson Jackson. May I ask who am I speaking with?"

The caller introduced himself. "This is Robert Kendall from the Kendall brokerage firm."

I looked over at the clock. Jackie still had an hour before she was supposed to be at his office.

"Hello, Mr. Kendall. My wife should be on the way to the bank to get the cashier's check and then down to your office. Is there something that you forgot to mention?"

The phone went silent for a second. He then cleared his throat. "Mr. Jackson, there must be some sort of miscommunication between you and your wife. She called last night to say that she was backing out of the deal. I was just calling to let you know that per our agreement your deposit will be forfeited since you backed out of the deal."

An Arctic blast housed itself inside of my body at that moment. I was numb and frozen still.

"Mr. Jackson, are you still there?"

After a few seconds I managed to respond. "Yes, Mr. Kendall, I'm still here" He seemed very disturbed.

"Well, Mr. Jackson please keep in mind that our company has accommodated you and your wife throughout this entire process. This deal should have been closed last week."

I began to panic. "Please Mr. Kendall, don't do anything. Give me twenty-four hours."

I rang Jackie's cell phone. A deep male voice answered the call. I pulled my phone away from my ear to check to see if I'd dialed the correct number. I had. I became enraged and responded. "Who the hell is this?"

The voice weakened. "It's me--Shorty?"

I felt awful. My son had turned into a young adult seemingly overnight and I had been too busy to take notice.

I tried to sound upbeat. "Damn, Shorty--what's going on with you, li'l man?"

His voice began to crack. He sounded as if he were afraid. "Big Man, the police are here and Jackie might be going to jail."

I was suddenly awash with a strong feeling of impending doom.

"Shorty, please don't get soft on me now--you have Jackson blood running through your veins. My attorneys will handle everything. It's going to be all right. Now don't mention anything to the police, and please don't say my name."

His voice hardened as he responded. "I got it."

I slammed the phone and reached for my shoes. The throbbing of my head and a sharp pain in my stomach caused me to fall to my knees.

I grabbed the edge of the dresser to pull myself up when the phone rang again.

That time it was Pops.

"Big Man, what in the hell is going on back there?" He was on vacation. How did he know that something was wrong?

I tried my best to control my breathing; however, my voice was shaky. "Pops, relax. I have everything under control."

He never noticed the tone in my voice because his breathing was heavier than mine. He began to yell. "Big Man, you need to get your ass down to my attorney's office ASAP. He says that you're under federal investigation and if you don't turn yourself in, they're coming for you!"

I grew nervous; my hands became unsteady, and I dropped the phone.

***

I never did report to the attorney's office. Instead, I went to Jackie's mother's house.

When I arrived on the block, the ambulance was leaving and Shorty was in the back of a police cruiser. I was a wanted man so there was no way I could stop. I was having an anxiety attack, so I eased my foot off the gas pedal and my truck began to cruise. I took long deep steady breaths as I coasted down the street.

Debbie waved her arms back and forth in an attempt to flag me down. I turned my truck around. Debbie was the neighbor. She was once a beautiful lady; however, she got mixed up with drugs and alcohol and they had taken a toll on her. She had aged about ten years. I could smell the scent of liquor on breath as she leaned inside my truck window. She tried her best to look sober, but her speech was slurred.

"Big, Man, Mrs. Scott and my mother are on their way to the hospital with Jackie. She was having trouble breathing and she passed out. The cops came to arrest Shorty. He and his friends are accused of robbing a gas station."

Debbie's words reverberated through my body and hit me like a ton of brick. I went into a daze. Shorty robbing a gas station....

"Big Man… Big Man…." Debbie shouted, "are you okay?"

Suddenly I was jolted back into reality.

I slammed the truck in drive and sped off toward the hospital. The world seemed to be closing in on me.

Less than a half hour later I was inside the hospital emergency room. Mrs. Scott's neighbor, Ms. Betty, spotted me as I walked through the door. "Jayson, hurry. They just rushed Jackie to the back."

As I was entering her private room, I was halted by the sound of Mrs. Scott's tearful voice.

"Jackie darling, please don't try and speak. Save your energy."

Jackie sounded sluggish, her words were faint, and she spoke slowly, but her persistence prevailed. "Mother, I have accepted my fate. I have known that I had cancer for a while. I didn't tell you because I didn't want you to worry. I'm a big girl. I'm strong. Just please take care of Shorty in the event that something happens to me."

Mrs. Scott sniffled. "Jackie, I won't hear of talk like that. I am a woman of strong faith and I know that you're in good hands."

Jackie continued to speak. "Mother, I want to apologize for the way I treated you throughout the years. Just because a child doesn't follow the path that their parents made for them doesn't mean they don't appreciate it. I love you, Mother--you really are the best mother a girl could ask for."

Mrs. Scott responded, "Jackie, I want to apologize to you for being so pushy. I never had a mother, so I tried to live my dreams through you. I love you and I'm proud to have a daughter with such a strong mind and spirit."

Jackie whispered, "Please go find out what's happening with Shorty. I can't leave him there. I want to see him. I need him."

Mrs. Scott said, "I'm going to step out into the lobby and try and phone his father. Your brother Jeffery will be here later this evening."

I stepped into the room after I heard my name. "Hello, ladies."

Mrs. Scott turned to me with a strained look on her face. "Jayson, I'm glad that you made it. I was just going to call you. So much has happened."

I looked at Mrs. Scott and tried to put her mind at ease. "I heard all about it. I'm sure it's all a big misunderstanding with Shorty. I'm confident that he'll be fine."

Mrs. Scott wiped her eyes and nodded her head. "I hope so." She then whispered to Jackie, "Princess, get some rest. I'll be back in a few."

I stepped over to Jackie's bed. She was hooked up to a breathing machine and appeared to be resting comfortably. I grabbed her soft hand and whispered her name. "Jackie, I came just as soon as I found out." Her eyes were closed and she was silent. "Jackie, get your rest, Princess. Big Man will be right here." Jackie still said nothing.

I sat next to her bed for hours and it was as if she didn't know I was there, because she never responded to me.

Her brother Jeff had made it in from California late that afternoon. He walked in and tapped me on my shoulder as I was resting my eyes. "Hello, Jayson--how is my sister doing?"

I hopped up in a panic. I was so tired that I had forgotten where I was. I shook Jeff's hand and replied, "I really don't know, because she hasn't said anything."

Jeff said, "Well, I'm here now. Please take a break. Go and get yourself something to eat or some coffee. You look really tired."

I looked at Jeff and said, "Thanks for being here."

As I walked out the door, I heard him call Jackie's name. It seemed as though I heard her respond, so I stuck my head inside the room. "Did she just say something?"

He looked over at his sleeping sister and said, "I didn't hear anything."

I nodded my head. "I guess I really am tired."

I was gone a little over an hour as I made phone calls and attempted to eat. I was unsuccessful at both. No one answered my calls and my appetite was gone.

Jeff sat next to Jackie's bed, holding her hand. When he looked at me I could tell he'd been crying because his eyes were red. "Did she say something while I was away?" I asked.

He hunched his shoulders and said, "She's been drifting in and out. She keeps asking to see Shorty." Jeff stood and said, "Jayson, the doctors are going to transfer Jackie to a room on the fourth floor. They said it would take a few minutes before she gets settled in. How about you and I go to the house so that you can grab her some things and I can make a few more phone calls? I really need to check on my nephew." We both stepped into the hallway. It was an awkward feeling, because I should have been the one checking on my son, but my hands were tied.

I cleared my throat, "Jeff, I really want to thank you. Since you're an attorney, you're probably the best man suited to handle this situation."

He looked at me and nodded. "You're probably right."

***

I grabbed Jackie a few pieces of clothing before I searched her entire bedroom. I didn't find anything but tons of shoes, clothes, handbags, and receipts. Her black bag and the money were nowhere in sight. I became worried because Jackie had all of our life savings and I had no idea where the money was.

I spent the night at the hospital. Mrs. Scott and I took rotating shifts inside her room. It seemed as though whenever I stepped out of the room she'd say a few words. When I would return, the silence resumed.

It was after eleven the next morning when Mr. Kendall called my phone. He needed an answer and he needed it fast. I was upset. He didn't understand. Things were out of my control.

Shorty walked in the room just as Mr. Kendall and I were having a heated exchange. I abruptly ended the call. I walked over to Shorty and wrapped my arms around him. He didn't reciprocate. His demeanor was cold as he asked the question, "Did you know she had cancer?"

There wasn't much that I could offer other than "She said that we were going to beat this."

Shorty sat next to his mother and grabbed her hand and looked lovingly into her eyes. He kissed her face and she still didn't move. "How long has she been out?" he asked.

"I've been here half the night and most of the day, and she hasn't awakened for me once."

"That's strange," he replied. "Nana say's that she's been asking for me all day."

I hunched my shoulders. "It seems like everyone has had a chance to speak with her except for me. I've been praying, but I haven't had any luck. Her doctor said that once her medication wears off, she would come to."

I looked down at my watch. I needed to meet with Mr. Kendall face to face. Shorty then said, "Why don't you take a break. When she wakes up, you will be the first person I call."

I headed to the door, "Shorty, have you by any chance seen Jackie's black bag? I went to the house last night and couldn't find it anywhere. There are some very important papers that I need out of there."

He responded, "Yes."

When I heard that word I felt a sigh of relief and I was beginning to feel as if all hope wasn't lost. "What did she do with it?" He then took his eyes off me and stared at Jackie as he answered. "She said something about going to her new place. Did you check there?"

I bowed my head as he was still speaking. I knew he couldn't help me.

I left the hospital and went straight to The Lady. A few ladies were getting ready to take the stage, the kitchen was open, and the music was playing when suddenly The Special Task Force unit burst inside.

The building was surrounded by law enforcement and there was no way I could escape.

The agent held up the search warrant. "Mr. Jackson, we promised you we'd be back. You've been under surveillance for a while. We had a few pieces to the puzzle that were missing and it was only a matter of time before we put them all together." He then laughed as he pushed me aside. "You seem to love beautiful women. We knew that it was only a matter of time before a scorned one turned you in."

When they came into my establishment, they knew exactly what they were looking for. They were not going to be defeated like they had been in the past. They went straight to the secret door and down to my spot. They busted the wall and found my safe. When they cracked it open, they found money, contracts, receipts, and bank statements. They confiscated the safe, slot machines, the gambling tables, and all the liquor. They then threw everyone out and padlocked the building. I knew right away who the scorned woman was.

I was taken to jail and released a short time later. I informed my attorney who had been a longtime friend of Pops, about my wife being in the hospital. He went before the judge and explained the situation, and the judge agreed to release me with restrictions. We didn't make it two blocks up the road when his cell phone rang. He made a few angry expressions as he continued to apologize to the person on the other end of the phone. When he ended the call, he looked at me with fury in his eyes and said, "Mr. Jackson, an attorney-client relationship should primarily be based on trust, and that trust must work both ways." He didn't need to utter another word. I knew what he going to say next. "I'm afraid that you will have to find yourself another attorney."

I buried my head in my hands. *Damn*, I said to myself. Jackie had hammered the final nail in my coffin. She released the divorce papers. His driver turned the car around and Pop's longtime friend quietly walked me back in the precinct.

That was the day my real suffering began. Jackie died that afternoon. I soon realized that the divorce, the wedding, the new beginning, and us opening up a new establishment were all a lie. She carefully orchestrated and executed her plan. She cleaned me out and according to our bank statement; she'd spent thousands of dollars on a private investigator. She knew everything all along.

I was hurt beyond measure because I never saw that coming. I was always known to stay one step ahead of the rest and the moment I let my guard down, I was beaten at the game I was known to play so well.

My head was unbalanced and I shut completely down. My love of money cost me everything. I was left with a long list of felony charges and a permanent scar on my heart from the woman whom I loved a little too late. I don't believe that I would ever forget the menacing look Shorty gave as I was being led away in handcuffs. I also thought about Pops. I was sure that he was disappointed in me. He had worked hard all his life to make sure that I wanted for nothing and in the blink of an eye, one stroke of a pen, my life had dwindled down to nothing but a prison ID number.

I was facing a long list of felony charges: operating an illegal gambling business, tax evasion, hiring minors to work inside of an adult establishment, and failing to send in payroll taxes. These were only a few of the charges. They had enough to send me away for a long time.

Pops spent a small fortune to pay for my legal defense. The attorneys worked tirelessly to get most of the charges dismissed. After everything was all said and done, some charges wouldn't go away unless I cooperated with the government. They really wanted the ringleader of the gambling operation. They wanted to know who supplied the tables and slot machines. I wasn't going to co-operate because that meant telling on my Uncle Buddy.

Uncle Buddy went into hiding after everything went down. I couldn't say that I blamed him. Although he was the total opposite of Pops, I loved him just the same. He was, and probably always will be a petty hustler. He never had any real money, but he always managed to get by. Looking back over my life, I wished that I had his free spirit. He was always happy and never seemed to stress about anything. Uncle Buddy was never a real threat to anyone. He was only a victim of loving the streets, and having a good time. I don't believe there's a real crime in that.

I was offered a plea bargain for eighteen months in a federal prison. If I refused to take it, I would have go to trial. If I lost, I would have been facing over twenty years. My attorneys claimed that it was best that I take it. I was left with no choice because some things just weren't worth the gamble.

***

Picking Up the Pieces

"All rise; court is now in session."

The judge takes her seat at the bench. News cameras flash as the Bailiff escorts Shorty into the courtroom. He doesn't look like the same scared child from earlier. His walk is tall and strong and he doesn't appear nervous. Jeff Scott wears a worried look. Shorty whispers something to him, putting him at ease. I am on edge, and torn up inside. Mrs. Scott closes her Bible and grabs my sweaty hand.

The judge clears her throat before speaking. "Mr. Jackson, now where were we?" Shorty holds his head up high and he speaks with confidence. He apologizes to Michael for the shooting and to his Nana and Uncle Scott for causing them pain, shame, and humiliation. Mrs. Scott and Jeffery both are proud, and my sick feeling is starting to fade.

Shorty then tells the Judge about a letter that he has written. She gives him permission to read it...

Missed Opportunities
I self-destructed at every chance
of being all that I could be.
Opportunities that I had,
slipped away from me.
My mother was a hustler,
my father was the same.
I considered myself a victim

because I needed to shift the blame.
So many people tried
to bring out the best in me.
Had I recognized it was tough love,
no telling who or what I'd be.
Then I was dealt a bad hand
that I was forced to play.
I hated everyone
when Jackie passed away.
My life had changed so fast.
My heart was ripped and torn.
I questioned my existence
and hated the fact that I was born.
But being locked away
has helped me to understand,
that making positive choices
will help me become a better man.
So if given a second chance
to be all that I can be,
I promise to jump every hurdle
that's thrown in front of me.

The entire courtroom gasps at his powerful words. Mrs. Scott can't hold back her tears. There aren't any words to describe how I'm feeling. It is the worst type of pain. The devil has administered one final hard blow to my gut.

I can no longer take it, so I hop up and run out of the courtroom.

When I make it outside, I push pass the protestors and run down the block in tears. I curse the Devil the entire time. "I hate you. I fucking hate you."

I stop on the side of the building. I slump my body in an attempt to catch my breath. I needed to calm my nerves, so I pull out a cigarette and eye the building from a short distance. Suddenly there is a small ruckus. The crowd disperses as the news cameras start following someone. It's Shorty. He starts running up the street screaming my name and chasing behind a cab. As I step away from the building I run into Jeffery Scott. He looks tired.

Jeff walks up to me and shakes my hand. He then says, "Jayson, they let him go." I look up and give a pleased nod. He hands me an envelope with pictures of my son James. "You have a lot of explaining to do." He then points at Shorty, who is headed in our direction with cameras in tow. I don't believe he realizes they're following him.

Looking at Shorty makes me think about Pops. He would have told me to stand up and take it like a man.

As Shorty approaches, I wonder what's going through his mind. I then ask myself, "How can I expect for him to accept me at my worst when I didn't accept him at my best?"

He stands directly in front of me. The news reporter's circles around us, causing us to look like two boxers in the ring. I am obviously the weaker opponent, because I didn't come to battle. We both have tears when Shorty reaches out to shake my hand. I reach in and grab him. We lock into a full embrace. I let out a full cry when he pats my shoulder and then he suddenly pulls away.

He calls for Jeff. "Let's get out of here, Uncle. I'm ready to go home."

They walk off with the news cameras still rolling behind him.

***

I don't know what to make of that situation.

Just when I thought that I'd reached my lowest, I found that I wasn't even close. I was at a breaking point. I could no longer face this alone. I needed help.

My therapist Sharon Baker's last words come to my mind.

"Jayson *please call me when it's over. It's imperative that we have our last few sessions. I owe that to your father.*"

I reach inside my pocket and pull out her card and glance at the address. I need to know what it was that she owed my father.

Her office is less than ten minutes away. I know exactly where the street is located.

***

I pull up to the standalone building. A strange feeling comes over me as I step out my truck. It's the former home of Vernon and Associates. The same building where I'd had my first encounter with Carla.

The big brown solid wood door hasn't been replaced. As I lift my knuckle to knock, I notice the big gold nameplate. It reads Dr. Winston Baker, MD. Family Practice.

I look at Sharon Baker's card and it has Dr. Winston Baker name as the logo. I shake the chill off my body as I walk inside.

The place has been remodeled to look like a doctor's office. The sign inside the reception area says "Out to lunch."

I look around the office. The huge plaque hanging on the wall catches my eye. I read the caption underneath.

I began to feel sick as I realize who these people were. How could these be her parents?

The photo is of Dr. Winston Baker standing alongside his wife and their three children. They smile for the camera as James Vernon's wife hands over a set of keys. The three children hold up a sign that says Grand Opening.

Suddenly I hear women's voices laughing as they enter the reception area. The older woman looks directly at me and I notice that she has a very distinct mole above her lips. I knew right away she was Blanche Callahan. Sharon looks alarmed once she sees me.

She whispers, "Mother, please go and get Mr. Jackson's file off my desk."

Her voice rattles as she says, "Jayson, I was waiting for your call. I would have come to you."

I stare at them both. The strong resemblance between Sharon Baker and Blanche can't be ignored. They were definitely mother and daughter.

Sharon begins to walk towards me and I slowly step back.

My voice is low and somber.

"Sharon, I trusted you. I really believed that you wanted to help me. You said that my father came to you. I don't believe that."

Sharon tries to speak, but I won't let her.

"Whatever it is that you came to me for, I sure hope you found it. I won't speak to you anymore, especially about my father."

Sharon looks distraught, but she never interrupts. Blanche then returns to the room and hands Sharon my file before she excuses herself.

My eyes follow her until she's no longer in sight. She was a very attractive older woman and it was easy to see why Pops fell in love with her.

My mind flashes back to that day in the bar when he told me all about their failed relationship....

"Blanche I want lots of children and I want them with you."

"James, we've been together for over a year and I have never gotten pregnant."

"James, I wanted to give you the child that Monica didn't give you."

"James, I can't come close to that woman because I can't have kids."

"James, I choose Winston Baker. He's a safe bet.

I want to run and catch Blanche. I want to shake her. I want her to know how bad her lies hurt my Pops and how he never got over losing her.

I turn to leave when suddenly Sharon grabs my hand and walks me over to the chair.

"Jayson, your father and my mother were old friends. He reached out to her shortly after you were incarcerated. They hadn't seen each other in years. He wanted answers that she could not provide so she referred him to me. He wanted to know why…"

I stood and cut her off mid sentence. I knew the story already.

"Sharon, I know all about your mother and my Pops. He had always been such a good and honest man. When he loved, he loved hard. Too bad that love was never returned. Sharon, your mother was the one woman that he never got over. I heard the name Blanche Callahan all the time. He still loved her even after she lied and claimed that she couldn't have kids. I'm glad that he forgave her and that they made amends before his death.

"Now if you'll excuse me. I have to get going."

As I walk toward the door, Sharon suddenly blurts out, "My mother never lied. Your mother Cheryl did."

I come to a complete halt and turn in her direction. "Excuse me?" I say angrily.

She starts to shake as she leads me over to the chairs. I am too exhausted to resist so I follow her lead.

She then tells me the real reason that my Pops sought counseling.

"Jayson your father came to me because he was on the verge of having a mental breakdown. He needed someone that he could talk to.

He blamed himself for everything that happened with his family. For over four decades he'd been living a lie. He believed that lie is what caused him to lose his entire family."

I stare her straight in the eyes. I remain silent as she continues to speak.

Sharon opens the folder. Pops scrapbook was the first thing that I saw. It was a timeline of his life. I remembered the day I found him putting it together. There was the old black and white photo of his parents, and the Smith family. There was a photo of Monica and him on the swings in Mississippi and there were several photos of Blanche Callahan.

As I stare at the photos I began to feel sad for Pops. He was used and betrayed by every woman he ever loved.

I think of what he told me about Monica and the baby that he claimed was his.

"James, we can get past this."

"It only happened one time."

"This baby needs you."

"You're the only father he knows."

I think about the love that he had for Blanche and his strange behavior after seeing her at James Vernon funeral.

"Blanche has a family."

"Big Man, my entire life all I ever wanted was a wife that I could grow old with and have lots of children and grandchildren."

Seeing Blanche with her family after she'd lied those many years ago by saying that she couldn't have children really tore him apart. He was never quite the same after that day.

I looked at Sharon and said, "The lies your mother told my father all those years ago really devastated him and he never fully recovered from them. As far as Cheryl---I really don't believe that he gave a damn about her and her lies. He was just happy that she left us alone."

Sharon bows her head and searches inside the folder. She then hands me several photos and posters of Uncle Buddy and Cheryl performing on the stage as Mississippi Soul. I had never seen those particular photos before. Their body language seemed a little too close for comfort.

A jolt runs through my body. I was upset so I shove the pictures back inside the folder.

"Sharon where did you get these photos from?" I ask. "Please cut the bull-shit out and tell me exactly what it is you are trying to say?"

Sharon looks frightened. I had never spoken to her that way before.

"Jayson your father went to Cheryl although it was against your wishes. He said that there were so many loose ends and unanswered questions. He needed to know the truth."

I let out a deep sigh. I was exhausted and didn't want to play any guessing games.

"What truth is that Sharon?" I ask in a disturbed voice.

"Jayson after your mother left, your father found these photos hidden inside a box that she left behind. He held on to them for all these years never mentioning a word to anyone about his findings. When he came to me I was the one who advised him to reach out to her. When he contacted her, she came clean. She admitted to him that she had a brief encounter with your uncle Buddy. She said that there was a slight possibility he could be your father. Jayson your father then connected the dots. It seemed that the writing was written all over the wall. Monica's baby wasn't his and my mother had three children and Cheryl took off and never came back. These were instances that he could no longer ignore. So he had a DNA test done. He'd planned to tell you his findings when you were released but unfortunately he never got that chance. Jayson, your father James was the one who couldn't have children. He was afraid of what you might think of him but he knew that he could no longer live with that dark and ugly secret."

I close my eyes and take several deep breaths. I feel vacant inside. I am at a loss. I wish that I could rebuke her claims but I can't.

I place my face inside the palms of my hands as my mind runs rampant.

I can clearly see Pops' face and hear his voice from all those years ago.

"Big Man, you act just like your Uncle Buddy. You have an excuse for everything."

"Big Man, you're the best thing that has ever happened to me. I wouldn't have it any other way."

I think of what Cheryl told him.

"James, I wish that I had met you before I dealt with Buddy. I hate wasting my time."

"James, I don't want to be a mother. I feel like a horrible person for saying this."

"James, this baby deserves a father like you."

"James, I want to travel the world and be a superstar."

Cheryl has to be the worst person who has ever walked the face of this earth. She walked away from Pops and me so freely and took her dark secret with her and never looked back. She pretended to despise Uncle Buddy when she was just the same as he.

Thinking of all this helps me to understand who I really am and why my life ventured so far off the course that Pops set for me. It's a part of my genetic make up. The women, the lies, the selfishness, the money and the deception are all innate. Pops tried his best to thwart what seemed to be predestined but it was no use. I'm just like Buddy.

Sharon sits beside me and rubs my back. "Jayson, your father wanted you to have that folder. There's letters, pictures and cards inside of it. I believe that it will answer every question that you have. He was extremely hurt once the truth was verified, but the love that he had for you and your son was unwavering. He didn't want to keep it a secret any longer. He believed that you had a right to know the truth."

I continue to sit with my head bowed and say, "What does my Uncle Buddy have to say about all of this?"

Sharon responds, "I've been working with your Uncle Buddy since your father's passing. Although he's made a tremendous amount of progress, I didn't feel as if it was my place to share this with him. I wanted to tell you because I know that's what your father really wanted."

I pause before I let out a huge sigh of relief. That is the best news that I've heard in a while.

"Sharon, I don't care what's inside that folder. I don't care what Cheryl says or a DNA test says. James Jackson is my father. He raised me, protected me and loved me although he knew I wasn't his biological child. That means more to me than anything in this entire world. My Pops was a remarkable man with great moral character, strength and integrity and it is an honor to be his son. I love my Uncle Buddy, but he could never measure up to the man that James Jackson was. Sharon you can pat yourself on the back, because we just closed that chapter."

I then grab Sharon's hand and I tell her about my son Shorty and Calvin. She holds me and cradles my head. I soon erupt into tears as I think about the irreparable damage that I caused my boys.

Sharon whispers in my ear, "Jayson, you are stronger than you think. You will get through this."

I squeeze her very tight. "I can't do this alone. I need you to help me pick up the pieces. I really want to start over. I know that it won't be easy but I promise that I won't quit. Just know that I am still a broken man, and far from healed, but I'm not weak. I am the son of one of the strongest men I've ever known. I won't let him down. From this day forward, no more excuses. I am a Jackson, and Jacksons don't make excuses or blame circumstances ever.

I rise up from under Sharon's embrace.

"Sharon, let's get out of here. I need you to accompany me down to the juvenile courthouse. I can't leave my son in that place…

CPSIA information can be obtained
at www.ICGtesting.com
Printed in the USA
FFOW02n0049311016
28911FF